IF THERE'S A WILL

JOHN W INGALLS

Editor -- LeAnne Hardy (www.leannehardy.net)

ISBN-13: 978-1979907163

ISBN-10: 19799007161

COLD-TURKEY BOOKS

27167 ENGEBRETSON ROAD

WEBSTER, WISCONSIN 54893

www.coldturkeyleftovers.wordpress.com

For

Leah, Anna, Abigail and Billie Kay

Preface

Stories beg to be told. We write them, we tell them, we share them, we read them, we listen to them and they move us and change us. Grandparents share tall-tales, parents read bedtime stories, children repeat what they have learned, teachers give examples and Jesus taught us parables but in the end, it isn't always the story-teller but the story itself which touches us.

I had to write this book but if I'm pressed to give a reason, I can't. I felt compelled to tell the story, but I don't really know why. Somewhere over the US-Mexican border flying at 30,000 feet it came to me. Not just a piece of the story, not just a crazy thought or idea, it was the whole story, beginning to end which popped into my head. After a week in Mazatlán, perhaps I could blame the sun or the sand or the guacamole or even the reunion with a long-lost cousin not seen for over fifty years. The sun had set into the Pacific and our plane was droning ever northward when it happened.

I turned to my wife and said, "Tammy, when we get home I'm going to write a novel."

Her response was less than enthusiastic. "Like the last novel you started and never finished?" She went back to playing solitaire on her phone. She made her point.

But write, I did. I wrote mornings before leaving for work. I wrote at noon, gulping sandwiches and coffee between paragraphs. I wrote in the evenings until bedtime and after the lights went out I took portions of the story to bed with me and rolled them around in my head like a rock tumbler smoothing edges and polishing characters. Then at dawn, I resumed my quest to get it all on paper.

In seven weeks, the entire rough draft, all 110,000 words, was assembled. I had built the house but it lacked paint and trim and carpet. Friends and acquaintances were called upon to read and digest and offer opinions and many responded with honest and telling remarks. To each and every one I am grateful for their willingness to jump into the muddied water at the deep end of the pool, not knowing what lies beneath the surface.

Tammy was my first reader and my first critic. She read some chapters multiple times asking for clarity but she was always kind. She even went so far as saying "I like your story better than the one I'm reading now." It was a book by someone. I think it was Grisfield, or Graham or Grisham or something like that.

The first non-family readers were Jim and Laura McCaul. The chapters were sent as they were written, rough cut, straight from the mill. It was a risk. Sending off my story raw and unrefined was akin to undressing in public. I felt exposed. But to my surprise, as each chapter was read, they begged for more. With encouragement and corrections, I sent the manuscript to others, Beth Afeldt, Amy Bloyer, Steve Pearson, Jim and Kathy Antilla, Danielle Panik and others. The insights and advice were remarkably similar from each. Some things were good and some things definitely had to change.

The next person in the chain of events was LeAnne Hardy, editor and friend. Her professional comments were clear and to the point, her friend comments were full of grace. Once I clarified the intent of my writing was not to seek commercial publication she softened her stance on some of my amateurish approaches to authorship. The story as it is written, should not reflect on her professional integrity as an editor. I am the rookie.

This book was written for my children as a Christmas gift, a long midwinter bedtime story. It is meant to tell them I love them more than life itself. It is meant to give meaning and depth to living, not just in the actions but the motivations behind the actions. It is meant to show that death and lost jobs and confusion about the next step isn't always bad, because good can and will show through. The story is designed to show life is meant to be enjoyed and celebrated on many levels in the context of love and serving others. It is my hope, when my story is done, they will write or tell their own to their children and their children's children.

I cannot thank my wife Tammy enough for her patience and understanding. She was graceful and kind when I ignored her company. She sat quietly for hours while my fingers tapped ceaselessly on the keyboard of my laptop. Although we have been married for over forty years, she remains my best friend. I have learned to say "I'm sorry" with humility and she says, "I forgive you" with grace. We make a good team.

To my children I cannot begin to thank each of them for the role they have played in shaping my life. To say "I love you" is a woeful understatement of what I truly feel but to say anything more would be a distraction.

And finally, I am so grateful to Jesus who is the greatest story teller. He took the art of storytelling and taught eternal truths through parables. He told the best stories and he is the subject of the greatest story ever told.

Table of Contents

Cast of Characters

Roy and Lola Ambrose. Aging and adventurous, they took an unconventional course in life and imposed a twisted journey upon their children when they were gone.

Earl Ambrose and Sandy Piper. Second cousin to Roy, Earl and Sandy live on the sunny west coast of Mexico in the city of Mazatlán.

Luella and Tom Tinker. Luella is the oldest of four Ambrose daughters. They have three delightful children, Maddie, age 10 and 7-year-old twins, Theo, and Zoe. They live in a small town just north of Stevens Point, Wisconsin. Luella is a nurse and Tom is a math teacher at the local high school.

Olivia and Harry Seymour. Olivia is the second sister. She and Richard live in Oak Grove Wisconsin, a small town near Pepin. Olivia works for a pharmaceutical company and Harry is a cattle breeder in the dairy industry. They have one daughter, Molly, age six.

Vera and Richard Dawson. Vera is a middle child, the third of four sisters. She is a pharmacist who owns a small retail pharmacy in the suburbs of Des Moines, Iowa. Richard is a physical therapist at one of the local hospitals in central Iowa. They have a daughter, Daisy who is best friends with her cousin, Molly.

Emma and Phineas Melquist. Emma is the youngest of the four sisters. She and her husband, Phineas live in Sioux Falls,

South Dakota. Emma works as a legal assistant while Phineas researches harmonic music theory as it applies to the natural world. He may never complete his PhD dissertation. They have no children.

Dag Rasmussen. Dag is the director of DEA counterintelligence, fighting international drug trafficking. He has one good eye, he grunts, he nods and he drinks twenty-year-old single malt scotch when he gets his man.

Javier Espinosa. Best known as "El Chico" he is the head of the ruthless Sinaloa drug cartel headquartered in and around Mazatlán, Mexico.

Pancho Hernandez. Hernandez is a rival drug lord based out of Chihuahua, Mexico.

Martin Garza. Martin is a coconut and t-shirt vendor on the beach in Mazatlán, but he becomes a reluctant messenger between the drug cartel and the DEA.

Petunia. Petunia is a massive 600-pound pig who loves donuts and is a friend to all children.

There are many supporting characters, lawyers, people doctors, animal doctors, good people and bad people and people in between. Meet them along with the Ambrose sisters as their paths cross and their lives change forever.

Chapter 1

Hot Air

Not all those who wander are lost. —J. R. R. Tolkien

Roy and Lola Ambrose stepped onto the gangplank and never looked back. Roy reached out with both arms, gripping the handrails to keep from falling. After two weeks at sea, he staggered and weaved like a drunken sailor. Mentally he deleted 'transatlantic cruise' from his bucket-list. It was over. He took a deep breath and exhaled slowly, relieved to be back on firm ground. With the sea behind and the Canary Islands ahead, he lurched forward, anxious, and excited about the future.

The security computer beeped monotonously as his bar-coded ID tag slipped under the blinking red light. He blotted out the background noise of fellow travelers, trying to grasp the next step. He had insisted on a hot air balloon ride, claiming it would be an uplifting experience, but Lola wasn't so sure. He watched her smile as her ID tag flashed under the light. He knew she was ready for dry land.

"Do you have the tickets?" Roy asked. "I told you to get them, right?"

"I don't have them, you do... Don't you?" She paused on the floating staircase, descending from the ship's main deck to the concrete jetty. "Should we go back to the room and look?"

"No, we need to go. It won't matter anyway." Roy was feeling impatient. He reached forward, urging her onward. She hesitated, acting unsure.

It had been his plan, not hers, to cross the Atlantic by ship. They had experienced several sailing cruises in the past but always in relatively sheltered environs. Athens to Istanbul, Scotland and Ireland, the Scandinavian Peninsula. Roy's bucket list was nearly complete. But as each activity was checked off, he added others. An empty list held ominous implications.

Lola reached out and gripped a signpost. She must be having as much trouble getting her land legs back under her as he was. Tourists buzzed past on rented motorbikes. Taxi drivers honked and pointed toward them, clearly seeking riders. Roy raised his hand and waved them on.

Lola glanced over the garishly colored carts and kiosks dotting the stone plaza along Front Street near the harbor. The street vendors were stocked and ready for a fresh wave of tourists coming ashore. Hawkers aggressively reached out, grabbing customers by the arm and shoving wares into their faces. Lola hesitated as they approached the first produce stand. "Roy, let's get some bread and wine. Maybe some fresh fruit too. We'll probably need it, wherever we end up."

Roy scanned the options and stepped forward. "Nos gustaría...une botella de vino...rioja." He paused and pointed to his choices. His Spanish was poor but adequate for a tourist area. The young man raised his eyebrows and pointed to the same bread and cheese, confirming his selection. Roy nodded. His hand shook slightly as he handed over the money.

"Gracias, Senor y Senora."

Bypassing the big exhaust-belching busses, they walked directly toward a waiting van. A short black-haired man held a sign, *AMBROSE*.

Roy focused on their journey and felt moments of frustration over Lola who loved to linger and watch people. Along the harbor she had many chances to observe, too many. Hundreds, perhaps thousands, of Americans and Europeans wandered up and down Front Street skirting the harbor. Open-air cafes, wine bars and gelato stands called out as they strolled by. As she looked at the people surrounding them, some made eye contact, others looked away. One man lowered his newspaper just as they went by, and Lola caught her breath as she glanced at his short rusty red hair and dark sunglasses. The stranger returned to his reading. She furrowed her brow and turned toward Roy.

"What's wrong?" Roy sensed a deeper anxiety building in Lola.

"Nothing." She paused, looking back toward the café. "I...um...never mind."

Roy reached out and held her hand. Their eyes met. Lola blinked a tear away as she turned to follow Roy along Front Street.

"I thought you were going to get some fruit or something," Lola said. She glanced again toward the man in the café. A folded newspaper rested on the table, its pages fluttering in the coastal breeze. A bottle of sparkling mineral water, half gone, stood on the table. The chair was empty.

"I can't remember everything. You should have said something when we were there." Roy felt annoyed.

"You get so upset when I remind you. Let's just forget it." Lola resolutely looked ahead.

"Do you want to go back?" Roy fidgeted and glanced twice at his wristwatch.

"No, we need to go. They're waiting." Lola cleared her throat. "Come on"

The driver grinned as they stepped into the mini tour bus. "You ready for adventure?" With broken English and boundless energy, he jammed the vehicle into first gear and headed west on the dusty road leading up to the launch site. "Hang on!"

Hanging on was easy, but everything they grabbed, came loose. The rusted white van had a hole in the side. Dust, dirt, and exhaust entered and exited at will. Without seat belts, Lola and Roy clung to each other. They arrived at the balloon launch intact but dusty. The view was wonderful. The rugged hills and mountains stretched from sky to sea, dotted with red roofed, whitewashed buildings. They stepped hesitantly from the minibus as the idyllic mountainous landscape beckoned.

An immense towering orb of fabric expanded and fluttered above the roaring flames of the burner. The balloon waited, tethered like a dog lunging at the end of its leash, desperate to be free.

"Buenos días, amigos. My name is Juan Carlos. I'm your balloon pilot today." The stocky black-haired man greeted them with a wide toothy smile. After introductions, he went through the safety precautions which he described as "muy necesario," very important. However, the entire set of instructions lasted less than two minutes. "Any questions?" They shook their heads, no. "The main thing to remember is hang on and don't fall out. If we go down quickly, we will all die."

It sounded simple enough. Lola looked ahead, but she knew Roy's eyes were fixed on her. A tear streaked down her face. "Are you sure you want to do this?" he asked.

Lola paused and nodded and stepped into the gondola. Roy made it sound as if she had a choice. The time for debate had ended long ago. They were ready for lift off.

"Roy...No matter what happens, I love you." Lola sniffed and wiped her moist eyes on her shirtsleeve. He reached out and held her hand and said nothing.

"Roy, how can you always be so confident?" She looked around. "Don't you ever wonder or worry?" Roy swallowed slowly and said nothing. He squeezed her hand; she squeezed back.

The driver of the van and two assistants on the ground released the tethers. The burner, perched just beneath the opening of the balloon, roared, sending a massive influx of heat upward.

The balloon responded. Silently they lifted above the hillside, catching a light wind from the hills, and drifted toward the sea.

They stared with wonder as the details on the ground shrank and the horizon expanded into endless blue. Far into the north, neighboring islands appeared as hazy hulks interrupting eternity. Lola slid her arm through Roy's. He embraced her. A string of brown pelicans and frigate birds, as large as kites, soared alongside, sharing the view. To their right the ocean stretched east, toward Africa. Yesterday lay behind them, and ahead was the great unknown.

#

The phone rang twice. "Bridge," Captain Caleb Beckett answered. "Beckett here." He listened intently to the caller and responded. "Have you checked their room? Is there a possibility they came aboard without checking in?"

"Yes, sir, we checked in their cabin and with security. Mr. and Mrs. Ambrose have not been seen or heard from since they went ashore this morning. All registered guests have returned except them." The ship's activity coordinator was concerned. The board of directors frowned upon lost customers, especially old people in foreign countries.

Beckett reviewed the scenario in his head. Missing or delayed passengers weren't unusual. Most of the time they were distracted, sometimes inebriated, but he had never lost anyone. "Check with authorities on shore to see if there have been any accidents reported involving an older couple with their description. We still have ninety minutes before we make final preparations for departure. We may have some leeway with the harbormaster but not much."

"We already did that as well, sir, but there's a problem. We checked with the tour company that handles our shore excursions. They told us, hot air balloon rides aren't offered on Tenerife due to unpredictable wind conditions. We also checked with their friends, the Nelsons in suite 205. They didn't know anything either. The tour company that handled Mr. and Mrs. Ambrose wasn't certified."

"Do we know who the tour operators are?" Captain Beckett asked.

"Local authorities know little about the tour operator, and no one answers the listed phone number. We are monitoring radio traffic for security reasons. An incoming flight at the airport notified air traffic control about a large brightly colored object, two miles out in the water. No flares or distress signals were reported. Search and rescue didn't find anyone at the site. They have been searching for several hours."

"Was it a hot air balloon?"

"Yes, I'm afraid it was."

"Let me know the minute you hear anything else. We need to file a missing person report. By the way...good job handling this. These things aren't easy." Beckett paused with a sense of dread. "I need to notify their emergency contact."

#

"Hello?" Luella yawned as she answered. She slurped quickly at her first cup of coffee. Luella was a night nurse at the local hospital. She had just sent her kids on the school bus and was trying to relax with a fresh brewed mug of Jamaican Blue Mountain coffee.

"This is Captain Caleb Beckett with Blue-Hair cruise line. Are you Luella Ambrose?" He paused before continuing, as if trying to gather his thoughts.

"Yes, I am Luella Ambrose, but my married name is Tinker, Luella Tinker."

"You are listed as the emergency contact person for Roy and Lola Ambrose, is that correct?"

Cruise ship captains didn't call to chat about the weather. Luella feared the worst. "Is something wrong? Did my dad have a heart attack or something? I told them to slow down...my gosh, they must be nearly eighty years old! Why are you calling me?"

"Ms. Tinker, your parents are missing. No one has heard from them for nearly eight hours."

"What do you mean, missing? They're old people; you shouldn't let them out of your sight!"

"Ms. Tinker, most of the time passengers get delayed or mixed up with directions, and eventually we find them unharmed. I'm sure we will find your parents soon. But I needed to let you know. We are doing everything we can to find them."

"Do you know what they were doing or where they were going?" Luella tried to think if they had left any kind of an itinerary with her. She couldn't recall anything specific.

"I am sorry to say, they may have been on a hot air balloon ride which landed in the ocean. No one has been recovered yet, but I assure you, we are diligently pursuing all options to find them."

A tight lump formed in Luella's throat. Her parents had done stupid things in the past, but this seemed more serious. She had to call her sisters. Luella prayed for the best but expected the worst.

Chapter 2

Bad News

Death is not the greatest loss in life. The greatest loss is what dies inside us while we live. —Norman Cousins

The girls agreed to arrive as soon as they could. With skills only a mother could manage, each made necessary arrangements for work coverage, day care and after school pick up for the older children. Devoted husbands likewise, cancelled appointments to be with their grieving wives and children. It was mutually agreed to meet at the home place, the house where they had grown up, the home of Roy and Lola in northern Wisconsin.

Olivia lived the closest to home, only a ninety-minute drive with light traffic, which was almost always the case. Usually the only traffic delays were logging trucks, tractors, and an occasional stray cow. There was none today. As Olivia drove, her mind raced back through memories and years. She desperately tried to control her emotions. It was helpful to have her five-year-old in the back seat, chattering away as only a five-year-old can do.

"Mom, why are you crying? Did you hurt yourself?" Molly didn't wait for an answer but simply lapsed into her own rendition of a Sunday school song, 'Heavenly Shunshine'. "Hey Mom, George said his mom cried once when he skinned up his knee. Can I feed Petunia when we get to Papa Roy's place? Huh, Mom? Can I?"

"Honey, Mama's sad because we don't know where Papa Roy and Grammy Lola are." It broke her heart to try and explain to a child that Papa Roy and Grammy Lola wouldn't be coming home. She choked back more tears and dabbed at them with her tissue.

"But I thought you said they were on a big boat?"

"They are, but they got lost." The tears flowed again. Unable to stop them she simply drove on, letting the tears run down her cheeks and drip onto her collar.

"But you said they went to heaven. Isn't that what Auntie Emma said?" The pudgy fingers held the crumbled remains of the donut in her hands. "Mom, I'm gonna save my donut for Petunia, OK, Mom? OK?"

"OK, sweetie, you can feed Petunia when we get to Papa's and Grammy's house".

Olivia turned into the driveway curving back through century old whispering white pines. The old family house perched on a gently sloping shoreline of the north woods lake. The weathered cedar shake siding made it appear more rustic on the outside than on the inside. It was home. Originally called Naygamukwa Lake in

11

Ojibwa, meaning 'bear with no hair' or 'naked bear,' the name had been transformed through the years to Namukwa Lake by European settlers who struggled with the native tongue. Most of the locals simply referred to the lake as "Bare-naked Lake" which aptly described some of the weekend swimmers at various cabins tucked in the pines. There was none of that now as Olivia gazed out over the calm water. It likely would never be the same here. No more picnics on the deck or beach parties or campfires or Papa's Swedish pancakes on Saturday mornings. No more hugs from Grammy, or cookies and splashing in the mud puddles. She clutched little Molly close and sobbed.

"Hey, Mom, don't cry, OK? Can we go feed Petunia now?"

"All right, let's go feed Petunia."

Petunia was the high point of Molly's visit to Grandpa and Grandma's house. Papa Roy had a crazy idea to raise a pig up to a thousand pounds. Petunia was the result. She topped out somewhere around six hundred pounds or so but no one was certain. Roy put her into a horse trailer once and tried to weigh her at the feed store. She scored about six hundred forty pounds, but he couldn't be sure of the accuracy of the truck scale. Since then, Petunia had been the princess of the place. When Roy was gone, one of the neighbor kids, Buddy Martin, fed Petunia. In return for his work, Roy paid him and allowed Buddy to show Petunia at the county fair as part of a 4-H project. She wasn't a show pig and never scored higher than third place. Neither Buddy nor Petunia seemed to care.

"Hey Petunia, look what I got for yah!" Molly waved the half-eaten donut in the air for Petunia's inspection. The pig's deep throated grunting rose to a squeal in anticipation of another pastry. Buddy hadn't been by yet, so Molly and Olivia dumped a pail of grain into Petunia's pink plastic feed tub and filled it up with water from the hose.

As the feed trough filled, a car horn honked near the house. Vera and Luella had both arrived. Emma likely was still a couple of hours out since she lived in South Dakota. Simple words of greeting were cut short by sobs and hugs. No words conveyed their hurt and loss. They were sisters and words didn't need to be spoken to be understood. Tom and Richard, husbands of Luella and Vera, herded the children and carried suitcases, pillows, and bags of food into the house. Harry, Olivia's husband, was on his way from Chicago, and Phineas had cancelled his classes to come along with Emma.

The children were delighted to be with their cousins again although a heavy cloud of sadness hung over the reunion. Molly led her cousins back to Petunia's pen so they could each feed her leftover pop-tarts, sandwiches, potato chips, or whatever remained from the trip. Petunia squealed in delight from the attention and treats. The adults slowly made their way into the house.

Luella was the first to speak. "Since I called each of you yesterday, nothing more has been found. I spoke with the local police department on the island of Tenerife, and they did find a hot air balloon in the water, but no people. They haven't determined if any local boaters may have picked up anyone. It has been about

13

thirty-six hours now, and if they don't find anything in the next twelve hours, they will call off the search." With that sense of finality, she broke into sobs. Each of her sisters did the same as they embraced, striving for some sense of comfort.

"Is there anything we should be doing?" Vera asked hopefully.

"I'm not sure there is anything we *can* do." Luella seemed frustrated. An air of hopelessness and helplessness prevailed. "I can't understand why Mom and Dad had to be so crazy! Why can't they be like other old people and play shuffleboard?"

Always the calm level-headed one, Richard offered words of comfort. "It's going to be OK."

"No! It isn't OK. My parents are probably dead, drowned or eaten by sharks, and your parents are alive doing paint-by-number at the senior citizen center."

Clutching Luella, Olivia said what everyone was thinking. "Why didn't we have normal parents like everyone else?"

The afternoon wore on. The sisters laughed, cried, and went through photos and old memories. Their children, ranging from four to ten years, spent their time sneaking donuts and pop-tarts out of the kitchen for Petunia. When the donuts were gone, they found an old broom handle in the shed and goaded poor Petunia each time she came begging for more treats.

When Emma and Phineas arrived, the crying and hugging started all over again. The same rhetorical questions, the same answers, and the same sense of loss. Each was so intent on comforting one another, they were startled when Luella's phone range.

14

"Hello?" she answered with anticipation. Everyone gathered around with hope, but that was slowly ebbing from her face. "OK, thank you for your help." She paused. "Do you have a phone number where we can get back to you? We need to talk this over as a family."

"I understand, miss. I am very sorry." The caller left his contact information and hung up.

"What's going on?" All eyes were on Luella.

"They found a backpack with Mom and Dad's luggage tag. It had the ship's ID card for each of them and a few personal belongings." She dabbed her eyes. "It was washed up on shore five miles from where the balloon was found. They called off the search."

Silence hung over them broken only by sobs and sniffles. It was finished. There was no more laughing or joking or recall of happy memories. It seemed too final.

"Emma, you are a legal assistant. Is there something we should do?" Vera was the first to break the sobbing silence. "We've never had to face anything like this before."

Emma thought for a few minutes. "Well, before anything can be settled, we need to have proof of death and a death certificate. In the United States it has been determined in the past that a missing person can't be declared dead until seven years have passed."

"Seven years?!" Vera declared. "We could all be dead by then!"

"Seven years has been the rule unless you can offer some proof or evidence to suggest the missing person has died. I hate to say it, but in my opinion, there is enough evidence now. We can pray for a miracle, but I don't think it's going to happen." Emma was very matter of fact about what they had already expressed to one another. Each nodded in agreement, a silent unified voice.

Over the next several days, life took on the ebb and flow of a roller coaster. The families stayed at Lake Namukwa sharing memories, and digging through boxes of old photos and mementos. Appetites were listless. Prepared meals were nibbled by children and slipped out the back door to the pigpen. Their pain was Petunia's gain.

They formed a list of things to be done. First, someone had to identify and claim their parent's personal belongings from the ship. The cruise line did agree to package them, and have them shipped, but a family member had to sign for receipt of the items. Secondly, they decided to contact a local lawyer to get advice. Although their disappearance was unexpected, Roy and Lola had made appropriate arrangements for their estate. A trust was established several years ago, and Olivia was listed on the joint bank account. Beyond that, the family had limited knowledge regarding property or assets. They found a safe deposit box key, but it was registered under the name of Roy or Lola only. They could not sign and gain access until a death certificate could be issued by the local judge. Unfortunately, it was Friday afternoon and any legal issues would have to wait. More time to feed Petunia.

Chapter 3

Court Hearing

Grief can take care of itself, but to get full value of a joy you must have somebody to divide it with. —Mark Twain

Small town living has its benefits. Namukwa perched on the northern shore of the lake from which it garnered its name. Home to a scant five hundred people except on summer weekends, it was possible to know most of the residents on a first name basis. So it was with Lenny Schyster, Esq.

During a quick stop at the local gas station and convenience store, Tom happened to bump into Lenny, filling up his boat at the same gas pump. News travels quickly in a small town, and when a descendent of one of the early pioneers goes missing, everyone is willing to lend an ear and spread the news, accurate or not.

Lenny Schyster was always alert for opportunities to make a buck. His plan was to put the boat in the water and casually motor over to the shoreline of the Ambrose home and offer his condolences. Despite no formal notification, most of the town had already written off Roy and Lola as fish bait. Lenny was no different. Most of his business involved estate planning, real estate, and an occasional personal injury claim. He wasn't against a bit of ambulance chasing, but increasingly, those cases were captured by the big-name firms out of Wausau, Minneapolis, Green Bay, Duluth-Superior and Stevens Point. Billboard advertising by law firms having six or seven hyphenated names attracted attention.

His official office name was Schyster and Son-Attorneys at Law. It sounded like a used car dealership. His one and only son was disbarred for an undisclosed reason and now ran a pawn shop in downtown Minneapolis. Rumors were many, but most believed he was using funds from a client trust account to pay for gambling debts. Green Lake Casino hurt the local economy as much as it helped. For some it destroyed their lives. Young Lenny was one of them.

"Tom, sorry to hear about your in-laws." Lenny put on his best sad face. Most people accepted him as being genuine with ulterior motives. He put his debit card into the gas pump and proceeded to fill his blue Seacrest ski boat as they talked. He stopped at half full. Since he had now contacted the family, there was no pressing need to put the boat in the water.

"Hi, Lenny, nice to see you." Tom answered. "Lenny, as a family—and I am speaking on behalf of Vera and her sisters—we need some legal advice. Are you available to meet with us while we are still up here at the lake?"

Lenny glanced at the calendar on his iPhone. "I'm in court on Monday morning, but I could meet with you all in the afternoon if that's OK? Call my office in the morning. Why don't we plan to meet in my conference room around two or 2:30. Would that work?"

"I'll let them know. Thanks." Tom finished pumping regular gas into his Toyota SUV and clicked the gas cap shut. At least one positive step forward.

#

Monday afternoon found the four sisters along with two of the husbands at Leonard Shyster's office. Phineas and Richard remained behind to monitor the kids while they got down to business, whatever direction that might be.

Lenny motioned for them to be seated around the oblong conference table in his office. He had his best suit on, only one small cigarette burn on the right lapel. His hair was slicked back, and his nose was as crooked as ever, realigned by an angry husband during divorce court. His thin mustache, carefully trimmed, had tobacco stains as did his front teeth and fingers on his right hand. The one-size-too-big suit helped to hide his thin frame, lacking any body fat from his stressful lifestyle and lifelong chain-smoking habit. But he was reliable and genuine if money was involved. He didn't have much of his own anymore after previous marriages had ended in divorce. He was on number four, this time marrying for money rather than love.

His assistant offered coffee, tea or bottled water, and they began. Leonard broke the ice. "I know or remember every one of you as you grew up in the local school system. The loss of a family member or a tragedy in a small town affects us all. I am very sorry about your loss." The girls glanced back and forth, waiting to see who would take the stage and speak first. They all remembered Lenny's kids in school, but Lenny himself hardly ever darkened the door of the school unless for a discipline issue with one of them. He had kids in the local school for nearly thirty years, having had children with each of his three previous wives.

As the oldest, Luella was the first to respond. "We know you are aware of our strange and tragic situation." She paused and dabbed her tears. "Mom and Dad are missing and the search has been called off. Personal belongings have been identified at sea, and they are feared dead. We don't know what to do and were hoping you could direct us through this very difficult time." Olivia, Vera, and Emma nodded in agreement but said nothing. A quiet sniffle was the only sound.

Emma spoke next. "I think the next step is to gather evidence and official documents and petition the court to issue a death certificate so we can proceed with appropriate transfer of their personal property." She looked around for approval, each nodding or looking to Lenny for advice. "Or is there something else we need to do?"

"Knowing that you were coming in today, I had my assistant do a search for legal documents, liens, titles, obligations etc. that are recorded in the court system. What I found is interesting. Roy and Lola had a will drawn up several years ago, but it was amended eighteen months ago and sealed. It is not available for review until the court recognizes their death. This was completed by the Minneapolis law firm of Snipe-Lempke-Ingram-Carlson and Kongsawatkoonapataporn. I am guessing that last partner is from Thailand. Anyway, the sealed document was filed in the courts both in Wisconsin and Minnesota as the firm is licensed in both states. They can be reached at SLICK-LAW.com. Appropriate contact information is on their website." He peered over his thin gold colored reading glasses at each of the girls around the table.

He coughed a couple of times and cleared his raspy, tobacco-ravaged voice and went on. "Their home here in Namukwa is part of a nonbinding living trust of which each of you girls are listed as equal beneficiaries. Likewise, they each had a modest IRA, and that money is included as part of the trust. Bank accounts and personal property are also part of the estate and by law should not be transferred or disposed of until the estate is settled. However, I will add that if there are items of personal interest within the home, you should work this out among yourselves. The court will not likely become involved in that unless there are items of high value or there is a dispute between you that you can't work out in some amicable manner."

He continued. "Because you are listed as equal beneficiaries of the trust, all will need to sign documents together, or we can draft an affidavit with your signatures authorizing a limited power of attorney, directing one or more of you to sign on behalf of the others so this process can move along as smoothly as possible. Generally, the items included in a trust can pass directly to heirs or beneficiaries and avoid probate unless there are unusual circumstances or the estate is unusually large. Because the will is sealed, you should contact the law firm that drafted the will."

Seeing and hearing no objections, he again proceeded. "This is a rather straight forward process, and it doesn't appear that we are dealing with a large or complicated estate. My usual fees apply for hourly work; here are my rates as they apply to situations such as this." He handed them a detailed form outlining fees from hourly rates of $450/hour calculated and divided into six minute increments, fees for mailing, copying, phone calls, responding to emails and, if necessary, fees for court appearance including travel time. Any filing fees required by the court would be in addition to any of his personal office fees. Any court appearance exceeding four hours in any given day would be charged at the full day rate of $450 per hour for eight hours plus a per diem of $100 for incidental expenses, food, drink or in his case likely an extra pack of cigarettes. Then there was the inevitable charge for research.

Olivia and Emma agreed to be the representatives of the family in part because Emma was a paralegal and Olivia lived the closest to Namukwa. Lenny added, "I will draft a letter with appropriate authorization for a release of documents by the authorities in Tenerife, Canary Islands. Since this is an international request, I don't expect it to move quickly. Hopefully we will have something official within three weeks, then we can schedule a court appearance. Again, please accept my sincere condolences. If I can be of any help elsewhere, let me know." The entire family nodded and thanked him as they exited the conference room.

As soon as they had cleared the exit, Lenny reached for a cigarette. Letting it dangle unlit from his lips, he waved at the departing Ambrose family and flipped his lighter. He wondered what they would find. Why would a small-town business owner file a will with a federal court in two states? Roy and Lola had a gift shop that sold knick-knacks, moccasins, fudge and beer and rubber tomahawks. Yet they were out of the country on vacations nine different times within the past three years, most of those for more than two weeks at a time. Something didn't add up. He coughed and took another drag on his unfiltered cigarettes. It just didn't add up.

#

Vera said, "Somehow I feel a small sense of relief at starting the process." She looked at the others. "But I'm willing to bet this isn't going to be quick or easy." Despite raw emotions compounded by poor sleep, everyone got along well. It had already been nearly ten days since the ill-fated phone call. She added, "I wish for once I could have just a normal day, whatever that is."

The cousins darted about in regular childlike fashion, and the parents did their best to ignore the inevitable minor mishaps. Feeding Petunia was always a good diversion. Arriving back at Papa and Grammy's house, everyone seemed to relax. They were back at the only home they had ever known since early childhood. No one expressed any interest in selling the property, and Vera hoped no one ever would. To those families from the Minnesota side of the river, the house was a cabin, to those in southern

Wisconsin and Iowa, it was a cottage, but to the girls it would always be home.

"Does Dad still have his wine cellar?" Vera wondered aloud. "I haven't been down there in years."

Olivia answered. "The last time I was home, I think he still had about two hundred bottles all labeled and categorized. Let's go downstairs and see." She led the way down the curved stairs into the lower level. In the middle of a painted mural on one end of the basement was a heavy paneled door. To anyone with basic art appreciation this was a very weak attempt to make a door look hidden. The door was secured with a simple sliding barn-door-type latch, no lock.

Slipping the latch, they entered the cool temperature-controlled recesses of the wine cellar. Three overhead lights flickered on. A tall, bright lamp on a center table illuminated tasting notes and Wine Spectator recommendations. Not knowing where to start, each of them surveyed the options. On the lower right was a line of French Bordeaux wines covered in dust. Six bottles of Les Forts de Latour, 2005, waiting for a cork screw. On the table was a log of wines entered and drunk. The price of the Latour was over $240 each. What startled them most was what came next. Three bottles of Chateau Lafite Rothschild, 1954, each worth $1200 and a half case of Chateau Lafite Rothschild Red Paulliac, 1954, with a price of $3600 per bottle.

The racks were full of wine, most from recent vintages, less than ten years old. Clearly the intent of the very expensive bottles was investment, but hundreds of bottles would likely exceed $200 in a high-end restaurant. No time like the present to sample the wares.

Emma piped up, "Hey everybody, let's have a good meal to remember Mom and Dad and celebrate their lives. I know it sounds kind of weird to be celebrating with them missing, but I need a break."

They all agreed a distraction was just what they needed to lift their hearts. Olivia wanted everything back the way it was. She knew it would never return to normal even if they desperately wished it could be so.

Each couple chose a bottle from all but the most expensive and oldest rack.

Emma hesitated as she spoke to the group. "Do you think Dad would be mad if we drank his expensive wine?" As if on cue everyone laughed at once.

Olivia responded. "Don't worry about what Dad would think. He wouldn't care, he loved a good party. But if you feel better about it, you can drink the cheap stuff."

Harry dug through the freezer. A case of lobster tails and several well-marbled ribeye steaks tried to dart out of sight behind the frozen green beans, but he rescued them from a lifetime of frosty obscurity. It was a celebration of life not to be repeated. Family life is easy when everyone gets along. It is even easier when the stories are supported with nearly $2000 of wine at a single meal. As hard as their loss was, they all expressed comfort at being part of a loving family. Their faith was strong and each held the belief that they would one day be reunited.

"Now look, I don't want to be a party pooper, but something doesn't seem right." Luella was often the first to raise an issue. "Mom and Dad had a simple little gift shop in town, right? Mom spent most of her adult life clipping coupons to save money. Dad drove his truck ten years before he traded it. So where did the money come from? People who sell trinkets don't usually have a wine cellar with $20,000 worth of investment grade wine, do they?"

Olivia tried to put a positive twist on the obvious. "Well, maybe they were just good at saving or investing."

"Are you kidding me?" Luella was getting geared up for a serious discussion. "Dad probably lost more money in the stock market than he ever made, and Mom never took a salary from the store because they couldn't afford it."

"Don't you remember when Grandpa died they inherited some money, or there was some life insurance or something like that." Emma looked over at her husband Phineas. "What do you think?"

Phineas was a lifelong idealist who tried to avoid controversy. And he always tried to see the best in people. "I think they found a lost Picasso at a garage sale and made millions." It didn't answer the question, but it was good enough.

#

The call came sooner than expected. Lenny had the certified documents from Tenerife, Canary Islands. The circuit court judge was willing to hear the case and set a court date for three weeks. Leonard Schyster reassured the family that the additional three weeks would work to their benefit because if nothing was found during that time, it would further support their request to have Roy and Lola Ambrose declared dead. As Emma handled the call, their request to have their parents declared dead struck her as weird and twisted. It wouldn't be easy.

#

"All rise," the bailiff addressed the members of the court as Pierce County Circuit Court Judge Michael East, presiding, entered.

"Please be seated." Judge Michael East addressed the court as he took his seat at the bench. The court reporter was seated and poised to record the proceedings.

"For the record, this is a closed hearing brought by the Ambrose family as beneficiaries of the estate of Roy W. Ambrose (DOB 9/20/1953) and his wife Lola H. Ambrose (DOB 3/28/1954). The request is to have the above stated individuals declared deceased based on evidence of missing person reports, failed search and rescue attempts and discovered evidence of the missing person or persons which would support the claim of loss of life. Is this the request that you bring before the court?"

"Yes, your Honor." Leonard was in his best form in court.

"How long has it been since the Ambrose couple disappeared?"

"Your Honor, it has been forty-three days since they were reported missing."

"And what evidence do you have to support your claims that the individuals are deceased and not simply missing? Forty-three days is a relatively brief time, and considering their personal history of extensive travel, isn't it possible they had a sudden change

27

in plans and didn't tell anyone?" The judge had a piercing look about him. He had a shiny shaved head, and his beard was dyed a distinct black and oiled to a slippery sheen. It was a perfect complement to his judicial robe. If you had any inkling to argue with the judge, his appearance was intimidating enough to change your mind.

"Exhibit A. We present information documenting the discovery of the remains of a hot air balloon in the Atlantic two miles off shore from the island of Tenerife, Canary Islands, on the date they were reported missing.

"Exhibit B. Further documentation showing that the individuals in question were in fact in the area of the accident and had purchased tickets for just such a tour.

"Exhibit C. Affidavits from fellow travelers supporting the fact that they were direct witnesses of the individuals in question traveling to the site of the hot air balloon launch. And they reported the individuals had in their possession a backpack matching the description of one found nearly five miles from the presumed crash site."

Each exhibit was handed to the judge for inspection and then to the court reporter for entry into the record.

The judge interrupted for a question. "Did you or anyone else actually see the individuals, Roy and Lola Ambrose, get into the balloon gondola and launch untethered from the ground?" He looked around at those attending the hearing. "Is there any clear evidence they actually lifted off from the ground?"

"No, your Honor, we have not identified any eye witnesses to document the activity you brought into question." Leonard went further. "The local authorities have not been able to find the balloon ride tour operator. However, we do have recovered evidence that was directly linked to Roy and Lola Ambrose. A backpack with a luggage tag identifying them as owners contained personal items. They were identified leaving the ship with this backpack and had it with them at the time they were dropped off for the presumed launch of the hot air balloon ride." He handed the judge photographic evidence certified by the search and rescue department of Tenerife.

"Your Honor?"

"Please address the court and identify yourself."

"Olivia Ambrose Seymour, daughter of Roy and Lola Ambrose. Your Honor, a disappearance like this is very atypical for them. My dad would walk off and never tell anyone, but Mom always let the family know everything they were going to do and when they would return. They must be dead, or we would have heard from them by now. We need some type of closure on this matter." Olivia pleaded with her eyes.

"Ms. Olivia Seymour, I know how difficult this may seem to you, but we want to make sure beyond a reasonable doubt before declaring them deceased." He thought for a moment. "Would you allow me twenty-four hours before I make a decision? I would like to think this through. Oh...I have one more question. Is there a pending claim against any life insurance policy of any kind?"

"No, your Honor," replied Leonard Schyster. "None that we are aware of."

"Ms. Olivia, on behalf of your family, are you aware of any insurance claims to be paid out, in part or in full, if the individuals in question, your parents, are declared deceased?"

"No, your Honor."

"Therefore, based on the evidence presented and the arguments regarding such evidence, I will make a final decision in twenty-four hours. My only concern is that no eyewitness has presented evidence to say they actually went for a balloon ride. You do see my concern, don't you?" A sharp rap of the gavel on the desk and court was dismissed.

Two hours later as the judge was leaving the traffic courtroom, the bailiff stopped him with a note regarding an important phone call. "I'll take it in my chambers."

"Hello, Judge Michael East, speaking."

"Judge East, we don't interfere with court proceedings, and we can't present evidence to support or deny the claims presented today regarding the Ambrose couple. They are deceased. I can say no more than that. I assume this will help you in your decisions. The Ambrose family are to have no knowledge of this conversation, is that understood?"

"Yes sir, I understand, but...who am I talking too?"

The phone went dead.

Chapter 4

El Quilete

The unexamined life is not worth living. —Socrates

La Casa de Mujeres (House of Women), Sinaloa Mexico, five years earlier

Traffic moved slowly in El Quilete. If the cobblestone streets weren't deterrent enough, drivers had to watch for goats and chickens and an occasional dusty kid. They didn't need speed bumps; the road was one continuous speed bump. Chickens scattered from their scratching and pecking in the shaded parts of the main street. Wide-eyed children stared from porches and old bicycles. Roosters crowed. A small church stood quietly by, observing life as it unfolded. A large wasp nest hung menacingly over the main entrance of the church, likely representing poor Sunday morning attendance.

"It's just up here on the right, great place to eat," Earl yelled out the window to Roy and Lola in the back of his truck. They nodded and waved.

Earl Ambrose was Roy's cousin, second cousin to be more specific. They hadn't seen each other for nearly fifty years. While Roy grew up in the Midwest, Earl had moved with his parents to the west coast, northern California. Earl's first wife, Hilda, had immigrated from Romania. She worked with her family as a trapeze artist or whatever you call circus people who make a living by swinging high in the air. Earl was a member of the Lions Club that helped sponsor the circus in a small town in northern California. That is how they met. She swept him off his feet. After six months, they were married. Although he had a good job as a math teacher, he quit to join the circus. He became their accountant, bookkeeper, ticket taker and even helped feed the elephants.

The way Earl explained it, the public wanted more thrill and less safety. As a result, the safety net used for the trapeze act was discontinued. Hilda fell to her death in a terrible accident. Earl was despondent and never able to put his life back on track. He moved to Mazatlán, Mexico, because he lost his pension from teaching. Living was cheap, and he got along.

During his time in Mazatlán he met Sandy Piper, another expat from the West Coast. Sandy was an artist, but unlike most artists, she wasn't starving. Her quiet, reserved façade contrasted with the mood of her paintings. But she always seemed to love good food and good times. She specialized in oils. Her subjects were people, usually women.

Earl scanned the street for chickens and children as he maneuvered his white Toyota truck to their destination, La Casa de Mujeres, the House of Women. Stiff from the forty-minute ride in the back of the truck, Lola stepped cautiously onto the bumper and then the uneven cobblestones. Roy followed. An enormous tree with smooth gray bark and large seedpods shaped like hundreds of ears hung over the plaza. Smoke from cooking in the back of the restaurant wafted up through the trees, bougainvillea, and disconnected red clay tiled roofs. The hot sun made everything slow. Roosters crowed somewhere back on the edge of town. The smell of barbacoa, Mexican BBQ, reminded everyone why they had come.

A little dark-skinned woman with twinkling eyes and a contented smile greeted them, "Buenos tardes." Her brightly colored dress was decorated with flour and grease marks. She flipped flour and corn tortillas onto the wood-fired grill and directed them toward the dining area. A young goat butted one of the village children, hoping for a bottle of milk. A chicken scratched at breadcrumbs on the floor between the tables, unconcerned about the sleeping gray striped tabby cat nearby.

The dining area was mostly open. Tiled roofs supported by rustic timbers sheltered the diners from the sun. The entire restaurant was open with no clear division between public and private spaces. One simply ran into the other. Along the back wall was a brightly painted mural and the reason for the name, La Casa de Mujeres. Brilliantly adorned local women were depicted dancing, working, playing, resting, and bathing. Like the small town and

33

restaurant where one space ran into another, the lives of the women were displayed in the same manner, showing a fine line between public and private. For Sandy, the mural was the culmination of two years of work.

Lola could see, Sandy was proud of her work and her arrival as a guest in La Casa de Mujeres excited the restaurant staff. Sandy and the others were seated near the mural as waiters quickly responded to any requests she had. Earl, Roy, and Lola were treated with equal dignity as her dining companions.

"Sandy, this mural is amazing. The colors are brilliant. The people look alive, like they are dancing. Can I ask a question about the mural?" Lola asked. "Did you volunteer to do this or did they pay you?"

She glanced about before answering. "I'll tell you later."

Earl, always the eager one to talk, leaned forward and in a hushed voice said, "We lived off the income from this painting for two years." Sandy gave him a look that didn't require translation.

Children came up to Roy as he was seated at the dining table, cherubs with big smiles and bigger baskets filled with trinkets for sale. Roy was quick to offer pesos but accepted nothing in return. From his position he could also see street peddlers perched on a bench in the shade but the usual beach vendor cacophony was absent. Two men, well-dressed, were seated near the back of the restaurant, one had a small glass of anjeo tequila, another had Pacifico. From Roy's vantage point, he could look out the window and down the street to the hacienda at the entrance to the village. In front of the hacienda sat another man, and down the street just

34

below the hill, near the cockfight arena or *peleas de gallos*, another man had the same casual but vigilant posture.

"Earl, what do you recommend from the menu?" Roy glanced over the offerings. "You told me you have tried everything more than once."

"Well, my favorite is the *cerdo a la barbacoa*, barbecued pork. But you really can't go wrong on any choice. Their seafood is wonderful. Any of the grilled items are great because it is all cooked over the wood-fired grill out back."

"Well, I'm having the barbecue." Roy looked over at Lola. "What are you going to get?"

"The bacon wrapped shrimp looks good, but I might just change my mind." Lola was never one to make up her mind until the waiter had taken the orders from everyone else first.

Always impatient, Roy excused himself from the table and went to the bathroom. Since prostate surgery, frequent rest stops had become a reality.

Walking around several tables, he found the bathroom near the rear entrance away from the street. The urinal was a wildly decorated statue of a pig with a trough carved into the back. Ice chunks were scattered about in the trough and the contents drained off somewhere. Standing at the pig, he could easily look out the window, down the street, toward the hacienda.

A black suburban pulled up slowly to the edge of town, windows tinted and reflective. It seemed oddly out of place in this dusty town. Probably a tourist from Mazatlán up for the day. Every door opened from the vehicle and several men stepped out. Roy studied the men. One looked familiar, but he couldn't recall exactly where he had seen him before.

Someone from the hacienda came out with a package. Sharp words were spoken, but they were too far away for Roy to hear, and he didn't know enough Spanish to understand anyway. What happened next, he did understand.

The two men from the hacienda were directed to turn around, and the young man from the front passenger side of the suburban, simply shot them in the back. No fighting, no discussion. Just 'Bang-Bang' you're dead.

Roy's heart skipped and fluttered. He ran back to the table, desperate to tell someone. The waiters were suddenly efficient and quiet as they came to the table. They no longer chatted among themselves and moved about quickly. Roy's sense of excitement and expectation were replaced with an aura of fear. His mouth was dry and he struggled to speak. Earl and Sandy looked straight ahead at their table and motioned for Roy to sit down and start eating. Lola's hands shook as she held the water glass to her mouth. The two well-dressed men in the back were gone.

The meal was eaten in unorthodox silence, and they passed up flan for dessert. There was no Mariachi music, and Earl's tip for the meal was uncharacteristically generous. They left quietly, no idle chatter with street vendors, no pausing to smell the flowers, and no time spent complementing the staff on a wonderful meal. They walked directly to the truck. By the time they had reached the small Toyota, the town had reverted to a sleepy wide spot on a dusty Mexican side road. Children chased each other down the street, and chickens resumed crowing and scratching.

Returning to Earl and Sandy's home, they went inside. It wasn't until the doors were locked behind them that they dared speak of the day's events.

Earl was the first. "Whatever you heard or saw or think you saw, try to forget it. El Quilete is one spot used by the Sinaloa drug cartel. The leader is Javier Espinosa. He is only twenty-five years old and is rumored to have killed more than a hundred people. They call him *El Chico*, the boy." He paused looking from Lola to Roy to Sandy. "As far as I know there are rewards out for information leading to his arrest and conviction, but no one here is dumb enough to try. The police can be bribed. Even if someone had the courage to speak against him there would be revenge."

Sandy spoke next. "The restaurant didn't pay for the mural, the cartel paid, probably Espinosa himself. We suspected the money came from the cartel, but we were paid to keep silent. We heard in a roundabout way, one of El Chico's women saw my painting in Poco Loco, a restaurant here in Mazatlán. She liked it so much El Chico asked the restaurant to have me paint the mural. Now you know. You need to be quiet as well. If El Chico suspects anything, there could be trouble." Sandy's hands trembled as she poured out a generous glass of tequila. There was no toasting today, she simply tipped the glass back and grimaced at the burn.

Roy now recognized the man who pulled the trigger as Javier Espinosa. His photo had been all over the US media with coverage of the Sinaloa drug cartel. For his own sake and for the safety of his cousin, Roy made a resolution to keep quiet. Everyone knew something happened, but only Roy saw it happen. Not until he was very certain they were safe would he even tell Lola. Maybe not even then.

Chapter 5

Avian Flu

I am not confused. I am just well mixed. –Robert Frost

The return flight from Mazatlán was nothing to write home about, at least according to what Lola wrote in her travel journal. She had numerous entries from their trip, different foods, people, places, weather, and spectacular sunsets, but details surrounding the day trip to El Quilete were absent. Of course, she wrote about the day, but her notes simply said, "We went to El Quilete and had lunch. It was a rather boring day. Not much happened."

During the flight home, Roy opened their travelogue intending to record his thoughts. He came across Lola's entry. With his pen in hand he paused over the page. "Not much happened." Those words ran over and over through his mind. "Not much happened." At the end of the page he wrote, "El Quilete is a nice little town, but I don't think I'll go back" and he signed his name, Roy A.

As the plane touched down in Minneapolis and taxied to the terminal, he resented being in third class. It wasn't third class, that didn't exist, but they always had the nonrefundable, cheapest seats usually at the back of the plane. More turbulence, less room, last on, last off. They did fly first class a couple of times, but it was on a complimentary upgrade because the airlines lost their luggage. He wondered at the tradeoff. Bigger seat, free drinks, no luggage, big deal.

As the line of fellow travelers thinned, they gathered their bags and headed to the terminal and processing through customs. The simple forms were completed. 1) What did you buy? 2) Do you have a pocket full of cash? 3) Did you visit a farm and get animal excrement on your shoes? And so on. Tired from the long day, they were anxious to get through the next few minutes and to the hotel where they were staying for the night.

"Next." The immigration officer at line number three, signaled. Lola and Roy stepped forward.

"Where were you?" He reviewed the customs declaration form. All items were "no" except a couple of gifts for grandchildren.

"Mazatlán, Mexico."

"Did you like the guacamole?" The officer loved to chat with travelers returning from foreign destinations.

"Oh, yes. It was always our favorite. Chips and guacamole at happy hour every day."

"That culture down there seems very interesting. Things are very different than here." Officer O'Brien flipped through their passports and stamped an empty page. "I watched a documentary on PBS about cock fighting that was fascinating."

"Oh, I know. We went out to one of the farms and watched a demonstration." As soon as the words slipped out her mouth, Roy knew they might be a bit late getting to the hotel.

Officer O'Brien reached over and hit the button to turn the light red on his lane. A friendly woman with a bulletproof vest and a gun to match approached. "Mr. and Mrs. Ambrose, would you please come with me." Lola didn't look back. Being led away into a closed room with three hundred airline passengers staring at you was an admission of guilt. It didn't matter what it was about; you were simply guilty.

"I need you to identify your bags and then follow me into this quarantine room." Ironically their bags were some of the first coming down the baggage carousel. Roy thought, "That never happens."

A low-level security person took the three bags with luggage tags identifying Roy and Lola as owners and placed them on the long low table behind the counter. They were instructed to have a seat.

"Do you know why you are here?" Her name tag read, "Officer Bridget H." She came across as a no-nonsense officer with a disarming smile. Roy bet the "H" didn't mean happy. It was probably the end of her shift, and she was missing a glass of wine at home with her feet up on the couch. "Mr. Roy Ambrose, do you know why you are here?"

"No, I'm sorry I don't know."

"Unfortunately, we have a crisis in the country with avian flu. Since you have been out of the country over the last fifteen days, about seven million turkeys were euthanized in Minnesota alone. I doubt you were being intentionally untruthful on your customs declaration, but you mentioned seeing a cock fighting demonstration. That means you were around domesticated birds of some type or another." Bridget snapped the latex gloves on her hand. Roy had a fleeting thought about getting searched, in areas that aren't normally searched unless you were visiting the gastroenterologist or prison.

"We take this very seriously since the CDC, the USDA and Homeland Security monitor all avenues of risk to our country through natural pathways as well as risks such as biological warfare. Now you look like nice little old people, innocent and all but the fine for failing to disclose being on or in the immediate proximity to any type of domestic farm, ranch or backyard chicken coop is $10,000 per person, per occurrence. In your case since you are two people, that amounts to $20,000.

"Now that I have your undivided attention we need to go through these questions in more detail. I am sure you will answer them appropriately and concisely and with enough detail to satisfy my curiosity."

Roy was tired. At age sixty-nine his prostate didn't function at the same level of efficiency as when he was thirty. The snap of the latex gloves didn't help matters.

"Mr. Ambrose, you seem a bit fidgety. Is there a way I can help you?"

"I'm sorry, can I use the rest room?"

"Of course. It's just down the hall." Bridget H. pointed toward the lighted restroom sign. "How long were you in Mexico?"

"Fifteen days."

The locked quarantine unit had meeting rooms, bathrooms, examination rooms and rooms to sleep. It was going to be a long night.

Roy and Lola were separated and questioned in detail regarding their stay in Mexico. Places they visited were of special interest along with names, dates, duration of stay and activities at those locations.

Officer Bridget was back to her usual pleasant self after the extended and detailed series of questions. "Now we want to see your camera and any travel journal or notes that you may keep about your travels. I don't need to get a search warrant to do this because this is a matter of national security."

"While we are going through these items, your shoes and clothing are being searched and will be irradiated to kill any potential pathogens which may be present." She paused. "We will be viewing your photos to document and correlate your stories. All your photos can and will be viewed. If you have photos of a personal or sensitive nature, be assured these will not be shared. All of what we are doing here today is an attempt to reduce the possibility of transmission of any biological agent to our agricultural industry or to the American people." Bridget talked on as if she had the script memorized.

"I believe you are both reasonable people on vacation, and you didn't realize the potential risk of your actions even though they were very innocent." She really seemed to come across as reasonable. Both Lola and Roy nodded politely, indicating they understood what was going on, but neither of them wanted to be part of it. Ironically the side issues of avian flu helped to distract them from their experience at El Quilete. "Once we are done with our final inspection and decontamination, you should be underway. I will need to get final approval for your release from my supervisor.

"Also, because every chicken and turkey farmer across North America is freaking out about Avian flu, this information will be entered into our national database so it can be referenced in the future. We are not keeping a file on you because you are a terrorist or drug dealer; this is simply protocol. Please have a seat in our waiting area as we resolve this matter." Officer Bridget motioned toward the chairs lined against the wall.

Roy and Lola settled back into the comfy metal folding chairs in the inspection room and sipped at the instant Nescafe coffee made available to people labeled as risks to the national security. Roy sighed and turned toward a very tired and discouraged-looking Lola.

"Well, kid, we did it again, didn't we?"

"Did what?"

"This, whatever 'this' is." He closed his eyes and thought back over the past couple of weeks. "Did you take any photos of that cock fighting chicken ranch?"

"Of course, I did. I have a picture of you holding one of the dumb things." She rolled her eyes. "We went out of our way just to see the dumb clucks and look what it got us!"

"What it got us? If you hadn't opened your mouth about going to the chicken farm we would be at the hotel enjoying a cold drink and a soft pillow, but NO, we must be friendly with the officer, mustn't we?"

"Are you blaming me for this? What about you? What about the time you were driving in the wrong lane, going the wrong way in New Zealand, and you killed the poor farmer's cow and you nearly hit the farmer?"

Roy rolled his eyes so far back they nearly got stuck. "What does New Zealand have to do with this? It's not my fault they drive on the wrong side of the road."

Lola was on a roll. "Or when you first came to a roundabout in Scotland, again on the wrong side of the road. You didn't know what to do so you went over the roundabout!" Now it was her turn to roll her eyes. "You blamed me for it, didn't you? You told the officer we were having a domestic discussion!" She continued. "The city magistrate let you off with a twenty- pound fine. They should have stamped your passport with big red letters that said IDIOT!" She was getting worked up. "Don't blame me for the little chicken dance. It was all your idea."

They were on the monitor and the detaining officers enjoyed the little sideshow. Everything checked out, and it was time to release these new domestic terrorists to the world.

Officer Bridget stepped away from the inspection area and approached Roy and Lola. "Mr. and Mrs. Ambrose, I am truly sorry for the inconvenience. I am sure you realize the seriousness of these little details. As I said before, this information will be available in the national database for cross-referencing in the future if necessary. Please drive safely on your way home."

Their little side trip caused them to miss the airport-hotel shuttle four times, but it came around every thirty minutes. Another short wait wasn't going to ruin the evening any further. With any luck, they wouldn't commit any serious crimes against one another.

After checking into the nearby Hilton Airport hotel, they were too tired and too angry to do anything other than get ready for bed. Reading the weekend edition of *USA Today* was a good way to relax and catch up on some of the happenings north of the border.

Suddenly Roy's eyes were riveted to a story on page three. A short article about the drug problem in Mexico and how it was affecting enforcement problems in the US. It wasn't the data about drug problems that worried him. He read further. Last week another undercover DEA agent was found dead in the Mexican state of Sinaloa. He had been shot in the back. Suspects include Javier Espinosa, leader of the Sinaloa drug cartel.

It wasn't the first time Roy had seen the man's face.

Chapter 6

Dag Rasmussen

I don't know which is more discouraging, literature or chickens. —E. B.White

Dag Rasmussen stopped in front of the black armored security entrance. He blotted a single bead of sweat just above his unibrow and adjusted his eye patch. His pulse was a steady sixty as he punched in his security entrance code. It was 4:58 AM. He ran the five miles to work in his uniform and combat boots. He didn't drive unless he needed to come in early.

Other agents in his office were already at their desks working. With Dag in charge you weren't late. Dag didn't waste words, preferring to communicate with grunts, gestures, or stare at you with one laser beam left eye. Maybe a nod.

"I want results today, people." When he spoke, people listened. But the results had been slow in coming and he was frustrated. He disliked puppies, his favorite food was hot peppered beef jerky and the only alcohol he drank was twenty-year-old single malt scotch, straight. But he never drank until he got his man, and he really needed a drink.

George B., the newest agent in the office, clicked on his computer screen and went through the security codes gaining access to the national database. Having graduated summa cum laude from University of Chicago law school, he gave up his law practice to join the DEA. After twenty years in the DEA, he was promoted to join the elite investigative branch under Dag. As the new kid on the block, he still needed to prove himself to Dag. No one gets a free pass. Dag would never verbally praise anyone, but if you did something good, he might give you the nod. Three of the other agents thought they got the nod in the past but were never quite sure.

Every day George ran the same search through the national database looking for any links, interesting facts or people that might give a clue to the death of the agent in Sinaloa, Mexico. George punched in the key words and took a long drink of cool coffee. Only 5:30 AM and already his coffee was cold. He needed a refill.

In Dag's office people didn't make small talk. If you had something to say, it better be important and pertinent to the mission. Chitchat was limited to hushed tones near the coffee pot.

"I heard the Cubs traded for a new starting pitcher last week." Phil Smith, a veteran of the office, glanced toward Dag as he whispered to George and poured himself another cup of coffee.

"Sounds good to me. I doubt they win the World Series before I die." George's favorite team was the Cubs. But like most Cubs fans, he was resigned to their destiny of 'always a bridesmaid, never a bride.'

Dag aimed his evil eye in their direction, and they parted as quickly as they could and returned to their workstations. George once made the mistake of asking someone what happened to Dag's eye. Co-workers reported that the room temperature dropped five degrees. No one answered. At a press conference several years before, an older woman made the same mistake. It was rumored that he kicked her cane out from under her. Two weeks later, off site in a locked room, late at night, Phil finally answered George's question.

"When Dag was young, about five or six, he was holding a pet chicken that belonged to a friend. Supposedly the chicken pecked him. He lost most of the vision in the eye. Dag wrung the chicken's neck. He hasn't spoken to his friend since. He still hates chickens. That was over fifty years ago." Even out of the office, Dag's presence hung over them.

Four thousand, three hundred thirty-seven hits showed up from the database search. George refined the key words and punched the search key. This time it narrowed to 157 items. Now came the hard part: reading.

Dag pulled out the bottom drawer of his file cabinet and carefully withdrew an unlabeled manila folder. Despite being immersed in high tech surveillance, terabytes of searchable files and every conceivable way to eaves drop on your neighbor, he still liked to hold something in his hand. The file folder held one newspaper article and one photo. The agent who died in El Quilete was his son, Paco. Dag had trained him personally, and he was good, one of the best. Dag was fifty-eight, his son was thirty-five.

Dag stared blankly at the photo as his mind wandered into his own past. He had served in a similar capacity in his early years with the agency. He was a liaison drug enforcement agent in Mexico when he met Maria Martinez. He wanted to be undercover, but a tall rusty-haired Dane doesn't blend too well with a small group of Mexican beach vendors. They had a relationship and Paco was the result. Dag had made certain that his birth took place at a military hospital in Texas so the boy was a US citizen. However, living in Mexico, the parents decided to give him the surname of his mother rather than Rasmussen. Growing up he developed all the strength and grit of his father but the physical appearance of his mother.

When Dag was reassigned back to the States, Maria stayed in Mexico. They had never married, but she played the role of an agent's wife. The stress and training that goes into making an agent successful in the mission goes completely against a stable relationship. Paco was in his teens at the time. Dag kept in contact for the benefit of Paco, but there was little likelihood he and Maria would ever get back together. When Paco became eighteen, Dag recruited him for DEA enforcement. He rose through the ranks quickly. He was a perfect fit for covert training and returned to Mexico.

The headline read "Otra Muertos," another dead. The photo told it all. If Dag had any tears, he would have shed them. He didn't.

George B. narrowed his brows as he read the bits of filtered information from his search. He took a quick slurp and put down his coffee. Immigration posted a possible avian flu virus exposure. Several days old, the information remained very pertinent. The key word was "El Quilete." He read the US customs report and jotted notes about the couple's personal travel journal. Collaborating photos with a date/time stamp were also uploaded.

The photos were fair quality and difficult to enlarge on his personal computer monitor, so he transferred it to the large conference screen at the front of the room. There before him was a photo taken by a tourist on the main street of El Quilete with a date and time which put them on the scene of the shooting. Seven photos were available. There was an older man holding a fighting cock, a small white Toyota truck with the words "Not for hire" on the side, and several more of the church, the town, and the restaurant. When he enlarged the photos of the cobblestone street, he saw in the background someone sitting in the shade outside the hacienda. Although the photo was grainy, he was sure he was looking at Paco, son of Dag Rasmussen, undercover agent for the DEA. Alive.

"Dag, I think I have something." To announce anything in Dag's office meant you better have something important. The boss put down his file and walked to George's workstation. The photo displayed on the screen didn't need explanation. "This was uploaded three days ago through immigration. It came up on my key word search."

Dag's eye pierced George. "What do you know about these people?"

"Old couple from Wisconsin, on vacation, went to a farm where they raise roosters for cock fighting." He glanced sideways at Dag. "Stopped at customs for possible avian virus contamination. The date and time stamp puts them on site around the time of the shooting."

"Who are these other people? Who is the guy with the cane?"

"Facial recognition software identifies this one as Earl Ambrose, originally from northern California area, and this is Sandy Piper. They are registered as permanent residents of Sinaloa, Mexico." Gesturing at the screen he pointed out Roy and Earl. "These two have the same last name."

Dag hated drug lords. He hated chickens even more. Having both together could be cataclysmic. Dag checked his pulse. Sixty-six. "Get me everything you have on Grandpa and Granny and everybody they visited, everyplace they went, and I want them face to face with me in twenty-four hours. And send an agent to visit the guy with the limp. Today." He nodded toward George. In this office the nod was as good as the Congressional Medal of Honor. George had arrived.

From Springfield, Virginia, to northern Wisconsin the flight took three hours and fifteen minutes. The Learjet-60 departed from DEA headquarters carrying Dag Rasmussen, special agent George Benson and one assistant. In flight they had plenty of time to review the files and get up to date. The Learjet had satellite communication capabilities, and they wasted no time in sorting information and discussing the implications.

"What do you know about the big guy with the cane?" Dag studied the photos and directed his question to the assistant

"Here's what we know so far. Earl Ambrose is sixty-seven years old. Grew up in a small town in northern California. He is a former math teacher. He was married to a woman named Hilda who was a circus trapeze artist. She died in an accident, and he lost his circus job. We assume he ran out of money, and he moved to Mexico because it was cheaper."

Dag shot her the eye. "Rule number one: don't assume anything."

"Sorry." The assistant continued with the briefing. "He moved to Sinaloa, Mexico, about six years ago, and met this lady, Sandy Piper. He had the knee replacement surgery in Mexico, and the payment for the surgery was cash. From what we have gathered, she is a very successful artist and paid for the surgery. Everything about her seems straight forward. Here's where the story gets interesting from our perspective." She looked up to make sure Dag and George were still following her.

"The knee replacement was botched. The surgeon put the artificial knee joint in reverse from what it should have been. Anyway, instead of the usual way, his knee bent backwards like a chicken." She paused to see if it was safe to continue. "They didn't discover it for a week until he had therapy. By then the swelling was so bad they had to wait to do a revision.

"He eventually had a second surgery, but there was so much scar tissue and damage they were unable to successfully remove the first prosthetic joint so his leg still bends backward. His bad leg is shorter than his good leg, and he lives in chronic pain. The surgeon wouldn't provide any more medication, and he has been getting something from a street vendor to control his pain."

"Any evidence hes dealing?" George was looking for an obvious link to the cartel.

"Nothing like that, but anything being sold on the street would most likely be coming from the cartel because they get really touchy about competition. A street dealer is small potatoes. I bet we would have to trace him back through three or four other dealers to get to anyone with direct links to the cartel and El Chico."

"OK. What about the Ambrose couple?" Dag was keen to know everything he could about them before the visit.

"Here is the printed summary of what we know." She handed him the file on Roy and Lola Ambrose. "Both grew up in the small town where they now live. High school sweethearts, they have been married since they were about eighteen or nineteen. They have four daughters all married, none of them living locally. They own and operate Roy and Lola's Knick Knacks, a small gift shop for tourists. Roy came into some money a year ago when his father died. Modest amount—fifty thousand roughly. They like to travel, but usually go for budget deals and offseason which is cheaper."

Dag glanced over the summary sheet. "Tell me a little more about their relationship with Earl."

"Second cousins. No evidence of any contact between them for many years. Then on social media there is a contact between Lola and Earl about two years ago. Everything looks like old relatives finding each other and getting reacquainted."

Dag commented on Roy's military past. "I see he was in the army, infantry. Served stateside, missed Vietnam. There was a Major General Ambrose, now retired, who was in the service then. I can't see how an infantryman missed Vietnam during the height of conflict. I wonder if there is a connection. Old Ambrose probably pulled some strings to keep Roy safe."

"Do you want me to check on that, sir?" George made a notation on his file.

"Nope, Old Ambrose wouldn't leave a paper trail, and it doesn't matter anyway. We are in a chess game, and Roy and Lola are just dumb pawns. If you want to win the game, we may have to sacrifice a pawn or two."

The plane touched down at a county airport with a runway long enough to handle the Learjet-60. A regional DEA official met them at the airport and drove them to the Ambrose residence. Time to make a move. Dag could almost taste the single-malt scotch.

Chapter 7

Red Rock Cemetery

Let's talk of graves, of worms and epitaphs. —
William Shakespeare

Luella felt her heart flutter and skip at the final rap of the gavel. It was over. Roy and Lola Ambrose were dead. They weren't dead on their own accord; they were dead because the judge said they were dead. Even though they disappeared nearly six weeks prior to the decision, the death certificates indicated the time and date when they were declared dead, and not a moment before. She wondered how it all made sense, but then again, she wasn't sure if government actions were synonymous with common sense. It didn't matter anyway.

The stress of the previous six weeks had left its mark on Luella and the rest of the Ambrose family. Someone said it was like trying to take a picture out the window of a speeding car. Nothing was in focus. Luella couldn't remember who said it, but they were right.

Despite the blurred view of life, she felt the outpouring of love and kindness from neighbors and friends was at times overwhelming.

Roy and Lola's Knick-Knack shop remained open. It basically ran itself with simple restocking and someone to take loose change from the weekend kids, up at the lake. Emma and Phineas adjusted their personal lives more easily than the others because they didn't have any kids yet. Phineas was a graduate student working on his PhD in music theory. They stayed at the lake home to help maintain some stability if that was even attainable.

The area neighbors and friends of the family were generous. At one point Luella counted four pans of lasagna, three roasted chickens, two loaves of bread, two jars of homemade blueberry preserves, and a tuna noodle hot dish. Some people in other places called it a casserole, but up here it was a hot dish. It tasted the same. On weekends or when time was available, the other girls and their families returned to help. There really wasn't much to do anymore but it was good for the soul. Hanging on to memories was the hard part, and a chance for another look back was dear to their hearts.

Emma broached the idea when everyone happened to be available for a summer weekend. "I think we need to consider a memorial service and some type of grave stone for Mom and Dad. Phineas and I have been up to the cemetery looking around. If they had died normally, they would have wanted to be buried up at Red Rock."

"Has anyone checked to see if they have plots already purchased?" Olivia went on. "I thought they were talking about that a couple years back."

"I called the cemetery caretaker last week because we were thinking the same thing. He said they had one plot in their name. He faxed a map of the cemetery to indicate the location." Luella pulled it from her purse.

Emma responded, "I did the same thing, but it didn't make sense. We drove by there, and I thought there was a monument already in place, unless we were looking in the wrong area. Why would they buy only one plot?"

Vera was the last to enter the fray. "Why don't we drive over there right now. It's a nice evening, and it can't be more than ten miles from here. The kids can run around while we look things over."

Despite ride sharing it still required three minivans to transport the unruly crowd. Big kids ran about, little kids toddled, and babies slept in car seats or vomited or pooped or drooled or whatever they wanted to do.

The cemetery wasn't as large as some, but finding the plot was difficult even with the map. Red Rock Cemetery was laid out in the mid 1800's, which meant there wasn't much in the way of planning. It sloped from west to east and covered about three acres. A large red sandstone outcropping crowned the hill, which, if scaled successfully, offered a stunning view of the area. The backside of the outcropping was very steep and unusable. The burial ground faced east and offered a gentle quiet place for grieving souls. Some claimed it was an old Indian burial ground; others claimed it was started by early pioneers. The earliest known marked grave was Fred "Old Man" Thompson buried behind the big oak tree. Ironically when he was buried, the tree didn't exist. The date on his gravesite was difficult to read but was discernable as April 1865, the same as Lincoln.

The adults in the Ambrose group spoke in hushed tones, commenting on the recorded dates. Some families had lost most of their children within one or two years likely due to diphtheria or small pox. Many markers had a first name and son of... or daughter of... or simply beloved. Luella reflected how the loss of others had a way of making your own pain bearable.

"I think it's over here," Emma called from the side near the highest point of the cemetery. "Lu, I assume your map shows the same place, here in the second row, the fourth plot north from the survey marker, right?"

There in front of them was an enigma, something they had never encountered.

CHARITY AMBROSE
1-7-1981 – 11-4-1993
THESE THREE REMAIN, FAITH, HOPE, AND CHARITY
BUT THE GREATEST OF THESE IS CHARITY
MATTHEW 7:7

"Who is this? Did Mom and Dad have another child that died?" Luella coughed and struggled to catch her breath. "What's going on?"

Despite the warmth of the day, Vera clutched her collar and pulled it snug around her neck. Luella and Vera locked eyes and said nothing.

"Emma, when you called the caretaker, did he say anything about the grave or who might be buried there?" Luella asked.

"Well no, but when I called, I didn't know what we know now, which I guess isn't much. If that makes any sense." Emma looked from person to person. "Luella, you're the oldest, do you ever remember any mention of someone named Charity, even from distant relatives?"

"Look, guys." Luella looked pale and weak. "I need to go home and think about this. Something doesn't seem right." The entourage silently returned to the vehicles as if they were leaving a graveside funeral of a love one. No one spoke again of the gravestone until the following morning.

Luella gulped her first cup of French roast coffee and spoke. "I couldn't sleep last night, this whole thing really shook me. So, I got up and checked for any information I could find on the Internet about Charity Ambrose. Here's what I found: There was a Charity Ambrose who died at birth or shortly after but that was in the early 1800's out east near Boston. There is an exotic dancer who goes by Charity Ambrose, and there is an Ambrose monastery in England that has a charity event once a year. I found a few others named Charity Ambrose, but I can't see any connection to us, and these people are still alive, not buried on Red Rock Hill." Luella continued, "The second thing that bugged me was the Bible verse. The verse and reference didn't match. I was too rattled to see it at first, but I took a picture of it yesterday and checked it last night. The verse is from Corinthians, and the reference is Matthew 7:7." She looked around to see if anyone else noticed the discrepancy. "And the third thing that really bugged me were the dates. I was born in July of 1981 so Mom couldn't have had another daughter born in January of the same year."

"Did Dad have any brothers or uncles or cousins who might have had a daughter around that time?" Olivia's reasoning made sense to Luella and the rest. The logical explanation was simple. This had to be another family, perhaps related but distant. "Well that's possible, isn't it? Dad's related to almost everyone around here in some way."

Vera chimed in. "What about the possibility of a child born out of wedlock, kept secret?" No one wanted to admit it but that was a possibility. "It doesn't mean she is our sister or half-sister, but this seems like a logical explanation." Looking around, "Let's face it, Dad could've had an affair; we don't know. She could have lived somewhere else and was sent here to be buried."

"Well, if that's the case, then she is our sister, and we should have known, but if she isn't, then who is she and where did she come from?" Luella held her head in her hands. "My life is getting weirder by the minute."

A search of online public records didn't solve the problem. No record of any Charity Ambrose who matched the dates on the stone, not anywhere in the states of Wisconsin or Minnesota or Iowa or South Dakota; nowhere. No birth certificates, no death certificates, no school enrollment, no social security numbers, no

61

church memberships, and no baptism records. The only place they could find Charity Ambrose was Red Rock Cemetery on the hill, out past the old Larsen farm. And she wasn't talking.

Chapter 8

Playing Chess

In this life, we are either kings or pawns, emperors or fools. —
Napoleon Bonaparte

"**W**hat are you doing?" Roy paced the floor, anxious about the
visit from the DEA. But he couldn't believe what Lola was doing.
"You're baking cookies and making tea? Do you think this is a tea
party? A social visit?" Lola, with her graying hair pulled back into
a bun, bent over the open oven, lifting out baking sheets covered
with soft, melted, chocolate chip cookies. Two sheets of cookies already sat cooling on the worn Formica counter top.

"Well the lady who called sounded so nice on the phone, I
thought this would make it more pleasant." It didn't matter anyway. Roy could see she was anxious and this was her way of dealing with it. The chocolate chip cookies did smell good coming out
of the oven. Roy had a habit of eating when he was nervous. He ate
four of them.

Petunia squealed loudly from her pen beside the garage as the black suburban with dark tinted windows pulled into the driveway. Always hopeful for a handout, she locked her eyes on Dag Rasmussen. Her nose, the size of a salad plate, twitched, searching for treats. Expressing her disappointment, she grunted and turned away as the visitors marched to the front door.

Lola clasped her hands tightly in front of her as she greeted the agents. "Oh, so nice that you could stop by. Please come in."

George did the introductions. Dag grunted.

Lola smoothed the front of her dress and motioned to the guests. "Would you rather sit here in the living room, or we could all sit around the kitchen table and have tea and cookies as we visit."

Each of the agents wore uniforms and a badge for a reason. It intimidated people. "Mr. and Mrs. Ambrose, I know this can be difficult, but we are here to get information, that's all. We are not here to arrest you. We don't believe you have anything to hide, and we are hopeful you can help us. Is that clear?" George smiled pleasantly.

"Oh, certainly we want to help you. Coffee or tea anyone?" Lola was relieved to know she wasn't in trouble. In typical grandmotherly fashion, she was ready and started pouring. Ignoring any protests, she placed steaming mugs before the new arrivals.

"No thank you, ma'am; this isn't a social visit." George pulled out his pen and legal pad and started writing some notes. It was arranged as a tag team approach. George was the good guy, Dag was the bad guy, and Rita, the assistant was there to keep the peace. "We need to find out everything you know about your recent visit to Mexico.

"First of all, we want you to know why we are here. The drug problem in this country is out of control. The Mexican drug cartels are a big part of the problem. Working together is the only way to get this under control. We are looking for any information you might have about the Sinaloa drug cartel. Even the smallest amount of information can be very helpful in putting these people out of business." George laid it all out so simple and clear, and Lola appeared to relax. He opened his attaché and pulled out some files. "We already have some basic information. Have you traveled to Mexico before?"

"Several times," Roy answered abruptly. It was clear to everyone, he wasn't interested in answering questions. He recalled the time he had to give a deposition and the lawyer coached him through the process. Short simple answers, don't volunteer anything and answer only the question being asked.

"Could you elaborate on that?"

"What do you want to know?" Roy was nervous and testy at the same time. His hand trembled slightly as he pushed his teacup toward the center of the table. He avoided eye contact with the agents. He eyes darted around the room, from the yellowed pine paneling to the dusty whitetail deer head mounted above the fireplace as if searching for a secret passage to escape.

"When have you been to Mexico in the past, for what purpose, where did you go and how long did you stay? Is that specific enough?" Dag was already impatient and wanted to get to the meat of the visit.

"Cancun 1987; Mazatlán 2004; Puerto Vallarta 2005, Mazatlán 2009; and again, this year. Each time we stayed seven to ten days. Fifteen days this time." Figuring some of these questions might come up, Roy was ready. "Always for vacation."

"What did you do on the most recent visit?" George continued to make notes. His black government-issue ballpoint pen quit working, and he reached for another.

"Do you want me to be specific or generalized?"

"Please be as specific as possible if you can."

Roy stared blankly out the large windows overlooking at the lakefront as he began. "On the first day we got up around 7:35 and had coffee, then we went for a walk on the beach going south for about half a mile and then returned to the condominium and read the morning news on the Internet. Then we talked to one of the beach vendors trying to sell blankets. We didn't buy one. Following that we played shuffleboard with another couple registered at the same resort. After that we sat by the pool and read a book. I don't recall the name of the book because it wasn't very good, but that was my opinion. At lunch..."

Dag's good eye twitched, and he ground his teeth as he clenched his jaw. "Let's change this questioning." He held out enlarged copies of the photos collected by the customs officer. "Who took these pictures?"

"I did." Lola spoke up nervously. "I took them."

"Please identify the people in the photo for me."

Pointing at the photos with a finger, she identified Earl Ambrose, Sandy Piper, Elizabeth Elkins, a friend of Sandy's from California and Roy Ambrose.

"Thank you. Now do you see anyone else in the photo that you might know?"

"It was just us." Lola seemed pleased with her answer.

"How about this person?" Dag stabbed his thick finger in the direction of Paco.

"Oh... I didn't realize there was anyone there at the time." Lola flushed as if she had been caught cheating on a school spelling test.

"Now after you took pictures what did you do?" He looked at Lola, ignoring Roy. She was talking.

"Well, Roy what did we do? Did we go into the restaurant, or did we walk around town and go to the church? Or did we go up to the chicken farm? I don't remember, it seems like we did quite a bit, didn't we?" Lola played with the corner of her napkin absent-mindedly.

"Lola, we went into the restaurant and had lunch." Roy answered. "From what I recall, we ate lunch, and then we left and went back to Mazatlán. Nothing more."

George stepped in. "Lola, you keep a travel diary, and you like to keep notes on places you have been. Am I correct?"

"Oh yes, I love to write things down. It's so easy to forget where you went and what you did. I have been doing this for years. Do you want to see some of my travel journals?" Her cheerfulness irritated Roy. He rolled his eyes but a glance from 'old one-eye' kept him in check.

"Lola, is this a copy of your travel journal?" George held out a rather large stack of photocopies held together with a hefty clip.

"Yes, that's mine. How did you get a copy?"

"From the customs officer at the airport. You were notified this information was going to be uploaded into the national database. You recall when you were detained at the airport, don't you?" George studied their faces for any response. "Ma'am, we reviewed your travel journal, and I find your descriptions of places and events to be quite interesting. If I do any traveling, I would like your recommendations."

Lola smiled toward the group as her travel diaries were discussed. "Thank you. I try to keep detailed notes about the places we've been. More than once it settled an argument between Roy and myself about places we've traveled."

"For example, on this day," George indicated one specific entry. "You described the traffic, the places you ate, the food, the smells and the weather. It all sounds interesting. And on another day, you talked about the beach vendors, the sunset and the 'gringo bingo' you played at the resort." He made sure she and Roy were following him before he continued.

"Now on this day, you went to El Quilete for lunch with your friends and all you wrote was 'not much happened' and Roy agreed. You have many days when you described the sunset and refried beans in exquisite detail but on this particular day, 'nothing much happened'. Don't you find this odd?"

Lola struggled to speak. "I guess I didn't know what to write."

"And why didn't you have anything to write?" Neither Lola nor Roy spoke. The only sound was the loud tick-tock of the old wind-up clock on the kitchen wall. The pressure to speak was building, but they kept their silence as they had agreed before the agents arrived. Roy had never told Lola about what he had seen out the bathroom window. It was his secret and he intended to keep it.

Dag leaned forward and focused his lone eye directly on Lola. She fidgeted in her chair and rubbed her hands together. "What do you know that you aren't telling me? What are you trying to hide?" He stared for a moment, watching her squirm. "Do you know what happened in El Quilete that day?"

"We heard a noise that sounded like gunshots." There she said it, and the emotions seemed to drain out of her. She cried and glanced at Roy. She had failed to keep her end of the bargain. "We didn't want to say anything because we thought it was related to the drug cartel or something like that."

"Did you think you were in trouble?"

"Yes! If the drug dealers think we knew something, then they might get us." Lola sobbed.

And Dag added, "If I think you know something important you aren't telling me, I will get you, too."

Roy tried to ignore the people, but the tick-tock from the old wind-up schoolhouse clock seemed louder and more incessant in the background. The questioning went on for another three hours, digging through details in the travel journals, exploring any and all ties with Earl and Sandy Ambrose and Elizabeth Elkins and repeated questioning about the day at the chicken ranch.

As the day wore on, there was little further helpful information forthcoming from Roy and Lola. It was time to wrap and begin the return flight to DEA headquarters in Springfield, Virginia. Roy didn't like the way Dag looked at him, and he hated Lola's chattiness. Roy ground his teeth and swallowed hard. He wasn't going to crack.

"Before we leave I want to remind you of one fact: withholding information from a federal investigation is considered a felony. I think you know something you aren't telling us. You aren't in trouble because you witnessed something, but you are in trouble if you fail to let us know." He paused for a minute before he went on. "I am reinstating the fine allowed by immigration of $10,000 per person for failure to disclose your presence in an agricultural setting and the risk of transferring the avian flu virus. That's $20,000. The penalty also allows for six months to two years in prison. You have up to sixty days to make the payment in full, or we will come knocking on your doors again. We will be in touch."

Lola sobbed. "Oh Roy, I don't want to go to jail." Roy clenched his jaw but refused to answer.

As the DEA entourage retraced their steps, Dag was deep in thought. The drive from the Ambrose home through twenty-seven miles of winding country roads to the small county airport was uncharacteristically quiet until he spoke. Dag talked quietly as if to himself. "I figured Roy witnessed something or knew something, and he's trying to protect himself, his family or more likely

70

someone else." George and Rita kept silent. They had received counsel to avoid interruption when Dag's one good eye was focused somewhere in the distance. "If Roy was an eye witness of the execution of Paco the DEA agent, and he's willing and able to testify in court, maybe we could get an arrest and extradition to the US for a federal trial. Without an eye witness the chance is almost zero." He quit thinking aloud and a nervous quiet settled over the group.

Finally, as the Learjet lifted off and reached cruising altitude, Dag began to speak again. "OK, here's our plan. Release information to our undercover agents in Sinaloa, about an American witness to the killing but don't let anyone know who. My guess is that Espinosa is well aware of who was in town that day. I am sure one of his flunkies kept track of the license plate and identified the truck of Earl Ambrose. We'll see if he makes a move." Dag went back into deep thought.

George spoke up. "What if Espinosa doesn't show his hand?"

Dag thought for a moment. "If El Chico doesn't kill Earl or Roy Ambrose, I will."

Chapter 9

Probate

The minute you read something you can't understand, you can almost be sure it was drawn up by a lawyer. —Will Rogers

The sisters sat like nervous schoolgirls awaiting their teacher on the first day of school. Knees together, hands clasped on their laps, eyes straight ahead and on the front edge of their chairs, in the conference room in the main office of SLICK-LAW. The Last Will and Testament of their parents had been filed with the appropriate legal authorities and was handled by the law firm of Snipe-Lempke-Ingram-Carlson and Kongsawatkoonapataporn. Today the Ambrose family was scheduled to meet with Gretta Lempke-Hanninin, attorney and daughter of founding partner Lyle Lempke.

"Good morning. I'm sorry I am a few minutes late." Attorney Gretta entered the room in a flurry, her heels tapping out a staccato Morse code of warning to anyone unfortunate enough to get in her way. "And you are the Ambrose family, or representatives of the family?" She glanced around the room looking for a response. "I realize this can be a difficult time. I understand what you are going through. My own father passed away about three years ago. Despite handling many similar situations, it always brings back memories."

"Yes, we are the Ambrose sisters. I am Luella and this is my husband Tom." Each went around and introduced themselves.

"Please be seated." Gretta motioned to the dark gleaming boardroom table surrounded by chairs. An eighteenth-century tapestry portraying a balanced scale symbolizing law and justice hung at the end of the conference room as witness to the meeting. The cushioned chairs skated noiselessly across the polished marble floor as they adjusted their positions.

Vera echoed the thoughts of the group. "Thank you for being able to meet with us today. It is difficult to arrange a time when we can all be together because of family and work obligations."

"Let's get right to the issues." Gretta arranged her notes and began. "First, since Luella originally contacted us about four weeks ago and provided certified death certificates of your parents, we have proceeded with the necessary notifications required by law. This allows any third parties with claims against the estate to present those claims to the court for appropriate review and settlement. I also understand that Mr. Leonard Shyster of Namukwa, Wisconsin, assisted you in getting the court to establish that your parents were deceased and not simply declared missing, is that correct?"

"Yes, that's right." Several responded by nodding in agreement.

"Well, so far we have received no unexpected claims against the estate, which makes the process easier. I also understand that one of you, is it you, Olivia? Are you listed on the joint checking account?"

Olivia nodded affirmatively.

"So, you are able to take care of incidental issues such as utilities and such? Are you having any problems with the account?" Gretta arched her eyebrows as she looked up from the Ambrose information folder in front of her.

"None so far." The formal oak paneling of the room didn't create a space for informal chatter. It was all business.

"I want to commend you on having parents who took estate planning seriously. Most of the controversies arise when no will or trust has been established and the heirs can't decide to get along and make reasonable decisions. Usually this is with large estates and a sudden or unexpected death in the family. I realize your parents died unexpectedly, but their attention to detail was good." She paused to open a bottle of Evian mineral water and took a brief swallow. As if by reflex or by a sudden granting of permission, others around the room took sips of water as well. "Based on our review of the living trust, the assets of their retirement accounts will more than cover the remaining small mortgage and any unpaid taxes and legal fees in the settlement. I expect you will be able to inherit the home and additional property they owned without any unanticipated expenses along with a reasonable amount of money.

I am estimating about $150,000, depending on the appraised value of the home, to include one fourth of the property value for each family after expenses.

"Now, before we go on to the will and assets, do any of you have any questions? If so, please feel free to interrupt me at any time." Seeing no objections, she continued.

"Here is the Last Will and Testament of Roy and Lola Ambrose, dated and signed about twenty-two months ago." She paused and took another long drink of water. "This is clearly out of the ordinary, at least in my experience. Most people bequeath certain unique items, usually listed in a will or assets designated to be dispersed in equal sums to their heirs. Your parents did neither."

Emma, the youngest leaned forward. "What do you mean by that?" She was hoping her experience as a paralegal would help to smooth the process. "I thought you said each family should inherit about $150 thousand dollars of value based on your review of the trust?"

"That was the Revocable Trust. The will refers to the trust, but also has another part to it. There are two separate exhibits or attachments that aren't in our possession. This will stipulates the estate will be divided and settled in accordance with the unanimous agreement of the heirs (daughters) or any surviving members thereof based on consideration of the attachments which are held in a safe deposit box at the Suisse Bank in downtown Minneapolis. We have this key in our position." She held up a key enclosed in a case engraved with the number and location of the safe deposit box.

Emma spoke up. "Is it possible that we can go to the Suisse Bank today and get the will?" Her tone made it clear to the group, she was hoping to get this settled, or at least as much as possible, before she returned to South Dakota.

"Certainly, it's possible. Did you bring the other key?" There was dumb look of stunned silence.

"What other key?" Luella glanced around at the blank looks of everyone else in the room. "Are we supposed to have another key?"

Olivia responded. "Don't you remember the safe deposit key we found? But it was to the local bank. I bet the Suisse Bank key is in there."

"That would make sense, but we can't get in there until it is cleared by the judge, and the judge won't clear anything until we have the will. And the will is in the Suisse Bank box. So, what can we do?" Luella felt dizzy with the circuitous reasoning.

"All safe deposit boxes at the Suisse Bank have at least two keys. One held by the bank and the other by the owner of the contents of the box. In this case, your parents rented one of the high security boxes that require three keys: one held in trust by us, a universal key held by the bank and one by the owner." Gretta glanced at the wall of blank looks around the table. "I may be wrong, but based on your quizzical expressions, you appear to have many unanswered questions." No one moved as she pulled out a note and began to read.

"There is an attached handwritten note stating, 'My children possess the key.' Is this your father's handwriting?" Gretta slid the note toward the center of the polished conference table. It didn't say anything about a safe deposit box at home or anything else regarding its whereabouts.

Vera answered, "Yes, that's Dad's handwriting. But...does anyone here know about a different safe deposit key?" Silence answered her question. Turning again to Gretta she asked, "Can we get the local judge to allow access to the local bank safe deposit box so we can work on getting the will?"

Gretta said, "All we can do is ask."

Olivia looked around searching for a flicker of insight. One by one they all expressed confusion and frustration. "Let me ask the obvious here. What if we can't find the key, what are the options?"

"Most banks will have the locks drilled out for a considerable fee of course. The Swiss are different. They generally won't do that unless you can present a compelling need and a court order and only after petitioning the bank to do this and a waiting period of one year has passed. They hope that during the passing year the key may be found. They take the security of their banks very seriously."

An air of resignation hovered over the group. While information about the will was helpful, it didn't resolve anything. Gretta continued, "We have requested a court date to meet with the judge to have the Last Will and Testament reviewed and settled." She flipped through the calendar on her smart phone. "That is thirty-seven days from now. Which gives you a month to find the key so we can get the contents of the safe deposit box for the scheduled probate hearing." She stood up signaling an end to the conference. "If you don't have the key within thirty days please let us know because it is pointless to go to court without the necessary documents."

"Gretta, may I ask a question?" Vera raised her hand as if asking permission to interrupt. "Do you know why our parents would choose a Suisse Bank over a local bank for a safe deposit box? It doesn't make any sense to me."

"Generally, any Swiss banking arrangements are limited to people who have international business relationships or substantial cash reserves or need anonymity. I don't mean to sound condescending, but, based on what I know about your parents, I don't see the need for a Suisse Bank safe deposit box unless they have something exceedingly rare or valuable or they have a special need for secrecy." As her heels resumed their clicking, she turned. "When you find the key, then we'll know."

Chapter 10

A Penny for Petunia

Wilbur didn't want food, he wanted love. —E. B. White

Summer was in full swing and the activity on the lake reflected it. The cool mood swings of spring were gone and life floated on summer bliss. Gone were the long mournful wails of the loons at sunset, replaced by fireworks, jet skis and laughing children. As husbands and children and work schedules allowed, each of the Ambrose sisters retreated to the shores of Namukwa Lake as often as possible to reflect and remember and search for the key—the key to the Suisse Bank safe deposit box. After a week without progress, frustrations began to set in.

Tom was out of school for the summer and spent as much time as possible at the lake. As a teacher, summer vacation never came soon enough. He welcomed it more now than as a kid. Being able to spend more time up at the lake was a bonus. He loved it. Luella could take a week of vacation time and some time off was allowed through the family leave act provided it was applied toward settling her parent's estate. The kids missed their summer soccer league, but spending most of the summer at Grammy's lake place was worth it. Swimming, fishing, sand castles, and fires on the beach with marshmallows were the best treats ever and ample replacement for missing soccer and softball.

Petunia blossomed. With more food scraps and plenty of attention, she lay on her side in the mud and let the kids scratch her back and her ears with a pointed stick. She roused from her blissful state only long enough to gobble a plate of leftover pancakes or a bag of stale donuts from the day-old stack at the bakery. If there was such a thing as pig-heaven, she had found it.

The home was still recorded as part of the estate, but each of the families began to think of it as their own. A gradual division of labor began to take place, each gravitating to their areas of comfort and expertise. The men worked on clearing junk that had accumulated over the past forty years from the sheds. They found pieces of odd lumber, jars and cans of screws, bolts, and nails all saved for that one day when you might need it. As with most junk, 'one day' never came.

Rick and Harry came up on weekends or spent valuable vacation time digging through closets, garages and archives in the basement looking for a clue to the elusive Suisse Bank key. When they tired of the search, they grabbed paint scrapers and paint brushes and went to work on the faded and chipped siding and trim work of the house.

Vera honked the car horn as she and Olivia coasted along the curved driveway. Kids glanced up from the sand castle construction site on the beach, and Petunia grunted in annoyance from being disturbed without so much as a treat. "Good news, everyone," Vera yelled out the car window as she pulled to a stop under the spreading limbs of the giant white pine near the garage.

"What news?" Tom yelled back from the inner reaches of the boat shed.

"Our lawyers petitioned the local judge to allow access to the safe deposit box, in Namukwa at First Miners Bank. Judge East reviewed the request and granted it because it seemed to be the most likely place for the other key to be located." Vera continued, "This means, tomorrow we can go to the bank and open the box! Now maybe we can get this whole thing going."

"Woo-hoo!" came the yell from inside the screen porch. Luella put down her glass of iced tea and ran out to give her sisters each a hug. "Good job, you guys. Emma should be up here again tonight. We can all go in after the bank opens and see what's in there."

The arrival of Emma and Phineas brought a new level of excitement to the group. They were a family that acted like friends. They laughed and cried and played together, and if there were disagreements or differences, they worked it out or let it pass.

The grill was fired, and the glowing embers begged for meat. Harry heaped on burgers and brats, and the smoke from the sputtering meat rose into the pines and drifted across the lake. Trips to Roy's wine cellar produced another taste test as the evening light faded across the darkening lakeshore. Phineas and his cello took center stage. As the campfires snapped and sputtered, the sweet, mellow voice of his cello mingled in delicate harmony with the mosquitos rising over the water. In the parting rays of sunset, a woodpecker responded in the percussion section, and the muted hoots of an owl in the white pine balcony was all the applause they needed. It was a fitting end to a wonderful day.

Tomorrow the key would be in their hands and the will would soon be settled. The house was always home in their hearts, but tomorrow would bring it one step closer to being their home legally.

Next day Olivia drove her minivan, and the other sisters rode along. When they arrived, the bank parking lot held only four cars. Three of them were tellers and the manager.

Olivia wondered aloud about the safe deposit box. "What do you think they have in there?"

Emma told stories about clients having diamond rings, loose teeth with gold fillings, birth, death and marriage certificates, titles to property and cash, jewels, and family secrets. One family discovered they had a sister given up for adoption, others believing they were biological children discovered they had been adopted. Old coins and stamp collections and valuable baseball cards were common. She wasn't aware of any clients through their law firm having a high security Swiss bank safe deposit box key.

Olivia hand carried the certified letter from the judge, authorizing access to the safe-deposit box. Already having the joint account with her parents, she signed for access. "Here's the key to the box," she said as she handed it to the bank manager on duty. He retrieved the box and placed it in a small room available for them to use privately. The curtain was drawn, and they paused to see who would open the box.

Luella was the first to lift the hinged lid. Inside was an incomplete inventory sheet of the contents. Birth certificates, title insurance for their home on the lake, four gold coins, each encased in plastic, sixteen silver half dollars, great-grandma's wedding ring, birth certificates for each of the girls and a tattered King James Bible with several lose papers stuffed between its pages. But no key. No mention of a Suisse Bank safe deposit box, no mention of a will or any directions for the girls to follow. Only mementos of her parents.

Vera let out a loud groan and said, "Well, Judge East did require that we provide a complete inventory of the contents to the court. So, we might just as well take everything with us." They gathered the items into a transparent evidence bag like those used at crime scenes, as requested by the judge. It was a quiet ride home. As much as they had hoped to find the key, this simply meant the key was somewhere else.

"This is so frustrating," Vera said as she stepped into the kitchen and dropped the evidence bag onto the dining table. "Where do you think they put the dumb key? And why would they hide it without letting at least one of us know?"

"You know, this reminds me of those crazy Christmas stunts your dad used to pull. Those were great; they really made me think," Rick reflected. "You don't think this was all his plan, do you?"

"You're crazy. He's dead and they died suddenly. Why would they do something like that?" Vera felt riddled. "If Dad did this to us intentionally, I'll kill him myself."

Phineas, the quiet one, suggested something simple. "Why don't we go through the contents of the box? Perhaps there is a note indicating where the key might be located. At least it beats sitting around feeling sorry and frustrated." They gathered around the kitchen table, but the expectancy that accompanied them to the bank seemed lacking.

Tom agreed. "This week we went through personal items, the small safe in the basement, the book shelves and even dresser drawers in the bedroom. I found a key ring in the shed with sixty or seventy old keys on it but nothing resembling a Swiss safe deposit key. At least going through the stuff from the bank will help us to see what they felt was valuable."

Luella dumped the contents of the evidence bag in a small heap in the middle. "Emma, why don't you be the accountant and write down a detailed inventory of everything we find."

Olivia grabbed the Bible. "Item #1, King James Bible." She fluttered through the pages and several loose notes and papers fluttered out.

Olivia picked one up. "What does this mean: 'Red rises the sun on those who sleep'? It must have been some sermon notes." She handed the note off to Tom next to her and reached for another item. "Here is a copy of "The Star-Spangled Banner." Wow! Like that needs to be kept in a safe deposit box? I think the old folks cracked."

Luella reached into the pile and pulled out a square sticker for the Red Cross. "Were Mom and Dad volunteers?" She didn't expect an answer and didn't get one. She pulled at the corner of the decal and passed it on.

Tom picked up a coin. "Hey, look at these. I collect a few coins and these gold coins are really nice." He turned the coin over. "This is an 1893 CC $20 gold piece." He admired the weight and the brilliant gold glint. The coin was encased in plastic with the letters PCGS and MS 62 printed on the margin. He punched in the security code on his phone and checked for coin valuations. "Listen to this. This coin is worth about $25,000!"

Vera picked up another. "What about this one? 1891-CC, MS60. What do you call this, a double eagle? And what is PCGS?"

"According to GOOGLE, PCGS stands for Professional Coin Grading System and is a way to certify the quality of the coin. They are locked in the plastic case to prevent tampering, otherwise someone could replace the good coin with a cheaper one, which would be fraud." He turned the next coin back and forth, watching the light glint off the face of the coin. "Wow! The 1891 gold piece recently sold for $38,775 at auction."

"You're kidding, right?" Olivia wondered. "Mom and Dad bought this house for less than that in the 1960s."

Tom reached out quickly, picking up the next coin. "This one's an 1883-CC. It says MS 62, and it's only worth about $22,000. And the last coin is an 1881. It says AU 50. What does that mean?"

Emma took one of the coins from Tom's hand and held the double eagle up to the light to see the reflection.

Tom was the resident coin expert, at least for the moment. "According to Google, AU means 'about uncirculated' and MS means 'mint state' or uncirculated. So anyway, this last coin has been circulated but is still worth about $45,000. If it was mint state like the others it could be worth $175,000."

A stunned silence hung over the group. So far they had found four gold coins with a conservative value exceeding $130,000, and there were more coins in the box.

Vera began to have doubts. "Where did Mom and Dad get these? Even if you add up the money they got when grandpa died, it doesn't explain the wine and the coins. You don't just find coins like these in mason jars and old shoe boxes."

Olivia joined in. "Even if they did inherit the kind of money to afford this, why didn't they pay off the house and put the money in the bank, or a mutual fund or something like that?"

Phineas voiced the question that was building in the back of Vera's mind. "Do you think there was something illegal going on? I mean... this seems so atypical. Your parents were the most honest people I know. They made Honest Abe look like a thief."

No one wanted to come home and find their parents dealing in stolen property or fraud or something even worse. Yet try as they might, there was no logical way to make sense out of what they were finding.

"What about this other stuff?" Luella looked over the small stack of Franklin half dollars. None of them were encased in anything, and each of them had varying degrees of wear and tear. It seemed obvious none of these carried a high value, yet they couldn't be sure. "I think we need to catalog all of this for the judge, and then get a formal appraisal of the coins. We may be mistaken about the value. Anyway, the court needs to have an accurate assessment of the value for probate or whatever you call this crazy process."

"Luella's right," Emma weighed in. "If we believe our parents were honest, then we need to be as well. Either way we need to get a third party appraisal. But what about all this other stuff?" She flipped through the papers. "Why would they have a copy of 'The Star-Spangled Banner'? They kept some weird things."

Various birth certificates and titles made sense in a safe deposit box, but not the National Anthem. And why an old King James Bible? Together they made a comprehensive list of contents.

1. 1891 CC double eagle PCGS, MS 60

2. 1893 CC double eagle PCGS MS 62

3. 1881 double eagle PCGS AU 50

4. 1883 CC double eagle PCGS MS 62

5. King James Bible

6. Star Spangled Banner

7. Birth certificates for each of the 4 girls, Luella, Olivia, Vera, and Emma

8. 16 Franklin half dollars in sequence from 1948 through 1963.

9. Wedding ring from Grandma Ambrose, Roy's mother.

10.   Title insurance for the Ambrose home.

11.   Three notecards of sketches that looked like doodling, found inside the Bible.

12.   Red cross decal

None of them made any sense out of the miscellaneous items before them. The coins certainly made sense as something valuable, and the documents had value, but most of the other items seemed like a collection of stuff from the back drawer of an old desk.

As the afternoon wore on, the contents of the safe deposit box were poked at, shuffled, and considered from all angles. But as much as they wanted to solve the mystery, they had children, and children demand to be fed and changed and played with.

#

Molly, always enthralled with Petunia, was constantly on the outlook for more food and more ways to entertain the giant pig. Nearly every day she skipped part of her breakfast or saved the end of her peanut butter and jelly sandwich so Petunia wouldn't go hungry. If a dog was considered man's best friend, Petunia and Molly were a close second.

"Hey, Mom, can I give Petunia a flower to eat?" Molly clutched a handful of crumpled dandelions in her smudged hands.

"Sure, but be careful. Just throw them in the pen, don't let her eat out of your hand, OK?" Olivia was somewhat confident that nothing would happen, but there was a big difference between a six-hundred-pound pig and a forty-pound kid.

"OK, Mom, I'll be careful. And can I color a picture for Petunia too? And look..." She held up a chipped rock with a small shiny spot. "I found this pretty rock, and I'm going to give it to Petunia. OK, Mom? OK?"

"Now be careful out there. If you want to give her the rock, just toss it into the pen." Olivia went about some kitchen chores all the while listening to the chatter of her, almost five-year-old.

"OK, Mom, I'll be careful. And can I give Petunia a penny? She doesn't have any money."

"I don't care, just get outside; it's a nice day." Olivia sighed and looked out the window at the boundless energy of the kids playing in the yard. It was always good to be at the lake. Molly was so proud of the flowers and treasures she had for Petunia, she was the center of attention as the cousins trouped out to the pigpen.

Chapter 11

Appraisal

All that is gold does not glitter. —J. R. R. Tolkien

The closest place to get a coin appraisal was Top Hat-Coin and Collectables in Ashland, Wisconsin. Close enough to make a day trip. Richard and Vera volunteered to bring the coins along with an explanation why the appraisal was necessary. It was easy to put Daisy, their four-year-old, in the car seat and drive. She was a great traveler and promptly fell asleep. It was also a good chance to have a change from excess family togetherness. As much as Vera loved her sisters, it was time for a break.

Vera called the coin shop prior to their arrival to explain the urgency of the situation. The certified coin grader agreed to do the full appraisal on a limited number of coins that day to prevent any delays.

Ashland was a wonderful break for Richard and Vera, however the beguiling sunshine had little effect against the cold wind coming ashore from Lake Superior. Some shopping for kid stuff, a stop at the local college scene coffee shop and a brisk stroll along the waterfront all helped to restore a sense of calm. Daily problem solving over the will, arguing with siblings and the constant closeness of too many people in a single house wore thin. Vera wanted to forget it all and have her parents back. She wanted to sit down on a Saturday morning to Dad's pancakes and a steaming cup of black coffee and let the world go by; to share recipes with Mom and laugh at old family photos; to face each day with a sense of peace and contentment. As Vera tried to take it all in, tears welled up in the corners of her eyes. She wiped the tears with her woolen gloves and blamed it on the brisk north wind off Lake Superior.

"Let's sit for a few minutes and talk." Vera sat down on the cold vacant bench along the waterfront. They were the only ones in the city park. The swings hung limp waiting for children, the empty seats pushed by the arms of the north wind.

"Hey, Rick, how much vacation time do you have?" She knew his job as a physical therapist with a larger hospital system, was always in demand. He had taken ten days off when Lola and Roy went missing. Vera was hoping they would have more time at the lake together, especially this summer.

"Not sure. I have some carry over from last year, but probably about fourteen or fifteen days remaining. What are you thinking?" Richard asked.

"Well...this whole thing is taking so much time, and I really need to spend more time in the store. I hired a replacement, but this is getting expensive." The store was her privately owned pharmacy in suburban Des Moines, Iowa. After graduation, she had worked for a pharmacy chain but found the work demanding and inflexible. Perhaps she had streaks of her father's wanderlust. Anyway, she found an older pharmacist ready to retire and bought the store on good terms. It was a good move, both for the family time and financially. But it was her store and she was responsible for its solvency.

"Vera, what do you make of this...this...fiasco?" Richard seemed frustrated. When his grandfather passed away, there were no court hearing, lawyer meetings, missing keys, and confusion. Certainly no surprises like thousand-dollar bottles of wine and rare coins. He sipped his steaming coffee as they sat on the park bench watching the seagulls. "Did your parents fall off the deep end, or do you think there is something strange going on?"

"Rick, I love you...I really do. But you need to understand my parents, especially my Dad. When I was growing up, there were a few times I thought he was three cards short of a full deck. Don't you remember at our wedding when he gave that ridiculous father-of-the-bride speech with one arm cut off his suit jacket? Mom was as wonderful and loving and solid as they come. She was the anchor in their relationship, and Dad was the dinghy trying to break loose and go for a ride in the storm. But as we get older and now that we have Daisy, I am starting to see things differently." Vera glanced affectionately over at her daughter, slurping on a strawberry smoothie. "Even when we were little, Dad did these crazy treasure hunts for Christmas, or he buried treasure outside and gave us a map to find it. Almost every day they told us 'I love you,' and even though I thought it was cheesy, I know they really meant it."

"Vera, I didn't mean to suggest your parents were crazy, I am just trying to understand what is going on." Richard continued. "To put this in perspective, my dad was an accountant and my mom was the school librarian. My dad wore a pressed white shirt and tie every day of his working life. On Saturdays he took the tie off. If my parents are plain vanilla, your parents are tutti-frutti, but I love it all. I'm just trying to wrap my head around this whole thing."

"I know; it's hard for everyone. Your love and the love of my entire family and my faith in God is what sustains me." She dabbed her eyes as the tears spilled over onto her cheeks. "I don't know how I could go on otherwise." With blurred eyes, she sat on the park bench and stared out over Lake Superior. Across the bay the small town of Washburn settled into the shadows. A large lake freighter moved silently in the distance, heading east to Chicago or Buffalo or Cleveland.

"Hey, Mom, can we get some donuts for Petunia? Molly always gets to feed her and I never get to." Little Daisy, a shadow to her older cousin Molly. Only three months apart, they had the same intensity for learning and sharing. They loved books, donuts and watching the food channel.

"OK, sweetie. We will get some treats for Petunia, but first we need to get the coins from Papa Roy's house, and then we can start back home."

"Yippee!" Daisy smiled and skipped as they walked together in the direction of the Top Hat-Coins and Collectables.

#

A tarnished silver bell rattled as the door swung open, forced by the gusty wind. The mustiness of the coin shop retreated briefly as the outside air rushed in.

"Ah... Ms. Dawson." The coin appraiser looked up from his work behind the glass counter. "I'm Cal Jensen. It's wonderful to finally meet you."

"Please call me Vera, and this is my husband, Richard."

He extended his hand to each of them. "The manager gave me your coins, and I did an appraisal as well as a report for each of them. Very interesting."

"What do you mean 'very interesting'? Did you find something you didn't expect?" Richard asked.

"Yes, I guess I did find something I didn't expect. It's in the report so I don't need to go over it all in detail now, but this was a very unusual set of coins."

Now he had Vera's attention. "Why unusual?"

"Please sit down. It will be easier if I go through my summary, and you can pass it on to the rest of the family. It is my understanding that you have several sisters. Is that right?"

Vera nodded yes as Cal motioned toward the small conference table in the back of the store. Though the store was dimly lit, over the table was a very bright light attached to a large magnifying glass on a hinged arm. "Please let me explain."

Cal carefully took the coins out of the package and reverently arranged them on the felt tabletop. Putting the gold pieces first and the Franklin half dollars next, he said something which caught Olivia off guard. "This is not a random coin collection. Most people have a random selection of coins often found in an attic. Occasionally, I run across a collector who tries to get a full set of coin types, or a date-series of coins. There is something about this set which makes me wonder." He held up one of the gold coins.

"These gold coins are of exceptional and rare quality. But I question why these four dates only. There are many other cheaper $20 gold pieces, so it makes me wonder. They are all similar quality. And then I looked at the Franklins. All circulated, many worn and with limited value. A dramatic contrast to the gold pieces. What's also interesting, this is nearly a full set except it is missing only one coin, the 1951 half dollar."

"What do you mean missing?"

"The coins were minted for sixteen years: you only have fifteen." Cal looked at the line of half dollars arranged from earliest to newest.

"But we had sixteen when we counted them yesterday. We must have missed one at home. Would this have made a difference in the appraisal?"

"No ma'am these coins are basically worthless for a collector. They're worn and damaged and are probably worth $5 apiece. But there is something unusual about these. Some of the coins have a small punch mark above or below one of the numbers, but not every coin. These marks were put there on purpose. It would be impossible for these marks to be random. I don't know what they mean, I guess that's up to you and your family."

He packaged the coins together, carefully wrapping the gold coins separate from the worn silver half dollars. "My appraisal is printed and included in the package. Your father had an interesting taste in coins." He walked with them to the door. "I would have enjoyed getting to know him."

Once in the car and on the road back to Namukwa, Daisy spoke up. "Mommy, who was that man?"

"Oh honey, that was a man trying to help us with Papa's coins. Did you think it smelled funny in his store?"

"Yeah, it was kinda stinky in there. What's he doin' with Papa's pennies?" Daisy kept talking as they headed east on Highway 2 and turned south. "Those are just like the big penny we gave to Petunia."

"What did you say?" Richard pulled their SUV to the side and turned to the child. "Did you say you gave a penny to Petunia?"

"Yep. Auntie Olivia said Molly and me could give a penny to Petunia. So, we gave her a donut and a big penny." Daisy seemed so pleased with herself. "She ate it."

They looked at each other in disbelief as they pulled back onto the highway. The setting sun in the west cast long shadows across their already tired faces. They both knew it was going to be an interesting conversation when they got home.

Chapter 12

Cocos Helados

I spent most of my life worrying about things that never happened. —Mark Twain

Martin Garza pulled back the latch on the door to his beachfront *palapa* and opened the door. Located along the Malecón de Mazatlán, he was one of many shack vendors occupying valuable real estate. Morning beach walkers marched by in colorful shorts and cover-ups fluttering in the morning breeze. Early morning in Mazatlán was typically quiet. Along the way fishermen hawked kilos of shrimp out of beat up coolers. As Martin hung gaudy T-shirts with lewd inscriptions in full view of the passers-by, no one paid him much attention.

He propped the sign, *Cocos Helados*, in the sand and stabilized it with a broken cement block. Ready for another day of business. Only one more thing to do. He checked the small drop box on the back of his beachfront store, just one message. As he tucked the note into his pocket, he involuntarily glanced up and down the waterfront. No doubt someone was watching; they always were.

"Buenos Dias." The falsely cheerful tourist crowd continually pawed through his wares, offering and bargaining for cheaper prices until it was pointless to continue. Rich Americans annoyed him, especially the fat ones. But most of his income was from these same fat, lazy Americans. At least that's the way it was until last year when the drug cartel started paying him for information. But that wasn't the whole story.

Martin pulled the red warning flag from the post near the lifeguard station and hung it behind his shop. A coconut vendor would stop by within the hour and sell him more coconuts.

A few months ago, while buying food in El Centro, the main street market in old Mazatlán, one of the vendors slipped him a note. Following the directions on the note he got on the Sábalo Cocos bus and headed east along the Malecón toward the Golden Zone. A graying man with broken English sat next to him even though there were several open seats. The man handed him a small package with a generous wad of cash. Thinking it was for drugs, Garza handed it back.

"*Tómalo*. Take it." He put it into Garza's pocket and hopped off the bus at the next corner. Fearing discovery or retribution or some type of violence against him, Martin didn't open the message until he was well alone and felt safe. It was then that he realized the Americans, or at least the American undercover drug agents, knew he was an informer for the cartel. They were willing to pay for the same privilege. Garza found himself to be a double agent without the slightest ambition to be either. The money was good but life was cheap. El Chico would turn him into fish food without blinking if he knew the Americans had him on the payroll, and if the Americans knew he was lying to them, they would let El Chico know and nothing else mattered. It would be over for him and his girlfriend and their little girl, Maria. He was forced to be an honest liar.

#

"The flag is up." One of the midlevel drug lords watched from the balcony of his suite in the El Presidente Hotel along the Malecón. From the fourteenth floor he and his men had a tremendous vantage point observing the ebb and flow of traffic below. They owned most of the beach vendors, and that was a great opportunity to launder money through a cash business and arrange drops and deliveries. A well-paid beach vendor was a good source to target rich Americans. Garza was reliable. His information helped the cartel avoid unwanted publicity along the waterfront.

A small dented pickup with the left front fender flapping like an injured seagull, pulled into the vacant spot along the walkway. The driver grabbed a large burlap bag filled with coconuts. Other than margaritas and beer, a cold coconut with the top chopped off and a tiny Chinese paper umbrella was the most popular drink with gringos. It's what brought them to Garza's shop, Cocos Helados. Dropping the bag at Garza's door, the driver went inside, out of the sun.

"What do you have?" The driver glanced behind him as he spoke, looking for followers. Garza, avoided eye contact until the lingering customers wandered toward the door.

"There is a witness."

"Witness for what? A prostitute? A drug sale?" He lit a cigarette and laughed in Garza's face. The cocky young man was too sure of himself. Martin had lived past midlife by being quiet and cautious. He wasn't sure this young man would make it.

"Here." Martin Garza handed the note to the guy delivering the coconuts. "There is a witness to the murder up in El Quilete. It was an American who saw Espinosa pull the trigger. The dead man was a DEA agent."

"Where did you get this?" the driver demanded.

"It was here when I opened. I don't know who brought it." Martin wasn't lying but he wanted to choose his words carefully. "What are you going to do?"

"What we do is none of your business, understand?" The young hotshot backed off slightly. "Does anyone else know about this?"

"Someone must."

"Someone might be talking to you today." He flicked ashes on the toes of Martin Garza's shoes and hurried out.

High on a hill toward the end of the street stood an odd shaped yellow building. A treatment center for addiction, it was also the headquarters for Alcoholics Anonymous for the state of Sinaloa. On the third floor, Fernando sat with a 50X spotting scope focused on Garza's palapa. After he witnessed the coconut delivery, he hit replay on his listening device and played back the conversation that just took place. The message had been delivered.

#

A knock sounded on the door, and Javier Espinosa released his grip on the woman. She was the housekeeper in the hotel, but her duties extended beyond the official job description. As much as he wanted her, there was business to do.

Two well-dressed men entered the room along with his oldest brother, Emilio. It was always intimidating to come into the room of Espinosa, even with an invitation. If you came in without an invitation, you placed your life in his hands.

"What do you have?" Espinosa lit another cigarette and flipped the cap shut on his lighter.

"The word is out about a witness to the shooting in El Quilete. The man who was shot was a US agent. An American saw it happen."

"I know he was an agent; that's why I shot him." A long slow drag on his cigarette allowed time to think. As he exhaled, a long slow curl of smoke leaked out his nostrils and wafted upward. "So, why should it matter if there is a witness? I own this hotel. I own this city and most of this state. I can do what I want to do, when I want to do it. I own the police. I own that worthless little rat in the shack on the beach. If you think his message should scare me, then you are as worthless as he is." Even though his eyes flashed with anger and agitation, his voice remained low and cool, like high explosives packed in ice.

"Emilio, what do you think?" Javier courted his brother's opinion as a courtesy to a family member.

Emilio looked away from the full-length tinted windows overlooking the waterfront and answered his younger brother. The oldest of three brothers, Emilio appeared as ruthless as Javier, but he lacked the fire and the will to dominate and kill. He had lapsed into second place in the cartel behind his younger brother. Ironically his name meant "flatterer or flattering" and that became his role, to say what his brother wanted to hear and to support his agendas.

"A witness here is meaningless. We can buy any judge, police officer and any witness. And if we can't buy them, we can kill them." Emilio turned from his brother to look out the window as if he were bored with the conversation. Then he added. "However, a witness to something like that can make the Americans dangerous. If they got you arrested and extradited to the US, then an American witness could be enough to put you away."

"Who's going to arrest me?" Javier raised his arm and gestured toward the bustling city street fifteen stories below. He had a brashness that allowed him to rise to the top of the drug cartel, but it never sat well with Emilio.

"Brother, I have seen the Americans work. The American government is powerful and can control how Mexico works. They are soft, but they have money, and they can pay more than we can."

"Then the answer is simple: We eliminate any witnesses before they have the chance to talk." Javier lit another cigarette. "Do we know who they might be?"

One of the henchmen spoke up. "We believe it is one of the five Americans who were eating at La Casa de Mujeres when you shot the rat." He hesitated before continuing. "We always keep track of any vehicles in and out of El Quilete. The only vehicle outside of the pueblo residents was this one." He handed a photo to Espinosa. A slightly rusted white Toyota pickup truck with the words "Not For Hire" displayed on the side. The license plate from Sinaloa was also clearly visible.

"It belongs to Earl Ambrose; his wife is the painter you hired at the restaurant." The man pulled out his own cigarette and used that as a pointer. "These people are relatives of his from the United States, and this is a friend of the painter." The lighter snapped shut and more smoke filled the room.

"Do we know where they are?" Emilio again turned from his position of staring out the window at the world below. "Are they back in the States?"

"Three of them are back in the US, but Earl and Sandy live here in Mazatlán. We have paid her well, and I doubt they will be a problem, but if it is their friend or relative, it could be more difficult to manage."

El Chico walked to the window and looked down at the sign in front of Martin Garza's hut. "Do you see that rat down there? He has a girlfriend and a daughter. I know he won't be a problem because we know where his girlfriend and his daughter live. I doubt the Americans will be a problem either because we know where their relatives live as well." After another long drag on his fourth cigarette in the last twenty minutes, he concluded the conversation. "Gentlemen, I think it is time to visit our friends, the painter and her husband"

Chapter 13

Moving Day

Love all, trust a few, do wrong to none. —William Shakespeare

The monthly meeting of the Mazatlán chapter of Alcoholics Anonymous neared its conclusion as the speaker introduced the latest member. "Hi everyone, this is Fernando. He is new here." Then turning to speak directly to Fernando Garcia, he asked, "Is there anything you want to say to the group today?"

"Hi. My name is Fernando and I'm an alcoholic." It seemed so canned and stupid to say it in this manner, but it worked. He was an alcoholic, at least for today.

"Hi, Fernando," the chorus replied.

"I'm...I'm not sure what to say. Just glad to be here, I guess." Diverting his eyes from making direct contact with any of the others in attendance, he simply sat down in the chair behind him. After a pause, the meeting began to break up, some staying for non-alcoholic refreshments and others heading down the stairs and out into the evening air. After several had left, Fernando excused himself from the remaining people and quietly slipped out of the room. The five-story faded yellow office building overlooked the main walkway along the Mazatlán waterfront. Much of the office space was vacant and served Fernando's purpose well.

Using his own key, he opened one of the unused rooms on the third floor and stepped in. The spotting scope was still in place, but he needed to retrieve his gun. Guns weren't allowed at AA meetings. He slipped the Berretta 9 mm into the holster concealed under his left arm and turned to leave the building. He knew from his own observation; the news was out. Now it was time to watch El Chico's next move.

#

In the waning afternoon sun, the driver of the delivery truck drove slowly, searching for house numbers. Tall trees in the street median harbored flocks of birds getting ready to roost for the night. As the truck moved along slowly, two or three birds deposited spots of white urates on the windshield.

"*Me cago en le leche!*" the driver muttered under his breath as he turned on the windshield washer and wipers. He wasn't having a good day. Then he found the address.

Like most homes in residential Mazatlán, the courtyards or entrances were enclosed with locked gates. He flipped off the radio and grabbed his clipboard. There was no bell at the gate, and it was locked, so he simply rattled the gate and pounded his clipboard against the chain.

"Buenos tardes." He continued rattling the chain. "Anyone home?" He shielded his eyes from the afternoon sun with his free hand and peered into the courtyard. Numerous potted plants in haphazard arrangements blocked the view into the house. A propane powered insect trap hissed quietly in the corner. A water hose attached to the faucet dripped slowly, and the rivulet ran toward the street.

Earl Ambrose opened the door slightly and looked out. "Can I help you?"

"Señor, I have a delivery for you."

"Delivery?" he opened the door further and stepped out. "I didn't order anything. What is it?"

"I'm sorry, sir. I am only the delivery person, but it came from the furniture store." The driver looked down at his clipboard. "It says you have ordered a new chair."

Earl turned toward the interior of the house. "Hey Sandy. Did you order some furniture?"

"No. Why?" She appeared at the door equally confused.

"Why don't you come out to the truck and see if this is something you ordered. If it isn't, then I will have you sign that you refused the delivery, and I will send it back. OK?"

"Sure." Sandy and Earl opened the gate. Earl limped forward without his cane toward the back of the truck. He cautiously stepped off the curb as the driver swung open the rear cargo doors.

Four strong men leaped out of the truck, catching Earl and Sandy by total surprise. Even before they could yell, the well-trained men clamped strong hands over their mouths and heavy zip ties gripped their wrists and ankles. They stuffed rags into their mouths, secured with a generous strip of duct tape. They couldn't fight, yell, or run. Earl's chicken leg bent backwards and he grunted with pain. Lifted and dropped into the cargo space of the delivery truck, they could do nothing but look at each other in fear.

With the cargo doors secured, the deliveryman calmly went about his work. He walked into the house and grabbed five cold beers from the refrigerator. Before leaving, he turned off the bug collector, the water faucet, and closed the door to the house and the gate.

As he entered the driver's side of the truck, he addressed the captives. "Don't fight us and you won't get hurt. OK?" They couldn't respond, and he wasn't listening anyway. A job was a job. He didn't like hurting the old man, but sometimes things happen. The men enjoyed Earl's cold beer in silence. The truck crept slowly down the street and turned left, moving into traffic.

Along the way, Earl and Sandy could only listen and think of what was happening. Unable to speak, they tried to shift into less painful positions. Earl's leg throbbed as he rolled onto his back to rest his knee. Thankfully his arms were bound on the front so he could lie back in the least painful position possible. His shoulder pushed against the toes of his captor's boots. They ignored him.

After an hour of travel the men began to chat quietly about un-related issues. Earl tried to follow the conversations, but his hearing wasn't good and the constant hum of the truck obscured enough of the words, he couldn't understand what they were talking about. Some of the time he drifted into a restless sleep, rocked by the continued motion of the truck.

Sandy remained fearful, wondering about their abductors. She had been mugged once in Central Park, New York, and this brought back memories. Then it was simply a young thug with a knife who had threatened her. After knocking her down, he had cut the strap of her purse and run off. This was different. It was quite clear they weren't trying to steal anything. She listened to Earl's quiet steady breathing. He was asleep. She recalled old spy movies where the hero or heroine, when captured, counted stops, and turns, which later allowed rescuers to find their location. After about a dozen such stops and starts Sandy was hopelessly confused about their location and their destination and gave up counting.

Several minutes after the truck stopped, the rear doors were finally opened. Earl and Sandy blinked from the glare of the overhead lights in the garage. The men used side cutters and released them from the bondage of the plastic zip ties around their ankles and wrists. Hopelessly stiff and uncomfortable from the cramped quarters, they needed assistance to get out of the truck. Earl nearly fell from the pain shooting through is bad knee. Despite the coolness of the night, beads of sweat formed on his forehead as he limped alongside his captors.

Out of the garage and into another building they walked without speaking. The only sound made by the group was the tapping and scuffling of their shoes on the stone floor and the occasional grunts of pain coming from Earl. One of the guards held his arm as they went, trying to prevent him from falling. There were no tell-tale signs or sounds or smells to disclose their location. Inside the building, it was quiet, almost too quiet.

"Here are your rooms. There is a bathroom across the hall." The smartly dressed young woman in the hallway motioned toward two sparsely furnished rooms. Each held a single steel framed bed with a couple of blankets and a stained pillow. One single chair was placed beside the bed and on the chair, was a pitcher of water, a glass and a towel, nothing more. Sandy wondered about the quality of the water, but she was too thirsty to care.

As quickly as the captors left, a door at the end of the hallway was closed and locked. Sandy and Earl stood in confusion and then carefully pulled the tape from their mouths. Earl pulled the rag out of his mouth and a line of drool slid down his chin. They could talk again.

"Where are we?" Sandy looked around in confusion. She tried to look out the barred windows of their rooms but was greeted only with visions of the night. Distant lights glowed against the low clouds, but there was nothing to reveal their location. "Earl, what's going on?" Now that the men had left, she felt a sudden release of emotion. She sobbed in fear as she leaned against Earl. Life wasn't supposed to end this way.

For three days they lived with monotonous anxiety. Confined to their rooms, a small central courtyard, and an area for eating they had nothing else. Anxious about their fate, aware only of their captors and their immediate environment, there was nothing else to do. They had no newspapers to read, no music to hear, no people to yell at and no tequila to help you forget. Every morning they were served scrambled eggs, refried beans, and tortillas, along with black coffee and water. Lunch was more of the same minus the eggs. Sometimes there was some cut fruit or corn. The evening meal was some type of grilled meat, tortillas, beans, and guacamole. No wine, no beer, no tequila, just water.

No one mistreated them, no one threatened them, but they knew they were being observed. They didn't know where they were or who abducted them. It wasn't until the fourth day of their imposed holiday that someone of authority addressed them.

At 7 PM while Earl and Sandy awaited their usual ration of beans and tortillas, an unexpected guest arrived. Anticipating someone with glossy black hair related to the drug cartel, they were greeted instead, by a tall man of northern European origin. His closely cropped reddish-blond hair, slightly graying at the edges was framed, by an intense stare, from one eye. He had a black leather patch over the other.

The benefit of a diplomatic passport and the vast unsupervised budget of the investigative branch of the DEA allowed Dag to come and go pretty much as he felt the need. His goal was singular—get El Chico. However, his means to accomplish that goal bent the rules of engagement, especially when outside the United States.

"Do you know where you are?" The one-eyed man bypassed introductions and went directly to questioning.

"No." Earl seemed cautious in responding. "Who are you?" Just because the person they were talking to wasn't Mexican didn't mean he wasn't involved with the cartel.

"You were in El Quilete when this man was shot." He pushed an enlarged photo toward them. They looked at it without any clear recognition. "What do you know about it?"

"I think I can speak for both of us. We don't know what happened." Earl was somehow hopeful that Sandy would not have to be dragged into the conversation.

"I heard his answer; what is yours?" His single laser-focused eye drilled into her. She flinched.

"Who took the photo?" Sandy asked. She was familiar with the small pueblo but not with the man in front of the hacienda.

"Here is an un-cropped image. Do you recognize anyone now?" Sandy, Earl, Elizabeth, and Roy were plainly visible and easily recognizable. The man seated in the shade near the hacienda had faded into the small details of the background. Lola had taken it.

For the next two hours Earl and Sandy were questioned with excruciating attention to detail about their life in Mazatlán and their relationship with the town of El Quilete. But no matter how Dag presented the questions no clearly usable information was forthcoming.

When they finally took a break, the usual supper fare was served along with a cold beer for each. It was late, but as soon as the food was eaten and the dishes taken away, the questioning resumed. This time with a bottle of aged tequila and three glasses. Sandy wasn't sure what this guy wanted, but she didn't complain about his methods. After four days of beans and tortillas, a respite from the mundane was welcome.

Dag grasped the bottle firmly in his left hand and poured a glass for each. When the glasses were emptied, another was poured. Dag began anew. "Do you know why you are being held?"

Blank stares were his only response. He swirled his glass and took another sip and tried another approach. "What do you know about Roy Ambrose, right now?"

"Nothing other than what I have already told you. Why?"

"At this moment, he is in the hospital in the intensive care unit. He could be dying. Do you want his death to be pointless?" Dag threw this out to see their response.

"What do you want from us?" Sandy expressed frustration. She wasn't even clear who they were dealing with. "Who are you?"

Dag changed his avenue of questioning. "Do you have children?"

"Yes, one daughter back in the States. Why?"

"Would you die for your daughter?"

"What do you mean by that?" A desperate feeling came over both Earl and Sandy. "Are you threatening her, as well?"

"Just answer my question."

"If there was no other choice, I would gladly die for my child. But that doesn't mean I want to die." Sandy furrowed her brow, puzzled by the turn of questioning.

"I am with the DEA, international counterintelligence measures. We are trying to stop the Sinaloa drug cartel from the continued exportation of death and destruction into the United

States and beyond. Whatever you or your cousin witnessed may be just the key to turning the tide. If we have a reliable US witness to an execution-type murder by a member of the drug cartel against a US citizen, then we may have sufficient evidence to extradite Javier Espinosa for a federal trial, which could result in the death sentence. If you witnessed something, I need to know." Dag laid it all on the line.

"If you are working for the DEA, then why are you holding us against our will?"

"El Chico knows there was a witness, and he knows you were in El Quilete at the time of the shooting. If we hadn't taken you when we did, you would be floating five miles off shore." He paused to look at each of them face-to-face. "You are currently being held in a safe house operated by the DEA and the CIA in Mexico City. If you want to go home, I'll call a taxi but we won't meet again."

"But what if we really didn't see anything?" Earl tried to look at the obvious.

"Right now, it doesn't matter. If we can get Espinosa to believe you know something, he might make a move and expose himself." He got up to leave. "If you want to leave, that is your decision, but trust me, you won't last long."

"Can I ask a couple more questions?" Sandy looked up at Dag. It was her turn to find out information. "Who was the man that got shot?"

"He was my son."

Sandy paused and took a deep breath. "How does the drug cartel know there is a witness?"

"I told them."

Chapter 14

The Other Side of the Coin

Or suppose a woman has ten silver coins and loses one... —
Jesus, Luke 15:8

Daisy was sound asleep when the Dawsons arrived back at the lake home. Most of the other kids were getting ready for bed, and Vera gently slipped her daughter into bed, clothes and all. Putting her to bed in her clothes was easier than trying to put on pajamas, and then convince her it was bedtime and not morning. Once Daisy was settled, Richard and Vera poured themselves a generous glass of chilled gewürztraminer from the Alsace region of France and joined the other adults on the screen porch. Everyone was anxious to hear the results of the appraisal.

"Well, how did it go?" Luella sat back in the rocking chair moving gently in rhythm with the lake waves against the shore. She sipped on her wine, eager for good news. "If you're hungry there is some leftover pizza on the table."

"Thanks, we already ate. The results are interesting, that's for sure." Vera stepped over some outstretched legs of her brother-in-law and found a vacant spot on the couch. "It's difficult to know where to begin. It seems with every question we get answered, three more questions pop up. Rick, why don't you explain it. You seem to know more about the coins than I do."

Richard opened the envelope with the printed and certified appraisal and passed it around. "The value of the coins is no surprise. In fact, he felt the gold coins were worth a bit more than we discovered from the Internet search. However, the Franklin half dollars are not worth much at all, probably $5 apiece."

"Why is that?" Olivia reached forward to refill her own wine glass. After a quick swirl of the contents, she took another sip. "Why would Dad keep four very valuable coins and sixteen basically worthless coins in a safe deposit box? It doesn't make sense." She considered her wine glass. "But then again sometimes Dad didn't make sense."

Most everyone chuckled in agreement. Sometimes things just didn't make sense, and you had to accept it that way.

Richard continued, "Cal Jensen, the appraiser, is convinced someone put marks on the coins, the half dollars, for a very specific reason. He made it clear, these marks were not random. But that's not the worst of it. We are missing a coin."

Everyone looked around, confused. "What do you mean missing? We all saw the coins and put them into the bag. How does he know if one is missing?"

Vera turned to her sister Olivia and began. "Do you remember Molly asking you about giving a penny to Petunia?"

"Vaguely, why?" Then the obvious hit her, and she flushed in a moment of panic. "Did Molly take one of the coins?"

"At least, according to Daisy. They took a 'big penny' and gave it to Petunia along with a donut. Daisy said Petunia ate it." Vera looked around at everyone staring back in disbelief.

Phineas broke the silence with a hearty laugh. "This is hilarious! You can't make this stuff up. What does it matter, the coin was probably only worth a few dollars? Look, the gold coins are worth $130 to $150,000. Cash them in and forget the lost one."

Tom chimed in. "Yes, I would agree, but what about these marks? If they were there for a purpose, then what purpose? We need to have another look at those coins and everything else in the safe deposit box. The more we know, it seems the less we know."

Olivia looked over at her husband, Harry. "It must have been your kid that gave the penny to the pig because my kid would never do that." They laughed at the absurdity of the whole thing.

Rick responded, "Why don't we open another bottle of wine. I recommend the Frei Brothers cabernet. It will help us maintain our sanity as we go through that pile of junk again." There was hearty agreement all around as most stood to stretch their legs and head back into the kitchen.

The items from the box were again arranged on the table for anyone to inspect, the appraised coins in sequence from earliest to latest. The other items were placed within arm's reach for anyone to pick up and inspect along with the itemized list. Luella then asked the open-ended question, "OK, what does this mean?"

Richard was the resident coin expert by virtue of discussing the findings with the appraiser. He started with the gold coins. "Do these dates mean anything to anyone?"

"What are they again?" Luella grabbed a pen and paper.

"1881, 1883, 1891, 1893."

"Well...I don't know if this is significant but those dates are exactly a hundred years from the birth years of each of us girls." Luella tried to find any other significance or connection to anything that made sense.

"Why would Mom and Dad do that?" Olivia pondered the possible connection.

"Dad was weird that way. When he needed to decide on a computer password, I know he often used the numbers in various combinations because he could remember them. Anyway, that's what he told me." Luella tried to recall anything in her past that would shed light on this mystery.

"OK. What about the other coins? The appraiser mentioned marks so we should try to identify what those mean or at least write them down." Vera looked at Rick hoping he would comment.

"Here they are in sequence. I made a list."

1948, nothing; 1949, nothing; 1950-M in America is marked; 1952-1 and 2; 1953-5; 1954-nothing; 1955-1; 1956-1; 1957-5, 7; 1958-5, 8; 1959-5; 1960-9, 1; 1961-1, 9, 6, 1; 1962-no numbers or letters--dot in the middle of Franklin's head.

"Does this make sense to anyone here?" Rick looked from face to face.

"Tom, you're a math teacher, what do these numbers mean to you? Anything?" Olivia looked over the list trying to decipher the sequence. "And why do some have nothing and some have letters? Some have more than one number."

Emma was half listening to the coin banter as she paged through the other items they found. "Luella, you took a picture of the grave up at the cemetery, didn't you?"

"Yeah, here it is on my phone. What made you think of that?"

"Well, I was paging through this King James Bible, and I noticed a couple of verses highlighted, and they sounded familiar." What she found was startling to her. "Hey, look at this. The same verse on that gravestone is the one highlighted in the Bible. "And now abideth faith, hope, charity, these three; but the greatest of these is charity."

"What? Are you sure?" Almost in unison everyone wanted to see the verse. "What about the other verse?"

"Matthew 7:7. Yes, it's highlighted too!" Emma found the passage and read it aloud. "Ask, and it shall be given you; seek, and ye shall find; knock, and it shall be opened unto you." Emma looked around at the others. "I don't know about you but this is creepy weird. Why would our parents have these verses highlighted in a Bible that are also on the gravestone of someone we don't know and have never heard of, and why would all this be in a safe deposit box?" The little hairs on the back of her neck stood up.

"You guys want to know something else that's weird?" Vera was staring at her smart phone trying to find any link with the Red Cross. "Look at this." She held out her phone for everyone to see. "Don't you see what this is?"

"It's the Red Cross symbol." Richard looked it over but couldn't see anything beyond the obvious.

"No, it's not. It is a flag. The only country in the world with a square flag, not a rectangular flag, is also red with a white cross. Switzerland." Vera was the only brave one to point where this was going. "Don't you see? Look at the note here in the Bible 'Red rises the sun on those who sleep.' All this points to the Charity Ambrose grave up at Red Rock Cemetery. That's where Mom and Dad hid the key."

Tom asked the next obvious question. "Are you expecting us to go and dig up a grave looking for a key? You're all crazy as far as I'm concerned."

"Why else would Mom and Dad go to all this trouble?" Olivia was hoping for some logical explanation to the crazy connections they were discovering.

"What trouble?" Tom asked. "Maybe you are reading too much into this. The key might be sitting in a perfectly obvious and normal spot, and here we go digging around in the night like a bunch of grave robbers. What are you going to tell the police if they show up?" The practical, math teacher side of him began to show.

Harry held up the coins. "What do these mean? We haven't figured that out yet." He flipped them over looking at the marks. He laughed. "I bet this is the combination to the safe that is buried in the casket of Charity Ambrose." The half-hearted laughs around the table did little to disguise their suspicions; it could be true.

Emma made a bold statement. "I don't know about you guys, but I'm tired. All this weekend stuff and the stress of it all, I don't feel too good. I'm going to bed, so good night." Getting up from the chair she stretched and yawned. "But tomorrow I am going up to the cemetery to plant some flowers. If any of you want to join me, you are welcome to bring a big shovel and come along."

Emma's plan didn't solve the problem, but it did give a sense of closure for the night. Each drifted toward the sleeping quarters, muttering and whispering to one another. They still had a little more than a week to find the key before the court hearing in Minneapolis.

The following morning a gray misty fog hung over the lake. Emma still didn't feel all that well, and Richard needed to head back to Des Moines. He had a job, and there was no way he could continue to stay at the lake and play games. This was getting old. No work, no pay. Vera's small pharmacy was going well, but they were using most of the profits to pay off the debt. He was the one supporting the family.

"Bye, everyone." Richard grabbed a travel mug for coffee and bent to kiss Vera and Daisy goodbye.

"Are you going to work?" Daisy always acted as though work was just around the corner. In this case going to work was a six-hour drive, and he wouldn't be back before the weekend.

"You bet, sweetie." He kissed her on top of the head as she munched on her bowl of cereal. "You be good, OK?"

"OK, Daddy. I'm going to save some cereal for Petunia." And with that she pushed her bowl away with a few remaining bits of soggy marshmallows and sugar chunks floating about. Slipping out of her chair, she announced, "Come on Molly. We gotta go feed Petunia before she gets hungry."

Vera walked out to the car to kiss Richard goodbye. "I don't think I can take this much longer. I cry at night because I miss my parents. I try to put on a happy face during the day, but I just want to run away and hide. If we don't find anything about this stupid key soon, I'm going to quit this charade and go home." She looked into his blue eyes hoping for some encouragement and clarity. "I try to understand my parents and why they would do this, but I feel hopeless. I'm so sad that they're missing and declared dead, and now this." She hugged her husband and cried into his sleeve. "I am so thankful for you. I don't know what I would do without you." She gave him one last hug, and he drove off. She knew he wanted to say things and fix it all, but for Vera, it was good to be heard, and that was enough.

As Richard drove off, Vera stood and listened. Somewhere back in the trees, a raven squawked an announcement to the rest of the forest. Blue jays screeched, bringing food back to their nests of young. A dove sitting on edge of the driveway made a soft mournful sound, and Vera cried.

The pea soup thickness of the morning fog began to lessen slightly as she walked back to the house. She picked up the water can but set it down again. There was no need to water the flowers today. She went inside and blotted her red puffy eyes.

Luella spoke up. "Look...I love you all, you know that, but I need to move on with my life. We need to get this stupid will settled." She leaned back on the couch and pulled her knee up close. Tom was off for the summer, and he could stay up at the lake with their kids, but Luella still had a job and even with a leave of absence, she needed to get back. Theo loved being at the lake, fishing, catching tadpoles and butterflies. Madeline was fine anywhere, with a book in her hand and a quiet place to read. Separation wasn't good for anyone. She caught the tears with her napkin before they drizzled down her cheek as she half-heartedly slurped her first cup of coffee.

Luella watched her kids and smiled a proud parent smile. Madeline, the oldest in fifth grade, sat in the corner of the living room, curled up on the tattered bear skin rug with a stack of books by her side. The eight-year-old twins, Zoe and Theo, chased each other in and out of rooms yelling, "You're it!"

"Hey, kids." Luella interrupted the flow of traffic. "When Auntie Emma gets out of bed, do you want to help her plant some flowers?" Luella figured it would be a good way to distract them and give them something to do other than chase each other and feed the pig. "Let's all go together. It will be more fun that way."

After Emma had parted her bedroom curtains and the morning pigpen parade was over, the fog began to thin. Emma finally felt better so they headed off. It always amazed Olivia how difficult it was to get the entire group headed in the same direction. Richard and Tom had returned to their homes for work, and uncle

Phineas volunteered to stay back and watch the twins. That left Harry to do the heavy lifting.

They stopped by the greenhouse on the way and picked up some flowers. Harry stopped by the Rent-All Hardware store on the edge of town and rented a metal detector for the day. Telling the clerk, they were looking for a lost ring. He left before any more questions were asked. It was awkward to announce they were going to the cemetery to dig up a grave.

Trudging up the hill with a metal detector, shovels, pails, flowerpots, kids, and folding chairs, they looked like a group just returning from the local flea market. At the graveside, they paused to address the uncertainty of the task before them.

"Where do we start?" Luella asked, looking from face to face for guidance.

"I say we start right here." Maddie sat down in the shade of a large oak and opened her Harry Potter book.

"I agree," Emma followed her into the shade and promptly fainted.

Chapter 15

Planting Flowers

The most beautiful adventures are not those we go to seek. —
Robert Louis Stevenson

"**E**mma!" They all responded in unison to Emma's collapse. "Are
you OK?"

Emma had barely slumped to the ground when she began to
regain consciousness. She was sweaty and trembled and for a moment seemed disoriented. "What happened?"

Luella, the nurse among them, responded in a typical professional manner. "I bet you're pregnant, aren't you?"

"Well, how could that be?" Emma was surprised. Pregnancy
was far from her mind.

"Do you want me to explain how that happens?"

"No, I don't mean that. It's just...we aren't ready to have kids
yet." She whimpered for a minute or two, and then just as

suddenly a streak of sunshine hit her. "Can we go back? I can't wait to tell Phineas."

"Why don't you wait until you have a positive pregnancy test. Besides we just got here." Luella could see through the turmoil and think logically. Harry, the only one without estrogen coursing through his veins, thanked Luella for her comments.

The grave was located on the far upper left corner in the sloping cemetery. Facing east, the high sandstone rocks jutted out behind them. From their location, they could see the entrance to the cemetery down the hill, but anyone entering through the gate could not easily see the grave of Charity Ambrose. Glancing quickly around the area, Harry slipped the strap of the metal detector over his left shoulder and flipped the switch. Tossing a couple of coins and his wedding ring onto the ground, he moved the search coil over the objects. The needle on the LCD display flickered, and the machine beeped. The unit responded differently for the penny and the wedding ring. Everything seemed to be in order.

"Let's pray for success." He put the headphones on and moved in a sweeping motion over the grave, around the head stone and the immediate vicinity.

"Hey, I got something." He stopped and hovered over an area at the foot of the gravesite. "Someone dig here."

Olivia grabbed the shovel and pushed it into the firm ground with her shoe. Two shovels full later they retested the loose dirt. The signal was still there. Further probing revealed an old rusty bolt.

"You didn't think it was going to be that easy, did you?" Vera was starting to feel cynicism creeping inward.

Finding nothing further, Olivia and Luella donned garden chore gloves and picked up shovels. "I hope we don't get into trouble." And they started.

The digging was not as easy as they had anticipated. The plan was to dig down a foot or two, putting the loose dirt into five-gallon pails and recheck with the metal detector since it could only detect metal through a relatively thin layer. The early afternoon sun burned the fog away, and the heat sucked away their motivation. Luella, Olivia, Vera, and Harry traded off with the shovels. Emma and Maddie supervised from the shade of Old Man Thompson's oak tree. Daisy and Molly ran around picking up pretty rocks, chasing butterflies and making up stories about Petunia.

"OK, let's stop and check the loose dirt, and see if we can find anything." Harry picked up the metal detector. Like a magic wand he waved it with hope over the clumps and clods of dirt. Nothing.

Starting near the foot of the grave they progressed systematically toward the headstone. They had long since filled the pails with loose dirt so they took a blanket from the back of the minivan and spread that on the ground. Pails were dumped onto the blanket and refilled from the digging. More digging, more probing, and more waving of the magic wand.

Twice the detector beeped, and again with renewed vigor they picked through the dirt with their hands. Instead of a rusty bolt, it was a 1964 nickel and a nail. Not much better.

Molly and Daisy took a respite from their wandering and came to offer advice. "Hey Dad, can I help dig?" Ever the optimist, Molly expressed hope they would dig up a dead person, because she had never seen a dead person before. "If we find somebody will he be a skeleton?"

"I'm scared of skeletons, aren't you?" Daisy stepped back from the edge of the excavation. "Don't you remember on Scooby Do when the skeleton chased Shaggy into the closet?"

"Yah! He went like this." Molly made her best imitation of the Scooby Do skeleton and jumped at Daisy. Unfortunately, Daisy's response wasn't so animated. She tripped against the stacked and overflowing pails of dirt and fell headlong into the hole. Tears mixed with dirt and two little girls with muddy streaks on their faces were forced to sit in the shade and be quiet. Luella took an inventory of the damages.

"Just a couple of scrapes and bumps. You'll be OK. Remember what Grandpa used to say, 'If you break your leg, don't come running to me.' Here have some gummy worms; we just dug them up." Luella reached into her bag and pulled out treats and a bottle of water.

"Hey, Daisy, let's save part of our gummy worms for Petunia. I bet she loves gummy worms." Even in the midst, of pain and chaos, Molly always remembered her big pig friend, Petunia.

"OK," Daisy agreed. "You save a green one and I'll save a red one." They stuffed the candy worms into their pockets along with a handful of pretty stones they had collected and raced off. For happy and active children, the world was an exciting mystery waiting to be discovered.

Once it was determined the kids were OK, everyone needed a break. Emma felt better, Maddie was on Chapter 21, and the ones doing all the work were tired. Lunchtime had come and gone. In their haste to start excavating, no one remembered to bring food. They surveyed the mess and realized it would be a while before they could leave.

Emma picked up the pails that had been knocked over. "Look what happened." She pointed to where the headstone was twisted. "The grave marker is broken loose from the base."

"I don't think it's broken, but it doesn't line up like it did before." Harry pushed dirt out of the way with his shovel and moved the remaining pails to the side. He grabbed the headstone and twisted it ever so slightly back into position. It gave a grating and screeching sound as if he were trying to loosen a corroded bolt.

"This doesn't seem normal to me." Harry sat back in the shade to mull things over.

"Nothing ever seems normal to you," Olivia goaded him. "What do you mean?"

"After high school, I worked one summer for a monument company. My boss and I would go to cemeteries and install headstones. When people died, we carved dates on stones with a template and a sandblaster. Once we came to a stone that was cracked because a big tree had fallen over on it in a storm. Anyway, as far as I remember the monument is anchored solidly into the concrete base. Nothing should move."

"Can't there be more than one way to do it?" To Vera there was always more than one way to get things done, even the wrong way.

"I'm sure there are many ways, but that's the only way I remember."

"Wait a minute, I have an idea." Emma thought for a minute. "Last night when you were going through all that crazy stuff with the coins, I was flipping through the papers from the box." She looked around. "Do you remember those little note cards with the sketches on them?"

"Refresh my memory, please." Harry said. "Remember I'm a cattle breeder. My work is simple. Identify the front of the cow, go to the back of the cow, job done. No sketches, no clues, no secret codes, nothing left to the imagination. In fact, with my job, imagination is better left at home.

Emma did her best to explain the drawings. "There were two cards, one showed two blocks stacked one upon the other. There was a cross on the top block. And in the second sketch the top block was turned so they didn't line up." She looked down at the headstone sitting slightly askew, engraved with the name, Charity Ambrose. "I think I know were the key is."

"How do you know that?" Luella seemed amazed how revelation had suddenly come upon her sister and the youngest one at that. "Well... tell us."

"Harry, don't you see it?"

"See what?" He was still stuck in cattle breeder mode. Front, back, no mystery, no clues.

"The headstone, the sketches, they show that the headstone unscrews or twists off the base. I bet the key is in the base." Emma grabbed the stone in her hands but was unable to make any progress. "Somebody help me. It has to be here."

Even working together, two people were unable to successfully move the monument. It was heavy, and there was no easy way to get an adequate grip against the carved edges of the stone.

"Wait, I have an idea." With a fresh infusion of enthusiasm, Olivia ran to the back of the minivan and returned with a short rope and a cargo strap. Putting two shovels, each on opposite sides of the headstone and then binding them together, she created a lever. Not perfect but adequate.

Now, with two people pushing and pulling on the shovel handles there was enough leverage to make a difference. The stone creaked and groaned as it reluctantly moved in a counterclockwise direction. One inch became two inches and two became four. After a near complete revolution it turned with relative ease. A space was widening between the marker and the base. Maddie put Harry Potter away to watch the proceedings. Daisy and Molly ate Petunia's gummy worms and returned to look for more treats and watch the dig. Everyone held their breath as the stone twisted five or six times around and then toppled onto its side onto the surrounding piles of dirt.

A heavy four-inch, stainless steel pipe was encased in the concrete base and the cap for the pipe was cemented into a carved space at the bottom of the headstone—a perfect hiding spot. The overhead sun illuminated the entire space of the pipe. There embedded in a block of wax to prevent corrosion, the key waited. The key would bring closure to the past. The key would help them move on. It was the key to everything.

Chapter 16

Mounting Pressure

Every man has his secret sorrows which the world knows not.
—Henry Wadsworth Longfellow

In the days and weeks following the DEA interrogation, Roy and Lola remained subdued. They limited their time in the public, avoided neighbors, and began skipping church. They kept the gift shop open with the help of employees but reduced their exposure to visitors. Even forays to the grocery store or the meat market were curtailed. They dug into the recesses of their chest freezer and sorted through old packages rather than risk conversation.

One weekend Tom and Luella invited them down for Maddie's birthday party. It would be a simple family gathering. But Roy was reluctant.

"Dad, why don't you and Mom come down for the weekend. We're planning a family pizza party for Maddie's birthday. It's going to be your anniversary soon as well. We can plan a night out, just the adults. What do you say?" Luella seldom needed to ask twice.

"Thanks for asking. Well... you know your mother, I think she is getting those headaches again." Roy referred to a long history of migraines in Lola's past.

"I thought she wasn't getting them anymore since the doctor prescribed something for her."

"Well, I think she's not telling the whole truth." Roy's voice trailed off.

"Dad, is everything OK?" Luella sounded worried.

"Of course, we're all right. I guess I just don't feel so good lately. I haven't been sleeping well." Roy sighed as he spoke.

"I thought you said Mom wasn't feeling well. Now it's you?"

"So, you're planning a birthday party. Is that for Emma?"

"Dad are you OK? Emma is my youngest sister, your youngest daughter. She lives in South Dakota. The party is for my daughter, your oldest granddaughter, Madeline. Maddie. You remember her, right?" Luella closed her eyes and leaned against the wall and muttered to herself. "I didn't think it would happen this soon.

"Dad, is Mom around?" Luella was practically begging for a normal conversation with her mother. After a pause, she could hear her father yelling for her mother to answer the phone.

"Hi, is this Luella?" Lola's voice sounded as if she had been just awakened.

"Hi, Mom, are you OK? Is Dad OK? What's going on?"

"Olivia...?"

"This is Luella."

"I'm sorry. Lu, I think your father is depressed. We just had a meeting with the undertaker about preplanning our funerals. Roy said he was feeling punk and didn't think we were going to live much longer."

"If he isn't snapping out of it, we need to get some help for him. I don't want to scare you but depression is a very common problem, especially in older people." She changed the subject. "I asked Dad about coming down for Maddie's birthday this weekend. Can you come?"

"Maddie? Is that your dog?"

"Mom! Are you both demented? Madeline is your granddaughter. If you aren't coming down, I am going to come up and get you." Luella made it clear, they needed help.

Roy and Lola muddled through the birthday weekend in reasonable fashion answering enough questions to calm Luella's internal anxieties. But not before Luella had sounded the alarm with the sisters. Now everyone was on heightened alert, like vultures perched on dead tree limbs watching the old folks circle the drain.

This went on for weeks. Roy and Lola did their best to hide all concerns from their kids, but sleeplessness and depression were taking a toll.

#

Dag Rasmussen kept up the pressure. He called several times weekly just to maintain contact. Dag ordered police surveillance of the Ambrose household, not because Lola and Roy were in immediate danger, but Dag wanted them to know they were being watched. In Dag's experience as an agent, psychological pressure was often far more effective than physical threats. Roy was a tough old goat. You could lead a goat to water, but couldn't always get him to drink. But Dag knew you could put some salt in his oats.

#

It was late when the phone rang. Olivia glanced at the caller ID and cautiously answered. Phone calls from hospitals after 10 PM were seldom good.

"Hello?" She listened for a minute and responded. "Yes, I'm his daughter." She clutched at her chest. The news sounded ominous.

"Can you tell me his condition? How serious is this?" The monotone voice of the hospital intern prattled on with indiscernible medical terminology. There were some concerns about his psychophonomognosis or possibly a pseudopneumophlegmatitis or something like that. The intern even speculated he might be suffering from a subacute sclerosing case of pan-encephalitis. Either way, according to the intern on call, at his age nothing was good.

"Should I come right now? Is he going to make it?" Olivia was frantically trying to get herself ready to leave, while trying to understand the intern. "Listen, can you call my sister, she's a nurse. She might be able to understand what you just told me." She heard a mumble and a click. Olivia was left to figure it out on her own.

"Harry, I need to leave for the Duluth hospital right now. My dad is being admitted into the ICU."

"What's going on?"

Olivia nodded as she blew her nose. Harry reached out his hand and held her shoulder.

"I'll stay here with Molly. Do you want me to call your sisters, or are you going to do that on the way?" Harry was a good solid husband, always calm and stable in a time of crisis. "I love you. I'll be praying. OK? And let me know as soon as you find out what's happening."

"I'll call Luella on the way and let her know. Maybe she can call Vera and Emma." Running on adrenaline since she got off the phone, now Olivia felt shaky. Hugging her husband goodbye, she left a big wet tear mark on his T-shirt.

As she pulled out of the driveway and onto the highway, Olivia hit the speaker on her phone and speed dialed.

"Olivia, why are you calling me so late?" Luella had concern in her voice.

"Hey Lu, they took Dad to the hospital in Duluth. I talked to the intern on call but he was a bag of nuts. I couldn't understand a word he said, something about pseudoflego something." Olivia paused as she looked for traffic, then continued. "I guess he's in the ICU. I'm on my way now."

"What happened?"

"I don't know. After I see Mom and find out something I'll call you back. Can you let the others know?" She added, "Maybe you can get ahold of Mom and see what's going on."

"OK, Olivia. Thanks. Drive safe; you don't need to speed. We'll be praying." Luella had that sick feeling in her stomach. Every health care worker knew the drill. Everyday someone, somewhere got a call because someone they knew was having a bad day. Every day was a lottery because you never knew when your phone was going to ring. Her phone rang today.

It was near midnight before Olivia could see her dad. Semi-comatose he was admitted to the ICU for monitoring. According to the on-call doctor, they were trying to rule out several possibilities including sepsis, stroke, heart problems, and some type of seizure disorder. So far, the lab results looked encouraging, and there didn't appear to be any heart damage. He was breathing on his own, and his pulse was regular, and his blood pressure was low but acceptable. He responded to questions by gestures, but he wasn't talking, just grunts and mumbles.

"Mom, what happened?" Olivia and her mother finally had a chance to sit and visit. Lola was visibly shaken.

"Well, your dad hasn't been feeling so good lately; I think you already know that." She continued with a low tremulous voice. "I went out to the garage to get something out of the freezer for dinner. I don't think I was out there more than a few minutes. When I came back in, he was sprawled on the floor and breathing hard." Lola trembled and blotted her eyes. "I thought he had a stroke. I didn't know what to do, and I'm not strong enough to get him up myself so I called 911." Lola closed her eyes and held her head with her hands. "It's all my fault; I should have been there for him."

"Mom, you did the right thing. It wasn't your fault. It's going to be OK."

"You promise?"

"Yes, I promise." Not so very long ago it was Lola comforting Olivia after skinning her knee or another breakup with a boyfriend. The tables were turning.

One day passed into another. The endless parade of doctors, consultants, specialists, x-ray techs, lab techs, float nurses, night nurses and custodians collapsed into a long blur. Despite many questions, there were few answers. More tests brought more questions and little resolution to the crisis of the moment. Finally, after the third day, Dr. Eno Antilla, MD, sat down with the family and tried to outline what was known and unknown.

"Mrs. Ambrose, I'm sorry about your husband. We are working hard to figure out what happened with Roy. So, let's start with what we know. First, he didn't have a heart attack or blockage of the arteries to his heart, and he didn't have a stroke."

"Dr. Antilla, I'm Luella, Roy's oldest daughter. I'm a nurse so I understand most of what's going on. Help me to figure this out. Dad collapsed and has remained 'out of it' for three days now. If he didn't have a stroke, what do you think happened?" Luella, like everyone else, was desperate for an answer they could understand.

"Well, that's the difficult part. We don't know. None of the tests are conclusive. There is no clear evidence of a seizure or metabolic disturbance. No evidence of head trauma, no evidence of occult or hidden infection, no evidence of any toxic substance, and no evidence of any vascular disturbance or heart arrhythmia. The only thing we have left is the possibility of some type of psychotic or psychiatric disturbance or fugue state."

"Do you think Dad is losing his mind?" Olivia turned to her mother. "Mom, all of us think you and Dad have been acting rather strange since you came back from your trip to Mexico. Did something happen?"

Lola diverted the conversation back to Roy and away from their experience in Mexico. "I think Dad is getting better every day. He seemed to be more alert this morning before all of you got here."

"How do you know that? All he has mumbled over the past two days 'tag, tag...Chico', whatever that means. I think he is delirious." Luella looked at the others to confirm her suspicions. "Mom, does this make any sense to you?"

"I wish I knew...I wish I knew."

At that moment, Roy had a sudden revival as if being awakened from a bad dream. His brief but animated resurrection added fuel to the speculation of psychosis. He sat up suddenly in his bed, staring straight ahead at the whiteboard covered in notes and patient vital signs. "DAG! DAG! I SAW HIM, DAG!" And then he slumped back into a catatonic state.

#

Dag Rasmussen was aware of the change in events surrounding Roy Ambrose. With local police and regional DEA field agents monitoring Roy's coming and going, Dag was kept current on his condition. However, being aware didn't resolve the El Quilete incident. It was time to talk to Roy again—before he died.

A quick overnight flight from Springfield, Virginia, directly into Duluth International Airport allowed Dag to get to the hospital before normal visiting hours. A quick check with the hospital physician on duty allowed him to estimate the level of awareness Roy may or may not have. In Dag's mind, any information even fleeting or fragmented was better than nothing. He needed a witness to stand up in a federal court and testify against Javier Espinosa. As of today, the only known eye-witness was Roy Ambrose, and he was flakier than a croissant.

Dag Rasmussen and George Benson presented their credentials to the hospital physicians and security and entered Roy's room at 6 AM. The sight of the one-eyed interrogator jolted Roy like a defibrillator. By 7 AM Roy was drinking coffee and talking freely. It was as if a great roadblock had cleared, and Roy was nearly back to his old self. Although confused about the events of the past several days, he was clear about what he had witnessed south of the border. By 8 AM they had a confidential taped interview and were on their way back to Virginia before Lola and the girls arrived for visiting hours.

Chapter 17

The Will

Judge not, that ye not be judged. —Jesus, Matthew 7:1

Discovering the key, elated the Ambrose clan. The meeting with the circuit court judge could go on as scheduled. The stipulation, per Gretta Hanninin, was clear. The will could not be opened and read until all beneficiaries were present before the judge. That however, didn't mean they could not go to the Suisse Bank and open the safe deposit box.

The trip to Suisse Bank in downtown Minneapolis was fraught with peril. One-way streets, full parking ramps, and roads closed to construction proved to be nearly equal in frustration to Charity Ambrose and her secrets. Multiple pedestrians walked into streets with little regard for life and limb. Screeching brakes and blaring horns added to the din of downtown noise. More than once the elusive Suisse Bank was spotted from streaked car windows as they circled ever closer. It was as if you knew where you were going, but you couldn't get there, no how, no way. Finally, as the last pedestrian stepped onto the curb and out of their way, a lane opened. They turned onto the last one-way street and into the parking ramp. Ten dollars for the parking ticket, and they were home free.

Attorney Gretta Hanninin was waiting in the lobby. Walking from her office through the downtown skywalk system saved her time and avoided another $10 parking fee. "Do you have the key?"

Luella and Vera were the family representatives at the bank, but the others were going to meet at the court. The stark but massive lobby gave an immediate impression of stability, strength, and confidence—just what you wanted from a bank specializing in secret accounts and high security safe deposit boxes. The three women followed the bank representative to the spacious gold colored elevators. A special code was entered, and they descended several floors from the lobby.

"Keys, please." Another attendant met them in the new lobby and checked their keys for authenticity. Once they met the appropriate criteria, a smartly dressed banker appeared to greet them. His well-tailored, three-piece suit was brilliantly accented with large gold cufflinks and a gold silk tie. His smile was disarming and pleasant.

"Good morning. I am Herr Fritz Gruber, one of the managing partners here at Suisse Bank. We always try to personally meet with our elite clients. I hope everyone is well today?" Not expecting an answer, he simply gestured for the small group to follow. They entered an elevator and descended five floors. From there they continued into the secured, private offices located immediately adjacent to the lower lobby. "Please have a seat."

Herr Gruber collected the unique keys, one held separately by the attorney's office and the other recovered from the cryptic recesses of the Charity Ambrose headstone. Together they fit into the separate locks on the high security bank box. The third universal key provided by the bank executive unlocked the box. The entire box was carried into the private room. Luella and Olivia hesitated, breathlessly. It was Gretta Hanninin who finally prompted the sisters to open the box as they were the lawful recipients of the contents.

Olivia tuned the latch and the lid popped slightly ajar. She lifted it and peered inside. She was greeted with two large sealed envelopes, labeled number one and number two with attached instructions. The directions were clear and unambiguous. Neither package was to be opened unless in front of a judge as a witness and only in sequence with number one to be opened first. That was it. No notes, no secret messages, no gold coins or gold teeth, no treasure maps, and no clue to what was enclosed in the envelopes.

"The court appointment is scheduled in two hours. I can take these documents with me to the courthouse or you can. Either way if there is any evidence of tampering, as decided by the judge, then the entire will may be considered void, and the judge can force the estate into probate." Gretta made sure they were aware of the seriousness of tampering with a sealed document.

"We understand. We want you to handle the contents of the box, and we'll meet you at the courthouse about fifteen minutes early if that's OK with you." Neither Luella nor Olivia wanted the responsibility of the envelopes.

"OK. See you soon."

The sisters discussed the use of the box with the bank representative and signed over the keys. They had no more need of the highly secured locked box. One milestone was behind them.

Judge Bjorn Bjornson, who presided over the fifth circuit court in Minneapolis, agreed to meet with the Ambrose family in his chambers. There was plenty of room for the sisters, their husbands, Tom and Richard, and the attorney. Harry was breeding cattle and Phineas was researching the effects of harmonic sound wave convergence on migrating hummingbirds.

"Good afternoon. I am Judge Bjorn Bjornson. You are the heirs of the Ambrose estate?" He shook hands all around as introductions were made. He was a big man with a deep voice, but he put them all at ease. "I understand how difficult these matters can be. Emotions and expectations can be overwhelming. I am hopeful your attorney and I can help you through this process and answer any questions you may have. Before we begin, is there anything else I should know about the estate or the deceased?"

The usual ten-minute summary morphed into forty minutes as they discussed the unfortunate events of the tragic demise of Roy and Lola Ambrose. Fascinated by the entire story the judge commented. "I don't think I need to tell you, but this is highly unusual." They all agreed.

Seated in a manner so that all could view the process, the judge opened the first of the two envelopes. It contained a rather thick stack of papers combined with certified checks made out to each of the Ambrose girls. On top of the will was a hand-written letter by their father, signed by both Roy and Lola Ambrose.

To our Family,

If you are reading this letter, it means we are no longer with you. We know what it is like to grieve the loss of a parent. Please don't grieve for us. Look forward to the day when we are reunited.

We hope and pray that the process of discovery for this letter and our Last Will and Testament was not too arduous and demanding. We suspect you were frustrated, but there was a purpose behind it all.

The gold coins you have in your possession from the safe deposit box are a simple representation of the beauty and value we see in each of our daughters. Though no earthly treasure can ever demonstrate your true beauty, always remember, in our eyes you are the most wonderful gift we could have ever gained during our time on earth.

Though we could go on with pearls of wisdom and advice for living, we won't. The best lessons in life are seldom taught but rather caught through experience. The true measure of living is not determined by the number of hours you live but rather how you lived during the hours you were given.

Until we meet again on that glorious day.
Roy and Lola Ambrose / Mom and Dad

The judge read the letter aloud. Even the crusty judge, after decades of sending criminals to prison, was misty eyed. He held the letter in his hands for a moment as he cleared his throat and passed it to Luella. Tears welled up and ran. Even Gretta reached for a tissue and blotted her eyes. When they had each had a chance to hold and review the letter, the judge asked if he could continue.

"Here in my hand is the document identified as the Last Will and Testament of Roy and Lola Ambrose. I will read the entire document, but you need to know if there is any concern on your part regarding inconsistencies or inaccuracies or what you believe to be false, you have the right to contest this in a court of law. However, based on the extreme measures to which your parents seem to have gone, you may have a difficult time convincing a judge. Are there any further questions?"

Seeing no objections, he began. After the initial statements about being of sound mind, he got to the meat of the matter.

"We, Roy Ambrose and Lola Ambrose, as husband and wife, bequeath the follow sums of money to each of our children. The sum of one hundred thousand dollars to each daughter and the sum of thirty thousand dollars to each grandchild. This amount of money will be held in trust until such time as the child shall cease to be a minor and is determined to be an emancipated adult." Enclosed in packet number one were certified checks in the amounts indicated, drawn on an account held in Suisse Bank in Zurich, Switzerland.

The document went on to discuss the disposition of personal property and real estate as indicated by the family living trust. There were a few other miscellaneous items to contend with in the main portion of the will, and then they came to the last page.

"The distribution of assets and property is clearly defined and available for use immediately on the final resolution of this Last Will and Testament. However, there remains a second option." The judge went on reading.

"Package number two is a second and distinct option from the first package. You may assume possession of the assets contained in package number two, if and only if, you decline package number 1. However, the contents and stipulations contained in package number two will not be revealed to you prior to a decision. You have twenty-four hours to make a decision.

"The decision to accept or reject package number one and choose package number two must be a unanimous decision among the four principle beneficiaries, Luella, Olivia, Vera and Emma (Ambrose). Beneficiaries are free to discuss the options, seek legal or personal counsel, but the decision must be made within twenty-four hours of the conclusion of this meeting. The court is bound by the stipulations contained herein.

"Choosing option number two results in the forfeiture of the money in option number one. If package number one is accepted, then package number two will be sent unopened by the judge pre-siding over this meeting to the legal firm Liakos, Economu, and Christopoulos, located in Athens, Greece. They have specific directions on file to manage the final distribution of the assets contained in package number two."

A rather awkward and confused silence blanketed the group. Emma was the first to voice her confusion. "I'm not sure I understand; please correct me if I'm wrong. We can have the money in package number one and reject package number two, or we can reject package number one and take number two, but we can't see what's in there?" She looked at the faces of her sisters, striving for clarification.

The judge responded as best as he could under the circumstances. "This is clearly an unusual Last Will and Testament, however the way you outlined it, is also the way I understand it. The big question is, What's behind door number two?"

Olivia was the first to speak up. "We aren't wealthy people. I'm not sure where Mom and Dad came up with the money, but this is a significant amount. It would be a difficult decision to give up something we know for certain and choose something we don't know much about."

Luella weighed in. "I agree, but why would our parents do something like this? It is so odd. Wouldn't you think they would be equal?" She looked for further input from Vera and Emma. "Well...what do you think?"

Vera was next. "I can't answer for Mom and Dad, but I have been doing some research. This Suisse bank they are working through is considered an exclusive bank. They cater to people with substantial means. They work within an area called 'private wealth management' for exclusive members only. I don't know where they got the money, but I sure hope it is legal. This bank won't work with individuals unless they have a net worth of at least ten million dollars."

There was a stunned silence around the meeting room. Even the judge was rather taken aback. Giving up five hundred thousand was not easy, but ten million was still ten million. However, there was no guarantee the second package held anything close to the value they had just discussed. It was entirely speculation on their part about the potential value. Even if package two did have a significant monetary value, that money may not be designated to them.

Emma cast the first vote. "I vote to keep package number one. I'm pregnant, my husband is in graduate school and we need the money."

"Are you sure you want to do that? What if we are looking at the possibility of millions of dollars?" Vera was lobbying for the second option. "Why don't you discuss it with Phineas before you decide?" Turning toward the oldest, she added, "Lu, what do you think?"

"We don't have much now and frankly, I didn't expect to inherit much from Mom and Dad anyway. They always taught us to take a risk, but not to make foolish decisions. We have already received the house together as joint heirs and to me that's enough. Anything else is a bonus. I vote for package number two. Sorry, Emma. I don't want to offend you or your decision, but I can't believe Mom and Dad would put something of lesser value in either choice. My guess is that they are at least equal." Luella voiced her thoughts, but she still had doubts.

Judge Bjorn Bjornson sat back in his mahogany and leather office chair. It made a slight squeak as he clasped his hands behind his head. "You do realize," he said, speaking to the group, "you have twenty-four hours to decide this. It doesn't need to be decided now."

Emma responded, "Yes, we know, but staying over in Minneapolis or leaving and traveling back is a pain. Let's make a decision today and be done with it."

Hearing that, the other three girls submitted their verbal vote for package number two. Emma paused to consider her options. She was the holdout. No matter which way they chose, no one lost out. Still the immediate use of money would be a huge benefit to both her and Phineas. On the other hand, she couldn't think of a good reason to not choose number two. It was the prospect of the unknown that loomed before them. "OK, let's do it."

The judge again asked for a verbal confirmation from the four heirs of the estate. "Hearing no verbal dissent and unanimous approval to proceed with the opening of package number two and to forfeit the contents of package number one as outlined in the Last Will and Testament of Roy and Lola Ambrose, we will proceed."

In a single motion that left no option to turn back, the judge grabbed the tab on the edge of the large envelope and ripped open the seal.

Chapter 18

Package Number Two

Anything that costs money is cheap. —John Steinbeck

Inside of the large sealed envelope was a polished wooden box made of exquisite bird's eye maple. The corners were held together with perfectly fit dovetail joints. No metal was used in the making of the box. There were no hinges, the tight-fitting lid lifted straight off. Inside the box an oblong object fit snuggly into the custom recesses covered with a thick, dark felt.

The girls held onto the edge of the conference table as a nauseous silence clouded the room. Luella dabbed her eyes and forehead, glancing about for a sense of clarity. Only one, Vera, dared reach out and grasp the object before them. As she gingerly picked it up, her hand shook slightly. This moment was a culmination of anxiety, confusion, and loss. It all came together in this, whatever it was.

"What is this?" Emma looked hopefully at Judge Bjornson.

"May I hold it?" The judge extended his right hand to pick up the object. The weight seemed out of proportion to the size of the device. It was heavy enough to hurt someone if you chose to use it that way. It was an oblong container made of polished brass and stainless steel. Somewhat in the shape of a large German summer sausage, it was encircled with several rings or bands engraved with numbers. "I didn't think these things actually existed. The only one I've seen was in a movie. They called it a cryptex. In the movie, it also had some type of fail-safe mechanism to prevent tampering." He handed the cryptex to Olivia.

"What do you mean by 'fail-safe' mechanism?" Emma wondered aloud. "Has anyone else seen anything like this?"

The judge continued. "In the movie, there was a vial of acid or something like that in the device. If you tried to cut it open or pry it apart, then the acid leaked and destroyed the contents, making it unreadable or unusable."

Tom wiped his forehead and spoke. "I don't want to burst your bubble, but you realize you gave up over five hundred thousand dollars for this. I hope you think it was worth it."

"Tom, that's not fair. We discussed this and agreed. It's too late to go back." Luella appeared resolute in her commitment, but she also expressed some doubt. "Judge Bjornson, what if we changed our mind?"

"I'm afraid I am bound by the agreement. The only way you could go back and choose the first package is to claim that you were coerced into making the decision, and you filed a legal challenge to the will, which would then go to court. The state would represent your parent's intent as outlined by the will. I don't see how you could win." Judge Bjornson seemed as confused as the others. In his thirty-seven years on the bench he had seen some very strange things, especially when it came to family and domestic issues, but this ranked up there with the most unusual. His normally, perfectly groomed hair had become as disoriented as the Ambrose family before him.

Once the initial bewilderment faded, the judge revisited the box. Under the felt covering inside the lid was a small sealed envelope. A collective murmur passed between them. Hope for an explanation was reborn.

Reading from the letter, the judge cleared his throat and began. "By now you have opened package number two, and we are sure you have many questions. Some of the answers lie within the cryptex and more will follow. As you may recall, at the bottom of the initial letter, Lola and I recorded a Bible verse, Hebrews 11:1. I am under the assumption you know what it meant or at least looked it up. Because of your decision to forfeit the money contained in package number one, you will be rewarded that same amount upon solving the puzzle of the cryptex. The full instructions are included within. You have been given the solution, or you know where to find it. Years ago, you were given a similar challenge. Each of you worked as couples to solve the puzzle. This time you must work together."

The judge rubbed his eyes and his temples as if trying to avert a migraine. "Did your parents do this before? Is this behavior normal for them?"

Olivia responded for the group. "Dad had this thing about making us think and search for our Christmas gifts. Every year he did something like that. It drove me crazy. But I loved every minute."

"Well, sisters, what do we do now?" Vera was hopeful for some direction. She was tired and desperately longed for a normal week in her life. As they filed out of the judge's chambers and into the main lobby of the courthouse, they mingled in the lobby, as if looking for direction.

Vera needed to return home to work. Olivia needed to be home to take care of Molly because Harry was scheduled to be at a cattle breeder convention next week. Luella was back in the night nurse schedule. It was either go back to work or risk losing her job. Emma was pregnant. She was a bundle of nausea and anxiety. She read every book on pregnancy and was anxious to begin her prenatal classes. She also needed to work because Phineas was busy doing research. Today was a Thursday, and everyone had the weekend off. If they were going to solve the puzzle, it had to be now.

Richard carried the box containing the cryptex. He was the quiet observer during the entire visit with Judge Bjornson. As they walked out, he looked at Tom who was still mopping his brow. "Are you feeling OK?"

"I'm sick." Tom replied.

Luella jumped in. "What do you mean? Do you have a fever?"

"Isn't it enough that I tell you? Do you want me to show you too? Should I deposit a green bilious mass on the smooth polished marble floor?" Tom held his stomach.

"Oh, stop it. You sound like a cheap novelist." Luella looked away.

"I'm better now. Not sure what hit me in there." Tom said.

"Probably too warm, and too many people in a small space." Richard was the calm and reassuring one, like an old golden retriever. Always reliable and quick to offer comfort. "So, what's your take on this?"

"A thought ran through my head when we were in the meeting. I believe I know the combination, but we need to stop back at Namukwa." Tom looked at the others.

"What kind of stop?"

"We need to take Petunia to the vet." The vertigo struck again, and he vomited in the courthouse lobby.

Chapter 19

El Chico

Being powerful is like being a lady. —Margaret Thatcher

Javier Espinosa didn't like being told what to do. The origin for his moniker "El Chico" derived in part from his fascination with the American thug, Billy the Kid. His actions reflected this. He didn't negotiate with people; he eliminated people. His reputation caused fear and concern, and the unmarked mass graves in the dusty hills of Sinaloa gave clear evidence of his ruthlessness.

"So... there is a witness, is that what you are telling me?" His steely calm voice was steady and unwavering like the dispassionate rambling of a surgeon before cutting your leg off. "What does it matter?"

"The Americans are trying to get rid of you."

"Do you think I don't know?" Not expecting an answer, he turned his back on the two lieutenant enforcers and looked out the window of his suite on the top floor of the El Presidente Hotel. The afternoon sun reflected off the windows, illuminating the paved waterfront walkway, the malecón below. Tourists and locals scurried along the walk searching for bargains—or suckers. Everyone wanted an edge, an advantage, a toehold to subdue and overcome one's opponent. War was fought on many levels, and Espinosa considered himself above it all.

Looking below, he focused on the Cocos Helados sign propped in front of the small thatched vendor shack below. "What does Garza know?"

"Someone left a message with him. An American witnessed the shooting of the rat up in El Quilete. We know who was there." He handed El Chico a list with the names of Earl Ambrose, Sandy Piper, Elizabeth Elkins, Lola Ambrose, and Roy Ambrose. "She's the painter." He pointed to Sandy's name.

"So, who is the snitch?" Javier looked around at the men. "We need to talk to them. If we can't determine which one, then we'll eliminate them all."

"We went to the house of Earl and Sandy yesterday. They are missing."

"What do you mean, missing?" Espinosa focused his squinted eyes at his henchman.

"Here is some more news. Garza gave us information today. It might have been Pancho Hernandez from Chihuahua. He has been trying to move in on you here in Sinaloa. Word is, he heard you were weakening and wants to gain territory."

"Hernandez is a dog. If we put the heat on him, he will cower in the corner with his tail between his legs. He won't try anything with us." Yet, a competitor didn't sit too well with El Chico. "If we find the painter and her husband, we'll make them talk. There is no easy way to get to the other Americans without raising suspicion." Then he added, "If you think Garza is lying to us, break his legs."

After the two enforcers left Espinosa, he sat back in his overstuffed leather chair and gazed out over the Pacific. With two packs of cigarettes already gone by early afternoon, he opened another and struck his lighter. The smoke leaked out his mouth and curled back up his nostrils as he inhaled. He didn't trust his lieutenants, he didn't want Hernandez around, and he didn't even trust the young housekeeper who provided more personal services than just cleaning his suite. He certainly didn't trust Garza, but that cheap palapa on the beach was a link between Espinosa and the Americans. Maintaining power and control was all that mattered. Money and death went hand in hand. In this business, there was seldom one without the other. Human life was cheap, power and influence was expensive. He had paid a dear price to rise to this level; no one was going to take it away.

Hernandez, "*El Perrito*," the little dog, was another issue Espinosa hadn't considered. Young and ambitious he was cut out of the same mold as Espinosa. Youth and reckless idealism could be trouble. Old criminals exhibited restraint borne out of experience. Young criminals showed no restraint. They killed with random apathy, little different than a video game. That's what made them dangerous; it was all a game.

#

Earl and Sandy frittered their days away with rising anxiety. Staying in Mexico City was not a realistic option, but neither was returning to Mazatlán. Sandy was sure their house had been searched and probably destroyed. Earl was even less optimistic. Reading about the ruthlessness of the drug lords was one thing; experiencing it first hand was another.

Several days had passed since the big Dane had grilled them. The people assigned to watch them and feed them were nothing more than drones, doing their duty, nothing more. Aside from access to cold beer and tequila, little had changed after the interview. They answered the questions to the best of their ability. If Dag Rasmussen wanted more details, they would have to lie.

"Sandy, help me think this through." Earl lay back on the squeaking iron framed cot that sagged in the middle like an old man's gut. The mattress felt more like a lumpy hammock, but it was better than the floor. "If we go back to Mazatlán, what can we expect?"

"You know exactly what to expect. Espinosa will turn us into chum." She took a long swallow on her Pacifico and thought aloud. "I bet they trashed our place already, and I expect they paid one of the neighborhood people to watch for us. If we so much as drive by, Espinosa will be all over us."

"What should we do?" Earl had been searching for answers but found little comfort in his conclusions. "The way I see it, we have three options: 1) go back and be tortured and killed, 2) stay here in Mexico City and get the same treatment or 3) go back to the States."

Sandy finished her first beer and cracked open another. Earl poured more tequila. The alcohol didn't make their problems go away, but they were less likely to lie awake at night and worry.

"Our passports were in the house. Unless you can convince old one-eye to issue new passports, we're not going anywhere." Sandy was always the optimist. "I suppose we could go to the US embassy."

Two more days passed and finally there was some activity. Earl and Sandy were awakened early and marched out of the compound and into a small waiting bread truck. Emblazoned on the side was the company logo, Bimbo Bread. Without explanation, a younger man with a jacket and a Chicago Bulls T-shirt jumped into the driver's seat and drove off.

"*Donde nos llevas*? Where are we going?" Earl tried to engage him in conversation, but the driver wasn't in the mood for chatter. Neither Earl nor Sandy felt threatened by the young driver, but he had a standard issue, 9mm Beretta, safely tucked into a side holster under his jacket.

"*Tu casa,*" was the simple reply. They were going home, and it didn't appear as if they had a say in the matter. The driver turned up the radio, and they listened to every possible signal they could receive in the hours-long drive back to the coast. There was news-talk commentary about the drug problems Mexico was facing. Music blared out from time to time, mostly with a Latin flare but also current popular music exported by the neighbors to the north.

Earl and Sandy talked softly between themselves, and the driver showed little interest. Whether he was on the payroll of Dag

Rasmussen or El Chico or both, they had little way of knowing. Either way, he smoked one cigarette after another and ignored the passengers. Not until they reached the outskirts of Mazatlán did the demeanor of the driver change. He speed-dialed someone on his cell phone, but no conversation took place.

The driver began to pay close attention to other cars and trucks. Nervously his eyes darted from one rearview mirror to the other and then back. Then abruptly, he relaxed and pulled on another cigarette.

"We live near the lighthouse." Earl offered directions.

"I know," was the driver's only reply. He drove with a destination in mind, but Earl was also aware the route taken was not the normal route. Randomly twisting and turning around El Centro, the main market area, he wove his way south and west toward the residential area. As the sun began to set over the ocean, the driver received another phone call. This time he listened and nodded. Suddenly his driving took on a new purpose, but rather than heading to the home of Earl and Sandy, he pulled to a stop in front of a dark, dilapidated building on stilts. The faded blue paint was chipped and peeling. The sign read, Stone Island Ferry, Closed. Announcing nothing, the driver opened his door and stepped out. Without looking around, he walked briskly and disappeared behind the ferry terminal. He never returned.

Five minutes turned into ten and then fifteen. Earl and Sandy glanced nervously about. This wasn't a good neighborhood to be in after sundown. As expat Americans, they would be especially vulnerable. No ferryboats were coming or going, no cars or headlights illuminated the streets, only stray cats, and the flutter of the frigate birds along the coast settling into their roosts. It was a forty-five-minute walk to their home from this spot, and with Earl's bad leg, the time would double.

"Earl, what should we do?" Sandy had a worried sound to her voice. When nothing further happened, they made the bold move of stepping out of the Bimbo Bread truck.

"I'm not sure, but we can't stay here." Looking nervously up and down the parking area near the ferry station, they saw no one. He winced from the pain of his bad leg and limped in the direction of the lighthouse. "Let's get out of here. I don't know what else to do."

At one end of the parking area, scattered old cars stood in crooked rows, like teeth in a jack-o-lantern. In the empty spaces between the cars, stray cats by the dozens gathered. Occasional rats, those fortunate enough to avoid the cats, scurried under rusted junk and old tires. The eyes of the cats glowed back at Earl, reflecting the dim light from the lone streetlight in the area.

Earl wiped the sweat from his forehead, partly from exertion and the rest from nerves; he had a very uneasy feeling. Suddenly, headlights came on and doors opened from a dark van at the end of the parking area.

"Are you Ambrose?" The well-dressed man was framed by the bright headlights behind him. Sandy and Earl blinked, looking away from the glare.

"Who are you?" Earl wasn't willing to volunteer any information.

"Are you Ambrose?" This time he was more insistent. He motioned to the men behind him. Two men with guns drawn stepped quickly to the side of Earl and Sandy.

Twisting Earl's arm behind him, one of the men kicked him behind his good knee, sending Earl to the pavement. His chicken leg bent under his weight. He screamed in agony. Sweat ran into his eyes, and he breathed heavily, trying to roll into a less painful position. The man held his arm and twisted harder.

"Are you Ambrose?" came the question again. Earl was too overcome with pain to answer. Sandy responded.

"Yes, we are. What do you want?"

"I ask the questions here." The man holding Sandy twisted both of her arms and kicked the back of her knees, sending her to the dirty pavement. Blood from her skinned knees trickled into the dust. A feral cat chased a rat in front of the van headlights, casting a surreal shadow over them.

The man asking the questions stepped forward and grabbed Earl's chin, yanking his face upward. He shined a bright light into Earl's eyes blinding him. "You know who I am." Then turning to Sandy, he reached out and held her right hand. "It would be hard to paint without fingers, wouldn't it?"

Shaking with fear, she didn't answer. El Chico had them. It didn't matter what they knew or what they said. She would never paint again. She tried to look away, but the same bright light was directed into her eyes as well.

"What do you know about El Quilete?" His steady cold voice cut into her memory.

"What do you want to know?" The bright light seared her retinas, blinding her. Sandy blinked, trying to see.

"I know you were there." Espinosa answered with a low menacing voice.

"When?" She tried to stall the inevitable.

"You know exactly when. What did you see?"

"I didn't see anything." She closed her eyes.

"What if I make sure you never see anything again?" He squeezed her hand until her knuckles cracked, and she winced in pain. "What did you see?" he asked again.

"Nothing, I saw nothing."

Then turning to Earl, El Chico directed the blinding light into his eyes. "What about you, limpy? What did you see?" Espinosa kicked the toe of his well shined shoes into Earl's bad knee. "Now you made my shoes dirty. You're going to have to pay for that." Grabbing Earl's ear, he twisted his head until Earl collapsed onto the dirt. A rat scurried out and sniffed at Earl's sweaty hair and then retreated to safety of the rusted pile of junk nearby.

"Do you know what I'm going to do? I'm going to kill you. It doesn't matter what you saw, or what your friends saw because dead people don't talk. It's as simple as that. I'm not even going to hide your body because it doesn't matter. I own the police. I own this country. We're going to throw you behind that pile of junk, and the rats will have you half eaten by morning and what the rats won't eat the seagulls and feral cats will."

With a contented smile, as if he had just finished dessert, he lit a cigarette and turned toward his vehicle. Motioning to his henchmen they pulled their guns and stepped forward. Looking across the water toward Stone Island, Javier Espinosa never blinked at the gunshots.

Chapter 20

A Snail's Pace

But in my opinion, all things in nature occur mathematically.
—Rene Descartes

Tom and Harry pushed and pulled and prodded Petunia up the ramp and into the small horse trailer. She wasn't a willing participant on the field trip to the vet. Moving a gigantic pig when it didn't want to move is no simple task. Tom put a collar around the fat that represented a neck and pulled until the veins in his own neck bulged from effort. Harry leaned into Petunia's massive hams and grunted as he pushed from behind. Petunia calmly expelled a voluminous pile of fragrant excrement, and Harry experienced it firsthand.

Molly cried out. "Don't hurt Petunia. Where are you taking her?"

"Molly, we're taking her to the vet." Tom looked over at Olivia to help with a good explanation. "She is going to see the pig doctor."

"Is she going to get her shots like me?"

Tom and Harry ignored her questions as they continued to wrestle with the massive pile of lard on legs. They reeked from the stench and sweat, but Petunia was no closer to entering the gate. If turning Petunia into a freezer full of pork chops and bacon was the answer, then it must be done.

"Why don't you just give her a donut?" What pearls of wisdom come from the mouth of babes. "Just give her a donut, and she'll follow you anywhere." Molly ran to the house and returned with glazed and sugar donuts in each hand.

Standing near the front of the trailer, she held out her little hands. Petunia squealed and marched dutifully into the back. Mission accomplished. Molly was the heroine. "Now what are you going to do with her?"

"Listen to me." Uncle Tom got down on his knees to look Molly in the eye. "Remember when you fed the big penny to Petunia?"

"Yep, she ate it." Molly recalled it very well, and she was she proud of it. "Mommy said I could, remember?"

"Yes, I remember. But now we need to get the penny out."

"Are you going to cut it out?" Molly started to cry. "Don't hurt her." Molly ran and hugged her mother.

Olivia bent down to comfort poor Molly. "No honey, they aren't going to hurt Petunia. The animal doctor is going to take an x-ray to see if the big penny is still inside of her." She looked expectantly at the men closing the gate to the animal trailer. "I promise, they won't hurt Papa's pig."

You don't just show up at the vet's office unannounced with a six-hundred-pound pig. The small animal hospital was prepared for their arrival. Petunia didn't fit the description of a small animal, but there were no other options within an hour's drive. Dr. Virginia Arbuckle, DVM, met them in the parking lot. She made her living by caring for dogs, cats, and an occasional pet rabbit. Since Petunia was technically a pet, she agreed to the visit. Petunia's immense size impressed her.

"When you called, you said she swallowed a coin. Are you concerned that she might be obstructed?" The vet was hoping she could offer an opinion without palpating the pendulous flanks of side pork. A glance into the trailer was enough evidence to demonstrate there was no obstruction. "What do you want me to do?"

"We want you to take an x-ray so we can see if the coin is still in her."

"That sounds simple enough, but my x-ray machine is for small dogs and cats. If you can lift her up on the table, I can take the picture." She laughed at the thought of anybody hoisting Petunia onto the small examination table.

"You can't just take an x-ray out here?"

"No, I'm afraid not. It doesn't work that way. The closest option for you is to drive to either Duluth, or Ironwood, Michigan. Both places have a large animal vet service. I can make a call for you if you want." Dr. Virginia was happy to refer her largest patient ever to someone else. "But why don't you just check in her pen to see if the coin passed already?" The simplest option is not always the most obvious. "With a pig this size, I doubt she is at risk of getting obstructed from a coin. She looks quite healthy." Petunia grunted her approval.

On returning to the lake, Petunia squealed with delight. The cousins waited expectantly. Maddie swung in the hammock, reading Harry Potter. Molly and Daisy were waiting at the picnic table with a bag of donuts and left-over bread crusts from their lunch. Zoe and Theo charged up from the lake with sand and water dripping from their hair. "Is she going to be OK?" Everyone wanted to know if they had to cut open Petunia to get the penny out.

With the prospect of more food, Petunia wasted no time getting out of the trailer. Once the gate was open she entered her pen and rejoiced at the food offerings from the girls. "Dad, did you get the penny out?" Maddie put down her book long enough to check out Petunia's return.

"Sorry, Maddie, we don't know. The vet said to check in the pen."

"You mean she probably already pooped it out?"

Olivia laughed. "So, you took her to the vet for nothing?"

"Well, that's the way it goes sometimes." Both Tom and Harry realized the folly of their trip to town. But they were already dirty; why not start digging in the pigpen now?

Modern hog factories have been sharply criticized about the small holding pens for pigs. But no one could say Petunia was restricted. Her pen stretched nearly seventy-five feet in two directions. In the center was a wide shallow depression holding the most wonderful mud a pig could love. If the coin was anywhere, it was there.

"Tom, how do you want to do this?" Harry looked for advice. He had no experience probing pigpens for lost coins. "Why don't we go back and rent the metal detector again? That would save us some time, don't you think?"

"Good idea."

Harry did the renting this time. He paid the deposit, avoided questions and eye contact, and hoped to get out of the store with some personal pride remaining.

Back at Petunia's estate, the entire clan gathered for the show. Kids with donuts and cookies, dads with rakes, shovels and metal detectors, and moms with cameras. Starting with the assumption that pigs spend most of their time in mud, they began there.

Over all, the process went much better than expected until Harry's boot got stuck in the mud and came off. Standing knee deep in mud with pig poop squishing between your toes wasn't on his bucket list, but it did make the family photo album.

"I think I found something." Harry held up the metal detector and put a stick in the mud to mark the spot. Unfortunately, Petunia also investigated and disrupted the entire process. Again, Harry waved the detector about and got a signal but rather than mark it, he simply dug in with both hands. It was an old rusty nail. Five times he got a signal and each time the results were disappointing. The sixth time it changed. Pawing through mud, water, pig slop and who knew what else, he found a round metal object. Swishing it back and forth in the pig's water bucket, a glint of silver appeared. Polished by the gastric juices of a porcine paunch, it looked better than the original. Victory at last!

Following hot showers and cold drinks, the mood of the group was light and optimistic. An abundance of sputtering sausages on the barbecue grill reminded them of the true destination of most pigs, a place Petunia would never know. Both Richard and Phineas joined the family for the weekend. The evening was shaping up to be a time of discovery.

"OK, how do you want to do this?" Richard carefully spread the coins in sequence from earliest to latest on the table. The coin with the most shine was the 1951 Franklin half dollar. Polished by Petunia's gastric expanse, it held the most interest from the kids.

"Tom, when we were at the courthouse, you said you had a thought about the coins. Do you want to share it with us?" Harry took a note pad and pen to jot down ideas.

Tom reached toward the line of coins and picked one up. "Remember the comments made by the appraiser?" Looking toward Harry, he continued. "According to his impression, the marks on these coins were not random. Someone made those marks, probably Roy, specifically for this purpose. If we write down the marks, or whatever the marks are trying to identify, then we should have the combination." Everyone hoped Tom was right, but nothing seemed straightforward since Roy and Lola had disappeared.

"All right, let's do it." Luella picked up the first coin and promptly realized she forgot her glasses. "You do it." She handed it over to her sister, Emma.

Tom held up the notes from the last time they did this. "I have it all written down from before, but we didn't have the 1951 coin. Is there a mark on that one?"

Emma put down the first coin and took up the shiny one. "It looks like a punch mark over the 9." She handed the coin off to Phineas for confirmation.

"That's what I see. It looks the same as the other marks." Setting it back on the table, he asked, "But what does it all mean?"

Harry had the marks recorded in sequence: 1948-N; 1949-N; 1950-M; 1951-9; 1952-1, 2; 1953-5; 1954-N; 1955-1; 1956-1; 1957-7, 5; 1958-5, 8; 1959-5; 1960-9, 1; 1961-1, 9, 6, 1; 1962-no numbers or letters but there is a dot in the middle of Franklin's head. "OK, who's the genius here?"

Vera looked over the list and asked, "What's the N on the list? You've N written by 1948, 1949 and 1954."

"Sorry, that means Null, nothing."

"What's the M?" Vera asked.

"There is a punched dot on the letter M in America."

"All right, here is another question. Some of the numbers have a punch above the number and some have below the number and some have right on the number. Do you think the location of the dot is significant?" Vera was doing her best to pay close attention to details.

Tom took the note pad and rewrote the sequence of numbers so it would be easier to see.

_, _, _, M, 9, 1-2, 5, _, 1, 1, 5-7, 5-8, 5, 1-9, 1-9-6-1, _.

"So, what can we deduce from this?" Tom looked around the table.

Olivia applied her deductive reasoning. One of her hobbies was solving logic puzzles and cryptograms in the Sunday paper. "I think the letter must refer to a name or word, but the numbers could be part of the combination. But there are too many numbers to fit the rings on the cryptex. Plus, there's a gap between the first sequence and the second sequence, which logically means they are separate."

"This is what I think," Emma said. "If we assume these numbers correspond to a ring on the cryptex then we need to have seven different numbers. So, what numbers are the combination?"

"I think the last coin with the dot in the head, means think. That's something Dad would do. Remember that Christmas when he gave us clues and one of the clues was false? Maybe some of these clues or numbers are meant to be false." Luella lapsed back into thought.

"Hey, anyone interested in a bottle of wine? Maybe that will help the gears turn better." Vera was already heading toward the cellar with Phineas and Richard in tow. They entered the hallowed chambers as the lights fluttered on. No matter what was happening in the rest of the world, in the wine cellar it seemed relaxed and quiet and worlds apart. They sorted through the racks and chose three bottles, aged to perfection.

"Hey, I like that sign your dad put up." Phineas pointed to a Bible verse carved into a slab of wood. 'And no one after drinking old wine wants the new, for they say, "The old is better." L 5:39. Then as the three of them looked at the sign, it was as if a ray of insight hit them. They headed up the stairway and into the group bound by confusion.

"I think we found a clue."

"In the wine cellar? How much did you drink down there?" Olivia looked up from her trance. She had the list of numbers before her and was trying to arrange them in a variety of ways but nothing was making sense.

"No. Look at this." Vera held up the sign from the cellar.

"I like the verse, but what does it have to do with this puzzle?" Luella wasn't seeing the connection. "Let's take a break and have a glass. Maybe then it will make sense."

"No." Phineas interrupted everyone. "Look at the reference. Now look at numbers from the coin sequence. M 9, 1-2, 5. Maybe it's a Bible reference. Your dad did that in the past, using biblical references for clues. That's not being disrespectful, is it?"

As the old wine was being poured, others offered their insight. "If it's a Bible reference, then there are four possible books: Malachi, Matthew, Mark and Micah. But the numbers don't add up." Richard tried to see the connection. He paused, thinking. "Maybe that's it. The numbers are supposed to add up, or subtract, or some other way of combining them."

Vera rejoined the others after pouring a glass of 1991 Caymus-Napa Valley Cabernet Sauvignon. Even the aroma was intoxicating. She sipped and swirled, wondering if the real treasure was already discovered in her glass. "I think the Bible verse is right. The old wine is better."

Olivia took Richard's idea and played with it. Assuming M meant one of the books that started with M, then 9 likely referred to a chapter. It would be simple enough with only four books starting with M to look up every chapter 9 under each book. It was a helpful way to pursue her ideas because there was no Malachi 9 and there was no Micah 9. Immediately she had narrowed her search. She read Matthew 9 but nothing seemed to fit with their search. She turned to Mark, chapter 9 and started reading. "I have it. I know this is it!"

"What do you have that's so important?" Luella didn't believe she really found something just reading.

"No really. Don't you remember when Dad had clues for us at Christmas time, and he arranged everything backwards. Well, I think this is the same verse only from a different book. Listen to this." She opened her Bible and read Mark chapter 9 verse 35. "'The first will be last and the last will be first.' Don't you guys remember?"

Tom caught on quickly and saw the connection. "M 9 1-2 5. Its Mark 9:35 if you add the one and two together. It could be a reach, but it's the best clue we have so far. Let's try to apply that to the rest of the numbers."

They took the remaining numbers and tried adding them, but no pattern was forthcoming until they started to look at the positions of the punch mark over the number. "On the 1 and 2 the dot is above the number, but when you get to the 1957 coin, the dot is above the 7 and below the 5. The next one the dot is above the 8 and below the 5. If you add the top and subtract the bottom you get '2' and '3'." Tom was beginning to see a pattern. "The next number is a 5 and the next one should be an 8."

"What about this last one, all of the numbers are punched." Emma did the math, 9+6-1-1=13. "But there is one more ring and no more clues. Any ideas?"

"I know what it is." Olivia looked around the room. "Tom, you're a math teacher, you should see it." She reached into the bird's eye maple box and took out the cryptex. Engraved on one end was a simple spiral and on the other end was a snail, beautifully embossed into the shining brass. The room was silent, waiting for the answer.

She reveled in her moment of discovery. She saw the answer and no one else saw it. Letting the anticipation build for just a moment, she poured herself another glass of wine. Ironically on the label was a printed spiral. The answers were everywhere.

"Way back around 1200 or so there was an Italian." She began.

"Quit already." Luella rolled her eyes. "You are starting to sound like Dad."

Olivia continued, "There was an Italian by the name of Leonardo Bigollo who discovered an amazing sequence of numbers that is reproduced throughout the natural world. It is seen in the ratios of the bones in your hand related to the number of fingers, in the petals of sunflowers, the sections of pinecones, the ratio of length to the position of eyes, fins, and the tail in dolphins. It is everywhere. It's called the Fibonacci sequence. It demonstrates that nature is not random, but there is an amazing intricacy and design. The numbers in the sequence is called the *golden ratio*."

"Of course!" Tom saw the answer. "It's obvious now that you point it out. The next number is 21. Each number is the sum of the two previous numbers. The dot on Ben Franklin's head is just as Luella said, we had to think."

Luella took the cryptex into her hands and turned the dials lining the Fibonacci sequence up with the snail. Nothing happened.

"Remember the reference. The first will be last and the last first. Do it in reverse."

Realigning the numbers in reverse order, she heard a distinct click and the ends of the cryptex separated.

Chapter 21

Stone Island

I didn't attend the funeral but I sent a nice letter saying that I approved of it. —Mark Twain

"Cobra-1, this is Cobra-2. Do you copy?"

Despite static in the ear piece, the sniper heard the transmission clearly. Perched on a rooftop, three hundred meters from the parking area, he readied his .338 Lapua magnum sniper rifle and 9X scope. He adjusted the bipod to accommodate his positioning. Obscured from detection by overhanging palm fronds, the sniper took several deep breaths and checked his pulse. Slow and steady, no tremor in his hands, he answered back. "Cobra-1 here. Is everything a go?"

"The package is in route and should be arriving shortly. Wait for my signal."

Cobra-2 was nearly four hundred meters to the sniper's left, located on another rooftop with a perfect view of the drop site. The escape boat was in position, and the tourists were gone. The trap was set.

Cobra-1 lay in a relaxed prone position, something he had done many times in the past. Afghanistan and Iraq mainly, but there were others that remained classified. His Swarovski binoculars gathered enough light in the early evening that he could see the wrinkles on a man's face at five hundred meters. But as the evening wore on he would switch to night vision capabilities if necessary. He was ready.

The Bimbo Bread truck pulled into the parking area near the Stone Island ferry. Moving slowly, it pulled to a stop. The driver got out and lit his cigarette. He looked straight ahead, walked to the ferry landing and disappeared. The package was delivered.

The din of the city behind him, faded into the background. A slight breeze blew on his cheek; a mosquito buzzed in his ear. Across the water on Stone Island he heard distant music and laughter, the sounds of happy tourists spending money. It always amazed him, how sound could travel so easily over water. But that wasn't his concern.

"The package is moving." The simple statement in his ear confirmed his own observations. The doors to the panel truck slid open, and two people stepped out. At the same time, bright headlights from a dark SUV illuminated the couple, sending long stark shadows across the parking area. A rat ran through the light, casting its own eerie shadow. Below him numerous feral cats began their evening prowl looking for rats, scraps, or conjugal visits.

Three men stepped from the van and walked forward. Unable to hear the conversations, Cobra-1 speculated on the exchange. He doubted they were chatting about the weather. There was movement and scuffling below. The man and women were both knocked to the pavement. As Cobra-1 adjusted his crosshairs awaiting the signal he felt movement and a tickle on his leg.

A voice crackled in his earpiece. "Get ready on my count of three."

A rat ran along the roofline and across his leg. Cobra-1 felt the whiskers and toenails of the rat investigating his bare ankle. "1...2..." The bare scaly tail of the rat rubbed against his leg. "...3".

The synchronized shots from the sniper rifles found their marks. The two lieutenants under the leadership of Javier Espinosa dropped without a sound. The drug lord stared toward the ocean, unmoved by the events behind his back.

As soon as he fired, Cobra-1 whirled around and grabbed the fat city rat behind the head and tossed it over the side of the building to the waiting pride of rabid cats below.

El Chico heard the gunshots but never flinched or turned. He gazed out to sea, looking past Stone Island toward the lights of a ship on the horizon. Another deep draw on his cigarette, his face lit up from the bright glow of the tobacco. Dropping the glowing embers to the pavement he snuffed it out with his shoe and turned toward the bodies.

Two shots had been fired and there in front of him were two bodies lying in their own blood. Expecting to see the bodies of Earl Ambrose and Sandy Piper, he found himself alone and unprotected. Life in Sinaloa was life in a war zone. He had witnessed many such executions and had survived attempts on his own life. But it was his own pride and arrogance that led to his capture.

The rest of the SWAT team descended upon him with precision and speed. Reaching for his gun was pointless. Any sudden moves and he would have been peppered with bullets.

"Don't move!" The leader of the capture team trained his assault rifle directly on the head of El Chico.

Standing motionless with his arms raised, he was caught from behind and forced to the pavement. With several guns trained on his vital parts, he lay still while a soldier quickly did a body search and took his Beretta 9mm pistol. They placed a gag across his mouth and zip-tied his hands behind him. Earl and Sandy remained silent and unmoved. Still kneeling in the dirt beside two dead bodies, they watched the apprehension of Javier Espinosa play out before them.

"Cobra-1, mission accomplished. Meet at the rendezvous point."

"Roger, Cobra-1 out." He disassembled the sniper assault rifle and climbed down the back stairs of the abandoned apartment building, descending to the street level. A quick check to avoid inquisitive eyes, he sprinted to the ferry landing and was on board without delay. Cobra-2 was already there along with three other members of the team, all wearing night vision goggles, flak jackets and non-reflective black clothing. Espinosa lay in the bottom of the boat, blindfolded, bound, and gagged. The bread truck driver started the engine, and they slipped quietly across the water to Stone Island, leaving Earl and Sandy behind.

The commando in the front gave a quick signal with his light and a similar response was received. All clear. He motioned to the boat operator. Despite a signal of being all clear, they remained hypervigilant for counter attack. As leader of a very well organized and well financed business, Espinosa had many connections and supporters. Money and power don't always make friends, but it can buy loyalty, for a time. They were prepared for all contingencies.

An ice cream truck backed up to the boat landing, and El Chico was half dragged and half lifted into the back along with the assault team. Once inside the truck on the floor, his feet were bound, and he was injected with a sedative to prevent fighting or any possible communications outside of the van.

The team remained quiet, monitoring the police and emergency radio frequencies for any information regarding the mission. They knew Espinosa had plenty of insiders within the police department, not only in Mazatlán, but also across the state of Sinaloa. Working with locals would have resulted in advanced warning and mission failure. It was a delicate operation on international soil but a necessary step to stop the waves of drugs and crime entering the United States across their southern border.

Forty-five minutes later the ice cream truck pulled up next to a Gulfstream G650 aircraft, waiting and ready on the tarmac. With diplomatic clearance, they were airborne as soon as the team was aboard. Javier Espinosa was on his way to a special federal detention center, maintained for international criminals who are a known risk to the citizens and government of the United States of America. Camp Delta, Guantanamo Bay, Cuba, was his new 'Casa Grande.'

Sandy and Earl were left wondering what happened. Events occurred so quickly they had little time to respond. They stood between the dead men, watching the ferry boat go quietly from the mainland area of Mazatlán over to Stone Island. It wasn't until several minutes had passed that they were aware of someone with them.

"Come with us." The two men in dark, casual clothes led them to a waiting vehicle on an adjacent street. Neither Earl nor Sandy could move well after the assault and injuries to their legs. Earl's limp was very pronounced and caused him visible pain. Sandy's knee was scraped and bleeding but no significant structural damage. She could walk without assistance.

"We are taking you to your house. Get just what you need, money, passports, but leave everything nonessential. It isn't safe here. You will be taken to another safe area until we can get a handle on the response of the drug cartel." The agents didn't leave time for questions and answers. When they arrived at their home, one of the men ran to the front door and shined a light inside looking for any possible evidence of unwanted guests. Seeing none he was back to the curb instructing Earl and Sandy. "Be back on the street in ten minutes."

Earl stumbled and fell as he tried to get out of the van. His chicken leg served him well. As he fell, the agent and Sandy bent to help him. A thunderous explosion gutted their house destroying everything. The force of the blast shattered the windows sending shards across the street. Flames and smoke poured out of the gaping hole in the front of their house. Earl's prize banana tree in the big clay pot by the door was gone. The explosion would have eliminated anyone inside. The agent had inadvertently triggered a delayed response detonator activated by a motion detector inside the window. Going home was no option. They had no home, no money, and no identification.

Chapter 22

Traveling Man

Some are born great, some achieve greatness, and some have greatness thrust upon them. —William Shakespeare

In the days and weeks following his release from the hospital, Roy was a different person. He had more energy and a better appetite, but he had changed. Normally a very social person, he became withdrawn and isolated himself, sometimes for hours at a time. Lola tried to offer solace, but he rebuffed her efforts. He fed his pig and went for long walks and spent hours in his boat alone.

Daily phone calls from the kids lapsed into weekly and then occasional. Efforts to crack the veneer around him were unsuccessful. In the evenings when Lola and Roy were alone, he would sit in his recliner and stare out the window. His companions were the fireflies, the stars, and the security lights from neighbors across the lake.

"Roy, what's wrong?" Lola pleaded with him to open up. She knew the answer, but if she could entice him to talk, it might help.

"Oh, nothing, just thinking."

"If you tell me, maybe I can help."

"You can't help, nobody can help."

"Are you depressed? The kids think you're depressed." Lola wanted him to know he wasn't alone.

"I'm not depressed," he snapped back at her. "I'm happy as a lark."

Three months after he got out of the hospital, the phone calls started. At first, they were brief, but someone called nearly every other day. Roy would take his cell phone out to the garage or go for a walk so Lola couldn't hear what was discussed. Lola checked his phone several times to get the number out of his phone log, but it was restricted. No phone number was ever recorded. Gradually the calls became less frequent, but lasted longer. Sometimes Roy would sit out on the lake in his boat for hours pretending to be fishing, but Lola knew he was talking to someone. If she tried to bring it up, Roy denied everything. He wouldn't talk about it.

Finally reaching a point of deep frustration at being shut out of his life, Lola confronted him. "Are you having an affair? Because if you are, you need to knock it off or I'm leaving!"

Surprised by her question, he laughed. He laughed so hard that he had tears. Her accusations brought a welcome break in the tension. "Lola, I am so sorry about what has been happening. I assure you, I am having no affair." He chuckled again softly. "I almost wish I was having an affair, it would be much easier to explain."

Then turning more serious, he took her hand and said, "I am going away for a few days. I am not leaving you. You must trust me in this. Someday I will explain everything, OK?"

"I don't know what you are doing, but won't you at least let me know so I don't worry so much?"

"I can't...not yet." He gave her a big hug, something long overdue.

Someone came and picked Roy up at the house. Lola stood motionless at the window and watched the car turn the corner out of sight. No explanation, no information, nothing.

He just left and came back as if he had gone to the hardware store. The next time it was five days and after that a week. Over the next several months the mysterious departures lessened, but he still offered no explanation.

Their relationship became strained. Lola sought refuge in volunteer work and church activities. She visited their children and stayed for several days, helping with the grandchildren. When she and Roy were together, they lived like strangers, chatting about the local news, the weather and about picking up bread and light bulbs at the grocery store. You could describe their marriage as friendly, cordial, and platonic but nothing more. No shared dreams or ideas. No intimacy. No reminiscing about good times. On one of his travels, Lola moved out of the bedroom and into her own room. There was no point in sharing a bed, nothing happened. The closest they came to physical contact was when one was snoring the other gave an effective jab with an elbow.

It was nearly nine months after he had been hospitalized when Roy began to relax, but he had one more trip to make. He didn't want to go, but he had no choice in the matter. It had already gone too far. As much as he wanted to confess everything, he couldn't.

"Lola, I am going away again, but this may be the last time. I don't know how long I will be gone, maybe two or three weeks or more. When I get back, I will tell you everything." He looked into her eyes and saw the hurt and fear. He was losing her and somehow the last forty-plus years didn't seem like enough glue to hold it all together. When the driver came and he walked out the door, she wondered if it was the last goodbye.

Roy kept at a distance because he didn't want her to feel the pain and anxiety he was feeling. His reasoning was simple. What you don't know won't hurt you. But Lola was hurting, and he prayed the hurt wasn't permanent. Everyone lives with some hurt, some disappointment, but left unchecked, the hurt becomes a cancer, spreading, and eating away everything good until there is nothing left. He could feel the cancer growing in himself as well.

#

"Roy Ambrose." The armed guard read his identification badge, comparing the photo to the face. "Date of birth?"

"9-20-1953"

The guard scanned the badge, and the computer database displayed a match and authorized clearance. "Go ahead." The guard stepped aside, and Roy entered the building alongside an impeccably dressed JAG officer.

It was the second week and Roy was restless. He would be taking the stand today, the star witness. For months, he had been secretly preparing for the trial of Javier "El Chico" Espinosa. It was no ordinary trial. It was being held at a military base and conducted as a military tribunal. It was not a trial by a jury of your peers, according to the standards of the US justice system. There were no peers.

Roy had flown by private jet to many different locations around the country, meeting with government officials. Lawyers, prosecutors, congressmen and women, military officials, CIA, FBI, DEA, and anyone else with a series of letters after their name. They were using him to lock away the criminal of the century, a scourge of mankind, because he was the sole eyewitness to the shooting of a federal agent. And he was the only one stupid enough to say so, under oath, in a court of law. Anyone fool enough to testify against Javier Espinosa was fool enough to dig his or her own grave. And there stood Roy with a shovel in his hand.

He knew about his cousin, Earl, but only because his legal representative told him. Earl Ambrose and Sandy Piper had been subpoenaed to testify about the attempt on their life and the destruction of their property. Roy was not allowed to see or correspond in any way with the other witnesses. The military tribunal wanted to avoid any evidence of collusion.

The first meetings were in Springfield, Virginia. Then later he was flown to Chicago; Fort Leavenworth, Kansas; Fort Hood, Texas; Washington DC and Guantanamo Bay, Cuba. Each time he was transported under armed guard in a private Lear jet registered to one government agency or another.

What he learned, surprised him. Private security had been watching him and Lola for nine months, providing a layer of invisible protection from unwanted intrusion. On several occasions, he dismissed Jehovah's Witnesses, pavement sealing companies and Boy Scout leaders, only now to realize they were part of the security team assigned to their protection. He wasn't sure if he felt safe or violated, knowing this. It was an odd sensation, knowing someone was always watching. He wasn't sure how Lola would accept it.

The courtroom was surprisingly stark. No Corinthian columns, no ornate bench for the judge, no scrolls or pictures of God or Moses holding the Ten Commandments. There were no visible symbols of the American justice system, just stern-faced people in military uniform trying to make a difference.

Roy glanced at the defendant's table. Javier Espinosa and his team of lawyers talked in hushed tones, ignoring the people responsible for his fate. Because of the Military Commissions Act of 2009, Espinosa had the right to challenge his detention and have his own team of lawyers represent him. But Roy had a fleeting sense of pity for them. As an attorney representing someone like Espinosa, you were hated because of your association. If you lost your case, you were a loser even though everyone hoped you would lose. But if you won the case, you were hated even more. Defense lawyers for people who have committed heinous crimes were a special breed—well paid, but in bed with the devil himself.

"All rise." The court bailiff announced the entrance of the judge into the courtroom.

"For the record..." The military judge began the court proceedings the same way he began every other day, 'for the record'. "When the court recessed yesterday, it was because the prosecutor wanted to call a special witness." Directing his attention to the prosecutor's table, he continued. "Is your witness available to take the stand now?"

"Yes, your Honor."

"Please proceed."

"The prosecution calls Roy Ambrose."

A trickle of sweat ran down the middle of Roy's back. He felt a cool clamminess in the palms of his shaking hands, and his knees were weak as he stood before the military judge. He swallowed hard as his stomach convulsed and tried to turn inside out.

"Mr. Roy Ambrose, raise your right hand. Do you swear to tell the truth, the whole truth and nothing but the truth?" He nodded affirmatively. "Mr. Ambrose, a nod is not an acceptable response, you need to answer the question directly. Do you understand?"

"Yes, your Honor. I swear."

The sweat on his back continued to run; his armpits felt swampy. His hands trembled as he took the stand and looked at the tribune of military officers staring back. He avoided eye contact with the defense lawyers and the defendant. But he couldn't avoid the fact: Espinosa was staring at him.

The prosecutor began with the usual identification questions, simple and straightforward. But once that was established, they quickly turned to the events that occurred in the streets of El Quilete. "Mr. Ambrose, will you identify the people in this photograph?" the prosecutor held out an enlarged photo taken by Lola in the main cobblestone street of El Quilete.

"The people in the photo, from left to right are Earl Ambrose, Elizabeth Elkins, Sandy Piper and myself."

"There is a date and time stamp from the camera on the photo, can you confirm that date to be accurate?"

"Yes. That is correct."

"Who took this photo?"

"My wife, Lola Ambrose."

"Is she here, in the courtroom?" The prosecutor continued confidently. A confidence, Roy didn't share.

"No, sir."

"Were you aware of anyone else in the photo when it was taken?"

"No, sir."

"Your Honor, I present this photo as evidence." He handed to the judge the enlarged photo, which was the subject of questioning identified as 'exhibit 122.' Taking another further enlarged version of the same photo, he held it out for Roy to view. "Is this the same photo you just looked at?"

"Yes."

"And do you see anyone else in the photo that was not visible to you previously?"

"Yes, sir."

"And can you identify that person?"

"No."

The questioning went on and on about seemingly minute details surrounding the location of people, the location of the hacienda, the angle of the sun and a hundred other things they had reviewed in the preparation for the trial.

"Now, following this photo what did you do?"

"We entered the restaurant, La Casa de Mujeres and ordered food."

The lawyer asked him to describe the restaurant, the people, and the entire setting to the best of his ability. "Mr. Ambrose, after ordering your food, what did you do next?"

"I went to the restroom."

"There are several restrooms in that restaurant, can you describe the one you were in?"

Roy described the urinal trough carved into the back of a giant pig statue, the window over the urinal offering a view down the cobblestone street and a clear view of the hacienda.

"And will you describe for the court what you saw out that window."

"A black Chevrolet suburban drove up and stopped in front of the hacienda. Three men got out. They had guns. Then two men from the hacienda brought out packages. The men from the car took the packages and put them into the back of the vehicle." He paused, feeling weak and nauseous. He wiped sweat from his eyebrows before it ran into his eyes.

"And then what happened?"

"One of the men from the vehicle ordered the two people from the store to turn around. He shot them in the back." Roy was shaking. He reached out to grab the rail in front of him so he wouldn't fall out of the chair.

"Can you identify that person?"

"Yes, I can."

"Is that person in this courtroom now?"

"Yes, sir. He is sitting right there." Pointing out Javier Espinosa was the hardest thing Roy had ever done in his life. Cold and emotionless, the drug lord fixed his black eyes on the witness, and his lips turned up slightly as if he were smiling. The killer's reputation brought waves of fear and anxiety over Roy. Whatever protection the court offered, left him feeling utterly vulnerable. No court of law could hold this man back. The long reach of evil slipped well beyond bars and barbed wire. Roy had just signed his own death warrant. He was a dead man.

Chapter 23

Unzipped

When I was a kid, my parents moved a lot, but I always found
them. —Rodney Dangerfield

Cracking the code of the cryptex opened more doors of uncertainty
and closed none. Dubbed "the snail" by Madeline, it was a source
of mystery and excitement. With a fertile imagination stoked by
the fires of Harry Potter, and Nancy Drew mysteries, Maddie envisioned vast treasures, hidden gems, dark dungeons, and distant
castles. When the contents of the snail spilled out, she was sorely
disappointed.

Two zip drives each enveloped in a sealed package fell out of
the snail and onto the tabletop. No coins, no jewels, and no treasure maps. No coded messages, nothing dangerous or intriguing, to
Maddie's way of thinking.

Vera picked up one of the cases holding a zip drive and pried
open the seal. "I have my lap top; let's plug it in."

Vera pushed the zip drive into the USB port and double clicked on the icon. The drive opened and several folders were displayed. Mostly PFD files, they contained pertinent information about the estate. One file was a video file, Vera opened the file with Windows Video Player and the screen flickered to life.

Suddenly there were Lola and Roy Ambrose in living color. It was a bit more than nine months since they had gone missing although at times it seemed like an eternity. The date on the file showed it had been recorded less than two years ago, slightly more than a year before they disappeared. It showed each of them sitting at the very same kitchen table with a steaming cup of tea, talking to the camera as if coming back from the dead was an everyday occurrence.

Vera and Emma began to cry, Luella held her breath, and Olivia gasped just a bit. Molly yelled, "Papa and Grammy," and everyone became fixated on the computer screen. It was surreal.

"Hi, family. I realize this is odd for all of you because you wouldn't be listening to this unless we are gone. Most importantly we want each of you to know, we love you all." Roy smiled and sipped his green tea. "We want you to believe that wholeheartedly."

"Hi, kids. This is Mom." Everyone laughed, as if they might not guess who was talking. "We miss you, too." It must have been awkward talking as if they were already dead.

Roy continued, "As you well know, we put some puzzles in your path, but there is a clear reason for it. The money is held in trust in a bank in Zurich, Switzerland. The account number is listed in one of the other files on this zip drive. We both commend you on deciding to forego option number one in the safe deposit box. It may have been difficult to give up the money for something unknown. But we know you likely did your homework and didn't decide based only on chance.

"According to instructions left with the will, the entire package is to be sent to the executors, Liakos, Economu, and Christopoulos, located in Athens, Greece. There is also a blank PDF form on this drive to be completed for each beneficiary, including the grandchildren. Take a digital photo of each person and import it into the form before printing. Every person listed as beneficiary needs to have a notarized signature and fingerprints on the form. If a child can't write or print their name, then they must scribble or draw a picture, and parents will cosign. If this sounds burdensome, we are sorry, but that is the way the law firm wanted it done."

"After they receive your forms, a hundred thousand dollars will be placed into separate accounts under your names. As you give that away, you will be rewarded the same amount. You don't get the money until it is given away. However, each of the grandchildren will receive thirty thousand dollars to place in a trust account until they are eighteen years old or older. The executor will work with you to make sure this happens."

Lola pushed her cup of tea to the side and looked directly into the camera. "We have given you information on several different children we sponsored over the years. Luella and Olivia, I think you may remember them. You wrote letters to them when you

were young. Vera and Emma, you may have been too young to remember, but that doesn't matter. We want each family to search
them out and visit them. We don't know if they are still living in
their original areas, whether they have married or even if they are
still alive. We want you to help them. If you cannot find them, use
your judgment and help someone else in a similar situation. Practice wisdom in the process."

Roy added his input. "Once the executor receives the certifica-
tion pages, each family has one year to give away a hundred thousand dollars. If you are not successful in giving the money away
within that time, the remainder of the estate will be distributed according to instructions already left with the executor. Here are the
rules. It must be given to individuals or small organizations. Also,
it must be given personally, not mailed, transmitted, or traded for
anything. You should not give it to any large charitable organization. You can't give it to your cousin, your mail carrier, or your
boss. You cannot give it in a manner that would profit you materi-
ally in any way. Our purpose is for you to invest your lives for the
benefit of those less fortunate. Remember what Jesus said, 'Give
and it will be given to you, good measure pressed down, shaken together and running over. For the measure you give, will be the
measure you get back.' We want you to succeed beyond your wild-
est dreams. When you have successfully given all four hundred
thousand dollars away, the remaining assets in our estate will be
distributed in full.

"It would have been far easier for us to simply donate this
money to a charity—any charity—but you would have missed the

wonderful joy of giving. I don't know if any of you remember what I used to say, but it bears repeating." Roy cleared his throat briefly. "Don't give until it hurts, give until it feels good."

"Goodbye for now. We love all of you so very much." And with that the recorded message ended.

A stunned silence hung over the kitchen. It was so wonderful to hear their parents again, but no one understood what was really expected of them.

"What do they want us to do?" Luella remarked. "It's like they expect us to give up our own lives and responsibilities to carry out their last will and testament. It's crazy, I can't tell the hospital to give me a week off every month to go to Honduras and feed some starving kids."

Vera was already working through options in her mind. "Remember the old cliché: if there's a will there's a way. Hopefully we can figure it out."

Olivia felt some of the same frustration as Luella. "This is not a will; this is a ball and chain."

Vera replied, "That wasn't quite what I meant."

"I know what you meant, but this is becoming a burden."

Richard glanced over the other files contained on the zip drive. The names didn't mean much to him but the locations did catch his eye. These were the people previously sponsored by the Ambrose family. Isabella Matamoras, a twelve-year-old girl living in an orphanage in Costa Rica; her parents died from Dengue Fever. Talia Safulu was a fifteen-year-old girl rescued from sex trafficking in Fiji. Giuseppe Benedetti was a seven-year old boy abandoned in the Cinque Terre region of Italy. The son of migrant workers from southern Italy, he grew up in a foster home. Chuenchai Bunyasarn, a refugee from Myanmar, had lived with a pig farmer and his wife in Chiang Mai, northern Thailand. No birth certificate existed, but she was estimated to be nine years old at the time they sponsored her. Marguerite MacDonald from St. Vincent, Grenadines. Age eight, she was the daughter of a single mother arrested in drug trafficking. The mom died in prison. Marguerite was left to an orphanage. The ages listed were at the time of sponsorship, which was seventeen to twenty-five years in the past. Finding these people now was not going to be an easy task.

"Before any of you get bent out of shape about expectations from your parents, you should look over the list. Costa Rica; Chiang Mai, Thailand; Cinque Terre, Italy; Vanua Levu, Fiji; the Grenadines. I wouldn't complain about going to any one of these places." With Richard's comments, the attitude of the group did lighten a bit. Suddenly they were thinking of possibilities and ideas on how to make it work.

For now, it was time to take ID photos and get fingerprinted. They had work to do.

Emma took her phone out of her handbag. "I've got my camera here. Why don't we take photos now? We can import them into the computer and get started."

"Mom and Dad have a laser printer in their office room. After we do the photos, we can print the forms. There is an inkpad here as well. We can do the fingerprints now as well. Then tomorrow we can all go into the bank and have Shirley notarize our signatures.

We can get this done." Olivia opened a new pad of paper. She loaded the printer and put a fresh color ink cartridge in place. "Good to go."

Emma set the camera on a tripod and hung a blanket for a backdrop. Suddenly the home took on a new sense of urgency. There was talk of packing, travel, vacation requests, who was going where and how were they going to do it all in a year. The kids thought the fingerprinting was the most interesting. Some of the ink made it from fingertips to face rather quickly, but no one cared.

It was good to see Mom and Dad again, even if it was just a recorded message. The air was filled with movement and chatter until suddenly Emma stopped what she was doing and held her stomach.

"Emma, is something wrong? Are you sick?" Luella, always the nurse even off duty, walked to her side. "Are you OK?"

"I just felt something strange. The baby has been moving quite a bit recently, but now my stomach feels crampy and hard." Emma pressed her hand against her lower abdomen and held it there.

"Hard and crampy isn't right." Luella pushed against the top of the fundus. "When did this start?"

"Earlier today, but I thought it was just from not getting enough sleep."

"I think you should go to the hospital and get checked for pre-term labor. You are only about thirty weeks along, aren't you?" Luella indicated to Phineas this was not something to ignore. "Phineas, you need to take her now."

"We are headed back home tomorrow. Can't it wait until then?" He wasn't in the mood to give up his easy chair and glass of wine just yet.

"You need to go now. It may be nothing, but don't take a chance. No matter what else is going on, babies take priority." She thought back to the events of the evening. "Even Mom and Dad's master plan will have to wait for this one."

"That's not the only thing. I might be losing my job. We find out this week about job cuts." Olivia had a ring of resignation in her voice.

"What company are you working for?"

"Igotchu Pharmaceutical Company. There has been talk of cut backs for months. We find out Friday." Olivia thought for a moment and lowered her voice to a whisper. "This whole thing with Mom and Dad has put quite a bit of stress on our marriage. Harry said if we don't get this whole thing settled soon, he doesn't know what he's going to do. I was thinking of quitting my job anyway."

"Boy...don't I know. The hospital is freaking out with all my time off. I don't have a single available vacation day for the next year." Luella stopped talking and blew her nose. "Vera, how are you guys holding up?"

"I wasn't going to tell anyone, but since you asked, I might have to sell the store. The mail order pharmacy companies eat into my business. The only medication I sell now is for headaches, coughs, and colds. I am losing money every day." Vera looked at her sisters. "Don't we sound pathetic. Mom and Dad left us hundreds of thousands of dollars, and we can't touch it until we give it away. The way they fixed it, we can't help ourselves until we help someone else."

Emma spoke up. "Dying isn't easy, especially for the people left behind." She caught her breath for a moment. "Ouch...that one hurts."

Chapter 24

Renewal

Things are always better in the morning. —Harper Lee

Following the trial, Roy's depression was worse. He had fleeting thoughts of suicide if only to protect his family. Yet he held hope that the conviction of Javier Espinosa would be enough to prevent any revenge. He discussed this with the DEA. However, his concern was not for himself but for Lola and his children. In his opinion, once the government got what it wanted, they would be less interested in his welfare. Nevertheless, life went on, and he had some repairing to do.

"Lola, we need to talk." His arrival at home was met with some skepticism. Months of poor communication created a divide. Lola was hurt. Not so much from the troubles Roy had been experiencing as hurt because of his reticence to involve her in the process.

"I have been wanting to talk with you for months." Lola was guarded but hopeful. "If you want to tell me the truth, I am ready.

If you want to avoid the truth and play games, like you have been, then turn around and go back where you came from."

"Lola, what do you think has been happening to me over these past months?" He hoped she already knew so it would save him some time.

"I think you are depressed, but I don't really know the whole story." So many of their conversations had started this way, but no meaningful substance prevailed.

"Where should I start?"

"Why don't you start at the beginning."

"OK, from the beginning." He took a deep breath and began. "Do you remember when we went to the restaurant in El Quilete with Earl and Sandy? I witnessed something, and it has been the cause of all my troubles." They sat on their screened porch listening to the afternoon sounds blend into the night sounds. He talked and she listened. When she talked, he listened. It was as if more than forty years of laughter and tears, dreams and promises were condensed into a few precious hours. The moon rose and set before they dried their tears and drifted off to bed. The earliest morning sounds were awakening, and the glow in the east promised a new day ahead. Roy was home.

Over the next year he made amends for his bad behavior. Although he probably wasn't entirely to blame, his failure to communicate compounded the stress and anxiety for both of them. He apologized to each of his children for his behavior, but he never told them the true reason for his depression and subsequent collapse. Although he was completely transparent with Lola, he made her promise never to reveal it to the children because he never wanted them to live in fear. His reasoning, whether faulty or not, was simple: what you don't know won't hurt you.

They traveled to New Zealand, Alaska, and points in between. They spent a month in Patagonia, Chile, South America during January. They did some shopping, and he restocked his wine cellar with good stuff. And on some days, he bought Petunia fresh jelly-filled donuts right from the bakery. He was happy again. However, he realized time was now the limiting factor in his life rather than money or resources. He made a bucket list and began checking items off. They made a will, transferred the house and property into a trust for the kids and talked about the future, whatever that may bring.

"Lola, guess what I just did?"

"What now?"

"I booked us on a transatlantic cruise." He looked at her, hoping for a flicker of acceptance before continuing. "Remember how we used to talk about it?"

"I think you were the one talking; I just listened." Lola had grown accustomed to his newfound impulsiveness. She was happy for his new lease on life, but she wasn't entirely comfortable where it was leading. "When do we leave?"

"We leave in a month. It is a spring transatlantic sailing cruise from Barbados to Portugal. It stops along the way at Tenerife, in the Canary Islands off the coast of Morocco." He flashed brochures and photos of the cruise, chatting excitedly about their upcoming adventure. "It's the Blue Hair Cruise Line. We went with them before."

Two weeks before they were to leave, they arranged for Petunia's care, held the mail delivery, and printed out an itinerary for their daughters. The girls were getting used to parents who suddenly skipped town and went on excursions. It didn't always give them a feeling of confidence, but the fact that Roy had a remarkable recovery from his bout with severe depression was encouraging.

It had been an easy winter in Wisconsin. The snow melted early, and warm southern breezes brought gentle spring rains instead of snow. Everyone seemed upbeat. Plans for their vacation were progressing nicely. Days were spent doing early spring tasks—put away the snow shovel, get out the yard rake, put out lawn fertilizer and pick up the sticks kind of days. They were relaxing, and the routine was a blessing after a tumultuous year. Lola prayed it would continue.

"Roy, come and look at this." She was watching the evening news. "You need to see this."

"What's happening?"

They both stood unmoving, fixated on the television, listening as the CNN news reporter began with their headline story. "Government officials expressed frustration and anger as a federal appeals court released Mexican drug lord, Javier Espinosa. An international human rights organization based out of San Francisco, California, filed an appeal on behalf of Javier Espinosa, claiming he was illegally detained, unlawfully transported out of his home country of Mexico and denied due process of law. And today federal appeals court Judge George Perez agreed. The United States government is required to provide personal protection for Mr. Espinosa and transport him back to his home country.

"Espinosa, known as El Chico, is the infamous drug lord of Sinaloa, Mexico. It has been speculated, he is directly responsible for hundreds of deaths across Mexico and into the southern US. In his absence his brother, Emilio Espinosa, has been rumored to be running the drug cartel, but lately there have been others rising in power including a rival drug lord, Pancho Hernandez, also known as El Perrito. El Chico's return to Sinaloa could increase tensions there as well as between Mexico and the United States.

"We asked the lead DEA officer his opinion, and he offer no comment. The governors of Arizona, New Mexico, Texas and California expressed strong opinions about Espinosa's release as their states bear the brunt of the illegal drug trade across the international border."

The screen diverted from the news anchor to photos of a war scene, the war on drugs. It pictured illegal aliens being escorted out of tunnels under the Arizona-Mexico border carrying packages of heroin, cocaine, narcotics, and other illegal street drugs. Photos of dead bodies, bound and executed, lying in streets did little to calm their nerves.

"Roy, what does this mean?"

"It means, we are going on a cruise, and we aren't going to talk about it." He wanted to believe no harm would come to him or his family, but anxieties have ways of taking root and growing. This would be a test of faith. "Let's go on this trip as planned, and when we get back we can sit down and figure it all out."

As Lola switched off the television, she noticed a slight tremor in her hand. As much as she wanted to trust Roy, God, and the United States Government, she was worried.

Chapter 25

For the Birds

Pay no attention to the man behind the curtain. —
L. Frank Baum

The emergency OB visit for Emma didn't quite go as planned. She was less than thirty weeks along and was starting to have contractions. Not a good thing. With a full three months remaining until she was considered full term, the obstetrician put her on strict bed rest. No travel, no work, no roller coaster rides, no lifting, and no sex until further notice. And no income.

Emma's life was measured in minutes. Relegated to the couch or bed, she spent her time counting and recording every twitch and tightening of her growing uterus. Minutes became hours and hours blended into days. Each day was an eternity of drinking water, counting contractions, going to the bathroom, and watching endless, mindless television. Sometimes the baby kicked, and she thought it was a contraction; sometimes she had a contraction and thought it was the baby moving. She tried reading but couldn't concentrate. She tried sleeping but discovered napping interfered with her ability to sleep at night. She tried eating and discovered she was good at it. She ate too much and gained weight. Without exercise, an ounce of chocolate added pounds to her hips and stomach. Then she was depressed. She and Phineas were happy expectant parents, but this wasn't what they expected. In every parenting class or book, women just walked into the hospital and popped out a baby and were back home before receiving the first round of guilt-inducing advice from grandparents. She missed her mother. She wouldn't be getting Mom's advice and at times like this she really needed it.

She had exhausted her entire maternity leave with preterm labor restrictions. Her employer was not willing or able to keep the position open indefinitely. They were pleasant about it all, but in the end, Emma knew she wasn't going back. Now she was stuck in bed paying high insurance premiums with no income. She didn't hold out much hope for Phineas filling in the gaps.

After seven years of working on his dissertation, he was no closer to finishing than when he started. Much of his research was rejected as lacking sufficient rigorous standards. His work experience was limited to washing dishes and flipping burgers. He could give music lessons with a variety of instruments, but living on this put them below the poverty line. Well below it.

But he could make a good meal, and that was a blessing for Emma. Or a curse. His favorite saying was, "God loves a good sandwich," and Emma agreed. Grilled chicken breast with bacon, avocado and melted asiago cheese on a toasted bagel worked magic. Two bites and she chased the preterm labor blues out the window. But after two sandwiches, the blues came rushing back, feeling the weight of guilt from over-eating. She couldn't win.

"Phin, what are we going to do?" Emma longed for a normal day. Each day was the same conversation, the same conclusion, and the same sense of dread. Every day she asked the same question, hoping for a different answer.

"I think we need to use some of the money from your parents rather than give it away. Your parents would understand." He had a point.

"I was thinking the same thing, but the people controlling the money probably won't understand. We don't even know who they are." She rehashed the rules in her head, frustrated by the limitations. If you don't give, you don't get. But if you don't get, you don't eat, you don't pay the electric bills or the baby bills. It was a conundrum they couldn't get past.

"Well, I have an idea." He leaned forward. Emma noticed an unusual uplifting tone to his voice.

"You have an idea?" She sat back with a perplexed look across her face. "You're going to get a job?"

"Better than that, I dropped out of graduate school, and I am starting a business selling bird houses." He sat back feeling very satisfied at finally sharing his grand idea. In his typical idealistic 'save the whales, stamp out poverty, world peace' ambitions, he was now going to confront their own looming trip into the abyss by selling birdhouses. Emma could tell by the contented look in his eyes, he was serious. Her sliver of hope withered.

"Are you crazy?!" She stopped to hold her gravid abdomen and breathe through a particularly troubling contraction. "Husbands shouldn't start businesses when their wives are seven months pregnant on bed rest. Phin, it's time to grow up and be a big boy now. Birdhouses? Are you kidding me?"

The big boy comment cut deep. He felt her disappointment but he understood. Phineas was a good husband and was going to be a good father, but what she needed right now was stability. She wanted a guy who carried a lunch bucket and punched a time clock. What she got was Peter Pan and the Pied Piper rolled into one.

"I'm sorry about what I said. I'm not trying to be mean." She blotted the tears running down her cheeks. She was so emotional. She loved and hated being pregnant. Every day was a bipolar crisis on hormones. "Look... why don't you make me a chocolate shake and another sandwich, then we can talk. OK?" With a faint glimmer of hope, her prince, the sandwich maestro, dashed off to the kitchen to save the day.

There is nothing like a load of chocolate ice cream to quiet the nerves of a pregnant woman. Phineas watched the ebb and flow of her emotions, and when the time seemed right, the birdhouse business plans were presented.

"Emma, I know this sounds crazy, but I have it all planned out." 'Planned out', meant different things to a man than to a pregnant woman. But the chocolate shake was holding so he plowed ahead. "You remember when the university rejected my research?"

How could she forget? Phineas spent two weeks listening to the blues with the curtains pulled. No visitors, no daylight, no hope. "Yes, I remember."

"Well, I submitted my results to the Audubon society. It was published in their quarterly journal last month."

"So...what does this have to do with feeding our baby?"

"Hear me out. My research was on the effects of harmonic music on the reproductive habits of blue birds." He paused to dab a speck of drool in the corner of his mouth. This was exciting. "Don't you remember what we did?"

"No, I had a job."

"We attached wind flutes and wind chimes to the bird houses so when the wind blew it would make a harmonic sound. They played major triads, minor triads, no music, and discordant triads."

"I have no idea what you just said."

"Think of it this way. We had wind flutes that made a good sound, a bad sound, or no sound. What we discovered was very interesting. In the houses with good music, they laid more eggs, and there was a better survival rate. The control group was the ones with no sound. And in the bad music houses they laid fewer eggs and had lower survival. The university rejected my research because there wasn't enough data to make it statistically significant."

"So, what does this have to do with birdhouses and making money?" Emma was trying to see the practical side.

"Don't you see it? The natural world can be influenced by music. The Freckled Finch Foundation wants one thousand houses with music pipes for their foundation members. The Audubon society wants five thousand. Now I have a business and no products. We need money to get started, but this could be our big chance."

"Until this starts to make some money, what are you planning to do?"

"I know this sounds weird, but I was talking to Harry."

"Olivia's husband, Harry?" Emma was curious about the direction he was going.

"Yep, Olivia's Harry. If we move over to Wisconsin, he would hire me part-time. Also, get this, he is interested to see if it works on cows." Phineas ran to the closet and pulled out a baseball cap. Embroidered on the front was "Happy Heifer Breeding Service." As he pulled it tight over his rather long hair, he asked, "What do you think?"

It brought Emma to a laugh. Not just a chuckle, it was a good deep belly shaker, something she truly needed. She envisioned her delicate handed, musical husband standing behind one of Harry's Happy Heifers, attempting to induce motherhood. It wasn't a pretty picture. He was afraid to stick his hand into the wide end of a tuba. She thought to herself, "You can't make this stuff up."

"I can't move now. I'm on strict bed rest. No lifting, no moving, nothing but eating and sleeping." She paused to catch her breath.

She felt huge now. It was hard to picture herself two months into the future.

"Yes, I know, but our apartment lease runs out in two months anyway. According to your doctor, if you go into labor after another month, it won't be a problem. You should be far enough along. When I called Harry, he said if I agreed to work for at least a year, his company would pay for part of our moving expenses." Phineas was on a roll. "Look here. These are homes for rent around your sister's place. Rent is cheaper there." He turned his laptop so she could see the rental listings for an area in northwestern Wisconsin.

"You have it all figured out, don't you?" Emma resigned herself to the move idea, but she wasn't too keen on going to a different doctor. She couldn't imagine Phineas going from a PhD candidate in music to a cattle breeder and birdhouse tycoon. There were just too many changes all at once. This was going to take some time to adjust. Another chocolate shake might help.

Chapter 26

Just Doing My Job

I knew who I was this morning, but I've changed a few times since then. —Lewis Carroll

"Luella Tinker, can I talk with you in my office?" Nurse shift supervisor, Betty Bludgen didn't sound cheerful, but then most night nurses aren't known for pleasantries. She was a tough-as-nails old school nurse who derived pleasure from broken bones and tap water enemas. She was the kind of nurse old small-town doctors loved to have around. Betty had a warm grandmotherly touch with children in distress, but if you came to the ER in the middle of the night with anything less than cardiac arrest or an amputation, she would likely accuse you of malingering and send you home. She had the same effect on coworkers, especially those under her supervision.

"Lu, what's the problem? Tom cheatin' on ya?" Betty wasn't one for a friendly chat over tea.

"I'm sorry, what did you say?"

"Luella, you are a good nurse, one of our best, but for the past month you have been acting like a ditzy co-ed on a first date. What's your problem?" She took a long swallow of cold coffee from a chipped Viagra mug on her desk. Luella couldn't tell if the rust colored stain on nurse Betty's fingers was from tobacco, dried blood, or betadine from swabbing a surgical patient. It was nearly 9 PM, six hours into the evening shift. Luella was working a double shift trying to make up for missed time.

"Betty, I am very sorry if I have been distracted. With my parents dying, and the kids, and now Tom is back in school, I guess it has been overwhelming." She glanced at her watch, realizing she had neglected to let Tom know she was working a double shift. He was usually home between 4 and 5 from school so it wouldn't be a problem with the kids. "Have there been complaints about my care?"

"A couple people whined a bit, but I set them straight." Betty slurped another shot of coffee. "Look Lu, I know what it's like to lose parents. I was 13 when my dad died in a farm accident. My mother went crazy and drank herself to death. After my older brother left for the war, I had to raise my six younger brothers and sisters. I know this sounds hard, but get over it." Betty laid it out straight. "I don't care if your kids are in hockey, volleyball, soccer and have a hundred school projects due tomorrow. But I do care if it affects your work."

"Are you going to write this up in my personnel file?"

"I don't believe in that crap. Files are for mamby-pamby administrators who don't have the guts to do their job. Just do your work without complaining and you'll be OK. If you don't, you'll be gone. Simple enough." Betty Bludgen RN, night supervisor, had a way with words and people. You always knew where she stood even if you didn't like it.

Luella bit her tongue trying to hold back her tears. It had been hard. Despite wonderful kids and a loving husband, she felt lost and overwhelmed at times. Her sisters seemed to always have it all together; she was the one with doubts and worries. Losing her parents was more difficult than she imagined. Almost like losing your past and your memories. Going home would never be the same. Perhaps she was shouldering more of the pain and sorrow because she was the oldest. She felt an obligation to be strong for the others. Even with the passing of time it still hurt.

"Here." Betty slid a box of tissues across her desk toward Luella. "Make sure you watch the gallbladder in 113. She's fat, diabetic and whiny. If that surgeon doesn't get here soon, I'm going to yank it out myself." Betty got up from her desk, signaling the end of the meeting. It was back to work.

Luella dabbed her eyes and cleared her throat. It was a good time to take a minute and check in with Tom and the kids. Grabbing her purse, she pulled out her phone and headed toward the staff bathroom just down the hall. Seeing a missed call and voice mail, she punched in her access code to listen.

"Hey Lu, I'm going to be working late at the school. Parent teacher conferences, I forgot to tell you earlier. Sorry. I expect to be home around 10. Love you." The message on Luella's phone was simple and to the point. The problem wasn't Tom; he was always good to let her now when he was going to be late. She was the one feeling the hyper-schedule overload.

She felt a rush of anxiety. Hitting the speed dial for Tom, she was frantic to talk to him.

"Hello this is Tom, leave a message." Luella started talking before the signal ended.

"Tom, why didn't you tell me you had meetings. I am working a second shift. Where are the kids? Did you get them?" She hung up the phone and redialed. Same response. She knew he had his phone on silent during the meetings to avoid interruption.

"Tom, answer the dumb phone." She yelled, hoping he would somehow know she needed to speak to him. "Oh, this is hopeless." She searched online for Luigi's Pizzeria, hoping she could find the whereabouts of her children. It was Wednesday and the church had a youth night pizza party at Luigi's. It was over two hours ago, and she was hoping someone from the church had taken her kids home. It was 9 PM, and she didn't know where they were.

"Luigi's." The hurried voice of the waiter left little doubt they were behind in their work and patrons were waiting.

"Hi. This is Luella Tinker. I had three kids there tonight with the church party. Do you know, by chance, if they are still there?"

"Oh, you're the parents of the lost kids?"

"Yes, are they there? Can I talk to one of them?"

"Look lady. The kids didn't know your cell phone number, and we tried calling the church number, but no one answered. After two hours of waiting, the manager called social services. We can't have kids running around here unsupervised."

"What do you mean, social services?"

"You know... social services. We had abandoned unsupervised kids here. If you want to know where they are, call the county courthouse and ask for child protective services." The phone clicked as the waiter hung up.

A fierce desire to find and hold her children overcame Luella. She had to leave and find them; there was no other option. Rushing down the hall, she met nurse Betty. Breathless with fear from losing her kids, she blurted out her story. "I have to leave right now. I don't know where my kids are."

Betty was unsympathetic. "Luella, I don't care if you're teaching Sunday school to the Pope's kids. You can't leave now. We are already short staffed."

"I have to go." Any mother would put herself in the path of death to save her children. Going directly against the nursing supervisor was no different.

"If you leave now, you are done. Understand?"

Without answering, Luella ran toward the employee break room to gather her things. As she headed toward the exit an overhead voice blasted in her head. "CODE BLUE ROOM 113, CODE BLUE ROOM 113." It wasn't a good day for the gallbladder lady either.

She tried Tom's phone again, still no answer. The only thing she could think to do was call 911. Missing kids, lost her job, can't get her husband to answer the phone, and as she dialed 911, it started to rain.

"Emergency dispatch." The perkiness of the voice on the other end of the phone didn't lift her spirits.

"I am Luella Tinker. My children are missing, and I was told, child protective services picked them up." She did her best to remain calm and rational.

"Ma'am, I will give you the after-hours phone number for the on-call social services officer. You can check with them."

"Thank you." She listened to the phone number and tried to memorize it. She didn't have anything in the car to write on. Immediately after ending the phone conversation she dialed the number. Of course, no one answered. She dialed and redialed. Finally, on the third try someone answered. The voice sounded as if it were a great inconvenience to be bothered at this hour of the night.

"Hi, this is Luella Tinker. I was told to call this number about my children."

"Ah, Mrs. Tinker. We have been trying to reach you for the past two hours."

"Yes, I am very sorry about that. It was a miscommunication between my husband and myself."

"I am sure you meant no harm, but now you have a problem."

"What type of problem?" Luella felt her anxiety level rising quickly.

"Well, let me put it this way. When children are abandoned..."

"My children were not abandoned." She felt agitated and defensive.

"Ma'am, I am only doing my job." The lady on the line smacked her gum and resumed her statement. "When children are left unattended for hours at an eating and drinking establishment, and we can't reach any parents or competent adults to get these children, then we are called. The children have been safely placed with an emergency foster home."

"Are you kidding me?"

"Your kids will be spending the night in the foster system until we can determine if you are competent to care for them." She paused just enough to let it sink in.

"I want my kids now!" Luella was yelling into the phone. "I have called social services a hundred times for neglected kids and never...ever have you responded as if you care. And now you are taking MY kids away?!" She burst into tears trying to understand it all.

"Where are they? I demand to know!" She was frantic at the thought of losing her kids. She began to shake.

"I can't tell you. It's our policy to protect the children from kidnapping."

"What? Now you think I'm going to kidnap my own kids?" She threw her phone down on the floor of the car. The back popped off and the battery bounced somewhere under the seat. She sobbed uncontrollably to the point where she could barely see the road as she drove to the school to find Tom.

Luella ran into the school with frantic determination to find her husband. Red swollen eyes and mascara-streaked cheeks caught the few remaining parents and school faculty off guard. Tom was aghast.

"What happened to you?" He grabbed his hat and jacket and flipped the classroom light switch off. He wasn't prepared for the angry sobbing outburst that followed. He felt a minor streak of relief to know someone took care of their children, but he wasn't comfortable about the process. "Why don't I call the number and talk to the social worker. Maybe we can get it all straight."

He dialed the number and the same gum-smacking, 'I've heard it all before' social worker answered. "Social Services."

"This is Tom Tinker. My wife called earlier about our children."

"Good evening, Mr. Tinker. What can I do for you?"

"I'm sure you know the reason I am calling. I would like to pick up our children tonight if you would be kind enough to let me know where they are." He was trying his very best to be calm and collected. "I can explain everything. This was simply a case of miscommunication."

"I am sure it was, but ..."

"But what?"

"We have a process we strictly adhere to, when dealing with neglect issues."

Tom raised his voice. "Are you suggesting I'm an unfit parent?"

"Mr. Tinker, I don't make determinations about your parenting ability. That's up to the judge and the psychiatrist."

"Now you think I'm mentally unstable? You're nothing, but a witch who goes around stealing children. What is your name? I

226

will do my best to make sure you never work in this county again. Do you understand?" Tom's anger was rising.

"Mr. Tinker, you need to stop right there. One more angry word, and I will have you arrested for interfering with a government official and endangerment of children. Do you understand?"

"Interfering with a government official? You haven't seen anything yet, but if I get my hands on you, there is no telling what I might do! You took our children without cause, and I'm going to get them back." Then it was his turn to throw his phone.

Neither Luella nor Tom were in a stable enough condition to drive alone, so they left one car at the school and rode together. Anger, frustration, and fear raced through their thoughts. "I don't understand what is happening. I just can't believe it." He drove toward home with a singular focus of getting his children back. Then in the rear-view mirror he saw the flashing lights.

Tom still couldn't believe it. He pulled to the side and opened his window. The county police officer walked cautiously to the side of the car. "Are you in a hurry tonight?"

"Yes, sir, I guess I am. I'm sorry if I was speeding." Tom had a defeated sound to his voice.

"I didn't see you speeding. You went through the stop sign at the intersection. Let me check your license and registration." Tom handed both through the window and leaned back in the seat, hoping he would soon wake up from the nightmare. The usual delay in checking Tom's license turned into something much longer. The flashing lights behind them were starting to give him a headache. Luella was no better off. She cried and yelled and cried some more.

The police officer opened his car door and walked slowly toward the Tinker's car. "Mr. Tinker, I need to ask you to come with me."

"For going through a stop sign? I'm perfectly willing to pay the fine."

"No, I'm afraid it's more complicated. While I was checking your license, a call went out for your arrest for threatening a government official and interfering with child protective services. Do you know anything about this?"

"Are you serious?"

"Yes, I am. If you don't come with me willingly then I will have to cuff you. You don't want that, do you? You could also be charged with resisting arrest. I'm sorry but I'm just doing my job."

Chapter 27

The Check is in the Mail

A banker is a fellow who loans you his umbrella when the sun
is shining but wants it back the minute it begins to rain.
—Mark Twain

In less than twenty-four hours Luella's entire life crumbled around
her. She lost the job she loved, her kids were taken away by a zeal-
ous social services worker, and her husband was carted off to
spend the night in jail. What was promising and exciting now lay
in ruins. She sat in her living room all alone, no kids, no husband,
and no clear way out of the mess.

The police officer was reasonable enough to allow them some
time to discuss a brief plan for the next couple of days. It was midnight now, but by morning she needed to contact the school to get
a substitute for Tom, call a lawyer, go to the county social services
office, and submit to a humiliating interrogation before the judge.
She would need to consider alternative employment options.

Walking out of the hospital during your shift when a patient was in serious need wouldn't be easy to explain. She knew she was wrong and she could have handled it much better. But a mother desperate for the safety and whereabouts of her children doesn't always think and act rationally. She grabbed a blanket and curled up on the couch, not even bothering to undress.

At midmorning Tom met with the district attorney who declined to file formal charges. He was released with the promise he would not verbally threaten social services again. The matter with the children took a bit more wrangling. Because child protection services were involved, Tom and Luella had to go before the judge. Thankfully the judge had children of her own and understood the story. In fact, she laughed out loud with the retelling of the lost child saga because a similar situation had happened in her own life.

"Mr. and Mrs. Tinker, I find your story interesting and sad. From my perspective you are good, dedicated parents. We need many more parents like you. I'm sorry you were caught in the system. You both work in professions where, first hand, you see the sad results of child neglect and abuse. I will direct our social services department to remove any record of your introduction to the foster system. While I applaud motivated child care workers, sometimes that zeal is misdirected." She whacked the gavel on the bench. "Case Dismissed."

Their children, Maddie, Zoe, and Theo were waiting in a side office. Happy to be reunited, everyone had stories and tears and laughs. Theo yelled out, "I thought we were being kidnapped. It was a good thing I had my Swiss army knife 'cuz I was going to cut my seatbelt and jump out the car window."

"You what?" Tom was hoping he didn't need another visit with the zealot.

"I had my Swiss army knife you gave me for my eighth birthday, remember? I told that lady if she tried to hurt us I was going to use my knife." Theo seemed proud of his bravery.

"Then what happened?"

"She took my knife away, but she gave it back to me this morning and told me never to hurt anyone with it."

"Now Theo, that was good advice, don't you agree?" Luella rubbed her temples trying to prevent a headache. She was relieved the story ended there.

It was twenty-three miles from the county courthouse to their home. Tom came to a complete stop at every intersection and looked twice in every direction before continuing. Homecoming brought a renewed sense of family, something they had taken for granted. A family is priceless, but it could be fractured and torn in mere minutes. With Luella out of a job, they expected more family time. Turning into their driveway, Tom stopped at their mailbox and retrieved the mail from the past two days. Quickly sorting, he divided the stack into absolute junk, maybe junk and stuff I better open. In the stack to keep was a larger package from Zurich, Switzerland. "I hope this holds some good news for a change." He handed the package to Luella and drove up to the house.

The cover letter was from the executor's office in Athens. It explained how the identification information had been received and was complete, no further information was necessary. Within the large package were multiple envelopes individually addressed. It included trust account information for each of the grandchildren in the amount of thirty thousand dollars each. Each daughter had two separate accounts in the amount of a hundred thousand dollars. Each account had personalized checks with instructions. One account was designated as a charity account. As money was drawn out of this account, the funds in the other account would be released, however, it stated, twenty-thousand dollars was immediately available for any personal needs. Everything was sent to Luella as the designated representative for the family estate.

"Please correct me if I'm wrong, but based on the video and other written stuff, we can use the charity funds to pay for expenses related to the charity, am I right?" Tom looked toward Luella for clarification.

"That's the way I understood it. But if any of us cheats, then we are all guilty of cheating and nothing further gets released. But none of us really knows how much money is in the entire estate. Besides, the executor reviews it all anyway." Luella separated out the envelopes by family and picked up her phone. It was time to make some calls.

"Hey, Olivia, this is Lu." Happy to hear a voice not connected with social services, Luella began to relax. "You are never going to believe what happened to us."

"Try me. I'm gullible." Olivia listened as the story unfolded. She couldn't help but laugh. To her way of thinking, Luella was always trying to be the super-mom, involved in every church or school program, and her kids were scheduled in some sports or enrichment program from the day school was out until the end of summer vacation. This past summer had been different, trying to figure out everything after their parent's deaths, but as soon as school started, Tom and Luella were, once again, up to their necks in commitments.

"Hopefully no harm done. The important thing is that we all learn something from it and hope it never happens again." Olivia changed the subject. "Have you heard anything yet from the lawyers or whatever they are over in Athens?"

"Yes, actually that was the reason I called. We got a large package today. There are checks and information about trust accounts for the grandchildren." She looked through the stack as she continued talking. "I need to get this to you as soon as possible. I guess if we are going to give this away, the clock is ticking."

"I know. It is a different feeling to be under a time pressure to give away money. I'm not sure how to handle it yet." Olivia closed her eyes and shook her head back and forth. "Harry and I have been looking through the people mention by Mom and Dad. Have you and Tom had a chance to sort through any of it?"

"Are you kidding? Our lives have been total chaos. Maybe now without a job I can settle my brain down and get refocused." Luella pressed the phone between her shoulder and ear as she thumbed through the calendar on the refrigerator.

"Are you going to be up to the lake anytime soon? We could get together up there and divide up the checks and paperwork or whatever needs to be done. Maybe Vera can make it up there too. I don't know about Emma. She is still on bed rest."

"I heard Phineas was going to work with Harry. Is that true? I can't picture Phineas standing behind a cow." Luella laughed.

"Harry is actually looking forward to it. He thinks Phineas is on to something with his research. Harry has been reading everything he can find about the effects of music on animal and human behavior. Now when Molly is acting up, Harry starts playing some weird native flute music sound tracks. It might work on the cows and birds, but it's driving me crazy."

"Let's meet at the lake and we can share some ideas. Just a minute, I'm getting a message on my phone." Luella paused to check her messages. After the fiasco of missed messages and lost kids, she wasn't keen on missing any more important messages. "Oh no! Emma's water broke. She's in labor."

"What do you mean, in labor?" Olivia asked.

"Well...I guess, the usual meaning of labor, why?"

"Harry took his big truck over to help them move. According to Emma, she was thirty-seven weeks along. The ultrasound was OK, but the doctor didn't recommend the move. However, if there were no other options, and she went into labor, the baby should be fine. They planned to leave South Dakota about 10:30 this morning."

"Where are they now? I heard on the weather channel about some storms and high wind somewhere west of here"

"I don't know."

Chapter 28

Number 451

Death, taxes and childbirth! There's never any convenient time for any of them. —Margaret Theo

Luella dialed and redialed but no answer. She first tried Emma's phone, then Phineas and finally Harry. Frustrated and worried, she called Olivia back.

"Hey, Olivia, have you heard from Harry? I tried everyone's phone, and no one is answering."

"No, I tried Harry, too. No answer. So, I called Vera and let her know. They said they would be praying and wanted us to update whenever we heard anything." Olivia sounded worried.

"Keep trying and let me know if you hear anything at all." Luella ended the call and updated Tom. People didn't usually worry about babies and labor unless it was your sister or yourself. But as a nurse, every problem that could go wrong jumped to the forefront of her mind. She experienced flashbacks of every labor and delivery that went bad under her watch at the hospital. It didn't calm her nerves.

#.

The drive east along Interstate 90 out of Sioux Falls, South Dakota, was uneventful. Emma and Phineas were surprised to find their small apartment held less than they imagined. Packed into a small one-bedroom space, it seemed to fill every crack and corner. But packed and loaded into Harry's cattle trailer there was room to spare. The enclosed space was a godsend because rain was expected, and in that area of the country the wind always accompanied the rain. Their belongings were safely packed into the trailer. Harry started out first with Phineas and Emma following in their tiny Toyota hybrid.

"Before we go, let's have a plan, OK?" Harry was the practical one. "My phone is nearly dead, and I forgot the cable to recharge it. You two follow, but if you need to stop at any time, flash your lights or your emergency flashers, and I will pull over."

Emma was confident but nervous. "I'm feeling fine, but us pregnant women need to stop more often. If you see a rest area, why don't you just pull over." First-time moms might appear as if they had it all under control until the contractions start, then you never knew what to expect. They had hoped to be on the road by midmorning, but Harry and Phineas were the only ones to pack and carry items down from their third-floor apartment. It was later than they planned, much later.

They hadn't traveled forty-five minutes out of Sioux Falls when Harry noticed the headlights flashing behind him. Pulling over at the nearest exit, Emma made a beeline for the restroom. Once she felt better, they resumed the pilgrimage east, stopping at every official rest stop and some truck stops in between.

Before they pulled out from the Albert Lea, Minnesota, rest area and continued their way east, Harry brought up his concern about the weather. "The radio is reporting some rather heavy rain and wind heading this way. I hope to cross over into Wisconsin before anything hits. Once we get into Wisconsin we will be turning north on state Highway 35 along the river. There are more turns there so try to keep close so I can see your headlights, OK?"

"No problem." Phineas was naïve and confident. He didn't have a clue. Emma was calm but anxious, and Harry was the nervous one. He didn't want to be caught out here with a pregnant woman, especially one related to his wife. Olivia had fast labors. Molly came so fast they barely made it to the hospital, and she delivered in the emergency room. Harry wasn't sure he could depend on Phineas if anything started.

Late fall storms in the upper Midwest could be tricky. Some brought thunder and hail, others could bring sleet. It all depended on which side of the weather front you were on. Once they started driving north, they could find themselves on both sides.

Driving north along the Great River Road they were soon past sunset and into darkness, compounded by storm clouds. Rain started heavy and got worse. Easing into Pepin, Harry's gas gauge hovered dangerously near empty. His one-ton truck pulling a cattle trailer used more fuel in a few hours than the little hybrid behind him used in two weeks. A stop would be a welcome respite from the wind and rain, and he could check on his travelling companions. He pulled off the highway into the parking lot of a Super America convenience store and gas station and walked back to Phineas and Emma.

"How are you doing?" Harry directed his concern toward Emma.

"Not too bad. That lightning and thunder about a mile back, caused me to jump. I can feel some contractions again. But not anything different than the past month." She got out of the small cramped car, happy to stretch for a minute or two. She never missed a chance to use the bathroom.

Harry and Phineas talked while Emma went inside. "Just a short way up the road we will be turning onto County Road CC. It's the shortest way to our place, but it's cross-country. It will likely take forty-five minutes or an hour to get to our place from here." Harry rambled on, wishing Olivia was along to calm his nerves. He didn't care for storms, and he was on edge about not having phone contact with his fellow travelers.

"No problem. We're doing fine." Phineas seemed unusually nonchalant with twenty miles per hour wind gusts, driving rain and lightning strikes close enough to make your hair stand up.

Once everyone was settled back into the vehicles they pulled out from the station and onto the highway. Phineas followed Harry through the small town of Pepin and turned right onto the rustic County Road CC heading north. They hadn't made it more than a half mile when Emma turned to Phineas and told him the news that set him on edge. "I had some bloody mucus when I went to the bathroom. I think this might be more serious."

"What should we do?" Phineas blotted a film of sweat on his brow.

"I think we just need to keep going. When we get to Olivia and Harry's place, I'll talk to her, maybe she can take me into the hospital." Then she gasped and felt an unexpected wetness. "Phin, we have a problem."

"What do you mean, a problem?"

"My water just broke!"

Phineas reached for the headlight switch and began flashing from bright to dim as quickly as he could. Harry couldn't see the lights changing. With rain and wind, and uneven roads the headlights appeared to flicker constantly. Harry kept driving. Phineas felt desperate even though there was little to do at this point. He tried pulling into the oncoming lane to flash his lights, and he honked the horn, but Harry was oblivious to both horn and lights. The winding road left no room to pass. Harry had his radio turned to the local stations trying to get any severe weather reports, but all he got was country music or static. Finally, a short stretch of straight road and Phineas pulled into the oncoming lane and raced beside Harry's truck, honking, and flashing his lights. This time Harry got the message.

Sensing urgency, he pulled onto the shoulder of the road and zipped his rain jacket before stepping out. The rain doused his face and ran down his neck. It was a cold. "What's wrong?" he yelled into the barely open window of the little car.

"Emma said her water broke, and she's in labor." Phineas tried his best to remain calm, but inside he felt helpless.

"The contractions are coming fast. They're getting stronger all the time." Emma sounded worried, and Harry felt stuck, and Phineas didn't have a clue. The winding road was too narrow to turn his truck and trailer around. They couldn't all ride in the hybrid, and it was too far to Plum City. The town didn't have a hospital, but they did have ambulance service.

"What should we do?" Phineas was hoping for answers. "Emma sent a text to Luella about her water breaking and hoped she would call, but I think the lightning knocked out the local towers. She doesn't have any phone service now. We don't even know if the text message was sent."

"There is a small wayside up the road about a mile or two. We can pull in there." Harry headed back toward his truck as he yelled over his shoulder into the storm. "Follow me."

Harry drove as fast as he dared on the wet winding country road. A big farm truck with a cattle trailer didn't allow for fancy maneuvering. With each twist and turn, he peered through the driving rain hoping for a sign to the roadside rest area. His wet hands gripped the steering wheel tighter with each bend in the road searching for the turn off. There it was.

As quickly as possible he turned into the small gravel parking area with Phineas and Emma close behind. Just as Harry was about to open his door to check on Emma a sudden severe gust of wind hit, and lightning struck the big oak near the gate. The huge ancient oak splintered and toppled onto the driveway. They were trapped. No phone service, no way to drive around the tree and no break in the weather.

Phineas jumped out of the car and ran to Harry. "Emma said the baby's coming!"

"Can we get her into the cabin?" The little log cabin wayside building was always open and a popular stop with tourists. Phineas was hoping for anything better than the front seat of his car.

"There is no power and all they have in there is a picnic table. Get her into the cattle trailer." Harry wrestled the rusty handle and the door creaked open. The wind and rain blew in. With the truck still running, they had dim lights in the trailer but barely enough room to move.

While Phineas helped Emma out of the tiny car and into the storm, Harry frantically moved boxes around until the couch was uncovered. He found a box labeled 'bedroom' and tore it open. At least he found some blankets. Throwing a blanket over the couch cushions, they eased Emma onto it. She groaned in pain. "I feel like I have to push!"

"It's not supposed to be this fast!" Phineas was paralyzed. All the books and movies on giving birth didn't include thunderstorms without power in a cattle trailer somewhere lost in Wisconsin.

"Phin, you stay with her. I'm going out to the road and see if there is anyone coming by. We need to get an ambulance. Find a box of towels or something; you need to keep her warm." Harry opened the back door and lurched out into the storm, hoping, and praying someone was crazy enough to be out driving on a night like this. Far down the road he saw a flashing light.

"Harry, the baby is coming!" Phineas yelled into the night. "What should I do?"

Harry didn't know what to do either. He had pulled calves, and he was there when Molly was born, but that went just as fast. Running toward the trailer, he heard it. A baby crying. No help from anyone but God, the little girl lay in a puddle of fluid on the blanket, screaming at the top of her lungs.

"Dry her off and wrap her in a blanket." Harry quickly closed the door behind him. He searched for something to tie off the umbilical cord. All he had was a zip tie, ear tag for calves. He clipped the plastic ear tag on the cord, she was now marked as #451. "Emma. Hold her close to you so she doesn't get cold. I'm going back to the road to watch for cars."

Back along the road he could see headlights and a searchlight inching toward them. It was the power company trying to find downed power lines. As they neared the wayside, he waved frantically for their attention.

The power crew could see the tree across the driveway. One member of the crew opened his door to check if everyone was OK. Before he could ask, Harry was alongside him. "Radio for an ambulance. We have a newborn in the trailer. Just born."

"A calf?"

"No, a baby! Born ten minutes ago. We don't have phone service."

The power company crew launched into action. Chainsaws chewed the broken oak into moveable pieces, and what couldn't be moved by hand was pulled out of the way with a winch on the big truck. By the time the roadway was cleared, a flashing emergency light could be seen traveling in the night. Help was on the way.

The men held tarps to shelter the back of the trailer. EMT's carefully moved Emma from the mess on the couch to the back of the ambulance. Finally, when Emma and the baby were in a dry and safe place, Harry broke down. Drained from the stress and emotion, he wept at the miracle of life, playing out before him.

Harry left the little car all alone in the parking lot of the Laura Ingalls Wilder memorial wayside and drove off into the night, heading home. Phineas, Emma and #451 were warm and dry and on the way to the hospital.

Chapter 29

Conundrum

To be, or not to be, that is the question. —William Shakespeare

El Chico's sudden and unexpected release from prison created a political maelstrom. The United States wanted him locked up or dead, Mexico didn't want him back, and Roy wanted to forget the entire thing ever happened. The president and senators alike rode the social media wave, adding official and unofficial comments, bolstering public opinion polls. The president's Twitter feed, flip-flopped from #liberaljudges to #rule-of-law. Ultraconservative and ultraliberal groups alike criticized the abuse of power in the hands of the government. Moderates called for calm and common sense, which was in short supply. The public called for action against crime and chaos. Dag Rasmussen adjusted his eye patch, clenched his teeth, and longed for a shot of twenty-year-old, single malt scotch.

A Shakespearean tragedy played out between Fox News and CNN. The most-wanted man in the Western Hemisphere was captured and convicted and then ordered to be set free on technicalities. The DEA and the US task force on drugs and crime appeared incompetent and humiliated in the media. The government with the most at stake was court ordered to provide transportation and protection during his repatriation back to Mexico. But the Mexican government didn't want him back and neither did El Perrito, the rising leader of a rival drug cartel.

Even Javier Espinosa had mixed feelings. In his absence things had changed. His brother was not the iron-fisted ruler Javier had been. There were defections within the ranks. Police bought with drug money no longer had an allegiance to El Chico. From the top down, Mexican authorities purged the military and police force. Nearly one fourth of the police in the state of Sinaloa were eliminated and convicted for accepting bribes or conspiracy to commit crimes. Purging the police force left a gaping power vacuum.

Espinosa couldn't stay in the US, although ironically, he was safer there. If he returned to Mexico, authorities would arrest him as soon as he was back on national soil. If he returned to his home area without being detained, he ran the risk of a challenge to his leadership. Despite the challenges he faced, Espinosa had some scores to settle, and he knew where to start.

Teams of lawyers, representing every possible interest group, engaged in legal combat on both sides of the border. Espinosa's release promoted a deluge of briefs, motions, lawsuits, and countersuits. One senator suggested some type of black-ops intervention.

However, when questioned on national television, he reversed his opinion. Such organizations don't officially exist. The United States doesn't condone such activity, which is illegal under international law.

#

Martin Garza did what he always did in the morning: he kissed his little girl good morning and had a shot of aged tequila. Anything else was a bonus. Since the international news about El Chico's pending release hit the streets, he had been busy passing messages. He felt like a post office. Garza found messages, coded, and sealed in the mornings, and by afternoon people acting as tourists or vendors picked them up. Never completely sure of the source or the destination, he cautiously kept to himself. But just like in Washington, DC, when pizza deliveries are up, something was happening.

Someone from the El Presidente Hotel was always watching his location, and he speculated others were as well. A week after the press conference covering the release of Javier Espinosa, Garza had the note. He pulled the red, tattered Peligro flag from the beach flagpole and clipped it to the back of his palapa. The coconut delivery truck was quick in responding. A large burlap bag was dropped at his door, and the vendor went inside.

"What's the news?"

"Tomorrow night," Garza said. That was all he had. The driver left without comment.

Espinosa and his team of lawyers managed a complicated repatriation process. The United States government refused to fly him back to Mexico City or anywhere else within the country of Mexico. It was a matter of national pride to the US. They would bring him to the border, but they weren't going to follow him into the snake pit. At the border he would be escorted under military surveillance and handed over to a Mexican military escort team. He agreed to fly by helicopter accompanied by a high-ranking Mexican government official to Mexico City. An escort helicopter with an armed guard and surveillance capabilities would document the return flight from the border. From there, the Mexican government planned to take him into custody until they could arrange for a trial.

Under intense public scrutiny and international media coverage, the process began. Espinosa was released from federal custody and flown to Phoenix, Arizona. From there he was taken under armed guard with air and land military escort to the border. The location where the transfer was to occur was never made public, but it didn't take a rocket scientist to figure it out. Nogales, Arizona, had more television broadcast crews on site than Hollywood.

Media companies loved every minute of the process. People around the world were glued to their computers, smart phones, and televisions. Airtime sold at a premium. Once the transfer of Javier Espinosa from US to Mexican authorities was complete and the helicopters lifted off, news programming shifted over to live commentary, opinions, and frequent replaying of the helicopter departure. CNN focused on the mishandling of the entire process under DEA oversight. FOX News harped on liberal judges and their lack of interest in public safety. Other news sources played and replayed film footage along with on-the-street interviews to gauge public opinion.

Just over an hour into repatriation coverage the programming was interrupted. "It has been reported by Mexican news authorities that the helicopter carrying Javier Espinosa and a high-ranking government official exploded in flames about three hundred miles south of the US-Mexican border. Just prior to the explosion two people were seen to parachute from the helicopter. It is not known who those individuals were, but one is suspected to be Espinosa. Five people boarded the helicopter in Nogales, three are presumed dead. The escort helicopter reported several military style vehicles in the area. It left the immediate area when it came under fire from antiaircraft missiles. US intelligence sources following the flight confirmed the explosion but had no further comments."

Dag Rasmussen turned off the computer screen covering the live satellite feed. He pulled the cork on his twenty-year-old, single malt scotch and poured just a taste.

Chapter 30

The New Normal

Wilbur never forgot Charlotte. —E. B. White

Mary Beatrice Melquist weighed six pounds and nine ounces. Emma named her Mary after the famed, Little-House-on-the-Prairie Mary and Beatrice after the grandmother of Phineas. She and Phineas had quite a debate about names. Her family had a strange tradition of naming children. Emma and her sisters were given names so the first letters of their first names spelled LOVE. She wasn't too fond of the idea of having enough children just to spell something.

Phineas' family usually chose names after an event or someone with notoriety. The family surname was Melquist, of Swedish origin, but the first names were odd or out of the ordinary. When Phineas was born, the doctor dropped him on his head. It wasn't a big drop but everyone heard him thunk, like a ripe cantaloupe. Despite the clunk on the head, he acted as any normal infant.

However, the injury prompted his father, Magnus, to name the child Phineas after the famed Phineas Gage who survived a bizarre head injury.

Olivia and Harry welcomed the Melquists into their home until they could adjust to a new way of life. Emma's days and nights were broken into short segments of eat, sleep, feed the baby, change a diaper, and repeat. She was very happy to have her older sister, Olivia, around to help and give advice. She missed the chance to learn hands-on childcare from her mother. It was something she dearly desired, but it was not to be. Olivia was kind and full of grace, gently advising when asked.

Thanksgiving and the avalanche of Christmas shopping advertising hit everyone quickly. Their first holiday season without parents brought memories and tears. The entire family elected to return to the lake. Petunia would be lonely, cared for by Buddy Martin, but little other company. The lake home also required some seasonal attention to make sure it was ready for winter. It would be a good time to reminisce and try to figure out the next step for giving. Time had a habit of slipping away. They were faced with a monumental task of giving away four hundred thousand dollars with less than ten months to complete the task.

Tuesday afternoon prior to Thanksgiving, Harry and Olivia loaded up their minivan along with Emma, Phineas and the baby and headed for the north woods. Molly was delighted to sit next to her new cousin, little 'Beat-rice' during the two-hour drive. The weather forecast called for snow, and it didn't disappoint. Large flakes fluttered down, the first of the season.

Turning from state highway to county road and finally the small township roads, they came to the home of Papa and Grammy. The afternoon light faded early and in the dim twilight they turned into the driveway. The headlights flashed quickly across the balsam trees already starting to bend from the accumulating snow. Two eyes glowed from the pigpen. They didn't look familiar.

"Hey, Dad, can I go feed Petunia?" Molly had her outing planned. She saved old bakery goods for a week and was ready to stuff the pig.

"Hold on a minute, Molly. Let's make sure everything is OK first."

"OK, Dad." As she spoke, a large black bear appeared from the pigpen and ran on the fringes of the yard before disappearing into the gathering night. "Dad, what was that?"

"Honey, I think that was a big bear. I don't want you going to Petunia's house tonight. Do you understand?" Harry had a sick feeling about what they might find. He looked over at Olivia hoping for wisdom. He added, "Molly, you go into the house with Mom and Uncle Phineas and Auntie Emma."

Harry made sure Molly was in the house before he checked on the pig. He found Roy's deer rifle, a 30-06, and some ammunition. A large bear poking around in the dark wasn't his idea of a Thanksgiving vacation, and he didn't want to be the one the menu. Most bears should be heading off for their winter sleep, but apparently this one wanted one more meal. Swinging his flashlight from side to side, he scanned the yard and the wood line adjacent to the

251

pigpen. The falling snow added to the stillness and quiet. He could hear his own breathing and feel the pulse in his head.

The yard was clear so he walked cautiously toward the fence. The top edge of the fence was bent and broken down. The bear had had little difficulty making his way into the pen. Petunia didn't fare so well. Although she weighed more than the bear, she had no defense other than running. At six-hundred pounds, running didn't come easy. The tracks and blood in the snow told the story. She had been cornered in the pen, and the bear attacked. Her entire side had been ripped open from the bear's claws. Steam rose into the night, and the falling snow melted on her massive flank. Harry was glad she had already breathed her last. He didn't have the heart to pull the trigger. In America, the lifespan of a pig was measured in weeks or months. For nearly three years Petunia had lived a life of porcine bliss, all the mud and donuts she could handle. But in the end, it wasn't a slaughterhouse but a wild black bear.

The oddity of it all struck him as he stood in the gathering snow and darkness, waxing philosophical about the life and death of a pig named Petunia. Did a pig destined for the table have more or less value than a pig destined to warm the heart, especially the heart of a five-year- old girl? Friendships and dreams take many forms, and to Molly, this gigantic pig was the biggest friend she would ever have. Petunia was dead, long live Petunia.

Molly waited anxiously inside the kitchen. Around the crackling wood stove, the coolness of the house gradually retreated. Harry put the rifle aside in the entryway and knelt on the cold kitchen floor in front of Molly. A big tear ran down her cheek and dripped in front of Harry. She knew but she didn't want to ask.

"Is Petunia OK?" Another tear followed the first. She sniffed.

Harry's voice cracked as he spoke. He flashed back to his childhood when a car hit his dog Benny. He saw it all and cried for days. "Molly... Petunia got hurt by the bear."

"Well...she's gonna get better, isn't she?"

"No honey, she isn't going to get better." He looked up at Olivia and Emma standing behind little Molly. They had the same streaks on their faces. "Petunia died."

"Oh, Daddy." She rushed forward and sobbed into her father's arms. "Petunia's in heaven with Papa and Grammy. What are we going to do?"

The next couple of days had a sullen mood. Olivia took Molly on a long drive up to Ashland to avoid the rendering truck. Petunia wasn't a pig, she was a pet, but don't tell that to the truck driver. The grunting and swearing of the driver as he winched the stiff bloody carcass into the back of the truck was anything but compassionate. Harry was thankful the fresh snow covered the mayhem from innocent eyes.

The arrival of the cousins helped Molly revert to being a cheerful child. They laughed and played in the fresh snow and made snow forts and snow people. The only moment of concern came at breakfast. Sausage, bacon, and Swedish pancakes were a morning staple at the lake. Olivia felt a twinge of angst as she turned the bacon in the pan, and Emma, still flush with postpartum hormones began to cry as she looked at the sausages, greasy and brown on the platter.

It was Theo who nearly ruined the day. "Hey, is this Petunia, we're eating?"

Daisy, Zoe, and Molly all cried; Maddie told him to shut up. Luella whacked the back of his knuckles with a mixing spoon and gave him the evil eye. Firm reassurance from Mom saved the day. "We are not eating Petunia." By the time a second platter of steaming Swedish pancakes with maple syrup were ready, the bacon was all eaten. Life went on.

Thanksgiving was a good time to reflect. It was fun to relax again with family. The past six months had brought sweeping changes to their lives. Every one of the girls had lost or changed jobs. Emma and Phineas had a baby, lost a job, and moved to another state. They were thankful for some of the money available to support their living needs, but it wouldn't last. They had to make some definite moves to meet the requests of the will. They had less than ten months to complete the charitable giving. None of them offered a clear way to start.

One evening around the fire, after the kids had been sent to bed, Luella started it off. "Since no one has made any clear decisions as far as I know, Tom and I decided to pursue one of the people listed in the will." She looked around. Everyone was listening. "We started to search for this girl, Marguerite MacDonald out of St. Vincent."

"Where is St. Vincent?" Vera was trying to recall the list.

"It's in the Caribbean, one of the southern islands." She took a sip of her wine, a nice five-year-old Napa cabernet, and continued. "Anyway, I wrote to the agency where she was staying when Mom and Dad sponsored her. She was out of their program when she was fifteen, and they didn't have any more information. So, I called the government office in St Vincent, but they weren't any help either. They couldn't understand why I wanted to find her. I tried to be polite and say it was just personal. They seemed suspicious, and I really don't think they wanted to help me. Has anyone else tried to find out anything?"

"Yeah, Richard and I tried to track down this boy from Italy. We found five people with the same name, and around the same age, but we haven't gone any further. I'm not sure how to do it." Vera was content to sit by the fire and sip wine. Searching the world for lost souls from the comfort of her chair wasn't so hard.

"So anyway," Luella looked toward Tom for reinforcement. She didn't want to do all the talking. "Tom called a private investigator."

"Where? In St. Vincent?"

"No. New York. It is a firm that specializes in international missing persons. They charged a basic fee of five hundred dollars for international searches involving public and private data searches. If it requires anything more, they will notify us, and we can decide if we want to pursue it further."

"When will you find out anything?" Olivia was interested in how to go about the process.

"We already did." Luella pulled out some printed sheets from her handbag. "Here's what we have."

Marguerite MacDonald

Age 26.

Marital status: single

Parents: Father-unknown, Mother-deceased

Children: One, Male, age nine, Bastian MacDonald.

Current address: Mayreau, Lesser Antilles.

Employment: none

Education: did not graduate from High School

Language spoken: English, Creole

Narrative Background: Mother was in prison on drug charges and died from AIDS while incarcerated. Marguerite lived in St. Vincent government orphanage from age five to seven and then went to live in a private orphanage run by an international relief organization, sponsored by various faith-based groups or individuals. She lived at this facility until age fifteen, at which time she was old enough to go back into a government sponsored boarding school.

Additional information from public sources: Criminal background check—no information found. However, she did have rape charges filed on her behalf by one of the school administrators. Police report indicated the above stated individual was raped in one of the dormitories by an unknown male. Complaint was filed but no person was ever arrested or charged with the crime. Marguerite was sixteen years of age at that time, and was seventeen with the birth of her child.

Following the birth of her child, she moved to Mayreau and continues to reside there. She did not finish high school.

"Do you know anything more about this rape charge?" Olivia asked.

"Well, yes and no. It seems teen pregnancies and marriages are quite common in the islands especially among the poor. We suspect nothing was ever done about it. Probably just another girl trying to make an excuse for an unwanted pregnancy." Tom and Lu had already discussed these ideas at home.

"So, what are you going to do?" Emma shifted her position in the chair as she nursed the baby. She was thankful little Mary Beatrice had a safe and loving family. It would be difficult to live with the uncertainties Marguerite MacDonald had to live through.

"Well, we gave it some thought. We are going there over Christmas vacation."

"This year?" Vera seemed surprised by the suddenness of it.

Tom spoke up. "Yes, we're leaving in about four weeks. The kids are coming with."

"The stipulation in the will puts the pressure on all of us. If we don't do it now, when will we?" Luella and Tom both agreed it was time to act.

It was as if Olivia suddenly realized they were serious. "How are you getting there?"

"Well, that is a problem. We discovered, you can't get there from here." Luella pulled out some travel information. "It looks like we need to fly to Barbados, then get an island hop to St. Vincent and from there we need to find a ferry or supply boat going to

Mayreau. The only place to stay on the island is a small six-room hotel on Salt Whistle Bay. But you can't book anything because they have no Internet, limited electrical power depending on generators and no one has answered my phone calls yet."

"You're crazy." Emma felt the motherly instincts well up within her. Six months ago, she would have sailed the world on a dare; now she just wanted to stay safe with her newborn baby.

"No. Mom and Dad were the crazy ones. Remember what Dad always said, 'The nut doesn't fall far from the tree.'" Vera reflected on the four nuts and their husbands, sipping wine around the fireplace. "Richard, we need to do it too. Mom and Dad are gone. Petunia is dead. We don't even know what normal is, anymore. What are we waiting for? You know...I'm proud of our parents. They did crazy things and they led exciting lives. They didn't sit around and wait until the time was right. I'm ready for a new chapter."

Chapter 31

Island Time

Time is an illusion. —Albert Einstein

In the frantic days before the Christmas holiday, Tom and Luella researched and devoured every detail they could find about the southern Caribbean. Maddie's new-found passion was cooking, so she watched every You-tube video on Caribbean cooking. Zoe wanted to know how the kids went to school. She was amazed most of the children wore uniforms. Theo checked out shark pictures and monkeys and stingrays.

Since Lu and Tom were getting into the act, Vera and Richard decided to jump in with both feet as well. With the aid of Internet resources and phone calls, they located the farm in northern Thailand where the refugee from Myanmar had lived. Surin Farm specialized in breeding pigs and selling the piglets to the villagers. Ironically the farm was owned in part by an expat named Crandall Jensen and his Thai wife, Nuch.

Feeling left behind, they made a quick decision. Within hours of chatting with Crandall Jensen and his wife, they purchased three airline tickets and were on their way. With passports in hand and uncertainty in their hearts, they were off. They boarded a 747 to Tokyo with a scheduled transfer to Bangkok and finally Chiang Mai.

Tom, Luella, and the children had far more planning, but their process went much more slowly. The first leg of their journey went from Minneapolis to Miami to Barbados. The customs official looked down at the three skinny blonde kids and smiled. In a big booming voice, he announced, "Welcome to Barbados."

"Dad, does he speak English?" Theo whispered loud enough so everyone could hear.

"Yes. I do speak English. Do you?" He took the passports and reviewed them one by one. "Is Barbados your final destination?"

"No, we are going to St. Vincent and then on to Mayreau."

"Mayreau? Why are you going there?" He looked back at them quizzically, obviously wondering why a family with young children was heading to such a small, remote island. "If you are going to Mayreau make sure you bring a book to read." His right hand grabbed the official stamp of Barbados, and he thumped each passport. Handing them back, he looked directly into the eyes of Theo and warned him. "You better watch out for old Moses on Mayreau." With a pleasant smile, he bid them good will and called for the next passenger in line.

They rushed as only a family with three young children can rush to the departure gate for the island hop to St. Vincent. But as expected, they missed the earlier flight, and the next flight was not until 9 PM. It was already a very long day, and it was getting longer.

"Lu, can you tell me why we are doing this, again? And what did the immigration officer mean to watch out for old Moses on Mayreau?"

"Tom, you know very well why we are doing this. Besides what a great chance to show the kids something other than ice and snow." She wasn't sure why they were doing this either. Trying to help a girl they never met, in a place they had never been. It all sounded crazy.

Arriving late into St. Vincent, they found a nice cheap cockroach-infested hotel and spent the night. Morning gave them renewed hope. It was a gorgeous day. The sun was bright on the water, and the palms swayed in the breeze. The kids had never seen anything like it in their lives. Anxious to avoid further delays they rushed about, stuffing their long-sleeved shirts and shoes into bags, exchanging them for sandals and t-shirts. It was liberating.

Hurrying out of their cockroach haven, they found a taxi and asked to be taken to the ferry dock in Kingstown. The driver laughed. "Ha Ha! You Americans, always in a hurry." He took the bags, slowly arranging them into the back of his pickup truck. "OK, Mum, you and da little girl ride in da front. Dad, you and da big kids in da back." Pointing toward the benches arranged sideways under the canopy in the back of the rusty Toyota pickup. The thirty-minute ride through street markets and busy intersections enthralled the children, but each start and stop gave Tom a reason to grab his kids to avoid being tossed overboard. The ferry docks were busy with boats and people coming and going. The driver indicated where to go to get their tickets.

"Da ferry goes at noon, dats what da sign says, but sometimes it does and sometimes it don't. You know what da T-shirt say: don't worry; be happy. You on island time now." Tom glanced at his watch, 9 AM island time. They had at least three hours to wait, maybe more.

They kicked back in the shade of the roof over the ferry dock and listened to the sea gulls. With fresh fruit from a street vendor and a loaf of bread, they slowly munched their breakfast on island time. Tom dozed off while Lu hovered over Theo and Zoe. Maddie retreated to a corner of the ferry terminal, which was nothing more than a roof on stilts along the water. In the early stages of her third Harry Potter book, she was oblivious to those around her.

The voice came over the loud speaker, shaking Tom from his reverie. "OK people, da Barracuda ferry is about to leave. Make sure you have your tickets. You may be on island time, but da Barracuda goes on my time, and Cap'n King don't wait for no one."

They joined the line of people stepping aboard the MV Barracuda under the watchful eye of Captain King. Theo was enthralled with the ship. Much larger than they expected, the ferry was secured to the pier. For the past two hours he had watched cars, trucks and fork lifts move equipment and supplies on deck for the islands. His only previous experience on board a boat of any type was Papa's pontoon on Namukwa Lake.

The horn sounded and bells rang as the MV Barracuda was released from its mooring and backed out from the pier. Heavy diesel engines shuddered and shook as the ferry turned toward the sea. Passengers lined the upper deck, waving at friends and family ashore. For others it was as routine as going to work.

"Safety announcement for passengers aboard the Barracuda. There are lifeboats on both sides and life jackets in the big bins on deck. So, if we sink, and you don't want to go swimming, get in the lifeboat." And that was the end of the safety announcement. Then the speakers cracked with new life with another announcement. "Mama King is selling roti on the upper deck. If you are hungry, better hurry."

"Mom, what's a roti?"

"I'm not sure. Let's give it a try." Luella grabbed two little hands, and they skipped up the narrow stairs to visit Mama King.

A plump lady with a big smile greeted them. "Mum, da children need some sunshine." She smiled as she looked at the little white-skinned kids peering over the counter.

"What's a roti?" Zoe wasn't shy about asking.

"What's a roti? It's da best food in da 'hole world. Dats a roti." She laughed as her hands moved quickly, putting food together. "Do you like chicken? Or goat?" Not waiting for an answer, she put both together. Roti was a thin sheet of handmade bread, much like a tortilla, loaded with curried chicken and some vegetables and rolled together. On a second plate, the same thin bread encased grilled spicy Caribbean jerk goat. "Der you go. Don' come runnin' back to Mama King 'les you want mo', OK?"

Luella paid with East Caribbean cash and carried the plates to a table on the deck. Maddie wrinkled her nose at the smell of curried chicken, and she wasn't so sure about eating goat. But she was happy to try a fresh slice of papaya and some bananas. Tom kicked back with a bottle of 10 Saints, a beer from Barbados, and Luella and the kids each had a bottle of Ting.

The first stop was Mustique, then on to Mayreau. Fifty minutes of travel from Mustique took them years into the past. Once the ferry was firmly tied to the jetty, they disembarked. One young man got off along with the white-skinned people from the US. Obviously familiar with the island, he trotted off the jetty and hiked up the road. Waiting on the jetty to board was an old woman with a bent back. She leaned forward using a cane to steady herself. A young woman, presumed to be her daughter or friend, held her arm and carried her small handbag. They exchanged places with the Tinker family, and the ferry pulled away.

Like a pile of mud at the end of a long dead-end road, the Tinkers sat on the jetty with their pile of suitcases, bags, and extra sunscreen. A single dirt and concrete road wound up the hill to a little cluster of buildings on the horizon. Three small fishing boats were anchored along the beach, and several naked boys, looking no older than five or six, jumped off the end of the boat into the aqua blue lagoon. No one appeared along the road or the beach.

"Dad, what are we doing?" Maddie asked the obvious question, but neither Lu nor Tom could answer it. They had landed on the smallest inhabited island in the Caribbean, no one knew they were coming, they had no place to stay and no idea what to do. Just some crazy idea about showing up and giving money to a strange girl and her family. Ten minutes stretched into twenty. It was as if quicksand grabbed their feet and reality hit them.

Shielding their eyes, the Tinkers looked up toward the village on the hill. One by one people began coming out of their homes. They gathered together, enjoying the spectacle of the new people in town. First one or two, then a dozen, and soon fifty or sixty people gathered, pointing down at the jetty. By the time thirty minutes had passed, a single rusty red pickup rumbled down the concrete path that doubled as a road. Without a muffler, they could hear it coming from quite a distance. It creaked and groaned as it turned along the beach toward the jetty. At the end of the road, the only road in Mayreau, the old black man turned off the key and opened his door.

He limped slowly toward the visitors, dragging his right foot slightly. His deep black skin, furrowed from years in the sun was a stark contrast to the wiry white hair on his head and beard. Behind the rusted and dented truck, the small crowd tripped over one another, jockeying for position to see the newcomers. Kids in blue school uniforms, young and old women with bright colored dresses, and old men as wrinkled and wizened as their host stood nearby with expectant smiles.

"Welcome." The old man held out his calloused, dusty hand to greet Tom and Luella. "My name is Moses Sinclair, the governor of Mayreau. We've been expecting you."

Chapter 32

Blank Check

A promise made is a debt unpaid. —Robert W. Service

As the new jetsetters circled the globe dispensing wit, wisdom and wealth, Olivia and Emma and their families returned home to Oak Grove. Making a single house into a home for two families can be a difficult transition, made more problematic with a newborn in the mix. Olivia enjoyed the company of her sister and little 'Beat-rice' as she was called. Harry had a more difficult time with the lack of privacy and new demands at work. He was trying to assimilate their family at home and Phineas at work, double trouble.

Work provided Harry with a good excuse to be out of the crowded house, and it also gave him some comic relief. Phineas was not comfortable around big animals. Even back at Namukwa, he contentedly stood aside and let the kids toss donuts to Petunia. Now, facing the other end of large animals, his anxiety intensified. The first day on the job, Harry utilized the talents of his brother-in-law for carrying the tools of the trade and note taking. By afternoon Harry began to realize the value of a gopher, and Phineas was very capable at running for this, carrying that, and keeping notes.

The second day on the job, Harry introduced his helper to some of the more intimate details of breeding dairy cattle. It didn't go so well, at least for Phineas. Harry carefully instructed him on how to stand and what to do. Phineas donned the full-length glove, reaching all the way to his right shoulder. He took a guarded stance behind the heifer as a fly buzzed on his eyebrow. Phineas flipped his free hand up to shush the fly away and knocked his hat off into the steaming brown cow-pie at his feet. Frustrated at his good luck, Phineas bent down to get his hat.

"Don't do that," Harry warned.

"What?" Phineas glanced up, not remembering the oft-repeated warning. A warm golden shower washed over him. Jumping up, he bumped the back end of the cow. The cow rewarded him with a sharp kick to the right shin sending him tumbling into the gutter across the walkway. Phineas was a fully baptized member of the cattle breeding business. Harry might have happy heifers, but he didn't have a happy co-worker.

Harry laughed so hard, he grabbed his sides to ease the pain. Helping Phineas out of the gutter and back on solid footing added to his joy. Phineas may have thought a few choice words, but he kept his tongue and never complained. Harry had always viewed Phineas as a preppy college boy who didn't know how to work. Maybe he still didn't know how to work, but they each gained a better understanding of the other. Just as soldiers are forever bonded to one another through the horrors of war, they had both been in the gutter and lived to tell of it. They were always brothers-in-law, now they were friends.

Back at the homestead, Olivia loved having Emma and the baby around. Molly was a precocious five-year-old who asked more questions than Olivia could possibly answer. She read at a third-grade level in kindergarten, but she didn't like to cuddle. With little Mary Beatrice around, Olivia could indulge her need to cuddle whenever Emma needed a break. It was so comforting and calming to hold a sleeping baby and rock her while gazing out the window at the winter snow. It was good to have a job and feel competent in her duties, but staying home doing the mommy thing didn't hurt her feelings one bit. Perhaps it was what she needed after the events of the past year. Rocking the baby gave her a chance to reflect on her own mother and what she had meant to Olivia when she was young. You take those moments for granted, thinking there is always tomorrow, always a chance to say I love you and I'm sorry and whatever else is in your heart. She didn't have regrets, but she did have a little empty hole in her heart, and baby Mary Beatrice was helping to fill it up.

The doorbell woke her from her daydreams. She handed little Beatrice off to her mom and went to answer. The rural mail carrier had walked up to the door with packages.

"Hi, Rhonda. Merry Christmas." Sometimes it is nice to be anonymous, but there is a simple joy of knowing your neighbors on a first name basis. In Oak Grove, neighbors made it their business to know your business.

"Merry Christmas, Olivia. We have been so busy with cards and gifts this year I haven't had time to think straight. I have a registered package you need to sign for. Looks like it's from Switzerland." She fumbled through another stack addressed to Phineas and Emma as well. "Looks as though Emma has the same thing." Olivia signed and then held the baby as Emma signed. "Have a good day." And Rhonda, their mail carrier for the past twenty-three years, drove off.

Emma went back to nursing the baby while Olivia sorted through the mail. Two days after Christmas and already they had spring gardening catalogs and spring clothing catalogs. Two Christmas cards from distant relatives. Olivia hadn't taken the time to send any. Surprisingly she felt no guilt. Most of the mail went directly into the garbage. Then she opened the mystery package from Suisse Bank.

"Emma, do you know how to get in contact with Luella or Vera?"

"No, I don't. Why, what's wrong?"

"We need to talk to Lu and Vera as soon as possible. I hope it isn't too late."

#

After twelve hours over the pacific, a three-hour layover in Tokyo watching sumo wrestling on the airport television, and another eight-hour flight to Bangkok, the Dawsons were finally in Thailand. But they still weren't where they wanted to be. The next leg of their journey was only an hour and fifteen-minute flight north, but it didn't leave until 7 AM. It was now 12:10 in the morning.

They were drained of energy, confused by language and culture, and felt lost. The enormity of their decision suddenly hit them. "Tell me again, why we are doing this?" Rick was ready to turn around and get on the next plane home. His question went unanswered.

The local time was 12:10 AM but in his stomach, it was 12:10 PM, lunchtime. Rick had always been a meat-and-potatoes kind of person. Plain, comfortable, and safe had been his unspoken motto. His favorite food before marriage was mashed potatoes with hamburger gravy. Then he met Vera. At the wedding she wanted something served from every continent. It was his first taste of sushi and wasabi. He would never forget it. Looking out at the crowds he suspected this was another excess wasabi experience about to happen.

Rick barely survived the spicy soup. Although he ordered the mildest version, it sent his Midwestern taste buds over the edge. It was so hot if he inhaled the fumes, it sent him into paroxysmal coughing fits. The first spoonful burned all the way to this stomach and sweat broke out on his forehead. It made his wasabi experience seem like oatmeal. Vera happily munched her papaya salad, and Daisy slurped down a bowl of noodles. The burning in his throat didn't begin to cool until they were boarding the next flight north.

The air in Chiang Mai was decidedly different than Bangkok. In the higher altitude it had a lighter more refreshing quality. Bangkok was hot and heavy, dripping with humidity. The atmosphere in Chiang Mai felt welcoming, in part because it was the end of a very long journey. Best of all they found a friend.

Crandall Jensen was waiting for them. Vera was a Facebook friend with him, and they had corresponded over the past few weeks. An expat, originally from the Midwest, he was now a one-legged pig farmer in Thailand. He lost his leg from an industrial accident years before, but he could out walk most people half his age.

"I hope your long journey was uneventful," Crandall greeted them, shaking hands with Richard, Vera, and little Daisy. "Welcome to Chiang Mai." His prosthetic leg creaked and groaned as they headed toward the exit. Daisy was fascinated by his mechanical leg, believing him to be some sort of robot. Crandall chatted on about the area and a bit about the culture as they loaded his car and drove out of town. It was an hour drive on a good day, much longer if the traffic was heavy. The Dawson family quietly sat back, trying to soak it all in.

"Daisy, look at the elephants." Vera held her up to the window. A line of five elephants worked in a field under the watchful eye of their handler. Ponderous animals with large slowly flapping ears, they moved in unison to the directions of the handler.

"Some of the farms and logging in the mountains use elephants, but increasingly they are moving toward machinery." Crandall pointed out other areas of interest including Buddhist

271

temples and monks draped in classic orange attire. They enjoyed the mountainous landscape covered in lush greenery.

Surin Farm was a pig farm in the truest sense although different from its American counterparts. Numerous large sows were bred, and when the piglets were weaned, they were sold. Daisy liked the pigs because of her fond memories of Petunia.

Once the Dawson's were introduced around and settled into the guest home it was time to talk. Crandall was fascinated by their story. "Tell me again, why did you come here to Chiang Mai? To give away money?"

"Yes, my parents put a stipulation into their will that we were unable to receive any funds from the estate until we had each given away $100,000." Vera went on to explain why they came to this place. "My parents sponsored a young refugee from Burma or Myanmar, who was in a Thai controlled refugee camp. It is my understanding you helped this girl as well, am I right?"

"You speak of Chuenchai Bunyasarn, a refugee from Myanmar. She lived here at Surin Farm for about eight years. She's a delightful girl and worked hard, but she's no longer here." He paused to pour some tea and offer it around. "Do you know the history of Myanmar?"

"No, I'm sorry we don't, or at least I don't." Richard joined into the conversation.

"To make a very long and complicated story as short as possible, let me summarize a bit. Most of the refugees belong to one of several ethnic groups or tribes. The leadership of Burma or Myanmar as it is known today, was brutal to these people. Many were

272

beaten or killed and driven out of their homes. Some were taken and forced into sex trafficking. The fortunate ones fled, many across the border into Thailand. Thais didn't want them either, and many were forced into refugee camps. Some have been living in these camps for decades. The camps are harsh, crowded, and unsanitary. It is no place you would want to go or stay. Some of these refugees have been living illegally in Thailand, but this isn't much better than the refugee camps. No one wants them." Crandall paused to see if they had any questions.

He continued. "Most of the ones who find work make very little money, the equivalent of three US dollars each day. But for many this is enough to buy basic needs."

"Could we give her some money? Is this a way we could help her or others?"

"Possibly, but this could be dangerous. If you gave her any substantial amount of money and others knew about it, she could be killed and the money taken. Secondly, she has no reasonable way of handling anything but small sums. She is a refugee. She is not a legal citizen here in Thailand, and she has no options for banking. A thousand dollars US represents more than a year's wages for her. There are many here that would want to take your money, but it would not be well spent. I am advising you to be very cautious." He thought for a minute. "You come here with very generous and kind intentions, but you must proceed wisely. Even though you want to help, if the Thai government found out, you could be in trouble with them as well."

"In what way?"

"If someone in Thailand were suddenly found to be in possession of ten or twenty thousand US dollars, they would be under suspicion of human or drug trafficking. I assure you, you don't want to be investigated."

Vera had a difficult time understanding what was being discussed. "Are you saying we came this far for nothing?"

"Not at all. There are relief organizations begging for help and money, but to help an individual as you have shared, could be more difficult than you think. Money isn't the answer to the world's problems."

Vera ran though several ideas in her head. "I know this sounds crazy, but what if I wrote a check to you and then you could dispense cash in appropriate amounts to those in need. Is that possible?"

"Why would you trust me? You don't even know me?" Crandall was clearly surprised at Vera's willingness to hand over thousands of dollars to someone she just met. "I would be happy to take your money, but what if I use it for my own benefit?"

"Mr. Jensen, I don't know you anymore than I know any of these relief organizations, but I believe you're a kind and generous person or you wouldn't have helped us, and you surely wouldn't have helped that refugee girl." She grabbed her handbag and pulled out the checkbook. "This sounds crazy but here is a check for five thousand dollars." She handed him a signed check. "Put it into your account, and use your judgment, and help these people in ways that won't raise suspicion or cause problems."

"What are you going to do?" Crandall reached out and took the check. "Is this what your parents wanted?"

"I'm not sure, but it's a start and I trust you. Think of it as a thank you for letting us stay at your guest house."

He took out his smart phone and took a photograph of the check. "Technology and internet banking has made living abroad much easier. With a simple photo of a check I can make a direct deposit into my own international checking account." He entered an access code and within a very short time the transaction was complete.

For a few minutes they relaxed, trying to adjust to the time changes. Daisy was sound asleep on a large pillow on the floor. Suddenly there was an alert on Crandall's phone. He checked his messages and looked across the room at Vera and Richard.

"Have you written any checks on your account to anyone else?"

"No, you're first. Why?" Vera wondered.

"I don't want to burst your bubble, but I just received a notification that your check is void. There is no account by that number."

Chapter 33

Back to School

They inspire you, they entertain you, and you end up learning
a ton even when you don't know it. —Nicholas Sparks

The words rattled around in Tom's head. "We've been expecting
you." But there wasn't time to figure it out. Once Moses Sinclair
contacted the strangers on the jetty, the dam broke. People poured
from the hilltop village down the lone road, singing, dancing, and
laughing at the arrival of the strangers. Maddie felt like an African
queen returning to her palace. People lined the road cheering and
waving. Zoe and Theo were holding hands and running with the
neighborhood kids before their luggage was loaded into the only
truck on the island. Luella wondered at the welcome; it wasn't
what she expected.

The truck rattled to life under the direction of the old man. He
ground the gears, turned around on the beach and headed up the
hill. Tom and Luella fell in behind the truck, their feet keeping

cadence with the singing and dancing. With the music moving them along, it was an easy trek up the hill to the village. Neither of them knew where they were going, and it appeared they had little choice in the matter. At the top of the hill Moses turned the truck to the right and drove off the road. There was only one road; everything else was a path. Moses followed the path to the right until it ended at a small house.

The doors to the house were ajar. The light blue shutters were open arms, inviting the ocean breezes in. Luella marveled at the bright lemon meringue walls surrounded by red bougainvillea and banana trees. By the time they arrived, Moses and some of the others had their belongings stowed in the house. No questions were asked, it was just accepted. Moses held out his hands, pointing the way into the home. "Please make yourself at home, relax and welcome to Mayreau. Tonight, we will have a pig roast."

"Mr. Moses, thank you so much for everything. What time is the party?"

"What time? Island time. We don't know what time it is. When the party is ready, you will know." With that announcement, fifty or sixty women and children burst into singing and clapping and dancing around the house. Old men stood behind them, clapping and singing. It was as if the prodigal son had come home.

The kids scurried around in the house, staking claim to beds and bedrooms. Maddie picked the small room looking down the hill toward the sea. Luella and Tom ejected Theo from the largest room, and Zoe wanted to sleep in the hammock on the porch. It didn't take too long to get settled. A quick change of clothing into light shirts, shorts, and sandals was all that was required. Then it was back outside in the Caribbean paradise.

Luella took the opportunity to lie back and relax, feeling the gentle sea breezes through the window. She loved the smell of the tropical air. It had a salty sweet quality to it, much like warm caramel popcorn fresh from an iron kettle. She felt so at home, she quickly lapsed into a nap.

Tom was ready to stretch his legs after a day of sitting. He hiked to the very top of the hill and looked at the school. It was a simple concrete block, three-room schoolhouse. School was already in recess at the end of the day, but the doors were open. He walked in. No high tech white boards or audiovisual resources, this was simple and basic. The blackboard in one room had elementary arithmetic problems, and the other room held the basics of English and spelling. Simple gray steel desks in tidy rows faced the front. Books were neatly arranged on the corners of the desk. Sharpened pencils stood upright in a cup set into a hole at the corner. Each desk was arranged to be shared by two students.

A tired, dusty, brown dog lay comfortably asleep on the concrete floor under one of the desks, seeking refuge from the tropical sun. He cocked his floppy ears and opened one eye to study Tom. Seeing no risk to his repose, the old dog let out a long sigh and drifted back to sleep. After twelve years of teaching high school mathematics with every new teaching aid and gadget, Tom wondered what it would be like to teach in a school like this.

Several children peeked in the door at him, but when he turned to look they giggled and ran off. In their place, Mr. Moses

Sinclair appeared. His shadow spread across the empty desks making him seem much larger than life. His big calloused hands brushed a few long rogue white hairs away from his eyes, and he smiled. "Was everything OK in the house?"

"Yes, it's fine. You are very kind to help us." Tom wasn't ready to talk about the reason they came so he tried to make small talk. "You have a nice school here. How many children?"

"We have about fifty children in the elementary ages. When they get big, they go to the boarding school in Canouan or St. Vincent."

"Mr. Sinclair, what kind of work is there for the people of the island? How can they support themselves?" Tom had seen no sign of industry of any kind.

"Please call me Moses. The people here are poor. Many have relatives on other islands that work and send money. Some sell to tourists, some work on other islands and return here when possible." He pointed out the many small houses dotting the landscape. "Most have gardens, goats or chickens. Some fish in the ocean and sell the fish to locals. Some are supported by the government."

Moses and Tom stepped out from the school into the open sunshine. Looking north, Tom could see ten or so yachts anchored in a sheltered harbor. "Do those boats belong to people here?"

Moses laughed. "No one here can afford a boat like that. They belong to rich people from America who live on their yachts and travel the Caribbean. They spend money here, and it helps us. We have a quiet secluded harbor. If it makes them happy, it makes us happy."

Their conversation seemed to stall, each wanting to ask more personal questions but neither seemed comfortable opening the door. At least not yet. They barely knew each other. Tom was hoping Luella would be the one to bring up Marguerite MacDonald. Asking personal questions three hours after arriving might appear impertinent. With the warm welcome, Tom didn't want to ruin their visit before it started. Yet their arrival seemed strangely welcoming, much more than he expected.

The warm afternoon sun slowly drifted toward the horizon. After parting company with Moses, Tom wandered about the village, wasting time. People came out of their homes and waved. Children followed him, giggling, and laughing. When he turned toward them they scattered as if to play hide and seek. Brightly colored chickens scratched and pecked in the yards and paths between homes. An old white nanny goat, tied to a post, bellowed, and strained against a frayed rope, hoping for a handful of grain or vegetable scraps. Tom smelled smoke and roasting meat. There was a sense of anticipation among the people.

Far down the hill, near the harbor, a woman slowly removed a line of colorful dresses and T-shirts from a rope strung between palms. No more rich tourists in fancy boats were coming to buy her wares. The day's work was done; she packed up and walked home. Tom returned to their home away from home.

Luella had a wonderful afternoon nap. She dreamed of her parents, and for a short time the world was right again. She was happy for the moment. "Tom, what is that wonderful smell?" She stuck her head out the window, gazing at the setting sun over the blue sea.

"They are having a pig roast down by the harbor." Tom pointed toward the jetty where the ferry had landed. People were starting to gather and walk in that direction. A fire burned brightly on the edge of the beach, kept alive by heaps of palm driftwood and scrubby trees along the shore. Three old women took turns rotating a pig and a goat on spits near the fire. Several tables, nothing more than old weathered plywood nailed to sawed off palm logs were draped with colorful cloths. Stacks of tropical fruit, vegetables and other dishes were arranged within easy reach.

Maddie and Zoe remained close to their parents, but Theo was already kicking a soccer ball around the yard with six or seven other young boys. In typical American fashion, the Tinker family hung back with a measure of uncertainty about joining the group without an invitation. But when the boys quit kicking the ball about and headed toward the fire, they joined the crowd.

This was no church picnic. The people laughed and danced and drank and ate. One old man played a type of bongo drum made from the end of a log. Another young man played a chipped and faded guitar, but it was the sweetest reggae beach music they had ever heard. The singing was joyous and from the heart. Everyone danced in the light of the big beach fire. Even Tom and Luella attempted some dysfunctional, out-of-rhythm, Scandinavian-influenced moves. In the flickering firelight, no one cared.

The hours passed into the night. There was fruit punch, rum, and some type of island beer. Someone hacked off the top of a coconut with a machete and poured in a generous dash of rum. One of each was given to Tom and Luella. It was the perfect complement to mountains of curried goat, spicy jerked chicken, and the island pig roast. The only thing that kept them going was the nonstop music and dancing.

The island generator was turned off and a glowing luminescence covered the island. Moonlight reflected by the calm sea lit their path back to the house. The big fire on the beach slowly burned down to embers and flickered out. Tom was exhausted from a very long day. He looked at his watch, the dial glowed two o'clock. As they worked their way slowly back up the hill, carrying dishes and leftover food, Moses Sinclair came up beside Tom and Luella.

"We'll see you at church in the morning?"

Not wanting to offend their host, Luella replied, "Church? Where and what time?"

"You'll find it, the time doesn't matter." And he limped off into the night carrying a large basket of items on his shoulder.

It was one of those nights when dreams are good and sleep is refreshing. Tom, Lu, and the kids slept so soundly they never heard a thing until a lazy rooster crowed them awake at 10 AM. Blinking into the morning sun, they pulled back the shutters and marveled at the view. Blue ocean on every side, chickens in the yard and swaying palms along the shore. It was their own little idyllic paradise, even if it was only for a short time.

Just as they had last night, people in colorful clothing walked along worn paths between scrubby trees and brightly flowered bushes to the gathering place. A small stone church stood on the hill, but few went in that direction. Instead in a clearing near one of the houses a handful of people assembled. Singing seemed to begin spontaneously and the sound swelled with the ocean breeze. A guitar joined, and then the same drums as last evening. The louder it got the more people came. Soon dozens were singing and swaying and clapping and dancing to the music. Last night Tom was sure the festive atmosphere was rum induced, but this was Sunday morning, and the same spirit moved the people. They had real joy in their hearts and life in their step.

Slipping from their lemon meringue cottage and into the fray, the Tinkers tried to blend in. However, if their white skin didn't give them away, their stoic Lutheran customs would. They just didn't have the swing and sway everyone else did. Zoe leaped into her mother's arms when a large black woman in a white dress jumped up and yelled "Hallelujah." Another stood and clapped her hands, and a man yelled something no one could understand. This seemed to go on for an hour, and finally it got around to preaching. The preacher was none other than Mr. Moses Sinclair.

When he got rolling there was sweat on his forehead and a spring in his step. Luella, being the observant nurse, realized at the height of his sermon, the limp went away. Moses Sinclair, the preacher, moved about with the agility of a cat ready to pounce on any sinners or heathens foolish enough to question the Word of God. He raised the Bible high above his head and spoke with authority and power. His black eyes seemed to look right though you. Just when you thought it was over, the women spontaneously broke into glorious song, peppered with a liberal dose of "Praise Jesus" and "Hallelujah" and "Preach it, brother" yelled out from the congregation. Moses wiped the sweat, drank some water, and got ready for round two.

Round two was shorter but no less dramatic. It was the call for all sinners to repent and turn from their wicked life and come to Jesus. It reached a feverish pitch as many came to Moses with arms up and their eyes heavenward. People danced and cried and yelled out to God. There was one great and glorious climactic ending, and it was suddenly over except for drying the tears and the sweat.

Moses Sinclair had one more thing to say. "People," he yelled out so all could hear. "You know we have been praying for a long time about something very important to all of us here in Mayreau. And God has answered our prayers in a glorious way!"

"Amen!" "Praise God!" "Hallelujah!" the people responded.

Tom and Luella waited anxiously to hear the answer to prayer. There was a sense of excitement and wonder in the air.

"Before you go into your homes today, make sure you welcome our new school teacher."

Everyone clapped and cheered and yelled, "Praise the Lord." Tom wondered if he would have a chance to meet the new schoolteacher. He wanted to compare his experience with their experience in a small isolated school. Then it hit him like a tsunami. People were lining up to greet him and welcome his family to Mayreau. He was the new schoolmaster.

Chapter 34

Give and You Shall Receive

It's not how much we give but how much love we put into
giving. —Mother Teresa

Tom and Luella weren't familiar with Pentecostal church prac-
tices. Being good Lutherans, the most response you got from the
congregation was a quiet murmur or a polite 'good morning.' Anything more was disruptive. When you combined island customs
and Pentecostal preaching, it was a fiery mix, like hot sauce and
120-proof rum in your tomato juice. It would have been impossible to fall asleep in church.

But falling asleep in church wasn't their concern. Suddenly
Tom had a new teaching job, and he wasn't looking for one. As the
Sunday gathering began to break up, Tom and Luella were
stricken with a sense of deception and panic. Neither of them had
ever disclosed their profession to anyone on the island. Was there
some inside information? Did someone on the island know

something they didn't? Even if the Mayreau islanders had been praying about getting a new teacher, did anyone ask Tom or Luella? What about their real purpose for visiting the island?

Once they were safely out of sight from the locals, Tom and Luella had a serious discussion about the next step. Tom put his opinion on the table first. "We need to have a direct conversation with Mr. Moses Sinclair since he is the one to thrust us into the public eye."

"Why would he even say something like that? No one asked us, did they?" Luella paced and back and forth within their tiny cottage. No longer were they staying in a lemon meringue cottage brushed with caramel corn breezes. It had melted into a very sticky situation. "I feel guilty about letting these people down. Somehow they expect us to live here and teach their kids, and we can't do that!" Even as she spoke, Moses limped in their direction from the church gathering place. They had to confront the deception now rather than letting it go unchecked.

"Mr. Moses." Luella opened the front door. A small breath of wind stirred the bougainvillea and sent the wind chimes into motion. "Can we visit with you for a few minutes?"

"Of course, I was hoping we could spend some time together today. My wife has made a nice meal, and we were expecting you as guests." He smiled knowing they had no other options unless they chose to go hungry.

"That's very nice of you, but it isn't necessary." Tom was still uncomfortable with the events of the past twenty-four hours.

"I know it isn't necessary, but you don't have any food. You aren't obligated to come, we just want to make you feel welcome." Without waiting for an answer, he simply turned and started walking away. They looked at each other and followed down the garden path. After all, if they wanted to discuss their dilemma, they should meet with the governor himself, Mr. Moses.

Moses stopped in front of a small pastel pink cottage with an open porch and a rocking chair. Flowers of every possible color bloomed profusely around all sides. Open to the tropical breezes, the windows were bordered by the same bright blue shutters. Inside the cottage was a very small kitchen filled with platters of fresh fruit, curried goat, Caribbean jerk chicken, conch fritters, baked yams, grilled grouper, and roti, warm and fresh from the oven. Two tables were set behind the house in the shade where several other people were seated, chatting about life. Mrs. Moses greeted them with hugs and invited them into the yard, through the house. "Happy Sunday to you. I'm Arbutus. Welcome to our home." If the people of Mayreau were anything, they were warm and hospitable.

Before anyone dared touch the food, Moses called upon almighty God to bless it. Then and only then, could they eat. The Tinker's were hungry, having missed breakfast, but that wasn't foremost on their minds. They needed to have time to be open and honest with the villagers.

The food was thoroughly enjoyed, and when the last bit of jerked chicken and roti was gone, Moses pulled out a box of cigars, offering one to any guest who wanted one. Two of the other men accepted as did Maybelle, the oldest woman on the island. Acrid cigar smoke drifted off through the village as the conversation reached a lull. It was time to talk.

"Mr. Moses, may we speak honestly with you and the others?" Luella broke the ice.

"Of course, there is no other way to speak."

"My parents died less than a year ago...and that's the main reason we are here." She stopped to think her way through the controversy. "They gave us money with the instruction we were to give it away. I know it sounds funny, but they didn't leave us any money until we learned to give money away. Does that make any sense?"

"Amen!" old Maybelle spoke from the shade. Two of the older men present also nodded and murmured their agreement.

"Mom and Dad gave us the name of Marguerite MacDonald as someone we should find and help. We searched for her and the last information we have, is that she is living on Mayreau." With the name of Marguerite MacDonald, everyone became instantly more attentive. It was clear by their response they knew something.

"How do you know Marguerite?" Arbutus wondered.

Luella and Tom wandered through every experience they had in the past year including the loss of their parents, the crazy clues and troubles trying to figure out what Lola and Roy really wanted and how they came to Mayreau. After more than an hour of dabbing tears, laughing, and spilling their innermost feelings, it was all on the table. Now the people of Mayreau knew they didn't come to teach, but they did come to help.

"Why did you think we were coming to teach at your school?" Tom wanted to know.

Moses responded. "My cousin works at the airport in customs. He checked you through. He called to tell me you are a teacher, and you are coming to Mayreau. I thought you were coming to teach. I should have asked, but I just assumed."

"I'm sorry if we aren't the people you were expecting. We don't want to disappoint you." And Luella ended her story. There was a long pause; no one spoke for several minutes. The children had already run off, playing with their newfound friends. Maybelle took a long puff on her cigar and spit into the grass beside her chair.

"Well, I declare, the Lawd works in mysterious ways."

Tom spoke up. "Can any of you tell us where we can find Marguerite MacDonald? Does she live here?"

"What if she don' wanna talk to you?" Maybelle seemed to be the most interested. However, the others listened carefully.

"Why wouldn't she want to talk?" Luella asked.

"I dunno, can't answer fo' her." Maybelle looked out over the low weathered picket fence dividing this yard from the next. "Hey, Bastian." She yelled across the fence. "Go find yo' mamma. We wanna talk to her."

There was a strange silence over the group as they waited. The comfortable chatter between the men, the women and the visitors came to a halt as they all waited for the arrival of Marguerite. As the silence wore on, broken only by the sea gulls and the children playing in the distance, Luella began to worry about what was happening. She wondered if they were over stepping their bounds trying to fix something that didn't need fixing or going places where they weren't welcome.

Finally, in the distance you could see the boy walking alongside a young woman. She appeared youthful and strong, walking swiftly along the path. Her long black hair was rolled into a bunch on the back of her head. Her face was impassive, neither smiling nor frowning giving no indication of her opinion at being summoned by the elders of the island. Her red dress fluttered in the breeze. By any worldly standards she was beautiful, marred only by a scar across her left cheek, near her eye. Her left eyelid drooped slightly compared to the right. A lone rebellious strand of black hair danced and flitted in front of her face, resisting her attempts to subdue it.

Marguerite entered the edge of the group and sat on a chair without talking. She looked over the group, mostly studying the Tinker family. Then she turned to Maybelle. "Gram, you wanted to see me?"

Maybelle set her cigar aside and turned to Luella and Tom. "Margie is my adopted granddaughter. She don' have no family."

"Marguerite, my name is Luella Tinker."

"We all know who you are."

"Yes, I'm sure you do." Luella paused hoping she wasn't treading on sensitive ground. "You were in an orphanage in St. Vincent several years ago. When you were living there my parents helped to sponsor you. They were named Roy and Lola Ambrose. Do you remember anything about that?"

"I remember some things."

Luella continued. "My sister and I wrote to you, and I sent you pictures of us when we were children."

Margie was quiet as if in deep thought. When she was a child, she had nothing to call her own other than the clothes on her back. She recalled those photos. She still had them. It was one of the first gifts she had received from anyone who seemed to care. "I still have them. They were very special to me." She was quiet again for moment, and then asked a question that stung Luella. "Why did you stop helping me?"

"What do you mean?"

"I was in the orphanage for one year when everything stopped. The people there told me you didn't care anymore, and you quit sending money." A slight edge began to form in her voice.

"But we didn't stop. My parents helped many children for years. I know they kept sending money, and we wrote letters, but there was never any response back." Luella suddenly realized what had happened. The organization designed to help some of these disadvantaged people was diverting the money for personal gain. Fraud in the worst possible way at the expense of helpless people.

"Do you know what happened to me?" She pulled the reckless strand of hair back. The scar was more visible and deeper than they had imagined. "I was released from the orphanage into a boarding school. I was beaten and raped, and when I got pregnant they sent me away. I didn't have any family, but Gram took me in. I call her Gram because she is the only family I know."

Luella dabbed at her eyes with a napkin. "My parents died this past year. They wanted us to come and help you. We can't change what happened, but we can help if you'll let us."

Marguerite looked at the aging islanders seated around them in the shade and then turned toward Tom and Luella. "I don't want your money or your help. It is kind of you to offer, but I don't need it." There were no protests or words to the contrary from any of the people present.

"May I ask why?" Tom realized the relative poverty the islanders experienced. By worldly standards, they had very little. But they required very little. It was clear, happiness had nothing to do with possessions.

"Whenever someone tried to give me money or help, they always wanted something in return. I can offer you nothing because I have nothing."

"Marguerite, we ask nothing from you, what we offer is a gift. Please let us help you."

The young woman thought for a few moments and then offered an unselfish alternative. "Mr. Moses has the only truck on the entire island. It is old and needs help. If you really want to help me, then help us all. Pay to fix his truck."

"Marguerite, if that is what you want, we can do even better. Tom and I will buy a new truck for the island. Is that OK?" Luella looked over at Tom for approval, but she already knew the answer.

Suddenly everyone had a new level of enthusiasm. People started chattering and laughing again.

"Moses, do you have telephone or radio contact with St. Vincent?"

"Yes, ma'am."

"Tomorrow is Monday. I want you to call and order a new truck to come on the next ferry. We will pay for it in full when it arrives. No problems. Is that OK with you?" Luella was pleased with the idea. It was a good plan. Tom agreed.

On Monday morning, Moses Sinclair was up and about extra early. He had never dreamed in his lifetime that he would ever have a new pickup truck. Over the phone, he could tell the dealer was skeptical but agreed to deliver a new shiny blue Toyota pickup on the next ferry. The dealer would have the paperwork complete and ready for a signature. Luella would have a check for the full amount. The truck was in stock, and he could have the truck on the ferry the same day. A new truck was coming to Mayreau; it would be another time of celebration.

The arrival of the ferry brought new excitement, more than the possibility of getting a new schoolteacher. Nearly two hundred people, almost the entire population of the island, gathered near the jetty as the ferry approached. There was singing and clapping and a clear sense of heightened expectation. And there it was, the shiny new blue pickup with only three miles on the odometer.

Moses smiled from ear to ear as he ran his hand over the glossy fender and tinted windows. He saved his biggest smile for the moment he sat behind the wheel and turned the key. The engine sprang to life and purred like a kitten curled up in the sunshine. Moses drove the truck off the ferry, up the hill and back down again. There was only one road on the island, and he had already covered it from end to end. Everyone broke out in cheers and clapping.

Luella went over the paperwork and wrote a nice big check for the entire amount. She understood what her parents were trying to accomplish. They always taught a simple truth. You don't give until it hurts, you give until it feels good. It felt good.

The entire island spent another day in celebration. Moses gave anyone who wanted, a ride up and down the road. The back of the truck never lacked for passengers. That evening he delivered all the food and people back to the beach for another party. More dancing, more roasted pig, more rum and more laughter. It was a day that Mayreau had never known.

Tuesday the weather changed. Gone was the bright sunshine, the sweet breezes and the and gaily colored flowers. The lemon meringue cottage took on a jaundiced look. Luella had a sense of foreboding and couldn't clearly describe her feelings. Even the children held back from the usual football with the neighbor kids. By midafternoon it happened.

Moses knocked firmly on their cottage door. "May I come in?" He didn't wait for an answer but stepped into the front meeting room. "I'm afraid I have some serious news."

"What's wrong?" Tom wasn't sure what to expect.

"The check you wrote on Monday is bad. No account exists by that number. The dealer won't take the truck back. You need to pay today or you will be detained here in Mayreau until you arrange full payment." Moses continued. "We don't have any means to pay for this, it is your responsibility. I'm sure you understand the seriousness of this."

Luella felt sick to her stomach. The account was bad. First, they let the people of Mayreau down because he didn't come to teach, and now this. Was the whole thing fraud? Did Roy and Lola know about this? Did someone steal the money? Did her sisters know about this? She owed twenty-seven thousand dollars to a car dealer in St. Vincent, and she had no simple way of paying. She suddenly felt nauseous and dizzy.

Chapter 35

El Perrito

Our envy of others devours us most of all. —
Aleksandr Solzhenitsyn

The helicopter operating under the authority of the Mexican military left Nogales with Espinosa on board along with two armed guards, Emilio Sanchez, head of the Party of the Democratic Revolution, and the pilot. The pilot registered a flight plan, heading 121 degrees southeast out of Nogales toward Monterrey, Mexico. This route took them directly over the state of Chihuahua. From Monterrey, they planned to land and transfer to a fixed wing aircraft with a destination of Mexico City. In Mexico City authorities were expected to apprehend Javier Espinosa, charging him with drug trafficking, murder, and a laundry list of other charges.

Putting Espinosa on board was risky to everyone involved. Releasing him to Mexican authorities concerned the United States and the DEA because they weren't sure who was on the cartel payroll. There was always speculation, but nothing could be proven. Many believed Emilio Sanchez was corrupt at some level, but again US authorities didn't know who owned him. The DEA knew and trusted the pilot. He had cooperated on numerous drug raids along the international border. The guards were unknown; however, with two guards there was less likelihood of problems.

The escort helicopter included a pilot and an independent film crew who were supposed to document the transfer of Javier Espinosa from US authorities to Mexican authorities. For three hundred miles, everything went according to plan.

Espinosa climbed into the transport helicopter and glanced at the people surrounding him. He couldn't recognize the pilot due to flight gear, helmet, and goggles. He knew Sanchez from past business arrangements. He could be relied upon to a point. The guards were likewise unrecognizable from his perspective, but that didn't mean they weren't under his influence. Once he was in his seat, the guards handcuffed him, binding his hands to rigging within the cockpit. A flight harness was placed over his shoulders, and he was securely strapped into this seat. One guard sat to his left and one behind him, each with automatic weapons. Emilio Sanchez as the ranking government official sat in the comfortable copilot seat. He had unrestricted two-way communication with the pilot and the guards. Espinosa was given hearing protection only, no communications capabilities. He didn't care; he was going home, or at least south of the border.

One hour into the flight the pilot began to relax. The guards remained vigilant and Sanchez simply enjoyed the view. He believed his participation in this prisoner transport would boost his standing with the US government and the Mexican government as well. Corruption meant little to any of them. The DEA knew corrupt officials and used it to their advantage. The drug cartel knew someone could be bought. It was money and power for the cartel if they delivered and death if they didn't. The Mexicans assumed everyone was corrupt, but they didn't always know who pulled the strings.

One of the guards checked his watch and activated the small discreet GPS device on his other wrist. Keeping a close eye on their position, he gave a single hand signal to the other guard. It was simple and professional, no wasted action or words. Guard number two took out a 9mm handgun and shot Sanchez in the back of the head. Before the blood began to run down the inside of the cockpit, the gun was trained on the pilot. He ordered the pilot to put the aircraft into autopilot hover mode. Then the pilot was efficiently dispatched as well. They were over the drop site. As the first guard unlocked the handcuffs from Espinosa, guard number two strapped on parachutes. Espinosa and guard number one were secured to one another in a double jump harness. Guard number two radioed the ground crew. At his signal, antiaircraft missiles and tracer rounds were fired in the direction of the escort helicopter. The plan was to fire close enough to force them off course but not to down the aircraft. International confirmation that Espinosa had escaped was essential.

Once the escort helicopter had retreated to a reasonable distance, they jumped. Espinosa who had no experience jumping out of aircraft was secured to a guard, and it appeared only two people had jumped out of the helicopter. Once they reached a predetermined drop altitude, they triggered on board explosives, and the helicopter was destroyed. Simple and efficient. The guards were professional at every level.

The drop site was a high mesa in the mountains out of the normal commercial flight patterns. It allowed for an unobstructed landing for experienced jumpers and a quick departure. Multiple military style vehicles were present at the drop site, but once their cargo was safely stowed, they split up, making it harder for satellite imagery to follow every possible escape vehicle.

Two hours from the drop, the truck carrying Espinosa slowed and took a sharp turn into the mountains. It pulled to a stop inside a tunnel area out of view from satellite surveillance. The mountain hideaway was equipped with radar and radio signal jamming capabilities. The entire complex was underground in the mountains, eliminating detection from infrared imaging. It had every intelligence measure and counter measure known to the Mexican military, but it wasn't military. It was the latest development by a rising power in the drug trafficking business. El Perrito's home base in the mountainous state of Chihuahua was well designed and almost completely unknown to most of the organized world. El Chico was the unwitting decoy, drawing attention from US and Mexican authorities. With so much attention elsewhere, Pancho Hernandez, El Perrito, had time and room to grow. This was his moment, his time to shine.

The mountain hideaway was nothing more than a carefully hidden bunker with exquisite attention to detail. State of the art electronic monitoring was present at every level. Facial recognition, retinal scans, satellite surveillance, audio and video transmission intercept capabilities and direct interface with law enforcement allowed Hernandez to follow his enemies and competitors in real time. Besides state of the art counterintelligence, it was a palace for the king. Luxury accommodations allowed him to remain hidden yet lacked nothing to satisfy his personal needs. State of the art food preparation, water sanitation and big screen entertainment met his every whim. Fresh seafood, dry aged beef and top of the line French and California wines were flown in regularly for his personal use and the entertainment of police, military, and government officials on his payroll. He enjoyed the finest aged Scotch and Irish whiskey as well as barrels of aged tequila.

The underground bunker had facilities so his guards and associates could be trained in the most rigorous fashion and to the highest level. Former Navy Seals and Special Forces operatives were employed as trainers of his own private military force. They were widely equipped with the latest and finest lethal weaponry available. Some of his operatives had weapons exceeding the capabilities of US Army Rangers. Pancho Hernandez was a country unto himself, and he was the king. It was this kingdom that hosted Javier Espinosa, El Chico.

The security team placed Espinosa deep inside the well-secured inner suite complex. It was complete with every comfort to which he had grown accustomed in his home state of Sinaloa. The bar was well stocked with his favorite drinks. Chefs and waiters were always ready to serve whatever he desired. No windows opened to the outside world, but large floor to ceiling flat screen monitors displayed live images through direct-feed high-resolution cameras. A climate control system automatically managed every nuance of the environment for the comfort of the guest. Four large diesel generators provided all the electrical needs of the miniature kingdom deep within the state of Chihuahua, Mexico.

Designed for the comfort and safety of Hernandez, it was also meant as a demonstration of power and influence. He expected El Chico to recognize his inferior position although he wouldn't likely accept it. During his detention by the Americans, Javier Espinosa, the feared drug lord, had lost much. Everything he lost, Pancho Hernandez had gained.

Espinosa's time in the American prison system did little to dull his pride and arrogance. He went to the bar and pulled out a bottle of the rarest aged tequila and poured himself a glass. Turning he looked directly into the surveillance camera and lifted his glass as if to salute his captors. He tipped the glass back and with one swallow emptied it. There was little else to do except wait. He wondered what the next move would be.

Hernandez and his people monitored the international news organizations, but no real information was forthcoming. It was a simple rehash of old news, differing opinions, and verbal tirades from low life elected pawns. Such public ranting did little to curb crime or limit criminals. Its sole purpose was to increase the public image of senators, congressmen and women and improve their chances at being reelected in the upcoming election cycle. It also boosted viewership and television ratings. More viewers meant more advertising revenue. Every new crisis delivered more time on Facebook, increased use of Twitter and every other social media outlet. People may talk about and pray for world peace, but if it truly happened, the economy would collapse. Every government needed a crisis, and every crisis needed someone like Dag Rasmussen deciding when and who would push the panic button. Pancho Hernandez sat back and watched. He felt no urgency to go anywhere or do anything.

Nearly every major media outlet tried to get Dag Rasmussen to comment on the current clash with Mexican and Columbian drug lords. He wouldn't comment. Reporters tried cornering him, shoving cell phones, microphones, and every mobile recording device into this personal space, but they didn't get much in return. He grunted for FOX news, he grinned on CNN and for the three network television stations he gave his nose an old-fashioned farmer blow—on live TV. Every possible interview was given the same response, no comment. If Pancho Hernandez wasn't concerned about El Chico, neither was Dag Rasmussen. They both knew exactly where he was.

CNN ranted and raved about the complete failure of American diplomacy in capturing Espinosa, even highlighting the likelihood of illegal activity on the part of American operatives. Dag Rasmussen and his DEA counterintelligence operation were emasculated on public television. Some left-leaning senators called for an immediate bipartisan congressional investigation into the actions of the DEA, FBI, CIA, and any other clandestine organization. Ultra-conservatives called for private citizens to arm themselves and take the law into their own hands if they or their communities felt threatened. Some ranted about government's failure to provide protection from lawless drug dealers. Libertarians fussed and fumed about the total lack of respect for a person's right to privacy. Even international criminals have a right to protection from illegal search and seizure. It seemed, no one was happy now that El Chico foiled the authorities and escaped in dramatic fashion on live television.

Javier Espinosa spent three days in his private suite without any outside contact other than his private butler and servants. He didn't suffer. Each morning he enjoyed crepes Suzette with fresh fruit, mimosas made with Dom Perignon and fresh squeezed orange juice. He preferred European cigarettes but smoked the Cuban cigars brought to him from outside. Lunches he ordered grilled cold-water lobster and drawn butter, with grilled asparagus, shallots, garlic, and coarse pink Himalayan salt. Perfectly complemented by a chilled white Bordeaux which was a blend of sauvignon blanc and semillon grapes. He also requested his daily shot of Rey Sol Anejo tequila. Rare and exceedingly fine in quality, priced at four hundred US dollars per bottle, he bragged how he and his wife bathed in it on their wedding night. Evenings he requested and dined on Wagyu beef, perfectly grilled to a medium rare and served with a ten-year-old Cliff Family Estate California cabernet, chilled slightly to 62 degrees. Evenings, he completed his day with a cup of caramelized flan topped with Cognac and another Cuban cigar. If he suffered at all, it was from over indulgence and lack of social interaction. He talked to no one, and no one talked to him other than his server. They were forbidden to interact other than to take his personal request for food and drink, nothing else.

Three days stretched into four and five and finally into seven days. Javier Espinosa was ruthless and worldly, but he was also suspicious and superstitious. He had a thing about numbers, and Pancho Hernandez knew this. On the morning of the seventh day, the server didn't appear. Hernandez took his place. El Perrito walked into the suite to a rather surprised guest.

Pancho greeted Espinosa pleasantly. "Buenos dias, good morning." Not waiting for a response, he chose a seat on an overstuffed tan-colored, ostrich leather chair with large rolled arms and a place to rest his feet. He stretched back, relaxing. Lighting a cigarette, he inhaled deeply and smiled. Reaching into his pocket, Pancho offered his own brand of cigarettes to Espinosa. Javier took one and lit it.

"So, we finally meet." Espinosa smiled at his captor. He inhaled deeply and smoke curled slowly out of his nostrils and dissipated into the air ducts. "Thank you for your hospitality; it has been quite pleasant. I would have enjoyed the company of a woman, but sacrifices must be made. Times aren't what they were, yes?"

Hernandez studied his competitor carefully as a rattlesnake coiled and waiting for the best time to strike. For a week he had watched every move Espinosa made. Espinosa was dangerous,

304

cruel, and cold as ice. He was known to kill women and children wantonly if it gave him benefit, hiding behind the idea that it wasn't personal, it was business. For Hernandez, it was both.

After a long pause interrupted only by smoking and sips of tequila, Hernandez spoke. "I have a business proposition for you."

"What makes you think we can work together?"

"Amigo, we both want the same thing. Together we can control much more. Rather than split the country, we can own the entire region." Hernandez spoke with passion. The rise and fall of his voice reminded Espinosa of Hitler or Stalin rousing the populace.

"What about the Americans?"

"What about them?"

"They have money and power, they could wipe us out if they choose."

Hernandez laughed. He knew El Chico was right, but he also understood what Espinosa did not. "The Americans are weak. They don't have a heart for fighting. They play a game of politics with their own people. If you want to get elected, you must give the people the illusion of power and control and money. Make promises on election day and afterwards throw them a bone."

"What do you mean?"

"They have hundreds of thousands of people trying to escape from reality. If it isn't the drugs we supply, then it is alcohol or pornography or video games or something else to ease the pain of living. Politicians want happy people and will give them anything as long as they can control it. They need us to send the drugs; they can't do it themselves." Hernandez spoke as if he had studied political science and human psychology. He had a great deal of wisdom and insight about human behavior.

"What do you want from me?"

"I have the names and personal phone numbers of US senators and managers in the CIA, FBI, DEA, state and local law enforcement and everywhere in between. I want your contacts, the names of your key people here and in America. If we combine our resources, we can be unstoppable." Pancho took another drag on his cigarette and got up from the ostrich leather chaise lounge. He walked to one of the high definition monitors and stood as if looking down the valley.

Javier responded, "I know the Americans too. We have tunnels, we have contacts, we have shipping options by land and sea. How can I trust you?" He resented being second place.

"We are brothers, you and I." Pancho Hernandez looked at his guest through partially closed eyes. Words may say one thing, but actions and body language another.

This time it was Espinosa's turn to laugh. He didn't expect to leave here alive and was surprised he had been treated so well. "I have unfinished business. I need to repay a favor for my holiday in America."

"We can work together."

"This is my battle. My revenge. I will finish it." Javier took a sheet of paper and wrote some names and directions. Folding the note, he sealed it inside an envelope. "Deliver this to my people. Cocos Helados on the Malecón. When it is finished, we will talk."

Chapter 36

Where the Wind Blows

In God, we trust; all others must pay cash. —American Proverb

Notifying Luella and Vera about the misprinted checks proved troublesome. International calling wasn't successful. Emails went unanswered. Facebook instant messaging wasn't working either. Olivia checked her email inbox several times daily, but there was no response. Finally, she gave up and went about her own business. She reasoned, that if her sisters were having some type of trouble, they would be the ones to try and contact her. But on the other hand, if they wrote bad checks it could cause problems.

"Emma, what do you think we should do? I have been trying to contact Lu and Vera but neither of them have answered." Olivia got up from her desk in the corner of the sitting room and flopped onto the couch where Emma sat holding the baby.

"Have you heard from anyone?" Emma asked.

"The only emails I have received over the last two days were spam and two messages from someone named Moses Sinclair which I deleted. Probably a computer virus or a 'rich Nigerian uncle' who wants to share the wealth." Olivia sighed.

"I guess I wouldn't worry about it. If they have problems, they can call us."

"Yeah, I guess so, but still..." She never finished her thought because her laptop computer beeped indicating a Facebook instant message. It was Vera. Olivia looked at the message.

Vera typed, "The checks are bad. Do you think this whole thing is a fraud?"

Olivia wrote back. "I just got a letter from the bank in Zurich. It was a printing mistake. The account is good. The checks had the wrong account number printed so they are void."

"So, the money is good?"

"Yes, but you need different checks."

"Oh, thank God...I was thinking something much worse."

"Well, I'm glad you guys are fine. I'm worried about Lu. Been trying to get in touch with her but no luck. Do you know anything about where they were going?" Olivia was hoping one of her sisters might have some idea about making contact.

"No, sorry. All I recall is that they were going to Mayreau in the Caribbean."

"Well...you have a good time, and I hope it works out OK without the checks until you get home." Olivia logged out and checked her email account. Still nothing.

#

Luella felt strangely uncomfortable. Her brief fainting was nothing compared to the heartache and nausea she felt once she was revived. Once she had a parking ticket she forgot to pay but nothing worse. No disorderly conduct, no breaking and entering, no fraud and abuse so the thought of being charged with writing a bad check in a foreign country, for more than twenty-seven thousand dollars was unsettling. That was fraud in a very bad way.

"Moses, do you have international phone service here in Mayreau?" Tom spoke up. Luella was not thinking clearly.

"Yes, we do, but service is sporadic depending on weather and tower signals."

"I need to make an international phone call with one of your phones. Mine doesn't have any service here." Tom checked his phone. The battery had died two days ago anyway.

"Yes, you can use one of our phones, but I assume you can pay for the phone call?" Moses was suddenly quite skeptical about the Tinker family. "I don't want to arrest you." Moses Sinclair was the governor, the Pentecostal preacher, and the sheriff.

Tom dialed the international codes, and Olivia's personal cell phone number. The recorded answer came back 'the number you have called is not in service.' He tried one more time, hoping the signal would go through successfully, but the fourth time was the same.

"Do you have internet service?"

"Yes, we do, but that is troublesome as well. You can use the computer at my home."

Knowing that Vera was in Thailand, he sent a message to Olivia. It was simple and straight to the point. 'The Swiss bank account is no good. We wrote a check for twenty-seven thousand dollars, and it won't clear. We need to pay the money as soon as possible, or we could be arrested for writing bad checks. Luella can't leave the island until we pay. Call or email as soon as you can so we can get this straightened out. Tom'. It was direct enough. No need to chat about the weather; they needed money clear and simple.

Until they had a way to pay the money there was little else they could do. Luella remained hidden in their little mustard colored cottage, embarrassed to be seen outside for fear of being labeled a fraud. Their kids played with the other kids of the island. Maddie had finished her book. She was looking for something else to read and decided to check out the school, hoping to borrow something.

Tom and Luella checked email twice daily, but there was no answer. By the third day, Tom and Luella were feeling very isolated and alone.

A great weight of guilt brought on by mistaken identity, check fraud and isolation in a foreign land, pressed on them both, but Tom decided to do something positive. Wandering up to the school, he met the one and only teacher present on the island, a young woman named Lillian. Her blue dress was the same as the uniforms for the students. Her glasses and hair pulled back into a neat bun gave her a professional look, like the librarian back in the school where Tom taught. When the students were on break, Tom asked her a few questions.

"Is it possible that I could help teach here at the school while we are on the island?"

She seemed surprised that he was willing to do that after the embarrassment of the public announcement on Sunday. "I don't think there would be any problem, but we can't pay you. That would have to be arranged through the government office for the school system in St. Vincent."

"I have no intention of asking for pay. I feel as though I need to do something positive. Especially after the events of the past couple days." Tom lowered his eyes to the ground. Lillian was sensitive to his embarrassment and looked away.

"We are supposed to have two teachers here; we have only one. I am a certified elementary teacher. I understand you teach math?"

"Yes, I am a high school math teacher." He stepped aside to let the old classroom dog find his way outside. His experiences at teaching didn't usually include resident pets with the freewill to come and go as they pleased.

"Would you like to start in an hour? The kids will be back from their lunch."

"Yes...I will be glad to start. I don't have a school uniform though." He hoped that wouldn't be a deterrent to his teaching. He had no doubt the children would pay attention to him. He was a novelty. A tall, skinny, white guy with a Midwestern accent, teaching math in an island world. It would be fun.

Luella was relieved they were finally doing something positive. If Tom felt guilty, she felt doubly so. All of this was her idea. Her family was the reason behind their folly. Despite their missteps, she appreciated the kindness and acceptance the islanders had shown to them.

She used the phone that had been offered by Moses. On the second try she got through. She was never so happy to hear her sister's voice as she was at that moment.

"Olivia, I'm so glad to finally talk to you." She almost didn't know where to begin. "Tom and I are stuck here on Mayreau…" She proceeded to tell the entire story, complete with the pig roast, the mistaken identity, and the problem of being on island arrest until she could pay for the truck. Olivia couldn't help but laugh. Lu was always the one in charge but also the dramatic one. Olivia thought it would have been fun to watch her squirm, but she quickly put the thought aside. Her sister needed help, and right now she was the only one who could do something about it.

"Hey, Lu, I have a plan that might work." She grabbed a scrap of paper to jot down a couple of notes. "I have the new checks from the Swiss bank in my name. I will write a check and deposit it into the account at your bank. Once that check clears, you have access to the funds, and you can write a check from your personal account to the dealer for the truck. Just give me your checking account number, and I can do it today."

"I think that will work. How long do you think it would take for the check to clear?" As Olivia talked, she looked longingly out to sea toward the neighboring islands. Stuck in paradise sounds delightful in theory, but she had a sudden flood of homesickness.

"I can ask at the bank, but I suspect it will be five days or more because it is an international account." Olivia wrote down the checking account number from Luella and stuck it on the refrigerator with a plastic pineapple magnet. "Also, I have been trying to send you emails, but you aren't responding. Are you getting them?"

"No. Like an idiot we changed our email and forgot to tell you. Here it is..." She spelled it out so there wouldn't be any more mistakes. Finally, they were back on track to do what they originally came to do and that was help someone less fortunate. She had discovered that helping people isn't as easy as it sounds. "Olivia, there is one more thing which is very important. Can you call Tom's school and let the principal know Tom can't leave until about seven days from today? They will have to get a substitute teacher until we can get home."

"What should I tell them?"

"Tell them, we got arrested."

Olivia made the same arrangements with her sister Vera in Chiang Mai. Once the issue of bad checks was resolved, they took advantage of Crandall and his wife Nuch. Under the watchful guidance of their hosts, they enjoyed the sights and sounds of the area. On the third day, they finally met the young refugee, Chuenchai Bunyasarn.

Vera was short by Midwestern standards, but she towered over Cheunchai. Barely scratching four foot ten standing on her tiptoes, she was a wisp of a woman. Despite being in her early twenties, Cheunchai had the look of a girl just entering junior high school.

Richard appeared as a giant beside her. His six-foot-two, wide-shouldered frame cast a dominating shadow over her. Yet even in that shadow, Cheunchai appeared strong and indomitable. Her bright and quick eyes took in everything. Her arrow straight posture identified a will to live and do it to the fullest possible in her circumstances. Richard and Vera had no easy way to understand the difficulties she must have faced, but they felt immediately drawn to her and accepted by her.

"Cheunchai... I hope I am saying your name right. My parents helped to sponsor you when you were in the refugee camp. Do you know anything about this?" Vera was hopeful her explanations made sense.

"Yes, I remember." They were quite surprised at her command of English. Although broken, it was very understandable. She appeared reserved. Vera realized this wasn't going to be a chatty afternoon.

"My parents died last year. They asked us to try and find you and help you if we can."

"I am sorry your parents died. My parents have been dead many years. I have new parents here." Nodding toward Nuch and Crandall. They had a look of mild surprise at being called parents, but Cheunchai likely had another name for them in her native language. Nevertheless, it was an adequate translation, and they accepted the title.

"Cheunchai, we came here to help you. We have money to give you, but if you prefer, we can give it to Crandall and Nuch. They can give it to you as you need it." Richard stopped to think for a minute. Then he added something they hadn't discussed yet. "Would you consider coming to America to live? If you want, we might be able to help."

Although Cheunchai may have considered it in the past, she gave no indication. She was quiet for many minutes then looked out toward the fields. "Do you see the flowers?" They looked where she pointed and nodded yes. Everyone could see the multicolored flowers, some tall, some short, some brilliant and some rather drab. "The wind blows the seeds into the field, and they grow. If you dig the flowers up, and move them somewhere else they might bloom as bright, but they might die. My teacher taught me to bloom where you are planted."

Everyone understood her point. Whether her wisdom was from Buddhist teaching or from an insightful schoolteacher didn't matter. It was clear and appropriate. The wind had blown her here, and she was trying her best to bloom despite rocky soil and adverse conditions. It was a good lesson to take home.

Despite the calm reserved nature of her Asian culture, it was the love and acceptance of a young child that opened her heart. Daisy, without saying a word, walked up to Cheunchai, and opened her arms. Hugging was foreign to the Burmese girl, but she welcomed it and melted in the acceptance and unconditional love of a young child. For the first time since she was a young child herself, Cheunchai cried.

When Vera, Richard and Daisy left Thailand and returned to the United States, they took with them much more than they left behind. They understood the resilience of the flower blooming where it was planted, despite harsh conditions. They understood love and acceptance, and they understood helping people doesn't always have to include money and material things. The simple unconditional hug of a child was far more valuable than thousands of dollars. It didn't erase years of hardship or an uncertain future, but it did give Cheunchai hope that no matter what happened she wouldn't be alone.

Chapter 37

Love Your Neighbor

Never to suffer would be never to have been blessed. —
Edgar Allen Poe

If donating the Ambrose inheritance did nothing but challenge
their comfort zones, then it was worth the effort. Tom jumped into
the island teacher position with energy and excitement he hadn't
felt in years of high school teaching. It was so refreshing to see students interested in learning. His uniqueness as a teacher may have
helped, but there was a different atmosphere on Mayreau compared to his home school. In his high school, the students were
more interested in prom dates, Facebook, and smart phones than
they were in school. The threat of violence was becoming more
real every day. Any attempts at discipline in the high school were
apt to be countered with threats from the students. School shoot-
ings brought new anxiety to teachers trying to do their job well. It
was always somewhere else, but everyone knew it could happen at

home. Instead of fire drills, they practiced school lock-downs and evading terrorists. School security measures and one-size fits all rules were applied without exception.

Once the truck payment was satisfied, apologies were issued and forgiveness bestowed upon the Tinkers. They returned to Wisconsin, changed within. Their American way of buying and working and being enslaved to the ticking clock every waking moment was seriously challenged during their relatively brief island stay.

Getting ready for school one morning after they returned to Wisconsin, Tom scurried about trying to find his car keys. Already late, he took one last slurp of his morning coffee. Luella bumped his arm and the coffee splashed onto his good jacket. It was cold outside and leaving the house in winter without a coat was foolish, especially up north. He grabbed his camouflage duck-hunting jacket and rushed out the door.

Arriving just in time, he flashed his magnetic ID badge at the monitor and hurried down the hallway toward his classroom. The school district administrator was giving a guided tour of the facility to several school board members and a representative from the state department of education. Tom did his best to slide past them in the hall, but he was one of the more seasoned teachers in the district and one of the board members wanted to ask him a quick question. He had his hands in his jacket pocket. As he pulled his hand out of the pocket to greet the guests, he immediately knew he was in trouble.

The button on his shirt cuff caught on the lanyard of his duck call. Like a stack of dominos, the duck call pulled out of the pocket followed by three shotgun shells. Spilling onto the floor for all the world to see, was live ammunition. Bringing ammunition onto public school property was serious. It was grounds for felony charges. Regardless of intent, the laws and rules accepted by the school board were clear. Tom was in trouble. The administrator knew Tom and realized there was no malicious intent, but he was bound by the law especially when scrutinized by the school board members and state officials. Everyone stared at the administrator and the administrator stared at Tom. Attempts at explanation were futile, he was guilty until proven innocent.

One shotgun shell was worse than a bale of marijuana. With marijuana, he could argue it was for personal use and get off with a slap on the wrist, and a misdemeanor charge if anything. Not so the shotgun shell. Ammunition on school property carried a mandatory 911 call and a school lock-down. The police escorted him to the police station in handcuffs. The world stood by and watched. He made the evening news in Milwaukee and Madison. Twitter and Facebook comments went wild. Conservatives protested, and the NRA threatened to sue the school district, the administrator, and the Department of Public Instruction.

Despite being a teacher in good standing and a member of the teacher's union, no one was willing to defend him. He was suspended with pay until he had a preliminary hearing in court. His attorney argued for a dismissal of charges because there was no intent to cause harm. Ironically the district attorney, a hunter and sportsman himself, agreed in principle, but he was bound by state law, which required mandatory charges in a situation such as this.

Then the state got involved. They argued it would be impossible to get an unbiased jury in rural Wisconsin because surveys showed ninety-eight percent of people thought he was innocent and seventy-six percent of homes in the county owned firearms. The state filed a motion to move the trial to Madison. Tom's attorney countered that there was a greater chance of antifirearm bias, filed a motion to counter the motion filed by the state. It degenerated into a national debate on school safety in rural areas. Before two weeks had passed CNN, FOX News and several local television stations came knocking.

Within a year, Tom and Luella had lost parents and run afoul of the law on two separate occasions, first with social services and now with a shotgun shell in his pocket. As a result, each of them had lost a job, a job they loved. He had enough. After two months of legal haggling and public embarrassment, Tom accepted a plea bargain and agreed he would not seek damages from the school district. He resigned from the school with all pay and benefits through the current date, and the state dropped all charges. Common sense was put on the shelf, and everyone lost. The students lost a great and dedicated teacher, the school district lost a solid family dedicated to education and community, and Tom lost his faith in the American justice system.

Some people protested by tossing road kill into their yard and putting up 'Killer' signs along their driveway. But like most things in America, the furor died down, and people went back to the next social crisis on Facebook. Then reality struck him. No one really cared, they just pretended to care. No one offered real help or assistance. No one tried to make a real difference. Despite being unemployed and socially eviscerated, no one cared enough to drop off a single pineapple upside-down cake.

If you lost your spouse to cancer, someone might drop off a tuna casserole. If you lost your arm at the cheese factory, you got disability and a severance package. If you lost your job, your social standing, and your self-respect, you got a dead woodchuck and a 'killer' sign in the yard. It suddenly dawned on him what Roy and Lola were trying to accomplish. Tossing a couple of tens in the offering plate did nothing. Sending a check overseas to an organization did the same. It was the up close and personal stuff that really changed lives. Now, he and Luella not only understood it, they felt it.

The Tinker family quietly moved out of their home. With the permission of the rest of the family they moved up to Namukwa and stayed in the old home place. It needed the sound of children and the smell of pancakes again. Their house sold within a month of listing with Century 21. Maddie, Zoe, and Theo were enrolled in the local school district, and Tom was regarded as a folk hero by the locals. People dropped by with smoked suckers and turkey legs and cold venison sausages.

Luella took a part time job as a school nurse in Namukwa. Her biggest problem as a nurse wasn't the latest medical treatment or procedure. It was head lice, and kids who didn't have running water, and kids who came to school without coats or socks or even underwear.

Tom volunteered at the local food shelf, and he came to love the people who stopped by. He and Luella made it their personal agenda to keep the food shelf operating and well stocked. Many weekends found them traveling to Duluth or Wausau to the big warehouse stores, shopping for the county. And true to the word of Roy and Lola, the more they gave, the more they got. They never lacked for anything and the relationships they made were priceless.

One evening after raiding Roy's wine cellar, they sat around the fireplace reminiscing. "Lu, do you ever think we were supposed to do this?"

"What do you mean?" Luella was feeling relaxed and dreamy in the dancing firelight.

"Well...do you believe in fate or purpose or some great design?" he paused and sipped. The French Beaujolais was delightful even on a cold night. "Do you think all of this was meant to be? Just the way it is?" He tipped his glass admiring the clarity of the red wine against the fire.

"Do I have to answer that?" She rubbed her eyes and turned back to the fire.

"You grew up going to church and all. I never did. How did you make sense of it all? It seems so complicated to me." Tom wasn't interested in solving the world's problems, but he was hoping for clarity.

"Well, let me tell you what my dad always told us. I'm not saying he was the brightest bulb on the tree, but he had a way of making complicated things easier to understand." Luella recalled many discussions around the supper table on ethics, religion, politics, free will, and who was most likely going to win the Super Bowl.

"So, what did he say?" Tom swirled his wine and stared at the red circular current in his glass.

"My dad always claimed it was simple enough even the people with limited intelligence could understand it, and so complicated that it would take a thousand lifetimes to begin to scratch the surface. He said the basic truth in life was 'Love God and Love your Neighbor.' When you break it down to that, he said we all do the same thing, we just do it in different ways." Luella hoped she didn't distort her dad's theology too much. "That way, no one is more important than anyone else because we all have the same job to do. Does that help?"

Tom was beginning to understand, but another glass of wine might help.

Chapter 38

Coffee Time

The world is a book, and those who don't travel only read one
page. —Augustine of Hippo

The winter was passing quickly, and Molly felt sorry for herself.
Auntie Vera and Uncle Richard and Daisy went to Thailand and
rode on elephants. Uncle Tom lost his job, and they moved to Papa
and Grammy's house. Auntie Luella was 'arrested' for writing bad
checks, and Maddie, Zoe and Theo played soccer on a tropical island and swam in the ocean with sharks. Molly helped Auntie
Emma with baby Beatrice, and she helped Uncle Phineas design
birdhouses, and she talked to Daddy about the cows, but she didn't
think she was having any fun. She wanted to go somewhere too.

"Hey, Uncle Phineas, can we go see some monkeys?" Molly figured talking to Uncle Phineas was the best way to get anything
done. When she asked Dad, he always said, "Go ask your mom,"
and when she asked Mom, she always said, "Go ask your dad."

Auntie Emma was busy with the baby so when she wanted to do something, she asked Uncle Phineas.

"Do you want to go to the zoo?"

"No. I want to go see monkeys where they live. In the trees."

"Emma, Molly and I want to go to Costa Rica and see the monkeys. What do you think?" It was always better to ask a difficult question if it appeared to come from a child. Phineas was learning the nuances of marriage.

Coincidentally, Costa Rica was the home of Isabella Matamoras, one of the children sponsored by the Ambrose family. She had been twelve years old when she was orphaned. Her parents had died from dengue hemorrhagic fever, a life-threatening viral illness transmitted by mosquitos.

"When?" Emma put Beatrice on the rug and stood by the sink, washing her hands. "Are you thinking of doing this now or sometime in the future?" First-time moms aren't typically enthralled with the idea of world-wide adventure, but she wasn't totally against the idea either.

"I was invited to speak at the University of Costa Rica in San Jose. They have a general conference on bird migration and reproduction in the setting of climate change. The sponsors of the conference liked my research. It's three days long, but I would be scheduled only one of those days. We might be able to find the girl your parents mentioned in their will, Isabella Matamoras." Phineas was already planning the trip; he just needed confirmation from the boss. Turning toward the kitchen, he yelled through the open door. "Hey, Olivia. Would you and Harry and Molly be interested in going to Costa Rica with us?"

Olivia quit chopping vegetables for an Asian stir-fry and stuck her head into the front room. She waved the big kitchen knife around and replied, "I'm game to go anytime, but I can't answer for Harry. When are you thinking about doing this?"

"The conference is next month."

It didn't take Harry too long to decide. He rescheduled some cattle breeding, and they made serious plans to head south. It was nearing spring break, which didn't typically affect travel to San Jose, Costa Rica. With the misprinted check problems resolved, they felt confident about the trip.

First class tickets all around, even baby Mary Beatrice. Molly got to sit in her own big seat and watch as many movies as she wanted on the trip. The nice flight attendants brought her all the crackers and juice she could possibly ingest over six hours. The group flew into Vera, North Carolina, and then switched planes. Despite minor turbulence, it was one of the easiest trips any of them had made. Molly fell sound asleep just before landing, and Dad carried her through baggage claim and customs.

Phineas was scheduled to speak on the first day of the conference. It was held at the Marriott, which overlooked an old coffee plantation on the edge of modern San Jose. While Phineas spoke about the birds and their music preferences, the rest of them gathered on the patio near the pool or in a small coffee shop serving fresh roasted Costa Rican coffee and wonderful pastries.

For nearly two hours they relaxed, enjoying the warm air and the wonderful coffee aromas. The young woman waiting on them was very attentive to their needs, and she spoke excellent English. After about an hour she came back to their table to check on them.

"Do you know those men sitting over there under the shade?" Maria the waitress spoke quietly and nodded in the direction of the men.

"No, we don't know anyone here. Why?" Harry glanced in their direction while sipping his coffee.

"They were asking about you. They offered me money for information."

"About us?" Olivia couldn't imagine why anyone from Costa Rica would wonder about them.

Emma spoke up. "What were they asking?" She lifted Beatrice to her breast and began nursing.

"They asked if your name was Ambrose."

"Why would someone from Costa Rica want to know if our family name was Ambrose?" Olivia looked across the table toward Emma and Harry.

Marie, the waitress, overheard her question and responded. "Miss, those men aren't from Costa Rica."

"How do you know?

"I am from here. They speak differently. You may not notice their accent, but it is obvious to us."

"Where are they from?"

"Mexico."

Chapter 39

Confession

Nearly all men can stand adversity, but if you want to test a man's character, give him power. —Abraham Lincoln

Compared to all the notes and all the contacts Martin Garza had made over the past couple of years, this one seemed different. He couldn't point to any objective evidence to prove it was different, but he had a feeling, a gut feeling you get when something is about to happen. It was a small note in a simple envelope much like the others. It didn't smell different, and there were no red lipstick prints on the outside, but he knew it was different.

Word on the Malecón was all about the daring escape of El Chico, leaping out of a helicopter just before it burst into flames. For some it was a sign from God; for others it was the devil himself. Either way the dramatic escape had set the city on edge. More than a week since the big story, no word was heard from the drug lord. Whether his lieutenants knew something or not was irrelevant to Martin Garza. He was the mail boy, the go-between, and nothing more. However, he reminded himself, he was a bottle-neck for information between the Americans, El Chico and his drug cartel, and Hernandez and the Chihuahua drug cartel. He didn't expect to live to a ripe old age. There was too much against him. He knew nothing, but he knew too much.

#

When Espinosa wrote the note, he had little hope it would be delivered and less hope it would be carried out. However, he was a marked person and had virtually no chance of getting home alive. His best opportunity remained with Hernandez. If Espinosa could convince the Chihuahua cartel he was an asset rather than a competitor, there was a slim hope. He also realized his current situation put him into a subservient role. He was no longer top dog, and never would be if El Perrito held all the cards.

When he handed the note off, he knew someone along the way was going to read it. There was no way he could send a coded message to his enforcers and expect them to win his release from the mountain top prison. But he still had his chance at revenge.

Old man Ambrose was gone, but Espinosa wasn't satisfied. He had been the king of the mountain. Now the king was deposed and exiled, and he didn't like it. Beneath his icy façade, fierce anger and hatred burned in his veins. Ambrose had kids. They might be innocent as little lambs, but sometimes lambs get sacrificed. At his peak power, El Chico could have sent death squads into the US and simply executed the entire family. Now his power was com-promised, but he held onto the idea of getting at least one of those little lambs. It was a scorched earth idea. But if he couldn't be happy, no one would be happy.

The note was simple and straightforward. Patience was the key to fulfillment. It read: Ambrose children, if they cross the border anywhere, torture and kill them. Hernandez had opened the note and read it after he stepped out of the room from his meeting with Espinosa. Sensing no threat to his position, he handed it off to the courier who would deliver it to Garza. Every person who held the note, read it.

Martin Garza now held the smudged note in his hands, the edges creased from being opened and folded many times. Meant for the boys on the fourteenth floor of the El Presidente, he realized this was important information for the Americans as well. Once the tattered red Peligro flag was tacked on the back of his thatched office, he went to the front door and looked about. He trusted no one, not even the poor fishermen selling shrimp from small brightly colored boats. They were always there, watching. He was never sure if they were watching him or the scantily clad tourists. He didn't care; someone was always watching.

He went to his battered and weathered Cocos Helados sign and turned it to the south, facing the lighthouse. It would be a busy day at the store. He might even sell a T-shirt or two. The early beach walkers went by at a steady pace. They were the retired tourists, desperately hanging onto a waning sense of fitness. Usually it was the women with flowing beach cover-ups, followed by pot-bellied, hunched over, old men with limps, their pockets full of American money and their brains full of memories of how good they were in years past. It was the same most days. Nothing unusual yet.

Three or four tourists were in the store when the coconut truck arrived. No words were spoken, the transaction took place quickly and efficiently. Garza handed the driver a few pesos for the bag of coconuts, with the note discreetly attached. The driver was out of the palapa and back into traffic quickly.

Two of the beach window shoppers left and returned to their beach walk, one young woman in a hot pink bikini remained. A big floppy beach hat shielded her face from Garza as she searched through his wares. She picked out a beach towel displaying the setting sun over the Pacific Ocean. In large bold letters, printed on the towel was Corona. It was just what she wanted.

She draped the towel over her arm. Pushing her beach hat slightly backward she handed Garza a hundred-dollar bill.

"I'm sorry, I can't give you change for a hundred US dollars. This is too much."

"I think you can." She slid the towel back exposing the business end of a 9mm Beretta with silencer attached.

"Take the towel. I have nothing here of value."

"The note?"

"What note?" Garza feigned ignorance, but he knew it was useless.

She moved her wrist and fired the gun. The silenced semiautomatic took out a stack of glazed ceramic pots at the back of the palapa. She moved the gun back in his direction, aiming just below the beltline and asked with her eyes. She raised her thin tweezed eyebrows slightly, but there was no need to speak. Martin Garza answered her question. An hour after the bikini lady, two others arrived asking questions. Garza never made it home for supper that night. Late business meeting.

#

The coconut delivery truck made its way slowly up the malecón, stopping at six other beach vendors, dropping off wares and picking up cash. It was his daily route and part of the cartel's way of laundering money. The driver knew the amount of cash handled by the beach vendors was very small in comparison to the entire operation. But many of the vendors sold prescription drugs, and cocaine along with crystal meth, PCP, and ecstasy. However, the big money was in the American cocaine market across the border from Tijuana into San Diego. From there it went to Los Angeles, Chicago, New York, and places in between. Twenty thousand dollars a day on the beach was nothing compared to the billions made with their neighbors to the north.

The coconut driver skimmed off several one hundred dollar bills and handed the rest to the security guard at the loading dock for the hotel. The note was attached, destined for the fourteenth floor. Emilio Espinosa was waiting.

From the back-door security guards, the note was transferred to one of the lieutenants and carried upstairs to Emilio. With Javier in exile, Emilio was in charge, but he didn't have the iron hand his brother had. Many things had changed. Javier was making contact, which created a new sense of urgency.

Emilio unfolded the note and read it. He understood revenge, and he understood power and control, but he was tired of the killing. Killing more innocent people wasn't going to give them any more money, any more power, any more anything. It didn't prove anything to the Americans or to the Chihuahua cartel. It was simple wanton killing because they could.

Emilio crumpled the note in his hand and threw it into the garbage. Turning his back on the room he lit another cigarette and went to the window. It was his place to think. He was in a prison of his own making, and his thoughts could fly free when he stared out the fourteenth floor window at the limitless expanse of the Pacific. As he drew in another breath his cigarette glowed brightly, reflecting in the window.

One of the enforcers in the room reached into the trash and pulled out the wrinkled note. Recognizing the handwriting, he announced to the others in the room, "Javier is alive. He wants revenge." His eyes darted around the room, and his trigger finger twitched.

"Enough killing." Emilio turned back from the window. "This will solve nothing. It will only bring more pressure from the Americans. Let it go. Javier can do nothing, he is being held by El Perrito." He was a changed person since the capture of Javier. When he heard of the parachute escape of his brother, Emilio went to the church and confessed everything to the priest. He didn't know what fate awaited him, but confessing his sins meant more than all the lies and money and power he had experienced over the past few years of his life.

"How do you know this?" One of the dark-eyed men in the room spoke up. "You have been withholding information from us?"

"Five days ago, I received information passed through Garza. It was a note from Pancho Hernandez. He is holding Javier in the mountains. Hernandez wants names and contacts from us, or he is going to kill Javier." Emilio went back to his window and looked west. He was trapped. Every day it was kill or be killed, eat, or be eaten. He was tired. "No more, do you understand? No more."

The henchmen had sworn an oath to the cartel. They pledged their very lives to maintain power and control for Javier Espinosa and the Sinaloa cartel. If Javier was dead, then they would obey Emilio. But if Javier was alive, and Emilio was challenging his orders, then Emilio must be put down. You didn't question orders. If Javier said 'jump,' you didn't ask why; you asked, 'how high?' Unquestioned allegiance was all that mattered. Money, control, power, loyalty.

"Javier wants these people dead. He has a reason. You realize what you are doing if you oppose him. Yes? Emilio?" These three were hand-picked by Javier for their sadistic minds and their black empty hearts. Cold and ruthless, they tortured children for sport. Loyal until death, they would carry out the orders or die trying.

Emilio Espinosa knew the consequences all too well. There were three men behind him in the room. His only option was surprise. He pulled his semiautomatic pistol out from his side holster and turned quickly, firing as fast as he could. One man went down with bullets through the chest and abdomen. A second was hit in the leg. The third man did as he expected. Emilio Espinosa crumpled to the floor, breathing his last. The tinted bulletproof windows withstood the onslaught of gunfire, but it couldn't hold back the spirit of Emilio. He floated out over the blue ocean, free at last from the killing.

Chapter 40

San Miguel

Why, sometimes I have believed as many as six impossible
things before breakfast. —Lewis Carroll

"Hey, Mom, I think I see a monkey. Hey, Mom, look out the window. Is that a monkey?" Inquisitive, precocious Molly stared out
the window of the prop plane, looking down into the rugged green
carpet below them. The rainforest along the Costa Rican costal
area was a thick green blanket over the rugged mountains. Occasional villages and buildings were visible through the misty ver-
dant shroud, but not monkeys.

Olivia leaned to her side and peered into the clouded rainforest. "I think you're right. I believe that was a monkey." She righted
herself and smiled. The prop plane pitched and bobbed in the turbulence, making her feel a bit queasy. She picked up a magazine
and quickly put it down. She didn't want to encourage any motion
sickness. Molly clung to her position against the window, riding

the airwaves like an amusement park roller coaster. She was thrilled at every turn. Mary Beatrice slept.

Once Phineas was done with his talk, they enjoyed the rest of the day around the Marriott Hotel. The presence of the Mexican men asking questions bothered them, but they had no knowledge of any past connection. Roy and Lola had never mentioned anything about the drug cartel, the trial, and El Chico. For Olivia and the rest, ignorance was bliss.

The next morning, in San Jose they boarded another small prop plane carrying twelve passengers. The plane rose over the western mountain range and descended along the coast. Following the Pacific south, they came to an airport of sorts.

To call it an airport was using the word in a very broad sense. It was a grassy runway beginning several feet from the ocean surf and extending inland at an angle until it stopped at the foot of the mountains. There was only one approach and departure route, and if the wind or weather wasn't cooperating, your only option was to wait for the weather to change. The terminal was an open sided thatched roof held up with weathered logs and frayed ropes. A generator sputtered and coughed behind the terminal, producing enough electricity to maintain communications, weather information and a beer refrigerator. A mile hike from the airport was the small village of San Miguel tucked under the rain forest canopy.

Most of the passengers were locals. Once the pilot turned the engine off, he opened the cargo doors and tossed everyone's luggage or belongings onto the dusty ground. The visitors from up north attracted attention. The orphanage had sent an old truck to meet them. Their driver was pleasant and quickly loaded their personal items into the back of the truck. The two women and baby Beatrice squeezed into the cab with the driver. No room for car seats. It was tossed into the back along with Phineas, Harry, and Molly. Harry clung tightly to Molly as they left the airstrip and wound their way along the rutted, dirt road through the jungle.

After only a quarter mile of bumping along, they came to the river. Running fresh and clean out of the mountains, it flowed into the sea. On a sandy spit jutting out into the river, sunning itself was a ten-foot crocodile. Another lay nearby half in and half out of the water. A handful of squirrel monkeys jumped and darted about in the trees over the river. The truck slowed imperceptibly and drove into the river. The crocodiles gave them no heed. The squirrel monkeys danced about, and a scarlet macaw squawked loudly as it flew over the river following the truck. Better than Disney World, this was real. Molly was speechless.

Even in the shade, the heavy humid air pressed on them. The hot damp cloak of the coastal rain forest replaced the cooler drier air of San Jose. Overhead there was an incessant humming or buzzing from millions of cicadas. Harry and Phineas felt the water drops from the trees as they drove on. Their shirts were damp and dark with sweat, great wet circles radiated outward from their underarms. The dust from the road flew up behind the truck and stuck to their wet skin.

The truck passed several people walking to and from the village. There were very few vehicles in the village because it was difficult and expensive to bring anything in. The project required hours of driving over treacherous and unpredictable mountain roads. It could only be done during the dry season and after washed out roads were repaired. During the rainy season, the village was isolated because the river was too high to ford. Then the only option was to come in by boat along the coast.

The truck stopped at Hogarcito de San Miguel, the orphanage of San Miguel. More than a dozen children rushed up to the truck laughing and pointing at the strangers. Most of the white people traveling through San Miguel used the area as a launching point for traveling further down the coast to eco lodges catering to the rising popularity of eco-tourism. Having the white visitors as guests was an honor to the village.

San Miguel was rustic and basic in every sense. One road led in and out of town, the only other way was by sea. The trail to the airport was a dead-end one-mile route. While the road system was marginally maintained even in good weather, the boats coming and going were the most reliable and the most comfortable.

"*Bienvenidos.*" Two women from the orphanage came out of the building and into the street, greeting the visitors.

Harry, Phineas, and Molly climbed out from the back of the truck and into the dusty road. Emma and Olivia and the baby unfolded themselves from the cramped pickup cab. Everyone was thankful it was only a mile ride.

"Gracias," Olivia replied. Her Spanish was passable for a resort area but limited here in San Miguel. They were all hopeful to find someone with English skills, even if rudimentary. One woman carrying a small child, walked to the group of newcomers.

"I am Isabella Matamoras. I was the one you wrote about." Her smile reflected a great honor at their presence. "Your family helped to pay for my care, many years ago. I can't thank you enough." She moved toward Emma and Olivia as though meeting a long-lost sister. She cried as they hugged. They were tears of joy as she found her family, a family she never knew. "Please, come and sit."

Leading the group to a small area under a thatched roof, Isabella sent someone to bring drinks and fresh fruit for the guests. The cicadas buzzed and whirred in the tall trees. The constant dripping from the trees seemed as though it was raining although the sun was hot and merciless. It was good to be in the shade, but there was no escape from the heat. The children of the orphanage and of the village gathered around, laughing, and pointing at the visitors. Once her guests had been served some type of chilled fruit juice, Isabella began asking questions.

"How did you find me?" She was amazed anyone would remember her or even care.

"Our parents helped to sponsor you when you were living at the orphanage. They still had information about you and this place." Olivia added. "Your English is very good." Isabella's was easy to understand even though she stopped and worked through her word choice, at times.

"I remember when your parents wrote to me. I still have those letters and pictures you sent me." She paused, thinking about her past. "My mother died when I was five. It was a very hard time for me. There was no one to take care of me then. I lived here in the orphanage."

"Do you still work or live here?" Emma asked, indicating the orphanage.

"Yes. When I became too old to be counted as an orphan, the directors let me be one of the workers because I had nowhere else to go, and they needed help." She stopped to take a drink of water and look around at the children. "Over time the other relief workers from the mission in San Jose left, and I was the only one. I became the director of the orphanage."

Behind them in the trees a pair of black and yellow toucans landed. To the locals, it was not a noteworthy event, but to the visitors it was exciting. Scarlet macaws cavorted with raucous squawks from the treetops and somewhere the other side of the building another macaw answered. A half-dozen capuchin monkeys with long black tails and white faces, swung and danced through the trees, descending toward the orphanage. It was as if Molly had walked into the San Diego zoo with no bars.

"Don't let the monkeys steal your fruit," Isabella warned. "If they get a chance, they come down and steal unguarded food from the children." With the arrival of the monkeys, two of the older boys in the orphanage swung into action. They stood guard like enlisted soldiers, holding large red super-soaker water guns, ready to fire at the monkeys if they came too close. "The monkeys don't like the water, and it is the simplest way to chase them off without hurting them."

As they discussed the monkeys, one jumped out of the trees and onto the thatched roof. "Get him away," Isabella directed the boys. The water guns shot out fifty feet, hitting the monkey squarely in the face. He sputtered off, retreating out of range, waiting for another opportunity to steal fruit.

Molly laughed and pointed toward the trees. This was better than a front row seat at the circus.

"May I ask you a question?" Phineas looked up into the trees away from the capuchins. "The dripping from the trees, is that water or tree sap or something else?"

"Ah...the dripping." Isabella followed his line of sight toward the treetops. "Do you hear the buzzing noise?

"Yes, that's the cicadas, am I right?" Phineas replied.

"You're right, but the dripping is pee...urine from the insects. They eat from the trees, and the tree sap passes through them. It sounds like rain, but it is really urine from the cicadas. I hope that doesn't bother you."

Everyone was silent for a few moments. Over the constant buzzing was the sound of "raindrops," all around them. It was raining bug urine. Despite the heat, Emma draped a thin blanket over sleeping Beatrice to shield her from the ceaseless dripping and inched herself further under the edge of the thatched roof.

Isabella talked to several of the older children and women working in the orphanage. She wanted them all to be on their best behavior. It was her chance to thank and impress the Ambrose family that had meant so much to her. The tour of the orphanage was brief, but enlightening. Six rooms with sleeping mats stacked against the wall. It was a simple arrangement for the children. Screens or mosquito netting were draped over the windows, and mosquito netting hung over the children when they slept. One larger room doubled as a meeting room, dining room and kitchen. During the rainy season, food was served indoors, but most of the rest of the year, the children were expected to eat outdoors and spend most of their time out of the main building. Nearby was a small, blue, low-lying, concrete block school designed to educate the elementary children of San Miguel. Its metal roof echoed the continual dripping from the canopy above.

Olivia asked, "How many children do you have at the orphanage?"

"We have seventeen children now which is more than we can easily care for." Isabella reached down to help one of the children at her side. Taking the corner of her dress, she wiped green sticky stuff from the corners of his eyes. "This one just came to us last week. His father was on drugs and his mother just left."

Next, the entourage wandered about the hamlet of San Miguel. Numerous small homes tucked in and out of the trees belonged to the residents of the town. Perhaps three hundred people called it home, fewer during the rainy season. Many who had the option, left the area because of isolation. Although flights came in and out of the area every other day or as needed, the river prevented supplies from reaching the town. Above the river was a walking suspension bridge. Any items that could be carried by one or two people could be brought across the narrow swinging bridge. No more than two people could go across it simultaneously because the oscillations of one person made it difficult for any others to cross at the same time. At intervals along the bridge, extending up the sides was netting to keep passersby from pitching into the crocodile infested river, thirty feet below. Much of the netting was frayed and rotten from the drenching humidity.

The river cascaded down from the coastal mountain range into the Pacific rim. Higher up, the water was cool and clear, but as it collided with the tropical heat, the water became stained and murky. Finally, the river morphed into pools and slack water areas along the coast with mangroves swamps below and rocky cliffs above. Sloths, gray-green with algae, lived in the mangroves. Their imperceptible movements were visible over days rather than minutes or hours.

Molly took it all in as only a six-year-old could. She looked skyward in wonder at the capuchin monkeys and scarlet macaws. It didn't take her long to adjust to the heat. While her parents were sweating with the least exertion, she accepted the invitation to join the other children, kicking balls, running up and down the dusty street and watching the older boys shoot the monkeys with water guns.

Afternoon slipped into evening. The orphanage had no room for visitors, but Isabella had arranged for a couple local families to serve as hosts. Other than some small lodges catering to tourists further down the coast there were no facilities in San Miguel. The visitors were at the mercy of the town's people. And they offered their homes warmly.

Nighttime found Molly sleeping in the same room as her parents. The homes were small, and they were fortunate to find a home with enough room to house a single guest. Sleeping together in the same room was fine with Molly. As the buzzing of the cicadas faded, the onslaught of the night sounds nearly drowned out the pounding of ocean surf a short distance away. Insects by the millions climbed over the windows. Frogs, crickets, and animals too exotic and numerous to imagine squeaked, croaked, and burped in the night. Down toward the river an occasional moan or groan from a crocodile echoed along the dripping, moss covered rocks.

Harry and Olivia slept fitfully under the cacophony of the Costa Rican night. Molly slept soundly and confidently with her daddy nearby.

Chapter 41

Molly

When you reach the end of your rope, tie a knot in it and hang on. —Franklin D. Roosevelt

The Mexicans were in no hurry. They knew the destination of the prop plane down the coast. There was one way in and one way out. The plane was scheduled in and out of the grassy airstrip every other day. Unless the Ambrose sisters were going onward by boat, the Mexicans expected to intercept them in the small town of San Miguel on the Osa peninsula. The four-wheel-drive jeep they rented pitched and jerked along the rutted and twisted mountain road. What took the plane forty-five minutes would take them over five hours of driving.

The message from El Chico was straightforward; the plan was simple. Revenge, first and foremost. Then departure by boat southward into Panama. Relying on known contacts from the various drug cartels throughout Latin America, they could easily

346

arrange a flight back to Mexico. With Emilio gone, they only reported to Javier Espinosa. They swore allegiance to the death, and death was their mission. Hardened professional killers in every sense of the word, they were heartless and sadistic. Different than most assassins who were quick, clean, and efficient, they toyed with their quarry as a cat plays with a half dead mouse.

And they enjoyed it.

San Miguel was a dirty, wide spot in the road, surrounded by mountains, mangrove-lined, mosquito- and crocodile-infested rivers, and the Pacific Ocean on the west. Snakes poisonous enough to kill a dozen people with a single bite and bugs the size of your fist lurked just out of sight in the forest duff. More than once along the rutted road, the Mexicans stopped to shoot at monkeys or boa constrictors. Well-armed and dangerous in their own right, they disliked the idea of spending time in the untamed rain forest.

They left San Jose in late afternoon, expecting to drive through the night. Extra water and fuel were stowed in cans in the back of the jeep. Other than that, they had weapons, satellite phones, some food and little else. They weren't on a holiday.

#

Molly woke at daylight and lay under the mosquito netting, entranced, and confused. The open windows permitted the dying night sounds to come in along with the early morning jungle noises. In the misty shroud of the mountains, a deep, throaty roar bellowed out of the trees. One howl was answered by another nearby. Molly shivered in fear and snuggled closer to her mom and dad as the black howler monkeys of Costa Rica welcomed her to their corner of the world.

Olivia hugged her daughter close as she listened to the noises on the edge of the village. Although Isabella had reassured them about the vegetarian habits of the howler monkeys, Olivia was convinced she would have her arms and legs ripped away, should she meet face-to-face with them. Between howls or growls, other noises harmoniously announced the arrival of a new day—their first full day in San Miguel.

"Buenos Dias," their host welcomed them awake. For breakfast, they had fresh baked bread, fresh fruit, juice and plenty of hot steaming local coffee served on a small table under the palms. Grown and roasted in the highland areas of Costa Rica, the coffee had a wonderful slightly sweet, acidic quality. Pushing the sleepiness of the strange and noisy night away, Olivia welcomed a hot steaming mug. She wondered how Emma, Phineas and the baby had tolerated the muggy night. For her, hot coffee and a cool shower did wonders.

The two families met on the main street, the only street of San Miguel, and compared notes. Baby Beatrice and Molly looked rested and ready to take on the world, but the parents had dark circles under their eyes. Phineas glanced longingly toward several hammocks strung between trees. Harry followed his focus and silently agreed with the idea of rest. It was morning in the Osa peninsula, and the heat index was already higher than an Iowa cornfield in August. They walked together along the road, toward the school and Hogarcito de San Miguel. Ahead of them a jeep pulled to the side of the road and stopped. A slight but fading cloud of dust settled behind it. No other traffic was seen or expected. They crossed the road in front of the small hacienda. Molly skipped between the trees looking upward for monkeys and birds and bugs and anything else that would capture the imagination of a little girl. She was never disappointed. If she didn't see something, her mind produced it.

Hogarcito de San Miguel was in full swing. After a morning meal, the children actively ran about. Isabella and two other women were clearly over-worked, but their faces reflected a sense of contentedness and dedication.

"I hope you slept well," Isabella greeted Olivia and Harry as they approached. Phineas and Emma were not far behind.

"Yes, we did, thank you." Olivia hid the truth of a fitful, sticky, noisy night. It was nothing like the clear, naturally air-conditioned breezes off Lake Namukwa, thousands of miles to the north. The orphaned kids welcomed Molly, and they all ran off playing, kicking balls, and skipping through the trees and dirt covered pathways. It was a good time to talk.

"Isabella, do you know the reason we came to see you?" Olivia asked as the others settled into chairs under the same thatched, open-aired room as yesterday. Emma made sure she was out of the drip line of the trees. Although the cicadas were warming up in the morning sun and hadn't begun their incessant urination yet, she wanted to be out of the way when it happened.

"No, I'm sorry. I don't know why you are here. We are honored to have you as guests." Isabella looked inquisitively at them. She hoped they expected nothing of her because she had nothing to offer.

"I am going to tell you a story about my parents. I hope it isn't too confusing. If you have questions please ask." Olivia began the long and sometimes twisted story of her parents. She included the years long past when they helped sponsor children in need. She told stories of their family, gathered on the lakeshore, around summertime bonfires. Olivia tried to explain winter, skating on the frozen lake and playing in the snow. Emma interrupted, adding comments when Olivia stopped to catch her breath or think for a moment. It was a condensed trip down memory lane. During it all, both Emma and Olivia realized just how fortunate they had been, growing up when and where they did. They had no choice in the matter; it just happened.

They also realized, Isabella had no choice in her life either. Orphaned from her parents, destined to live most of her childhood in a small concrete orphanage, it's walls damp with condensation and crawling with insects, mosquitos buzzing and biting though the night, the persistent threat of malaria and dengue fever. Life wasn't fair.

"We came to see you because we want to offer our help. Our parents left us money and told us to find you and help you." Emma felt incredibly blessed as she looked at the happy, healthy baby asleep in her arms. In a few days, she would be back on US soil, away from howler monkeys, crocodiles and mosquitos carrying death threats. Isabella Matamoras and the bouncing, smiling children would remain here. No amount of money or encouragement would change anything.

"Thank you for your kindness, but I can't offer anything in return." Isabella wasn't sure what to expect.

"We don't want anything in return. I hope we can help you for a few days, and perhaps we can return in the future and continue to help you. None of us knows what the future may bring." Olivia reflected on the sudden turn of events in their own lives over the past year. Life was truly a day at a time.

After a couple of hours of visiting, some of the children tentatively began hovering around their location. No longer bouncing and smiling, they appeared guarded. Finally, one of the girls about the same age as Molly blurted out something in Spanish to Isabella. Her response seemed worried.

Isabella turned to Olivia and Harry.

"Do you know anyone else here in San Miguel?"

"No. Why?"

Isabella nodded toward the little girl who did the talking. "Maria said, two men called for Molly by name, and she went with them. The men are not from around here."

Olivia leaped to her feet. "What? Where did they go?" A shock of anger and maternal fear shot though her entire being. Her mind raced with frantic thoughts and confused ideas. Children were abducted on the streets of New York and São Paulo and Miami, not in dusty remote villages. It couldn't be happening here.

"Show me where she went?" Harry and Phineas were on their feet as the children pointed up the road toward the river. Running as fast as they could in the stifling heat, the men saw nothing on the road. The jeep that had been seen earlier was not in sight. Very few vehicles belonged to the villagers. Harry ran in the direction where the jeep had been. He felt lost, and a deep sense of dread gripped him.

"Molly, Molly!" he yelled, a desperate edge to his voice. "MOLLY!" No answer.

Olivia screamed her daughter's name into the hills and trees. The only answer was the mindless pissing and droning of the cicadas. Isabella gathered the children, trying to get any helpful information from them. She knew the risk of an unattended child in the rain forest. They had lost a child in the past; a boy fell into the river, and the crocodiles took him. A helpless little girl unfamiliar with the area would not survive the night.

"Run, get your friends and anyone who can help find her." The children scattered, looking and calling for their new friend, Molly. Throughout the village, between buildings and behind boats and trees and piles of garbage they ran, searching desperately. By this time most of the village was alerted, and they also joined in the search. The few people who owned trucks, headed up and down the single dirt road in and out of town hoping for a clue. After an hour of searching, nothing was heard, nothing was seen, and nothing was found.

Olivia sobbed uncontrollably in Emma's arms as Harry and Phineas continued the frantic search. Emma clutched her own baby as tightly as possible, fearing the child would be wrenched from her arms. Their desperate and fading hope was slowly washed away by the dripping trees. Throughout the village and up and down the road, Olivia could hear the people yelling Molly's name. Even the howler monkeys and the white-faced capuchin monkeys clung to the forest canopy, intent on the activity below. The toucans were silent, and the macaws departed. A single three-toed sloth, high up in a tree along the river, slowly turned its head toward the yelling children. All of creation waited expectantly and fearfully for Molly to appear. There was no answer.

The initial frantic search from the villagers yielded nothing. People began to gather back at the orphanage, asking questions. Olivia yelled, "Can we call the police?"

"No, I'm sorry," was the only answer Isabella could give. "We have no police, no ambulance, no doctors. I'm sorry; it is just us." Isabella hugged Olivia tightly as they both grasped for any help. They prayed silently and aloud, calling upon God to deliver the helpless little girl, unharmed. Still there was no answer.

Then there was an answer. A child came running down the road, yelling something Olivia couldn't understand. She waved a note in her shaking hand. Tears washed narrow trails through the dust on her cheeks. Her black hair fluttered behind her as she ran barefoot down the rocky road. She was bleeding from one big toe-nail. Her dirty hands clutched the paper, and she handed it to Olivia. Unable to read the note, Olivia gave it to Isabella. Isabella read aloud as she translated from Spanish to English.

"The girl is at the bridge. Your life for her life. In six hours, she will be thrown to the crocodiles if you do not show."

Olivia screamed for Harry, desperate for help. They had to save their little girl, their only child. Isabella yelled for the other men in the village to get help, and they ran and drove as fast as they could in the direction of the river crossing toward the landing strip.

"Molly!" Olivia yelled as they came to the river. Vehicles could cross the river by driving through the shallowest portion, but a short distance up stream, between moss and vine-covered rocky outcroppings, a narrow rickety suspension bridge hung precariously over the river. Barely visible from the road, only when you had gone around a point on the river did the bridge come into full view. There, hanging from the middle of the bridge was Molly, her arms and legs flailing about grasping at thin air. A rope was wrapped around her as a makeshift harness and held in place with copious amounts of duct tape. Her hair was matted and tangled. She was crying.

"Daddy, please help me. Daddy! I'm scared!" Molly screamed and then was quiet for a few moments. It was obvious she had been crying and screaming for a while before the would-be rescuers had arrived. From her makeshift harness, the rope extended to the top of the suspension bridge and across to the end of the bridge. One of her captors stood in a guarded position behind some rocks at the end of the bridge. The other man was at the opposite end of the bridge. Each cradled a high-powered semi-automatic weapon, ready for use.

Harry, frantic over his daughter, rushed along the trail toward the river. Two rifle shots rang out, one striking the river and the other hitting the muddy trail at his feet. He lurched to a stop, confused and desperate. Another shot hit above his head on a tree.

"Ambrose." The voice yelled from the end of the suspension bridge. In passable English, he continued. "We killed your parents, now we will kill you."

No one dared move. Olivia and Emma were dazed. Who was speaking? Who had killed their parents? Why were they doing this? Nothing made sense.

"Who are you?" Olivia screamed as loudly as she could.

Molly heard her voice and cried, "Mommy, help me!"

"You know what your father did. Now you must pay with your life as he did."

"What do you want?" Harry called back. He didn't dare move for fear of drawing another shot. The next time they might not miss.

"Give yourselves up. You have six hours. Every hour we will lower the child until she is in the water. You don't need to ask what will happen then." Even now below Molly a crocodile lay motionless on the surface. Another sunned on the bank, unfazed by the verbal exchange.

Heat bore down on the river. Trees shaded the riverbanks, but poor Molly hung in the sun. Flies and mosquitos tormented her. She swung her arms and kicked her legs without effect. They only seemed to attract more insects. The heat was insufferable, and she cried out. Her dry mouth made it more difficult to call for her mommy and daddy. She cried until she could cry no more, and then mercifully lapsed into sleep, exhausted from fighting the heat and the bugs.

"One hour." The voice yelled out, and he jerked the rope, startling poor Molly awake. She slipped closer to the river. The crocodile moved, his long, scaled tail undulating in the water. The other captor tossed a dead chicken into the river. With a large swirl in the murky water, the chicken and the floating crocodile disappeared.

"Daddy, help me!" Molly flailed about again and then became still. Weakened by heat and dehydration and constant fear, she was losing strength.

"Harry, do something!" Olivia was ready to sacrifice herself if she knew for certain Molly would be OK. Olivia was desperate. She yelled out to anyone who could hear, "Can anybody help? Is there anybody who can help?"

Harry yelled back at the Mexicans. "If you pull her up and release her, I will come to you."

"If any of you try to attack, we will release the girl into the water." And the man lowered the rope another foot.

"NO!" Harry yelled back.

The onlookers were shocked to see such a brazen heartless attack on the little girl. The children of the orphanage cried in fear seeing their new friend in trouble. Isabella tried to gather them and usher them away from the river, but as much as they hated to see such a horrible sight, none of them dared avert their eyes. The horror clutched them and repulsed them in the same instant.

Olivia knelt in the dirt, calling out to God for mercy. She was on the verge of collapse. Emma clutched Beatrice and knelt beside her sister, praying, and crying, seeking a miracle. Helpless against the evil and nowhere to turn, they had no other option.

The Mexican holding the rope was barely visible where he sat in the shade of the rocky outcropping at the edge of the cliff. The man on the left was hidden in the trees. From his position, he could signal the first man if anyone attempted to attack. The rope holding Molly was tied off against the railing of the bridge. Periodically the man pulled or hit the rope to aggravate Molly and stir up the parents. But like a cat playing with a mouse nearly dead, he bored of the game and wanted to move it along.

Harry, Olivia, and everyone present desperately considered every possible option. One man in the village was trying to figure out a way to ambush the captors. No one had weapons, certainly not guns. Someone in the town had a spear gun for scuba diving but that wasn't going to be helpful. Two or three people suggested killing goats or chickens and throwing them into the river upstream to attract the crocodiles away from Molly. Harry feared this would do nothing but attract more crocodiles into the water. One or two were already deadly. Adding to their numbers would not alleviate the problem.

Several had binoculars, and they tried spying on the men, hoping to find any possible advantage. There were none, at least none that they could think of. Every passing minute was critical. Heat, insects, crocodiles, and fear clutched at little Molly. She was no longer crying. Her breathing was shallow and rapid, and then she appeared to stop breathing altogether. Olivia was crazed with fear that Molly was already dead or nearly so. Six hours wouldn't matter.

"Fer-de-Lance," one of the local men with binoculars spoke softly and then repeated himself. "Fer-de-Lance." He pointed toward the man controlling the rope.

A group of capuchins climbing through the trees near the end of the suspension bridge suddenly became animated. They hung above the man, descended slowly, and then retreated quickly into the tree canopy. Several times this happened, each time the monkeys became louder and more agitated.

Harry, unable to watch his beloved little girl suffer any longer, stood and walked into the sunshine along the river. He fearlessly glared at the executioner on the cliff. It didn't matter anymore. A decision between life and death wasn't an option. He chose life for Molly, and in doing so he was willing to give his life with the hope Molly would have hers.

"Kill me and let her go," he yelled at the man by the bridge. Harry closed his eyes, waiting.

"NO!" Olivia screamed. She heard the rifle shot as she collapsed in the mud along the river.

Chapter 42

For Love or Money

We never know the love of a parent till we become parents
ourselves. —Henry Ward Beecher

Javier Espinosa paced within his palace prison, agitated, and
bored. His note wasn't likely to be delivered, but it didn't matter.
Revenge was all he had left. Hatred, fear, anger, power, and death
marked his life. He had reached the pinnacle, and it was everything he fought for and nothing he expected. Billions of dollars at
his disposal, all of it, blood money. Bought and paid for by thousands of little people. People who struggled to provide daily neces-
sities for themselves and their families, and when it was over they
were dead, pawns in a great game of chess, sacrificed to save the
king.

Their lives were a small price to pay for his glory, his achieve-
ments, his power. And now his life would be sacrificed—sacrificed
to his god, the god of power, the god of money, the god of lust and

rage and ruthless oppression. He laughed as he poured a large glass of aged tequila. Would it be his last? The burn in his throat warmed him and brought false courage. He poured another.

#

Dag Rasmussen stepped from the oncology office in Springfield, Virginia. It wasn't as he expected. Once you hear the diagnosis of cancer, you hear nothing else. It didn't matter if treatment options exist. It didn't matter if it was a lazy slow-growing cancer. Nothing really mattered until you were able to wrap your head around the C-word—cancer. Once you could get past the C-word, then you could begin to think and act rationally again.

In his mind it wasn't really cancer, it was leukemia. Hairy cell Leukemia, to be more specific. What troubled him the most was how the oncologist approached his treatment options. "This is a type of leukemia which can be treated, but we don't consider it a cure." Dag asked more questions and more answers followed. "Basically, you learn to manage it. You use whatever means available to control it, but you can't ever say it is cured. You learn to live with it and it lives with you."

Dag was a black and white kind of person. If you painted a picture of the way his brain worked, it would look like a checkerboard, black and white. Very few gray areas existed in his cerebral cortex. When confronted with evil, you got rid of it. When faced with an enemy, you killed it. Managing or controlling was a cop-out, a compromise. Training and living in a kill-or- be-killed, eat-or-be-eaten environment didn't allow for half measures.

360

He never considered applying the leukemia management principle to his work. It was a foreign concept. Stamping out evil did not allow compromise. It was either right or wrong, not halfway, or part way. When the oncologist discussed the hairy cell leukemia coursing through his veins and the options for controlling it, Dag recalled an unpalatable political option which the United States faced not so long ago. Saddam Hussein wasn't a Sunday school teacher by any stretch of the imagination. To Dag's way of thinking, Saddam needed to go. Good-Bad. Black-White. No other way to look at the problem until after the problem was solved. Then the world was faced with a worse problem. Radical Islam became a virulent cancer invading and destroying, not just in the Middle East but anywhere and everywhere. It was an aggressive metastatic cancer. There was no way to kill the cancer unless you killed the host.

As head of DEA counterintelligence, fighting against international drug trafficking, he was faced with an incurable cancer unless you killed everyone. Unless you killed everyone directly or indirectly connected with the drug trade: drug lords, mules, addicts, tainted politicians and police, and everyone in between. You can't just kill the head and expect the rest of the disease to whither. It mutates and grows on its own. After his own leukemia experience, he saw the wisdom in the method, but it still turned his stomach. If he could eliminate the most aggressive cancer, perhaps they could manage the less aggressive cancer.

Once Javier Espinosa was captured, Dag set in motion a series of discussions and agreements that he thought would help to manage drug trafficking across the Mexican-American border. Dag agreed to deliver Javier Espinosa into the hands of Pancho Hernandez if certain conditions could be met. He basically traded all his values and all his ideals for a world devoid of right and wrong. It was only better or worse depending on your relative perspective. It was a deal with the devil.

#

Two of the local men circled around the riverbank, doing their best to avoid detection. They hoped to approach the armed Mexicans from the side or behind without making the situation worse. One went up the north side of the river and another went up the south side. The advantage went to them because the Mexicans were unfamiliar with the area. The Mexicans cradled their rifles, cocky and confident with their superior firepower. No one in the village had anything other than spear guns for fishing.

The jungle was thick with vines, leaves, and dead wood at the ground level. Due to the heavy treetops, little light infiltrated to the ground so little underbrush existed. This made it more difficult for the villagers to approach unseen. The man on the south of the river had crawled within fifty or sixty yards of the Mexican when he heard the yell from Harry, "Kill me and let her go."

The Mexican assassin was intent on his target. Sitting in the shade against a tall flat rock, he was comfortable and able to watch the throng of people down river. The top of the rock where he sat was just above his head and in the sun. The Mexican stood and shouldered his rifle, carefully aligning the crosshairs of the sniper scope on Harry.

At that moment the Fer-de-Lance, one of the deadliest pit vipers in all of Costa Rica, lashed out, hitting the Mexican in the face and eye. The snake recoiled, and struck again, as sudden and unexpected as a lightning bolt. The rifle fired, but the shot was far wide of the mark, hitting the river.

Frantic and confused, the enforcer flailed his arms and grabbed the snake as it struck for a third time. He lurched forward onto the suspension bridge. His fumbling and stumbling caused Molly to dance in the air like a marionette. The rope securing her to the bridge came loose, and she fell precariously toward the water, stripping the loose coils of rope from the bridge decking.

"No!" Harry screamed.

Molly plunged toward the water. The rope caught in a gap between the boards of the walking bridge. Molly's unconscious body jerked to a stop inches from the water, her bare foot dipping into the current above the crocodile's patient, unblinking eyes.

A second twelve-foot crocodile rose from the bank and slid into the water with barely a ripple.

On the bridge above Molly, the Mexican shrieked as he struggled with the viper. He tripped on the railing and tumbled over the edge, still clutching the snake. Screaming and thrashing, he fell thirty feet into the river. The large reptiles turned from Molly's toes toward the thrashing in the water. The man screamed again as the first crocodile took him by the leg and the second his arm. Under the surface the water convulsed, and a trail of red drifted down stream.

The pit viper slithered ashore.

The second assassin witnessed the entire event and ran across the bridge to loosen the rope and finish the job. The man from San Miguel picked up the rifle dropped in the trail and fired. Three times he fired without aiming, but the first was enough. The Mexican fell onto the bridge, inches from the rope.

His movement caused Molly to bob up and down, her foot dipping in and out of the river. With blood in the water and frantic activity, more crocodiles arrived on the scene.

Isabella saw the child. There was only one hope for her. She ran as fast as she could up the riverbank and jumped in as one of the prehistoric beasts opened his jaws around Molly's leg.

"Salve niña! Save the little girl!" Isabella yelled to the villager on the bridge. She splashed and thrashed and created as much noise as possible. The crocodile left Molly and turned toward Isabella and the noise. Quickly the man on the bridge pulled Molly to the bridge deck. Only then did Isabella turn and try to climb out of the muddy river.

But she wasn't quick enough. Before she could pull herself out of the mud and the slime one of the beasts grabbed her. In an instant, she was twisted and pulled back into the river. Isabella and the crocodile disappeared under the frothy surface. Everyone watched, too stunned to react. Ten seconds turned into twenty seconds. The water boiled as if a titanic struggle were going on beneath the waves. Finally Isabella gasped and heaved herself out of the river, cut and bleeding on her lower leg. The skin and muscle was torn away and white bone lay exposed to the mud and debris of the river.

Harry gasped. Evidently the crocodile had released its bite, attempting to get a death grip on its victim. Isabella prevailed but at a terrible cost.

Harry and Phineas and the rest of the villagers rushed to pull her to safety. Olivia raced as fast as she could up the riverbank to her little girl.

Ripping and tearing the tape away she was relieved to find Molly still breathing. "Somebody get a doctor!" she yelled clutching her child. "Everything's going to be all right," she whispered into the unhearing ear of her baby. "Everything's going to be all right, Mommy's here now."

Two of the women arrived at Olivia's side holding her and praying. One of the women was a nurse. The small village had a medical clinic, but the doctor visited only three times a month. He would not come for another week. But they did have medical supplies and a radio.

Isabella and Olivia, holding Molly, were helped into the back of a truck and hauled as quickly as possible to the clinic. Molly was dehydrated and unconscious, but the nurse could find no direct evidence of injury. She did her best to start an IV into the collapsed veins of the little white arms. On the second try she succeeded. The normal saline began to drip into Molly's arm. With no other options than IV fluids and prayers, people gathered around murmuring, singing, and praying. They held a vigil long into the night for the brave little girl and the orphaned woman who helped save her.

Isabella needed surgery. The large artery in her foot was spared, but to anyone with the courage to look, she was losing blood. A big flap of muscle and skin lay open like a dog-eared paperback. Blood dripped out from the fleshy pages, pooling in the bed where she lay and dripping onto the floor. The nurse radioed the medical evacuation center. Help was on the way, but would not likely arrive for two hours. It would take an additional two or three hours to reach the hospital. Every minute mattered.

Both Emma and Phineas had basic EMT first-aid training. They did what they could, cleaning and irrigating the wounds and holding pressure to stem the flow of blood. Everyone hoped it would be enough. The local nurse started an IV on Isabella with the same saline Molly was getting. The doctor on the other end of the radio ordered IV antibiotics for each of them. The small medical clinic didn't have much, but what they had was put to full use. Now all they could do was wait. And pray.

It was near midnight before the med-evac helicopter could be heard up the coastline. A large fire was built at each end of the grassy runway, and people stood to the sides with flashlights to illuminate the safest landing area. The generator sputtered behind the thatched terminal and all three lights were turned on. Even the small beer refrigerator was called into service. The fifty-foot extension cord was stretched to the limit as the cooler was brought out as far as the cord could reach and the door propped open.

Clouds of insects dipped and darted around the lights. Huge bugs, attracted by the light, flew kamikaze style into the fires, sizzling and sputtering in the flames. The rain forest cacophony was at full volume just out of sight from the stage lights along the runway, nearly drowning out the noise of the helicopter rotors. The primeval chorus gave a sinister backdrop for the life and death drama.

Molly regained consciousness but was feverish and delirious. Her speech was weak and disoriented. Nothing she said made sense, but she was speaking and alive. The saline IV fluid continued to drip. Her little body had already taken in nearly a half liter of life saving liquid. Isabella had been given nearly a liter of IV saline, but she was losing blood. Molly was gradually moving more, but Isabella was going the opposite direction. Initially she was alert, offering advice and encouragement to those who encouraged her, but over time she grew weaker and tired. The adrenalin, which served her well at the beginning, was gone, and she was down to her reserves.

Two paramedics and a pilot sprang into action immediately after touchdown. A second IV access was started on each patient. Molly winced and cried, a clear sign of improvement from the medical clinic. Isabella was weaker and barely responded. Blood pressures were obtained while trying to fit the victims into the tight space of the med-evac unit.

"Are you the mother?" One of the emergency workers looked directly at Olivia. "Normally we would want you to come with us, but we don't have room, and we barely have enough fuel to get back to San Jose and the trauma hospital." She paused. "I'm sorry. You won't be able to come with us."

Olivia clutched at Molly, gradually loosening her grip as the paramedic carried the listless little girl into the helicopter and strapped her down. Molly flickered awake and looked out into the night. She saw her mother's muddy, tear streaked face looking back.

"Mommy?" She cried as her little hands tried to reach out. "Mommy, don't let them take me away again."

Olivia let go, and sent Molly off into the dark night—the darkest she had ever known.

Chapter 43

Recovery

I don't think of all the misery but of all the beauty that still remains. —Anne Frank

Hernandez hit the mute button on his phone and slipped it into the breast pocket of his black Gucci seersucker and silk tailored suit. He flipped his finger and brushed away a speck of lint on his lapel. He was now the king. He was the leader of an unholy alliance, and the world was under his command. But he had made a deal with the devil. The United States government was on his side if he was on their side. Power, glory, money, he had it all. But image was as important in the drug cartel world as it was in Hollywood. Truth didn't matter; perception did. If everyone viewed you as the best, then you were the best.

Javier Espinosa was done. His few remaining loyalists were easily rooted out. The final transfer of power was simple. Hernandez displayed the torture and execution of El Chico on the internet. The details were graphic, and Hernandez himself pulled the trigger to demonstrate his mercy. By the time Google pulled the video, it had been viewed nearly a quarter of a million times.

Just as Hernandez lived in a world of intrigue and lies, so did Dag. Political power and influence were hard masters. Success hung on back room alliances, fear and public perception. Truth was twisted and manipulated to mean whatever you wanted it to mean.

Garza seemed untouchable. Dag needed him as a link, a go-between for local communication. He was paid by both sides and became the richest coconut and T-shirt salesman in Mazatlán. But he was stuck in the game. Hernandez used him to pass information and instructions, and Dag did the same, like third graders passing 'I like you' notes during arithmetic class. Both sides bypassed Garza for anything important, and over time he became less relevant. One day he disappeared and wasn't heard from again. Neither side claimed any responsibility for wrongdoing.

Dag circulated a rumor about how Garza obtained false ID's for himself, his girlfriend and his daughter. They were now living somewhere in Chile or Argentina, but no one could confirm it. No one was talking and in the end, it didn't matter. Just like Garza, Earl and Sandy had disappeared. No trace, no trail; they just fell off the earth. If Dag new anything he wasn't talking.

Dag was good at managing his arranged marriage with El Perrito, but he had concerns about freelancing and outliers. He was very troubled when he heard the news about the attack against the Ambrose family in Costa Rica. Roy had been his 'ace up the sleeve' and was the key to putting everything in motion. Without Roy, he didn't have the political influence to detain Espinosa. Without holding Espinosa, he would have never had the chance of meeting or managing Pancho Hernandez. Without Hernandez, Dag would be back in Springfield, Virginia, brown-nosing politicians, begging for funding to support his programs.

The politicians didn't seem to care one way or another. Drugs, gambling, prostitution—it was all the same unless some special interest group got their undies in a bunch. These vices had been around for thousands of years and would persist long after democracy or totalitarianism or any other form of government ceased to exist. Manage it, control it, buy it, borrow it, use it for political gain. They used whatever means they had to boost approval ratings before the next election.

As the publicity surrounding Mexican drug trafficking began to fade, public money to fight it, dried up. The public was fickle. It didn't take long before another hot button issue was all the rage on Facebook or Snapchat or some other social media platform. Dag used drug cartel money to fight drug trafficking, at least superficially. Hernandez was smart enough to see his opportunity. When Dag needed publicity, Hernandez would send some poor defenseless mules through a Tijuana drug tunnel with enough drugs to make the arrest significant. Dag was notified of the time and location. Arrest made. Drugs recovered. No one got killed. Dag got his man. Hernandez got free use of alternate routes, and everyone was happy. Until the news of Molly's abduction hit social media outlets.

Once Molly and Isabella were safely evacuated from San Miguel, the local people banded together and found reliable vehicles capable of driving Molly's parents, as well as Phineas, Emma, and Beatrice back to San Jose. It took two four-wheel drive vehicles six hours to negotiate the treacherous, poorly maintained road out of the Osa peninsula. Phineas and Harry took turns driving while the women rested. Two women from the village went with them to assist Isabella in her recovery.

By morning Harry, Olivia and the rest had made it to San Jose. The tense and tedious journey was finally over. On their arrival at the hospital, the staff met them. The parents were taken immediately to Molly's room. She was sound asleep. Only one IV still ran into her left arm. She was cleaned up and her hair brushed. The bug bites on her face were still red and puffy, but her cheeks were pink. Olivia sat on the edge of the bed and wept. Losing her parents was nothing compared to the anguish and terror she had experienced over the past twenty-four hours. She reached out her hand and touched Molly. The girl's slow easy breathing startled just a bit, and she opened her eyes.

"Mommy!" That's all she said. It was all she needed to say.

The staff brought food for Molly and the rest of the family. It was good to feel safe and alive again, all of them. No one wanted to speak; it was just good to be together.

A polite knock sounded on the door to Molly's room. "Excuse me. The police are wondering if they could ask you some questions. Can I send them in or would you rather meet them out here?"

Harry and Olivia's eyes met. Their primary concern was for Molly. They didn't want to discuss or review anything when she was listening. If Molly asked questions, they would answer. If she didn't ask, better. Harry got up to meet with the police, but first he bent down and kissed Molly on the forehead. "I'm going to visit with someone, OK? But Mommy is going to be right here. We aren't going anywhere."

"OK, Daddy. I'm better now. I love you."

Harry wiped the tears from his eyes as he stepped out of the room. He tried to clear his voice as he introduced himself to the police investigator. Extending his hand, he said, "Good morning. I'm Harry Seymour."

"Mr. Seymour, may we ask you some questions? Can you tell us in your words, what happened in San Miguel?"

Harry tried to be objective in his response, but the crushing load of exhaustion and emotions pressed heavily. He choked up, unable to speak for several minutes. Then slowly, bit-by-bit the story came out. Several people stood around the police listening intently.

"Mr. Seymour, are you aware that someone from San Miguel recorded part of your daughter's abduction?"

"Why would someone do that?" he looked around suddenly confused and lost. He had just survived a nightmare; he didn't want to relive it.

"I can't answer that. No one is perfect. Many people of Costa Rica are poor, especially by American standards. I'm sure whoever posted the video hoped to benefit somehow."

#

Isabella made it through surgery fine. She was young and healthy, and the doctors expected a good recovery if there were no problems with infection. However dirty water and a reptile bite increased her chances of complications. In the days following her evacuation and recovery, Olivia and Harry and Molly finally had a chance to sit and talk, quietly.

"Isabella, we can't thank you enough for what you have done."

"Miss Olivia, you would have done the same for me or any of my children if you knew what to do." She grimaced mildly as she shifted position in the bed.

"I want to remind you why we came. We came to help you and help the orphanage." Olivia held Molly tight in her arms. If Isabella hadn't offered her life in the river, in exchange for little Molly...Olivia couldn't bear to think what might have been.

Harry joined in the conversation. "Can we help you and the orphanage? We can get medicine, mosquito nets, new buildings, whatever you need."

Isabella thought aloud. "You are both so kind. We don't need your money. We don't have much, but we get along. But there are many in our village and in our country who have nothing. Any help would be appreciated."

"As I told you before, our parents expect us to give this money away. I know this sounds funny, but we are going to give you money, and if you don't want it, make sure you give it to someone else. We will make sure the orphanage gets anything it needs." Olivia was amazed. It was easy to give money away. It was nearly impossible to give it to the people who really needed it.

As they visited, a representative from the hospital entered the room. "Ma'am, there is a television crew here to ask you some questions. Will you talk with them?"

Isabella responded, "Why would someone want to interview me?"

"I'm sorry, I was asking you, Mrs. Seymour."

Chapter 44

Chaos

Life is 10% what happens to you and 90% how you react to it.
—Chuck Swindoll

"Mrs. Olivia Seymour, I'm Gabriela Lorenzo from CNN affiliate station KRZY in San Jose. May I ask you a few questions?" She stuck the microphone close to Olivia's face, expecting a response.

"Questions about what?"

"Was your daughter captured by Mexican drug lords?"

"How do you know this? Who told you?" Olivia looked around, wishing Harry was with her. He remained in the hospital room with Molly, safe from the media for the moment.

"Did you see the YouTube video clip of your daughter?"

"No, I didn't, and I have no desire to see it. Whoever posted that, did not have our permission. It isn't right." She felt anger at being paraded in front of the world for a publicity stunt.

"So, you don't deny it happened?" Gabriela Lorenzo was a professional. Given enough time she would get the story and the scoop.

"Is this your daughter?" CNN correspondent Lorenzo pointed to a video playing on a laptop computer. Olivia was transfixed. She began to tremble and sweat.

"Turn it off!" She turned and ran out of the lobby and up the stairs to her husband and child. It couldn't be happening again.

Turning toward the television camera Gabriela spoke into her microphone, "We have just confirmed the story of Molly Seymour, the little American girl hung as bait over wild crocodiles. Her mother, Olivia Seymour, was too distraught to continue our interview. This much we believe to be true: Molly Seymour, a six-year-old first grader from rural Oak Grove, Wisconsin, United States, was abducted by Mexican drug lords in the small village of San Miguel here in southwestern Costa Rica. What happened next would stop the heart of any parent out there. As you can see from the short video segment we played for you earlier. The details about why Molly's parents and grandparents were being threatened by these men remains under investigation. I'm Gabriela Lorenzo reporting live for CNN."

The YouTube clip went viral. Within the next twenty-four hours it had more than four million hits around the world. CNN had the scoop, and it was the topic of discussion on every newscast. Back in Des Moines, Iowa, Vera, and Richard were relaxing at home trying to shake off the events of the day. They turned on CNN. Vera nearly choked on her wine. There on the screen was

377

Molly hanging from a rope, waiting to be eaten. Then the frantic cries of Olivia. They saw Harry walking out from the trees yelling at someone, "Kill me. Let her go." It was surreal and horrible and unbelievable.

"Where's my phone? I have to call Lu and Tom." She found it on the coffee table and hit speed dial.

"Hello." It was Luella.

"Lu have you seen the news? Molly and Olivia and Harry are on CNN!"

"What are you talking about? We don't have a satellite dish here. All we can get is local news. What's going on? Are they OK?" Luella was confused. She didn't have a clue anything was happening.

"Go on your computer and log onto CNN. You'll never believe it. I can't even talk about it." Vera was in shock trying to take it all in. "I guess I called to warn you before someone else tells you."

"I'm trying to log on now. I'll call you back after I watch it. Thanks for warning me." But it was too late. Anderson Cooper was already on the way.

Following his live evening broadcast Anderson Cooper left the CNN main office and traveled by company jet to Minneapolis. Following a brief night in a hotel, he along with an affiliate CNN broadcast team maneuvered the roads of northern Wisconsin, first to Oak Grove and then to Namukwa. Pulling into the driveway they parked by the vacant pigpen and adjusted their satellite dish for a live feed. Tom was already at the food shelf, and Luella had just returned from dropping the kids off at school. She was sitting down to a second cup of coffee. Her computer logged 147 new Facebook messages, and she had 39 new emails. Still distraught over the news about Molly, she was blindsided by a knock on the door. Anderson Cooper was looking through the screen, with his coifed white hair and a chipper smile.

When she opened the door, he held out his right hand. "Good morning, I'm Anderson Cooper from CNN."

"I know who you are. What do you want?" She was not enthused to spend her morning with America.

"I'm sure you are aware of the unfortunate circumstances surrounding your sister and your niece. Do you have ideas why it happened?"

"Look, I know you are just doing your job and all. But I don't want to be on television. I will agree to talk with you when my husband comes home, but it must be off camera. Is that OK?"

She was too polite to slam the door in his face and pull the curtains. It only got worse. By the time Tom arrived back home, two other television vans had arrived and were setting up shop. Tom could barely get into the driveway. He was expecting something because everyone who stopped by the food shelf had more information than he did. This was big news.

As he was trying to open his car door, a short fat bald guy with bad breath shoved a microphone into his face. His voice sounded like he was from Fargo. "Can you tell us why your niece was abducted by Mexicans?"

"What are you talking about?" Tom fought his way to the house. Two more television reporters crowded around.

"What connection do you have with the Mexican drug cartels?" "Tell us about your in-laws." "Why did you lose your teaching job?" "What were Harry and Olivia Seymour doing in Costa Rica?" "Tell us about Roy and Lola Ambrose." The questions kept on coming. He felt like a boxer in a ring, dodging microphones and people.

Finally getting inside the house he was greeted by Luella, their gray tabby cat, Howard, and Anderson Cooper. He didn't know what to expect.

"Tom, this is Anderson Cooper from CNN." Luella introduced him as if they were old friends.

They shook hands, and Tom stepped on the cat's tail. The shrill yeow from Howard broke the tension in the air. Luella poured Tom a cup of coffee, and he sat down.

"Tom, I agreed to talk to Mr. Cooper if it wasn't on camera. Is that OK with you?"

"About what? What is all this about?" Tom needed to catch up on the drama. As Luella and Anderson Cooper started talking, Tom sat awkwardly to the side, and Howard sulked under the rocking chair.

When the questions started coming, Luella realized CNN knew more about their family than she did. "What do you know about my parents?" Luella was surprised by what she heard.

"This is a photo of your father; am I correct?" Anderson slid a glossy 8X10 black and white photo across the table. It appeared to be a photo taken by a security camera. Her father, Roy Ambrose was dressed in a black suit with a light-colored shirt and tie. He looked dapper, even in the grainy black and white photo. Surrounded by several people also in suits and armed security, he was the center of attention.

"Yes, that's Dad. Where did you get this?"

"And do you recognize this person?" He handed them another glossy color photo of Javier Espinosa.

"No, I'm sorry. I don't. But he looks familiar."

Tom looked at the photo. He knew. "That's the drug lord from Mexico. Don't they call him El Chico?"

"Yes, this is El Chico. His real name is Javier Espinosa. He was arrested and tried for drug trafficking and murder. The trial was closed to the public. The United States verses Espinosa. Your father, Roy Ambrose was the key witness in the trial. He was the reason Espinosa was indicted."

"How do you know this? We don't even know about this." Luella was dazed at the information she was hearing.

"CNN operates on an international level. We have many sources. It isn't difficult for us to get information."

As they talked, the noise outside grew. More vehicles were pulling into the driveway and onto the lawn. Tom pulled the shades over the windows, but he couldn't hide. Photographers were encircling the house, and reporters recorded clips for the evening news.

"Do you know this man?" One-eyed Dag Rasmussen stared back at them. His flat-topped military style haircut bristled, and his jaw muscles bulged in the portrait. One glance and you knew he was an all-meat-no-potatoes kind of a guy. Luella looked at the photo and looked away. She didn't answer.

Cooper continued. "He is Dag Rasmussen, head of DEA counterintelligence and international drug trafficking. We believe there is a connection between him, the Sinaloa drug cartel and your father."

"What are you saying? That my father was involved in drug trafficking? That he was some sort of drug lord? You don't know my parents. They might be eccentric, but they are good people. They would never do anything like that." Luella was in tears as her mind raced.

Tom jumped in. "This interview is over. Just leave us alone."

Cooper was quick to calm the waters. "No, I'm not implying anything. We believe your father was a very brave person to testify against a drug cartel. And that was why he died."

"Do you mean my parents were killed?" She grabbed a napkin from the kitchen table and held it to her eyes. "Why? Are you saying the drug cartel had them killed because he testified against El Chico in court? Who told you this, and why didn't anyone tell us? His children? His family?"

Luella was overwhelmed. In a single moment, nothing made sense. The cute comfortable memory of her delightful aging parents on a Sunday outing was gone. She wasn't sure what to believe or whom to trust. Did her parents just disappear into the ocean? Where they tortured or shot or drowned? If these thugs went after poor little Molly, where would they stop? With her? With her children? Would anyone be safe ever again?

Then for a fleeting moment, everything started to make sense. Her parents knew. They recorded the message, they planned the activities, the events of the past year. They expected death could come, and yet they lived with dignity and didn't cower in fear or hide in the closet. They didn't want their children to shrink from living and breathing and seeking to do good.

Luella wanted to run and hide and forget that pain and suffering existed. She wanted to shove Anderson Cooper and CNN and everyone who wanted to exploit their suffering for ratings, out the door and down the road. But she didn't. No one was immune from suffering and pain and loss. Not her, not Molly and Olivia, or her sisters or her parents. The world was full of good things and suffering. She resolved in her mind to continue to live and breathe and do what her parents taught her to do. She would do as her parent did, love God and love your neighbor.

Luella took a deep breath and cleared her throat. Then she looked Anderson Cooper directly in the eyes and began her story. She told it all, right or wrong, about her family, her values, and the tasks she felt called to do. She told about the requirements of the will, to give away before anyone of the family could receive. And she told the reason her sisters and their families were in Costa Rica for that very purpose, to help, and to give away what they could not keep.

#

Everyone who traveled to Costa Rica returned safely but not anonymously. Most major news organizations were waiting at the Minneapolis/St. Paul Lindberg terminal when the plane touched down. Unaware of the intense publicity surrounding their experience, the family was deluged with reporters as they stepped from the secured area into the baggage claim on the lower level. Cameras flashed and recorded their every move and word. Attempts at avoiding recognition were fruitless.

Molly had recovered from her physical wounds, and if she had any emotional scars, they weren't yet apparent. Olivia and Harry weren't so fortunate. The mental image of Molly's limp body hanging over the waiting crocodiles was forever branded in their minds. Olivia tried to be polite with her refusal for an interview; she only wanted to go home and have a normal life. Harry was not so courteous. He had a few choice words for some reporters invading his comfort zone. Security was called and eventually helped the travelers extract their luggage and leave the airport without further interruption.

The CNN story hit prime time the night they returned from Costa Rica, complete with video footage of Molly and her parents picking up their luggage and leaving the Minneapolis airport. If they had any concerns about finding suitable recipients of their inheritance, the problem was resolved. Once CNN reported on the reason for their travels to Costa Rica, the entire family was bombarded with requests for donations.

Telephone calls, letters, emails, and recommendations from friends, neighbors, and acquaintances were overwhelming. Ironically the needy didn't always want help and the greedy demanded it. Requests for donations ranged from new tools to fix a Harley Davidson motorcycle to a grandfather dying from cancer, and the only possible treatment was from a specialist offering a cure... in Tibet. They received thousands of requests for help with debt, expensive health care and countless other gut-wrenching stories.

In the end, it was Olivia who suffered the most. Almost overnight she withdrew. She had lost her parents and nearly lost her daughter to a hideous and sadistic attack. Harry struggled to find ways to connect. She feared intimacy and lacked compassion. She became cynical and calloused to those requesting help. Getting out of bed each morning became a chore. Some days she didn't. Molly was her sunshine and after she went to school, Olivia went back to bed or locked herself away. Even Harry was shut out.

When the letter came, she refused to open it. She wanted no part of it. If they forced her, she might end it all.

Chapter 45

On the Edge

Life is either a great adventure, or nothing. —Helen Keller

To say life returned to normal was a broad stretch of the imagination. None of the Ambrose sisters had a normal day, compared to what they had before. Before Costa Rica. Before Mayreau. Before Chiang Mai. Before everything. Vera and Richard remained almost normal. Richard continued working as a physical therapist, but he quit hospital work and started doing home physical therapy. It gave him more flexibility and allowed him to meet people on their own terms. He liked that. Vera also made career changes. She loved having her own store, but it had become a ball and chain. She gave up the store and found freedom to travel and work in different areas. She became a freelance pharmacist, working as a fill-in. When someone was gone, she stepped in. She enjoyed the variety and had the option of saying no. And she started saying no more often.

Tom and Luella and their three children remained in the old family home in Namukwa. They both loved their former jobs but neither wanted the fallout they experienced. They learned lessons from the experience in Mayreau. They found it was easy to get by with less and were very satisfied with a shift toward simplicity. Tom loved his volunteer work at the food shelf, and Lu gradually worked into a full-time school nurse.

Emma and Phineas adapted to rural Wisconsin life. His idea of a birdhouse tycoon waned. He hoped to pursue his passion of applied music theory in the natural world, but he had a family to feed and it changed his priorities. Harry was a sympathetic employer. He and Phineas worked well together, and there was hope for a long-term work relationship.

Harry was grateful for Phineas because his hands were full at home. Olivia struggled with anxiety, depression, PTSD, anorexia, borderline personality disorder, schizophrenia, insomnia, constipation, diarrhea, and rabies. That's what Harry figured out from his Google search. He typed in her symptoms and out came a list of probable diagnoses. Luella and Vera were the only family members with health careers and became Harry's go-to support group.

"Has she been willing to see a doctor about this?" Luella questioned Harry over the phone.

"Yes, but she won't listen to them. She thinks everything is OK, and she doesn't need any medications or help. She just wants to be left alone." The tone of Harry's voice betrayed his frustration and concern. He'd nearly lost Molly, and now he was losing his wife.

"What does she talk about?"

"Nothing." Harry coughed and cleared his throat. "She sleeps in the guest bedroom. She hangs onto Molly until she goes to school, then she retreats to her room until I pick up Molly after school. She's moody all the time; she doesn't want to eat. I think shes losing weight."

"What does she say about the letter?"

"She doesn't care. That's my biggest concern. She acts like she doesn't care about anything. Two days ago, she was talking about her parents, your parents. She was wondering what it was like to be dead or what you would think about if you knew you were going to die." Luella heard his voice crack. She heard him sniff and blow his nose. After a long pause with neither speaking he simply hung up.

Luella went and sat with Tom. He saw the worry on her face. "Any good news?" He asked, not expecting anything. Her eyes said it all.

"No. Olivia's the same." She put her fingers to her scalp and massaged her temples. "Tom, when you were a teacher, if you thought a student was at risk for suicide, what would you do?"

"Well, it isn't easy. You notify people, especially family. Get social services involved. Hopefully you get them assessed by mental health professionals. If you think there is an imminent risk, you can get a twenty-four or forty-eight-hour detention by calling the police. But if you save her life, it's worth the risk. Do you really think she is a risk for suicide?" Tom had known Olivia for many years. She was different. But stress, especially what she had experienced, could change people. But he had been surprised in the past.

Luella went to the kitchen and opened a bottle of red wine. It didn't need to be anything special. She just wanted a glass of wine to quiet her mind. Yelling back toward the living room she asked, "What should we do about the letter?"

The letter was a summons of sorts sent by the executor of the Ambrose estate, Liakos, Economu, and Christopoulos, law firm in Athens Greece. The one-year anniversary of the opening of the will was soon to pass. In keeping with the original intent, the entire family had to be present for the final transactions. Money was being released from the estate for the family to travel to Athens, Greece. According to the original will, the entire family must be present or the executor had the option of declaring the will, null and void. The only reason anyone could miss the final closing of the will was a physician certified document indicating serious health reasons.

"What do you want to do about the letter?" He thought aloud. "What can you do?" Tom looked longingly at the bottle of cabernet on the kitchen counter. He helped himself.

"It is my understanding, we have a period of sixty days to travel and complete this transaction, or it is all void. I'm not certain when the sixty-day period begins, but either way, we have a limited window of opportunity. Olivia's refusal to go, changes things." Luella ran through various options with Tom, but nothing appeared easy. If Olivia refused treatment, Luella doubted a doctor would write a letter. Also, Olivia likely wouldn't let Molly leave without her. And Harry wouldn't go and leave his wife, especially if everyone thought she was unstable. If they didn't go, then it was pointless for anyone to go. It was over and done. Give the money away and get on with life. They still didn't know if there was any money, all they had was speculation.

"Hey, Lu, what about this?" He looked at her, hoping for a resolution to the problem, or at least a plan. "School will be out in a week or two. Why don't we call everyone and have them come up to the lake? We can relax and talk this thing out. What do you think?"

"I don't have a better plan. Maybe Olivia will agree. Maybe a change in scenery will help, I don't know." Luella swirled the remnants of her wine and downed it with one gulp.

Everyone wanted to come to the lake except Olivia and Harry. Harry didn't want to go because of Olivia. He was tired of fighting the battle. Depression doesn't just affect one person; it affects everyone around them. Olivia finally consented to go, but Harry wasn't sure if it was a good sign or a bad sign. Her first reason for not going was another doctor appointment. She always went alone. Then when she suddenly decided to go to Namukwa, Harry was concerned she wasn't going to the doctor anymore. Harry always wanted to go with her and begged to go, but she refused. Days and weeks ran together, and they muddled along. No high points, no low points just bland mediocrity.

Molly enjoyed getting back with her cousins. Petunia wasn't there, but that didn't seem to bother her. She was resilient and happy. Only the adults were morose. On the bright side, according to Emma and Phineas, Olivia agreed to go to Greece. But she was done with this whole idea of giving money away, especially if it meant dying.

#

Summer vacation brought vacationers back to Namukwa. Luella decided to reopen the gift shop. It brought her full circle. As a kid, she loved it. Helping her parents, buying penny candy. She fondly remembered the tinkling of the little bell above the door, when visitors came in. As a teenager, she changed. She despised the little bell. It reminded her of her parent's wasted life spent at a ridiculous stupid little gift shop. In her mind, her parents had no dreams, no goals, and no life. Their existence revolved around the tiny silver bell above the door. When it tinkled, they came running.

Now she saw things differently. The bell gave her security, rootedness, and contentment. It was good to dream, but it was better to be content, wherever those dreams led. Throughout their high school and early college days, each of the girls longed for something different than what they had. There was 'save the whales,' 'stamp out world hunger,' the 'human genome project,' and 'a cure for cancer.' Gradually idealism faded from sight and pragmatism stared back. The tinkle of the silver bell held new meaning. Suddenly the simple little things in life meant so much more. Saving the world became synonymous with sharing a loaf of fresh baked bread with your neighbor.

#

A summer bonfire was a sure ticket to lift spirits and relax the mind. The men gathered firewood and laid the foundation for an evening blaze. The women assembled the supper options. Hotdogs, marshmallows, and beverages. With a strike of the match, paper and birch bark curled up in flames and started the mound of branches and firewood on fire. It was good to be back at the lake.

Emma worked the hardest to build bridges with Olivia. "Is there anything you want to talk about?" It was about as simple as she could get. Olivia simple nodded her head 'no' and continued looking out over the lake. "Olivia, I don't know what you are going through, but I want you to know I love you as my sister. If you ever need to talk, I'll be here for you. OK?" Emma sat beside Olivia, quietly holding Mary Beatrice, saying nothing. It was all she could do.

"The fire's ready if anyone wants to roast a hot dog," Richard yelled to anyone within hearing range. The kids came running. The adults gathered, quietly talking. Olivia slowly wandered toward the group. As she came near, the others whispered and mumbled as if trying to hide their words. Olivia was awkwardly quiet. Her normal bubbly self was subdued. Everyone tiptoed around her as if on eggshells. Attempts at engaging her in conversation were awkwardly one-sided. When Olivia failed to respond as everyone had hoped, they ignored her as if she didn't exist. The kids were having a great time, but for the adults, it was like attending a funeral for a good friend. Everyone wanted to say something, but no one knew how to say it.

"Look, everyone. I know you care, but I'm just in your way. I don't want to ruin your evening. I'm going to bed." Olivia hung her head and slowly drifted toward the house.

"Olivia, we care. All of us. But you can't shut us out." Vera walked toward her, trying offer a hug.

"Leave me alone!" She pushed Vera away.

"Olivia, just knock it off. We aren't the problem; you are." Luella had a way with words. Many times, she said what everyone else was thinking, but it didn't always come out smoothly.

"Not one of you saw your child hanging from a rope. No one! Don't you dare tell me you understand because you don't." Olivia lashed out blindly. "I hate you! I hate all of you! Leave me alone!" She ran into the house slamming the door behind her.

The flames died slowly. No one wanted to add more fuel to the fire. The family, just like the fire, was in danger. One of the cousins poked at the coals with a hot dog roasting stick. She turned to Molly and asked. "What's wrong with Auntie Olivia? Is she OK?"

"My mom is just scared about something, that's all."

"What's she scared about?"

"I think she's scared I was going to get eaten by the big crocodiles." Molly seemed very matter of fact about it all.

"Weren't you scared?"

"Yeah, I was scared, but I prayed to Jesus, and then I fell asleep. I dreamed a pretty lady with a shiny dress came and helped me. She told me I was going to be OK." Molly looked through the flames toward the others sitting around the fire. "That's all."

No one dared speak for the rest of the evening. The fire flickered out, and the remaining adults and children drifted off to bed. Harry didn't dare interrupt his wife. He roamed the dark corners of the house and eventually faded into fitful sleep on the couch.

In the morning, the sun was shining through the east windows. He blinked and prayed for a better day. No one was awake so he quietly made some strong black French roast coffee. After slurping down his second cup, he finally had the courage to check on Olivia.

Slowly opening the door, a crack, he peered in. Expecting to see her sleeping in bed, he was startled. The bed was made, and a note was on the pillow.

"I'm leaving. Molly is with me."

Chapter 46

Icaria, Greece

End? The journey doesn't end here. —J. R. R. Tolkien

"Hey, Mom, where are we going?" Molly slipped her arms into the straps of the little pink backpack. It was summer, but the breeze off the lake gave her a shiver. She zipped her jacket up to her chin. "Are we going to have a picnic?"

Olivia didn't answer. She was lacing up her hiking shoes and thinking. The parking area was mostly empty, but it was morning. One of those bright clear mornings which made people feel alive. It made everyone else feel alive, but not Olivia. She was listless and sad and angry and apathetic. She felt everything, and she felt nothing. She wanted it to end.

"Mo-om, where are we going?" Molly's repetitive questioning snapped her back to the moment.

"Oh, honey. We're going for a walk. This is where Papa and Grammy used to take us every summer. I wanted you to see it."

She was always happy here. It was a place where she dreamed she could fly. She wanted to fly, to fly away and never come back. "Ready? OK, let's go."

"Mommy, what does that sign say?" She looked up at the trail sign for Tettegouche State Park on the north shore of Lake Superior.

"The sign says this is where we are going to walk." Olivia traced her finger over the long winding black line heading out along the shore. "The name of the park is Tettegouche."

"Tat-ta-gooch. Did I say it OK, Mom?"

"Yup. You said it perfect."

The trail had changed since Olivia was a girl. The rough, washed out gravel path had been repaired and replaced with boardwalks and steps. It was easy going with the morning sun, shining across the vast blue lake. They encountered few other hikers along the trail to Shovel Point. They moved along at a brisk pace for a six-year-old hiker. Molly stopped to smell the wild roses, throw rocks, and pick up bits of birch bark and funny looking pebbles.

The long climb up twisted rustic steps was taxing to Molly. She stopped to rest several times because her short legs couldn't keep up with Olivia. Finally, at the top, she looked back over the narrow path and the long view back toward Duluth in the southwest. It was beautiful and frightening.

Shovel Point was before them, a sheer drop, hundreds of feet straight down to crashing waves and icy water. It was a popular draw with rock climbers who hung precariously from bright nylon threads, dangling over the deep. It was this edge that drew Olivia. Molly held back. Without a guard railing it meant sure death. Olivia wanted to fly. She wanted to feel the wind and put her life's troubles behind.

"Mommy, don't get so close. You might fall." Molly loved the view and feared the heights. Olivia didn't hear her. She stepped closer. The wind was fresh off the lake as cool as the sun was warm. She closed her eyes and let the breeze take her away.

#

Sisters Lilja and Evangelika worked diligently preparing the inn for new guests. The law firm from Athens had booked the entire inn—all six rooms—for the meeting. Perched on a rocky hillside overlooking the Aegean, the white walls were a stark and beautiful contrast to the deep blue of the sea below. The wind blew constantly, a welcome respite from the torrid sun. The easiest way to get around on the island was walking. People walked everywhere. Vehicles occasionally hauled heavy items, but goat carts, bicycles and sturdy sandals served most residents very well. It kept people young.

Life was slow on Icaria. Time was recorded in weeks and years not hours or minutes. People slept in late, ate fresh vegetables and thick yogurt, and drank copious amounts of homemade wine. They were always working and always relaxed. Everyone had time for their neighbor or their friend. Children and chickens ran free; only the goats were tethered so they didn't destroy the gardens.

Visitors didn't frequent Icaria. It was out of the way. An uncommon destination, it required a three-legged journey from most places. Athens to Naxos; Naxos to Samos; Samos to Icaria. The ferry didn't run every day. Most visitors were other Greeks visiting relatives. A couple from America or Europe wouldn't be entirely unusual, but an extended family from the United States was odd. Lilja and Evangelika weren't sure when the guests were due to arrive. The ferry came yesterday so it wouldn't be today, maybe tomorrow or next week. Time wasn't that important.

#

"Could you take a picture for us?" The young couple sporting a baby backpack huffed and puffed up the winding stairs. The view from the top of Shovel Point was stunning. Molly stepped aside as they moved toward Olivia. The young dad, intently tapping the icons on his phone tripped just as Olivia turned toward them. Pitching forward, the infant slid out of the backpack and bumped into Olivia's feet, just a short distance from the edge.

"MY BABY!" the child's mother screamed.

With a quick instinctive movement, Olivia reached down and grabbed the baby, jumping back to safety. Olivia trembled as tears flooded her cheeks. She clutched the child close, clinging tightly even as the mother approached.

"Mommy?" Molly's eyes reflected the fear and uncertainty in her mother's face. She reached her small hands up and gripped the finger of her mom.

For several moments they all stood still, shaking at the sudden and stark realization of what could have been. The young parents, dumbstruck with fear, clutched the baby and started back down the trail. In a split second, life and death and the fine line

398

separating them was revealed. It shocked Olivia. It cut to her core and shook her. She trembled with the realization of how close death lurked.

She knelt and hugged Molly. "It's time to go home. Is that OK with you?"

"OK, Mom. Let's go."

Back at her car, Olivia dialed Harry. "I'm OK. I'm coming home."

#

"I am Angelika Stephanopoulos, office manager for the law firm handling your parent's estate." Her thick black hair glistened in sharp contrast to her perfectly white teeth. Her rings sparkled in the sunlight as she extended her hand, greeting each adult by name. "I believe I have all of your names, including little Mary Beatrice." She handed Vera a list confirming the names. The Ambrose family clustered together in a corner of the lobby of the Hotel Bretange, Athens. Another place, another country another requirement. It was wearing thin, but each held hope the end was in sight.

"Can you tell us why we were obligated to come here instead of finishing this in the United States, somewhere closer to our homes?" Vera was frustrated by come-here, go-there demands. "I don't mean to be ungrateful, but I feel you owe us some explanation. We are still grieving the loss of our parents and these demands seem to be endless. Can you explain this to us?"

"I am sorry. I know this sounds like I am avoiding your concerns, but I'm not. I am only the office manager. I'm afraid you will have to discuss that with Mr. Nicholas Economou, one of the senior partners. He is the one handling the estate." She stopped and arranged her papers into a leather attaché. "Normally he would be here to meet you, but he was delayed in court today. A representative from the office will meet you at the Paradeisus Inn on Icaria."

"How are we getting there?" Luella wondered.

"Years ago it was very difficult to get there from Athens. It was a long ferry ride over night. The journey typically took at least two days. Now we have a flight into Naxos and then a relatively short ferry ride. Or you can take a small plane directly into Icaria. Because you are a rather large family group, we chartered a plane into Naxos, and there someone will meet you and take you by ferry to your destination. The plane will be leaving around midday tomorrow. A tour company will pick you up in the morning here in the lobby and take you to the small private airport."

After answering a few more questions, Angelika left, and the Ambrose clan was on their own in Athens. All voted for a tour of the Acropolis and then Greek coffee with baklava. The sheer amount of history was incredible. Thousands of years of accomplishment lay everywhere before them. A small outdoor restaurant offered a pleasant corner to rest and reflect. After gyros and coffee and baklava, Olivia smiled. Everyone smiled back.

The flight from Athens to Icaria was uneventful. No controversy, no arguments, no delays or turbulence or cranky fellow travelers. Olivia wasn't back to her normal disposition, but she wasn't as subdued or melancholy as she had been either. The kids loved it. From Maddie to Mary Beatrice every child looked out the window, enjoying the deep blue blanket of the Aegean Sea below them. Naxos was a wonderful relaxing place, but it was only an interim stop. From there they were transported to the harbor and stepped on board the ferry from Naxos to Samos and then on to the rocky isolated shores of Icaria.

"Welcome to Icaria." Lilja and Evangelika greeted the Ambrose family with warmth and love. "We are so honored that you are able to be here with us. How was your trip?"

Emma was the first to answer. "It was a good trip, but we have been traveling for several days. It is good to rest."

"You will have plenty of time to rest here. Icaria is a wonderful place of rest. We often say, we are always working but forever at rest." Evangelika brought out a pitcher of cold water and fresh fruit. She had a large crock of thick Greek yogurt and a pot of raw honey. "Here enjoy yourself. Relax. We will get your belongings moved to your rooms. You can take a nap if you want."

"Do you know anything about the meeting we are supposed to have?" Luella wanted to have some sense of organization.

"Yes, I think someone else is coming to talk with you, but I don't know any details."

"What time is dinner?" Richard wanted to know. He was looking forward to a good nap, but he didn't want to miss the evening meal.

"Sometime this evening. We don't know what time. We don't have a clock here." Lilja and Evangelika looked toward each other and shrugged. They weren't slaves to the clock. People ate whenever dinner was ready.

Everyone found their own niche to relax. Some went to their rooms and found a pleasant uninterrupted nap. The kids were ready to explore.

"Mom, can we go for a walk?" Maddie was eager to run around and see what they could find.

"It is very safe here. No one will hurt you. Just don't fall off the rocks into the sea." Lilja interjected. Icaria was a great place for kids.

"Come on, let's go." Daisy and Molly went behind the inn to play in the garden. Maddie and her sister decided to search the quiet corners of the Paradeisus. Theo ran toward an old man herding a few goats in the small orchard along the path. Chickens scattered, and an old cat woke up from her nap and yawned.

The Paradeisus Inn was more like someone's home. The rooms had simple furnishings, nothing fancy. Small original oil paintings hung in most of the rooms. Murals on some of the walls reflected the idyllic life on the island. The windows opened toward the sea on one side and the olive grove and gardens on the other. The vented blue shutters closed, shutting out the wind and the sunshine, but when open, song birds and butterflies moved in and out of the rooms as extensions of the outdoor world.

The evening meal was delightful. Grilled goat, chicken, and sea bass along with heaps of fresh vegetables sautéed in olive oil. Small loaves of warm crusty bread fresh out of the wood-fired brick oven smelled wonderfully inviting. They tore apart steaming loaves of bread dipping the hearty chunks into ceramic bowls of olive oil and garlic. Platters of olives, feta cheese and crusty bread adorned the tables. The girls served pitchers of chilled local wines along with fresh fruit juice and goat's milk for the children. Dessert was cold thick yogurt with nuts, drizzled with dark sweet raw honey.

The evening meal never ended. It simply blended with the night. People gathered on the stone veranda sipping red wine and ouzo, eating olives and feta, and baklava. Everyone talked and laughed. Men and women alike played dominos or chess or other games. Locals aimlessly drifted in and out, chatting, laughing, and drinking. It was as relaxed and unpressured as anyone had felt in a very long time. Luella laughed as some of the local men tried to engage Tom and Harry in a traditional dance.

Emma noticed another man who seemed to remain outside the continuous camaraderie. A rather tall man walked into the edge of the veranda glancing around quickly as if looking for someone. He disappeared out of sight and then reappeared an hour later, sitting by himself off to the side at a small table near a lemon tree.

He looked about, as if taking note of everyone present. Evangelika went to his table and poured him a small glass of single malt scotch. He wore a patch over one eye, but his good eye darted around the room. Emma's eyes met his, and he nodded, raising his glass in salute. A faint smile tugged at the corners of his mouth. He downed his drink and slipped out of sight into the night. The party went on.

Emma stopped Evangelika as she walked by. "Who was the man with one eye?"

"Yorrie calls him 'the Dane' but I think his name is Dag."

"Who's Yorrie?"

"Yorrie is the caretaker and gardener. His wife, Anastasia, cooks for guests in the mornings. You will meet him tomorrow. He will know more. You can ask him." Evangelika paused waiting to see if she had any more questions. Hearing none, she went on to the other guests.

Emma checked with her other sisters. They had noticed the Dane as well, but he didn't disturb their evening. Still on Midwestern time, the Ambrose family drifted off to their rooms and shuttered their windows to the night but not to the sounds. The veranda gathering lingered until two or three in the morning. And then there was quiet, interrupted only by the Aegean surf and the gentle ocean breezes swaying the olive branches.

Olivia was up early. She had slept well and for the first time in many weeks she had a sense of anticipation and hope. Slipping out of their room, she put on her sandals and walked the path through the olive trees behind the inn. Birds sang, chickens clucked and scattered at her approach, and a white cat pounced on a grasshopper. From the hilltop, she could see the neighboring islands of Samos and Naxos to the north and Patmos to the east looking toward the coast of Turkey. She reflected on the apocalyptic stories that were written on the island of Patmos. It was more than a story, the places were real.

The morning was quiet and few people were up and about. Most of Icaria seemed to have been up all night. Near the orchard an older man raked and scraped at the gardens. As she watched him, he turned and looked her way. He had a familiarity about him, but he quickly turned back to his work. Olivia found a bench looking out to sea. In the morning sun, she relaxed and remembered good things and good times. An old man with a bad leg and a cane limped by. He carried a basket of vegetables and flowers. A short young woman was at his side. They chatted busily to each other, laughing about life. They didn't notice Olivia until they nearly bumped into her.

"Good morning."

"Good morning to you."

"Are you American?" Olivia asked. "Forgive me for asking, but you don't sound like you are Greek"

"Yes, we are Americans." They looked at each other as if it were a big secret. Everyone else on the island knew they were Americans. "My name is Nick." He said as he extended his big calloused hands.

"I'm Jacqueline." She smiled pleasantly. "Maybe we can visit later. Where are you staying?"

"The Paradeisus Inn." Olivia turned and pointed behind her. She watched them move slowly down the path toward the village and turned back to staring across the deep blue Aegean. She closed her eyes, enjoying the sun, and the wind across her face and hair. She thought of Shovel Point. The wind had taken her away to Icaria and a small seed of peace was growing within her.

People were beginning to stir at the inn. A long banquet table was being set. Evangelika covered the rustic worn wooden tabletop with linen. Fresh flowers were set in crockery vases. Olives, feta, and thin cuts of meat were arranged on platters. Warm food smells escaped the kitchen area. Faint aromas of goodness warmed Olivia's heart. She went to get Molly and Harry. It was time for breakfast.

They were all there. Luella and Tom seated on one end of the table. Next to them were Emma, Phineas and little Mary Beatrice perched in a highchair, sucking her hand, and staring around with big blue eyes. Olivia sat next to Harry. Vera and Richard were seated at the opposite end of the table. The children, Maddie, Zoe, Theo, Molly, and Daisy gathered at the separate table.

Luella surveyed the scene. "This is amazing. It's like Thanksgiving dinner used to be up at the lake." There was a good feeling in the air. She heard a sound and turned. Behind her an older couple walked onto the veranda and sat down. At another table, the one-eyed man sat alone.

Lilja and Evangelika brought out steaming pots of coffee, American style. They were about to say something when the one-eyed man stood and approached the long table. He cleared his throat and spoke.

"I don't know how to tell you this, so I'll just say it." He adjusted his eye patch as if he had a sudden case of nervousness. He wasn't the nervous type. "I knew your parents, Roy and Lola Ambrose." He stopped talking and looked each one in the eye. "I'm responsible for their deaths."

A stunned silence hung over the veranda. The butterflies and birds disappeared as the cloak of death was unfurled. No one moved. No one spoke. A yellow petal came loose from one of the flower arrangements and fluttered to the tabletop. Everyone focused on the Dag Rasmussen; no one noticed the kitchen door opening.

A shaggy gray-haired man with a short goatee stepped from the kitchen carrying a large steaming platter of Swedish pancakes. Close beside him a petite woman carried jars of homemade jams and a pot of honey. Her light brown, gray-streaked hair was pulled back in a long ponytail.

"Hi, Papa. Hi, Grammy." Daisy knocked over her glass of orange juice, fresh from the tree, and ran into their arms. It wasn't every day you saw your grandpa and grandma come back from the dead.

The response was electrifying. Leaping to their feet, everyone jumped for joy, laughing, crying, talking, and asking a thousand questions a minute. Someone spilled a pitcher of goat's milk all over the floor, and no one noticed but the cat. There was no way to describe the sudden and unexpected appearance of Papa and Grammy. Missing and declared dead for more than a year, this was a resurrection to behold.

Lola went to each grandchild hugging and kissing and crying over each one. She held Mary Beatrice so close and so tight, Emma feared for the baby's safety. Once Lola was done crying over the babies, she went to each of her daughters. The laughing and crying and questions started all over. Then it was the sons-in-law. To each were given the same family treatment, kisses and hugs and tears.

As the melee subsided, Roy raised his arms to quiet the crowd. Wiping tears from his eyes and his cheeks, he struggled to speak. "I know we have much explaining to do. But we have plenty of time to do it. Now eat these pancakes before they get cold." Food was passed along with excited chatter. As everyone enjoyed the breakfast Roy introduced the others. "Lilja and Evangelika, you know them." Pointing toward the side of the veranda was Nick and Jacqueline. "This is my cousin Earl, from Mazatlán and his wife Sandy. We try to remember them by their new names, Nick, and Jacqueline. And this notorious fellow is Dag Rasmussen."

Vera interrupted. "You told us, you killed them." She was looking directly at Dag.

Roy explained. "I guess we might as well tell you now. Mr. Rasmussen works for the United States Government. If he tells you what he does, he might have to kill you, too." A nervous laughter flitted around the table. "I'm going to make a very long story as short as possible. Your mother and I along with Earl and Sandy became witnesses of a murder in Mexico. I had to testify in court. Remember when I went a bit crazy? To safely testify against the drug cartel, Dag had us enter the witness protection program. There was a very large reward, but we feared for your lives, not ours. We couldn't tell you about it until it was safe. We went away for your benefit. We died so you could live."

"But Dad, why Icaria, Greece? Why not Kentucky or North Da-kota?" Luella wanted easy answers. But some questions in life don't have easy answers. Some don't have answers at all.

Roy shrugged his shoulders but said nothing.

"Is that how you got the money?" Olivia was beginning to see clearly.

"Yes, honey. That's where the money came from. It was much more than we could possibly spend, and it's all for you. Dad wanted to make a big treasure hunt for you, but we wanted you to learn to be generous as well. Earl and Sandy and Dad and I split the reward money. It doesn't take much to live here. Use it for good. We know you will." Lola paused and looked concerned to-ward Olivia. "How are you feeling?"

"Oh, Mom." Olivia looked at her sisters. It had been a rough couple of months since Costa Rica. "Not so good."

"It will be better in a couple weeks." Lola smiled. "You're preg-nant. I can see it in your face."

Astonished at her answer, Olivia wondered. "How do you know?"

"I may be dead, but I'm still your mother."

Epilogue

A lifetime of celebration was condensed into the days following the resurrection of Roy and Lola, now known as Yorrie and Anastasia Pappas. Glasses of wine and ouzo were raised in salute to wonderful memories and lessons learned, and to a new beginning. New friendships were bonded, and Dag Rasmussen was forgiven for killing Roy and Lola.

As the time drew near for their return trip, Vera hugged her parents and didn't want to let go. "Dad, will we ever see you and Mom again?"

"I would love to sit in the screen porch on a summer's night and listen to the loons over Lake Namukwa. But this is our home now. Each of you has learned to live well and love others. Our job is done. Everything we have is yours. We know you will use it wisely." He wiped the tears from his eyes and hers. "You can come and visit here any time you want. But, you never know about us. We might surprise you."

They took a long lazy walk around the village, through the olive grove, past the vineyard, through the old cemetery and down to the ferry dock, every one of them, parents talking and laughing, children running, chasing grasshoppers and chickens. Even Sandy and Earl with his cane and chicken-leg knee came. Passing through the cemetery, Luella noticed a new grave marker.

Charity Pappas
These three remain Faith-Hope-Charity. And the greatest of these is Charity

Luella smiled to herself. Some Greek kids were in for a wild ride.

IF THERE'S A WILL

THEN...

THERE'S A WAY

COMING 2018

Photo by Drew Walsh, used by permission, Northwest Passage Ltd. Webster, Wisconsin.

About the Author

John W Ingalls MD is a small-town family physician in northwestern Wisconsin. He lives in the same area settled by his great-great-great grandparents, Lansford and Laura Ingalls who are grandparents to the famed and beloved author, Laura Ingalls Wilder.

Dr. Ingalls graduated from Webster High School, Webster Wisconsin in 1976. Following three years in the US Army, he attended the University of Minnesota, graduating with a BS degree in biology. In 1985 he and his family moved to Madison, Wisconsin where he attended the University of Wisconsin. He graduated from the University of Wisconsin, Medical School in 1989 and completed a Family Practice Residency in Eau Claire, Wisconsin. Dr. Ingalls returned to his home town to practice medicine where he remains today.

He currently serves on the board of directors for Northwest Passage, a nonprofit organization committed to hope and healing for youth through innovative mental health services, education, the arts and hands-on interaction with nature.

Married to his wife, Tammy they enjoy all things related to the great outdoors, extensive travel, fine dining, and time spent with close friends. Together they have four wonderful daughters, Leah, Anna, Abigail and Billie Kay. Each of the girls are married to gracious and loving husbands and they are now raising their own families and writing their own stories.

79152286R00237

Made in the USA
Lexington, KY
18 January 2018